THE CHARITY SHOP DETECTIVE AGENCY

An absolutely gripping cozy mystery filled with twists and turns

PETER BOLAND

The Charity Shop Detective Agency Mysteries Book 1

JOFFE BOOKS

Joffe Books, London
www.joffebooks.com

First published by Joffe Books in 2022

Cover art by Nick Castle

ISBN: 978-1-80405-693-6

PROLOGUE

Wrenching the handbrake, Ted pulled up outside the house of his favourite customer. He always looked forward to this delivery slot — it put a grin on his face as wide as his windscreen. No other customers would offer him tea on his rounds, there just wasn't time. But Sarah Brown of 64 Stourview Way was from the frugal make-do-and-mend generation. She'd make a flask of tea first thing in the morning, so she only had to boil the kettle once to save on electricity. As soon as she heard his van pull up, she'd have a hot, steaming cuppa waiting for him on the kitchen counter.

Ted licked his lips at the prospect of refreshment. He lifted the crates of shopping out of the truck and made the short but careful walk down her front garden path, made back in the day when crazy paving was a thing. Today it would be deemed a trip hazard. Goodness knows how Sarah traversed this low-slung obstacle course with her walking frame.

He rested the crates on her front step and knocked on the door. It didn't open straight away but that was to be expected. Not being too good on her feet, it would take a while for her to get there.

"It's okay, Sarah. Don't rush," he called out. "I'm ahead of schedule."

He waited. The door didn't open.

Maybe she was upstairs, in which case, the stairlift would be taking its sweet time sliding her round the tight bends of her staircase like the world's most sedate fairground ride.

1

Still the door didn't open.

"Sarah, would you like me to start putting the shopping in the kitchen?" Sometimes she'd leave the door unlocked to save him waiting for her.

No response. Maybe he should give the door a try. The clock was ticking, and tea-drinking time was a-wasting. He twisted the handle. The latch clicked open.

Bending over, he picked up the crates and nudged the door wide with one elbow. Then he dropped them all, spilling shopping over the front step.

Sarah Brown was in her hallway face down. Ted swore and rushed in, assuming she'd had a fall.

In a second, he was by her side. "Sarah! Sarah! Can you hear me?" Her lack of response led him to believe that she must have hit her head and knocked herself out.

Ted flinched, panicked, not knowing what to do. He felt her neck for a pulse. He'd seen it a million times on the TV. That was what they did first, wasn't it? Fumbling with two fingers, he sought out Sarah's carotid artery.

All he found was cold skin. Then he noticed the damp, dark patch below one shoulder blade. In its centre, a deep narrow wound, wet with blood.

His breath caught in his throat. Hands shaking, he reached for his phone. As he fumbled to dial for an ambulance, something made him jump.

A small, dark object slid out of her left hand.

A domino with a name scratched onto it.

CHAPTER 1

Fiona Sharp liked her life.

She liked that both her knees still worked and, although they would sometimes creak like a Victorian staircase, neither felt as if they would need replacing anytime soon. Her hips were fairly serviceable too.

She liked being retired, specifically retired in Southbourne, a small suburb hemmed in by Bournemouth and Christchurch. It had a traditional sweet shop that sold gobstoppers, lemon drops and other confectionery the way they were meant to be sold, from large, dusty glass jars perched on shelves reaching up to the ceiling. The shopkeeper would decant them into little striped paper bags, which he would hold by each corner and flip over before handing them to you. She liked the local hardware store, where men in brown overalls still bustled behind a scuffed-up counter, fetching whatever you wanted, although Fiona had never had the nerve to ask them for four candles.

She liked Southbourne's pretty side roads and avenues, lined with large, stout and sturdy Georgian homes. She liked that they led to a grass-topped cliff standing guard over a sweeping bay of blond sand, soft as Demerara sugar.

She liked volunteering at the Dogs Need Nice Homes charity shop that raised money for, well, dogs that needed nice homes. She liked the people she worked with. It made her feel part of the community, rather than a permanent tourist, as some retirees felt.

She liked Simon Le Bon. Not *the* Simon Le Bon, you understand, but her diminutive, scruffy terrier cross — crossed with what was anyone's guess. He was so scruffy that he often looked as if someone had used him to clean their house. Adopted from Dogs Need Nice Homes, she had named him after the New Romantic because his messy hair had instantly reminded her of the singer's mulleted mass of gravity-defying highlights.

Best of all, she liked coming home at the end of the day to catch the dying western sun on her veranda and sip tea — or something stronger — while turning the crisp pages of one of her crime novels, Simon Le Bon dozing at her feet.

There were only three things she didn't like about her life.

The first she could see up ahead as she rounded the corner, clenching the shop keys in her pocket.

The second would be along very shortly.

The third . . . *She never dared mention the third.*

After the charity shop had closed for the weekend, the public would think it quite acceptable to dump their donations outside, piled against the plate glass window. Nothing irritated Fiona like donations left unattended, causing an eyesore. They weren't really donations either. It was mostly junk because people couldn't be bothered to go to the recycling centre. The unsightly clutter of boxes and bulging bin liners would usually only be fit for landfill.

It had led Fiona to put up a massive sign in the window that was almost always ignored. "What part of 'Do Not Leave Donations Outside When We're Closed', do they not understand," she muttered under her breath.

Fiona's day was about to get worse as she witnessed the second most annoying thing in her life: Sophie Haverford from the Cats Alliance, a rival charity shop across the road. Fiona had nothing against other charity shops. She had nothing against cats. What she didn't like was Sophie Haverford. It was as if some higher power had worked out the most

4

efficient way to irritate Fiona and then formed it into a single human being. Sophie was a self-righteous, pompous snob who thought and spoke far too highly of herself, sashaying around as if she were the Queen of Southbourne, flinging air kisses around with wild abandon like confetti at a wedding.

As she strode purposefully across the road, Sophie's black, velvet, hooded cape billowed out behind her theatrically. For goodness' sake, it was only Monday. But it was what she was carrying in her arms that turned Fiona's tinnitus up to eleven. No charity shops were immune to donations being dumped outside over the weekend, not even the Cats Alliance. However, rather than disposing of them, Sophie had decided to give herself one fewer box to deal with by taking it from her pile and adding it to Fiona's.

"Hey!" Fiona quickened her pace, Simon Le Bon tugging on his lead. "I see you, Sophie Haverford! I see you! Stop that this instant!"

At the sound of Fiona's voice, Sophie dropped the box on top of the pile outside Dogs Need Nice Homes. She spun on a balletic heel, sending that ridiculous cape swishing around in a wide arc like a pantomime villain, then hastily hurried back across the road to the safety of her own shop.

A few moments later, huffing and puffing, Fiona reached the stacks of boxes and bulging bin liners outside Dogs Need Nice Homes. She had a cursory root through the one Sophie had fly-tipped to see what kind of junk she'd left. One mouldy foot spa (a charity shop donation staple and cul-de-sac of retail technology — nobody ever wanted them, because nobody ever used them), which jostled for space with a toasted sandwich maker, minus its plug, and rusted all over. There was never any need for either product when they were new, which meant nobody ever wanted them when they were old.

Fiona rummaged further. Towards the bottom of the box was an object that sent a tremor of shock across her shoulder blades.

She blinked and her breath hitched.

It was a knife. Smeared with blood.

5

CHAPTER 2

Fiona stared at it for several seconds, trying to make sense of what she was seeing. A large paring knife with a sturdy black handle and a blade about six inches long and one inch wide. Paring knives were normally used for chopping vegetables, so why was it bloody? Some of it had dried and some of it was still fresh.

She had to corral her thoughts. Maybe it wasn't blood. Perhaps it could be something else.

Fiona's mind had been shaped by years of reading crime novels. Conjuring up dastardly scenarios came easily to her. No matter how hard she tried, the idea kept pinging back into her head — had Sophie stabbed someone and was disposing of the evidence? If so, she hadn't done a very good job. Plus, Sophie wasn't the type. Smarmy, yes. Stabby, no. It would be far too messy for her, and she certainly wouldn't be stupid enough to hide the weapon in a box of charity donations where it would be easily discovered, even if she had left it outside someone else's shop.

But that begged the question, did Sophie know about the knife? Had seen it and wanted to get it away from her shop, to make it someone else's problem? Possible but not probable. The knife had been stashed in the bottom. Highly unlikely that Sophie would have dared to soil her regularly manicured fingers by delving down that far. One look at the foot spa and sandwich maker would've been enough for her to turn her nose up.

Fiona told herself to be sensible. Stabbings didn't happen in Southbourne. Okay, the knife was bloody, but a lot of people donated things without cleaning them. The shop had a washing machine and several bulk-bought bottles of washing-up liquid under the sink for that very reason. The knife had probably been used to prepare meat and then tossed in the box of donations ready for the charity shop. Yes, that was a far more rational explanation.

A few niggles with that theory flicked away at her brain. Judging by the wet blood, the knife had been used recently, and from what Fiona could see, it looked fairly new.

Simon Le Bon pulled her from her thoughts. He was on his hind legs, stretching up to the pile of unwanted donations, sniffing the air, trying to get closer to the bloodied weapon.

"Get down, Simon. *Down*."

He obeyed. Okay, it had piqued Simon Le Bon's interest. But that didn't mean it was human blood. It could be an animal's, or it might not be blood at all. She had to be sure before she called the police.

Fiona left the box where it was, conscious that she didn't want to disturb anything, and made her way across the road to the Cats Alliance, Simon Le Bon by her side. She shouldered open the door and was immediately distracted by the smell, or lack of it. Anyone who'd been thrifting in charity shops knew their distinctive tang, a musty, lived-in odour. Regardless of location, whether in Dorset or Doncaster, nationwide and possibly worldwide, they were united by their pungent second-hand fustiness. Eau de Charity Shop. All except for the Cats Alliance in Southbourne. It had no such smell. Fiona didn't know by what sorcery Sophie had eradicated the collective odour of other people's unwantedness, but she had. It didn't look like a charity shop, either. It was light and airy with standout items tastefully displayed on plinths. A clean and uncluttered retail experience.

The ambience of the shop had momentarily diverted Fiona from her mission. She locked eyes with Sophie, who was leaning against the counter, arms crossed. Fiona noticed Gail in the back room, Sophie's monosyllabic assistant and hamster of a woman. She was hunched over a futuristic phone and appeared to be fixing it with a slender screwdriver.

"Hello, Fiona. What a lovely surprise," Sophie drawled, smiling like an assassin, and looking like one, with her rigid jet-black bob — dyed, obviously — and blood-red lipstick. And, of course, that cape still draped across her shoulders. "To what do we owe the pleasure?"

"You *know* what. You dumped one of your boxes outside my shop."

Sophie feigned hurt. "Oh no, dear. It was already there. I saw that it had toppled over, causing an obstruction on the pavement and, like a good citizen and fellow charity worker, I picked it up and placed it safely back on top of the others." Before Sophie had retired, she had worked in PR, and could spin a nuclear winter to make it sound like Christmas every day. "That's what happened. Isn't that right, Gail?"

"'S'right," Gail mumbled, not sounding at all convincing.

Fiona stared at Sophie, unflinching. "You're lying. I know you're lying because I saw you."

"No, no, I'm telling you that's what happened, isn't it, Gail?"

"'S'right," Gail muttered, giving Fiona the impression that her stock answer was a result of Sophie bullying her into agreeing with everything she said.

Fiona wasn't deterred. "Well, that box has a knife in it that happens to have blood on it." She watched Sophie's face carefully to see how she reacted to that piece of news.

Sophie's face dropped. It didn't look like she had any spin prepared for that one. "W—what?"

"There's a kitchen knife with blood on it in the bottom of the box left outside your shop."

8

Swiftly regaining her composure, Sophie smiled. "Oh, Fiona, you do worry about the silliest things. One, it wasn't outside my shop, it was outside yours. And two, you know the sort of rubbish people throw away. It's probably pig's blood. Someone killed a pig and then didn't want the bother of washing up."

"Who kills pigs round here?" Fiona pointed out. "This is Southbourne, not *Clarkson's Farm*. And why throw out a perfectly good knife?"

Sophie put her hands on her hips. "You know, some people are so unsustainable. It makes my heart ache for the planet. I'm trying to do my best to change it, but me and Greta Thunberg can only do so much."

Fiona nearly choked. "Sophie, you drive around in a diesel Range Rover."

Sophie wrinkled her neat little nose dismissively. "Only to Waitrose and back. Where, I might add, the majority of my shop ends up in the collection for the food bank. And it's not Waitrose Essentials I put in there, either. I donated a nice jar of garlic-stuffed olives the other day that I wouldn't have minded keeping myself. But, no, I thought. I want a single parent to get a taste of the finer things in life, rather than living off Greggs steak bakes and the like."

This was getting Fiona nowhere. Every situation that presented itself to Sophie, she spun into an opportunity to pat herself on the back and congratulate herself as the world's most wonderful human being.

Fiona's tinnitus cranked up a few notches, causing her to wince.

"Are you okay, dear?" asked Sophie with faux concern.

"I need to get back over there and report this to the police. There's a potential murder weapon sitting in a box."

Sophie blew out air from between her lips like an inner tube puncturing. "So melodramatic. Are you sure you want to bother the police with a dirty knife?"

"Positive. And once I've told them where the knife came from, which would be *you*, and they've taken it away for analysis, you can have your junk back."

9

"Well, I really don't think that will be possible. The items in that box aren't right for my shop — *if* they had been outside my shop," she added hastily. "They don't fit with my edit, dear."

That was the main difference between Sophie and Fiona, that word "edit". Though Fiona used to work in publishing, she would never have dreamt of using the word to describe what was essentially rummaging through second-hand stuff in a cardboard box. And Fiona would rather die than call someone "dear".

"And what exactly is your *edit*?" asked Fiona, then instantly regretted it.

Sophie giggled. "Certainly not sandwich makers and supermarket clothes, that's for sure."

"So you did look in the box, then?"

"I may have had a cursory glance. And what I saw wouldn't have been right for my edit. It's more upmarket, like the Bang & Olufsen home phone that Gail is fixing."

Gail looked up from her work. "'S'right."

Sophie stepped closer to Fiona, speaking in a hushed tone. "Gail's not too bright but is an absolute darling at mending stuff."

"Well, I think anyone who can mend a phone is very smart indeed," Fiona replied, loud enough for Gail to hear.

Gail allowed herself a self-conscious smile, until Sophie shot her a look laced with barbed wire and broken glass.

"Anyway, I'm calling the police," said Fiona. "So you'd better get your story straight because they will be paying you a visit."

"You know, I donate to so many police charities, it will be nice to catch up with one of their officers."

Fiona ignored her. The woman was as slippery as she was insufferable. She needed to get out of there fast. Sophie made her stressed, and stress aggravated her tinnitus, which was currently squealing at a pitch that only Simon Le Bon could hear.

CHAPTER 3

Fiona stood guarding the offending box and other dumped items. She hadn't dared move them again, knowing that you weren't supposed to touch a thing in case you contaminated it. Although that procedure was strictly for a crime scene, she thought it better to err on the side of caution.

Half an hour later, a police car pulled up. An officer with a thin face, who looked young enough to be delivering newspapers, stepped out. But Fiona knew it wasn't true that police officers were getting younger and younger these days. They were the same age as they'd always been. At seventy-six, it was Fiona who was getting older.

"Hello," said the constable, turning the chatter down on his Airwave radio. "Are you Fiona Sharp?"

"I am."

Simon Le Bon jumped up on the officer's leg, wagging his tail.

"And who's this cute little fellow?"

"That's Simon Le Bon."

The officer looked blankly at Fiona, as would anyone born after 1993, then said, "You reported finding a knife with blood on it in a box donations."

"Yes. Well, no — sort of. It wasn't one of my boxes, it was from the Cats Alliance over there."

Glancing across the road, the police officer returned a confused look. "How did it get over here?"

"When I came into work this morning, someone from the Cats Alliance was dumping her unwanted donations on top of mine. I was about to take it back over when I saw the knife and the blood."

Fiona could tell by the look on his face that he thought this was nothing more than a petty squabble between rival charity shops, which, to a certain extent, it was.

The officer sighed. "Are you sure this person—"

"Sophie Haverford. Her name's Sophie Haverford. Make sure you write that down."

The officer didn't write it down. "Are you sure this Sophie Haverford wasn't winding you up? Just a prank."

Fiona hadn't thought of that, but it was highly likely. Both of them had retired down here from London, and ever since Fiona had arrived, Sophie had taken an instant dislike to her, passive-aggressively hinting that the position of glamorous bohemian-type from the big city had been taken. Fiona couldn't have cared less. She didn't want that position and would hardly have classed herself as glamorous. In misshapen cardigans over roomy floral dresses and Croc-ed feet, Fiona had a strictly-for-comfort dress code. She maintained that if she couldn't manage a two-hour stint shopping in a garden centre in what she was wearing, then she wouldn't wear it. She couldn't for the life of her figure out why the uber-glitzy Sophie considered her a threat.

"It's possible, Officer. We do have a bit of friendly rivalry going on. Why don't you ask her?"

"Let's take a look first, shall we?" From his pocket the officer retrieved a pair of nitrile gloves and snapped them on. "Which box is it?"

Fiona pointed. The officer crouched and carefully picked his way through the junk. He stared at the offending article, then went back to his car and returned with a clear plastic tube and a large transparent evidence bag. Removing the knife with his gloved fingertips, he placed it inside the tube, sealed it up and scrawled on the outside with a marker pen. "I'll take the box too, just to be on the safe side." The whole box was placed in the large, clear evidence bag and also sealed. He took a few details from Fiona and turned to leave.

"Er, aren't you going to question Sophie Haverford?" Fiona asked.

"Not at this stage. Not until we're sure it's blood. Could be jam from slicing up a Victoria sponge." He chuckled.

In her head, Fiona scoffed at that idea. She knew her cake, and if that were the case, then where was the buttercream filling? Honestly. "Have any knife crimes been reported? Any stabbings?" she asked.

"No, not for a while. If it turns out to be something more serious, then we know where to find you."

"And Sophie Haverford."

"Yes, and this Sophie Haverford. I'll be in touch if we need anything else." The officer placed the evidence in the back of the police car, slid into the driver's seat and pulled into the morning traffic.

Fiona stood on the pavement, unmoving, her brain attempting to analyse what had just happened. Had she over-reacted? Was this the result of her crime-fiction brain seeing felonies everywhere when, in reality, nothing bad ever happened around here? And, as the officer had said, no stabbings had been reported, making her feel like she'd just wasted police time. He didn't think it was anything to be worried about, and he certainly didn't seem interested in Sophie, the one who'd actually put the box there in the first place. What was it about that woman? No matter what happened, she always came up smelling of roses.

Fiona glanced over the road. Speak of the devil. Sophie was standing in the window of the Cats Alliance staring back at her, a sickly half-smirk, half-pitying expression on her smug face.

CHAPTER 4

Once the front door was unlocked, Fiona put the box down and unclipped Simon Le Bon from his lead. He scampered in and did his usual circuit of the shop, sniffing in corners and rooting around, checking that everything was the same as when they'd closed up on Saturday afternoon. Satisfied that all was well, he curled himself into his bed by the till.

As far as charity shops went, Dogs Need Nice Homes had a rather handsome interior, due to the fact that it had been an old-fashioned jewellery shop before the owner had abandoned it without warning. When the charity had taken it over, they'd changed very little. First off, they didn't have the money to spend on anything so frivolous as redesigning the interior, and second, it wasn't really necessary. Dating back to the early forties, the walls were clad in elegant dark-wood panels with a large clock set into the back wall, solemnly doling out slices of time into the musty air. If it had a fireplace and a Chesterfield, one might retire for the evening to sip sherry and tug on fat cigars. There were no sofas or a fireplace, but Fiona had added a circular table and chairs in one corner for her older, less mobile customers to take a load off. Fiona thought of her shop as a box of delights, enticing and appealing, and full of forgotten treasure. Which

14

probably annoyed the hell out of Sophie, as her shop was little more than a bland white box, no matter how often she painted it or how many PR strings she pulled to get Z-list celebrities to reopen it.

Fiona began ferrying the other boxes and junk into the shop. She needed to stay busy. Keep her mind and body occupied, that was the key. If she slowed down, *it* might come back again. *It* was the third thing she didn't like about her life. The thing she never dared to mention.

One by one, she manoeuvred the boxes past the spinning racks of clothes and overflowing bookshelves, and into the storeroom to add to all the others awaiting "the sort".

"The sort" was a phrase that struck terror into the heart of even the hardiest charity shop volunteer. The never-ending task. The boulder that had to be pushed uphill only to rumble back down again, or the painting of the Severn Bridge, if the Severn Bridge had been made from mountains of splitting cardboard boxes and bin liners haemorrhaging clothes. The rate at which donations came in exceeded the rate at which they went out, creating an endless backlog. Still, better that than the other way around, Fiona thought.

Donations were split into five categories for resale: clothes and accessories — by far their best seller; books and DVDs — DVDs were getting rarer by the day and video cassettes had not been seen since Jeremy Kyle got axed; toys, games and jigsaws (jigsaws had to be stickered with either "checked" or "unchecked" on pain of death — the distinction was crucial, as hell hath no fury like a dissectologist denied the last piece of the puzzle); crockery and small household items; and miscellaneous. Anything they couldn't sell would be bagged up for recycling or landfill.

Fiona returned outside the shop to collect more donations. A small runabout in need of a wash and possibly some work, judging by the demonic and guttural shriek emanating from its exhaust, screeched to a halt. Gears ground and the car threw itself into reverse, backing into a space with urgency and abandon. The engine shut off and out popped the energetic figure of Partial Sue, one of the shop's volunteers. Thin as wire but with big, bright and clever eyes, Fiona had nicknamed her Partial Sue, not because of her slight build but because every time she expressed a like for something, it was preceded by the word "partial".

She stepped out of the car. "Did you see that? I am partial to a good parking space. Right outside."

"Morning, Sue," Fiona replied, picking up a heavy box that had to be supported from the bottom in case it split.

"Morning."

Partial Sue went straight for the pile of boxes, helping Fiona carry them in without having to be asked, for the simple reason she was also partial to a bargain and would want to get her hands on anything good inside.

As they took the first lot of boxes into the storeroom, Fiona filled her in on the morning's events.

Partial Sue gasped. "A bloodied knife! And the box definitely came from over the road?"

"Saw it with my own eyes. Of course, Sophie denied it."

"Hey, do you think Sophie stabbed someone and was getting rid of the evidence?"

"Much as I would like Sophie to be the villain in all this, she genuinely didn't know it was in there."

"But you know how good she is at twisting the truth."

"I do, but initially it shocked her. She was lost for words. First time I've ever seen that."

"And it would be out of character for Sophie," Partial Sue replied. "If she were to stab someone, she'd get someone else to do it. Wouldn't want to ruin her nails."

Fiona giggled. "Exactly. And stabbing's not subtle enough for her. I think poison's more likely to be her weapon of choice."

"Yeah, she'd have one of them special rings with a top that flips open, so she could drop it in your tea."

"I think we deserve a cup of tea ourselves," Fiona said. "Minus the poison."

"Now you're talking."

While Fiona put the kettle on, Partial Sue dived into one of the boxes, churning over its contents of more items destined for landfill.

She suddenly gasped.

"What is it?" Fiona hurried over. There, among the junk, in mint condition, sat the new Val McDermid crime novel. In hardback, no less.

Partial Sue loved crime novels as much as Fiona, and the pair had access to a never-ending supply of their favourite fiction, donated on a daily basis. Heaven for two crime-fiction fans. "I am partial to a good Val McDermid."

"Me too," replied Fiona.

They'd hit the mother lode. Both knew the other wanted to read it first. They stood staring at it, almost frightened to touch it. After all, it was written by the queen of crime.

"What are we going to do?" asked Partial Sue. "Who gets first dibs on it? I don't think I could wait while you read it."

"And vice versa."

"How about we take it in turns," suggested Partial Sue. "You read a chapter then I read a chapter. Alternate."

"Brilliant idea. You go first. You found it. Once we've finished, it goes in the window. We could easily fetch a tenner for it."

"I'm not going to argue with that." Partial Sue picked up the book, feeling its heft and slowly turning it over in her slender hands to take in its majesty. She flipped gleefully to the first page. "I'm going in."

The little brass bell above the door tinkled. Simon Le Bon grumbled at the appearance of the Wicker Man, as he always did.

"Good morrow, dear ladies," he said in his deep, rich voice.

"Would you like tea?" Fiona asked.

"Ah, to partake in such delights would be—"

She cut him off before he got carried away. "A simple yes or no will do."

"Yes, that would be simply marvellous."

The Wicker Man had a shop next door selling second-hand furniture. His name was Trevor, but everyone called him the Wicker Man, because he had invested a lot of stock in old-school wicker from one of his dodgy contacts who had a lock-up full of the stuff, thinking that it would make a resurgence. It never did. Everyone wanted modern rattan, not the stuff gathering dust in his shop. The nickname had stuck, a bit of a blessing, as before that he had been rather cruelly known as the Dickensian Dickhead, due to his penchant for using flamboyant turns of phrase. This was a complete mystery as he came from Clacton and used to work for the electricity board. With his slightly dubious connections, Fiona had a theory that he was on the run and had adopted his Terry Thomas persona because he'd had to reinvent himself.

For all his Dickensian ways, the Wicker Man dressed fairly normally in a V-neck sweater and shirt, although he always wore odd socks and had been known to sport a cravat whenever he had a sore throat and needed to "mollycoddle the old tonsillar region that was in the grip of an Exorcist-level event". Although his sore throats always seemed to coincide with meeting someone he wanted to impress.

Fiona and Partial Sue brought out the teas and joined the Wicker Man at the round table. Before any of them had had a chance to sip their teas, the front door flew open. Daisy, the third member of staff, stood panting and wheezing, attempting to form words without any breath to back them up. She shuffled in, shoulders hunching up and down, as she gobbled air into her oxygen-starved lungs. Fiona and Partial Sue rose from the table to support her and guide her in the direction of the table, still puzzled as to what had caused all this exertion. The Wicker Man pulled out his chair for her to sit and recover.

Daisy collapsed into it. "S-sorry for being late."

"Oh, don't worry about that," said Fiona. "I don't mind you — or anyone being late." Fiona added *anyone* in that sentence to be diplomatic. At a mere sixty-seven years old, Daisy was the baby of the bunch. A dreamer who had an obsession for cleaning things, she was easily distracted and never on time for anything.

"A modicum of tardiness never troubled anyone," declared the Wicker Man.

Fiona went into the kitchen and returned with a glass of water for Daisy. She drank deeply.

"Did you run all the way here?" Partial Sue enquired.

Daisy nodded, although this was probably an exaggeration. Daisy never ran anywhere. It had probably been more of a hasty amble. Living in maxi dresses, it was the most she could hope for without tripping over the hem. However, she'd certainly overexerted herself for some reason. Her complexion was more peaches than cream, and those peaches were on the verge of becoming red apples. She had a sweet, open, round face and a mop of grey curls that never behaved themselves. From her bag she pulled out a blue-grey inhaler, gave it a shake and sucked down two doses of medicine.

After a few minutes, when her wheezing had subsided and her breathing had returned to something more normal, she finally found her voice.

"Sarah Brown's been murdered."

CHAPTER 5

"Are you sure?" asked Partial Sue. "Did you see an ambulance? Maybe she's just feeling a bit poorly and had to go to hospital."

Daisy shook her head. "Her body was completely covered up when they took her out."

Hands clamped over mouths to contain their shock.

"Oh my gosh," gasped Fiona. "Who would do such a thing?"

"I can't believe it." Partial Sue got to her feet and started to pace. "Our dear friend, murdered."

Sarah Brown was well-liked by everyone. The eighty-six-year-old had been a regular customer at Dogs Need Nice Homes, making the walk from her home around the corner, always preceded by her walking frame. Chatty and spirited and never one to complain, her outlook was always sunny and positive. She was a keep-calm-and-carry-on poster personified. Growing up in the Second World War, surviving the Blitz, she had seemed indestructible. A stiff-upper-lipped survivor who would soldier on for ever.

Daisy cuffed a tear. "Horrible, it was. Horrible and upsetting. The road was blocked off with police tape. Cars and vans everywhere. Radios blasting. I could see police going in and out of her house in haphazard suits."

"What?" asked Fiona and Partial Sue.

"You know, haphazard suits. They have hoods and face masks. Make people look like skinny polar bears."

"Oh, you mean hazmat suits?" Fiona offered.

Partial Sue's eyes widened. "If they were wearing hazmat suits, and going into Sarah's house, that definitely means . . ."

"They suspect foul play," said the Wicker Man, not holding back on the opportunity to be melodramatic.

"F-foul play?" Daisy stuttered.

"Another word for murder," Partial Sue replied. "And Fiona found a knife with blood on it this morning."

CHAPTER 6

Daisy didn't want to come, and who could blame her. She'd had enough shocks already that morning and decided to hold down the fort. The Wicker Man had gone back to his shop to open up for the day, so it was Partial Sue, Fiona and Simon Le Bon who made the walk through Southbourne's pretty avenues and past its handsome houses with their obligatory hand-painted plaques brandishing romantic house names such as the Old School House, Dairy Cottage and Fir Tree Hollow, plus a few that should have never been allowed such as Thisilldous and an old doctor's surgery called Bedside Manor.

The poor taste in names did nothing to lighten the mood as they turned into Stourview Way, where Sarah had lived. The recent past-tense nature of her status sounded odd and uncomfortable in Fiona's mind. At once they were confronted by a chaotic scene quite out of character for the usually serene roads of Southbourne.

The whole road had been blocked off with blue-and-white caution tape stretched across either end. A couple of police officers stood guard, stopping people from going any further. A small crowd had gathered, some of them holding their phones aloft, popping off shots. It was the same scenario at the other end of the road. One guy had a proper SLR camera. Fiona wondered if he was a press photographer. In between the cordons, it was just as Daisy had described — white-hooded figures with masks darting in and out of the house, carrying things in labelled plastic boxes to put in the back of police vehicles parked at odd angles.

"Do you think those two will tell us anything?" Partial Sue nodded towards the pair of officers standing by the tape.

"Not likely," Fiona replied. "We need to tell them about that knife. It could be connected. But let's be subtle. We need to establish how she died before we start going on about a bloodied knife. She could have been pushed down the stairs for all we know."

"A horrible thought." Partial Sue shuddered. "But yes, softly, softly."

They sidled up to the police tape, then edged along it until they were level with the two officers.

Before Fiona had a chance to speak, Partial Sue blurted out, "How did she die?"

Fiona glared at her. So much for the subtle approach.

"And who are you?" asked one of the officers.

Fiona stepped in to answer. "We work on Southbourne Grove, in a charity shop, Dogs Need Nice Homes. Sarah Brown used to come in a lot. She was our friend."

"Oh, well, I'm very sorry for your loss."

A wave of sadness broadsided Fiona, the sudden loss of a customer and a good friend still raw. She'd miss her company, her stories and her green-fingered generosity. Before her back gave out, Sarah would grow the juiciest tomatoes by the bucketload, and make gallons of the tangiest jam and chutney, ensconced into jars of all shapes and sizes, all freely given to anyone who would want them.

Then Partial Sue ruined it again. "We found a knife with blood on it."

Fiona was sure that her colleague's enthusiasm, for not just spilling the beans but spraying them everywhere with abandon, was caused by overexcitement at standing before

23

a real-life crime scene. She'd become a teenager at the front of a pop concert.

"Did you report it?" asked the other officer.

"I did," said Fiona.

"That's good. You did the right thing," the officer replied.

"Is it connected with this?" Partial Sue asked, almost shaking.

One of the officers gave her a sympathetic smile. "I'm sorry, we can't reveal anything about this matter. We've only just got here ourselves. Put on crowd control."

"We know as much as you do," the other officer added.

They were interrupted by a flustered mum with a baby in a pushchair, the back laden with supermarket bags. "I need to get to my house, and he needs changing. If not, I'm going to have to change him here in front of you."

"Okay, just calm down," said one of the officers.

A delivery driver appeared on the other side of them, holding a small box. "Any chance I can get this to number fifty-six? I'm running late."

"That's not going to be possible," said the police officer nearest to them.

"Well, can you take it for me?" He held out the package.

Fiona and Partial Sue removed themselves from the heated discussions erupting around them about nappies and next-day deliveries, edging away from the tape.

"He didn't seem very interested in our bloody knife," Fiona said.

"No, it's not like on the telly, where they rush over to tell the senior officer, then the senior officer hurries over to question us, the members of the public who have vital information about the case."

"Maybe that's just it. Our information isn't vital. Maybe Sarah died some other way, and our knife isn't relevant."

"But how do those officers know it's not relevant? They didn't seem to know anything."

The pair went silent for a while, mesmerised by the sight in front of them. Instead of finding it thrilling, compelling and irresistible, and all those flashy adjectives you see plastered on adverts for blockbuster thrillers, the experience left Fiona cold and numb. Real crime was depressing and left a large empty hole. A friend had been murdered and she didn't like it, not one bit.

A well-dressed female with slicked-back hair stepped out of the house. Tastefully outfitted in a tailored wool coat with a slim pair of slacks and sharp heels, the woman had style and a businesslike way about her. She was followed by a greying middle-aged man dressed in casual sportswear. Bordering on scruffy, he looked as if he'd just finished a shift at a hand car wash. He had the gaunt face of someone who worked out too much and ate too little saturated fat. Cake would solve that problem, like it solved most problems.

"Those two look like they're in charge," Partial Sue remarked.

"I'll say. Probably a couple of DIs, or a DI and a DS. Pity we can't talk to them."

Police officers and hazmatted figures orbited the pair, taking it in turns to check in and run things past them. Busy and in demand, they multitasked, speaking on the phone while handing out instructions simultaneously.

Fiona and Partial Sue watched them for a good quarter of an hour, until they disappeared back into the house.

"I don't think there's much else to do here." Partial Sue sniffed, her initial excitement subsiding into a more subdued mood.

"One thing I do know," Fiona replied, "is that they'd better catch the swine who did this."

CHAPTER 7

The sombre mood of yesterday lingered, spilling into Tuesday and infusing the musty air. Not good, as Tuesdays were coffee mornings at Dogs Need Nice Homes, which Sarah Brown had regularly frequented with her fellow octogenarians and a few nonagenarians. By ten o'clock, you wouldn't be able to move for walking sticks, frames and the odd wheelchair. The shop would ring with the happy chatter of people who lived on their own and hadn't talked to a soul all week, collective mouths going ten to the dozen. Today Sarah Brown would be sadly conspicuous by her stinging absence, made all the worse by the fact that she'd been the inspiration for the coffee mornings in the first place.

It had all started with a rattly Transit. More specifically, the rattly Transit minibus that would round up pensioners and deposit them at the community centre once a week. They would often complain that the minibus was too hot or too cold, too draughty or too stuffy, and definitely too uncomfortable. The rust bucket was in the garage more than it was on the road. However, that tired old Transit had been their lifeline, bringing them all together once a week, where they'd swap advice about bunions, complain about the government and have a jolly good game of bingo. But then everything changed.

At the start of the next financial year, the budget for the community centre took a hit. Something had to go, and the minibus got the chop. Stranded in their homes and unable to make the trek to the community centre, a lot of people in their eighties and nineties were left miserable and alone. No more human contact, no more socialising and nothing to look forward to except week after week of their own company. Solitary confinement with no hope of appeal.

Not one to sit and mope, strong-willed Sarah Brown had decided she didn't need the minibus and was determined to walk to the community centre, aided only by her walking frame. On her first attempt, she made it as far as Dogs Need Nice Homes.

Fiona had spotted her outside looking worse for wear. She'd ushered her in, sat her down and made her a cup of tea so she could recover from her exertion. Undeterred, over the weeks that followed, Sarah Brown had tried to make the trek several times more, concluding that she merely needed to build up the stamina. Sadly, every time the limit of her range was always the charity shop.

This had given Fiona an idea. Why not create a mini version of the community centre right here in the shop for the older folk down this end of Southbourne? The shop didn't really have the space, but she could make some, do a bit of creative rearranging. Fiona, Partial Sue and Daisy cleared one corner and acquired a table and mismatched chairs, donated, of course, rather reluctantly by the Wicker Man. And so, Tuesday coffee mornings were born.

They were an instant hit and Fiona would regularly have seven or eight and sometimes even nine pensioners squished around the table. She'd ply them with tea, coffee and cake. More importantly, they could see their friends again. Heartening for the socially starved.

Would any of them know about their friend's untimely death? It had been on the local news that a woman had been found dead in her home, discovered by a supermarket delivery driver. They were the only details. There'd been no mention of the victim's name. For people who didn't get out much, it was highly likely they were unaware of Sarah's demise. Should Fiona be the one to tell them?

They had a right to know. She would break it to them, as gently as she could.

Daisy and Partial Sue had gone mute, knowing this would be a difficult morning to get through. Not wanting to engage in conversation, Daisy busied herself in the storeroom with her favourite pastime, cleaning. She fed musty clothes into the washing machine and wiped down surfaces that she'd already wiped. Partial Sue sat at the till, nose deep in the Val McDermid novel, distracting herself from a real murder by reading about a fictional one.

It was with some relief that Oliver, the baker from a few doors up, broke the silence. Dressed in his smock, he elbowed the door open, followed in by his similarly dressed son, Stewart. Their hands were full of industrial-strength cake tins piled up to their chins, like they were carrying miniature cabers at a Highland game.

"Good morning, Oliver," they all managed to say.

"Is it?" he replied. Oliver had no neck of which to speak, and with a rather rotund bald head, he bore more than a passing resemblance to a Henry Hoover, except far less happy. His mouth had been stuck in a perpetual grimace since 1990 and he had a short temper, acquired from a previous high-pressured job in engineering, which he'd left to pursue something less stressful — baking. It hadn't done much to quell his temperament, which was not helped by standing in front of a searing oven from five every morning and sharing a cramped flat above the bakery with his son.

Stewart had a similar face, except with hair. Being in his mid-to-late twenties, his scalp had yet to be ravaged by his father's genetics. When Stewart wasn't reluctantly learning how to bake from his father or being sent off on errands at all hours of the day, he never took his eyes off his phone screen. The device was never out of his right hand. Even while carrying the cake tins, he was still managing to thumb the screen.

Simon Le Bon appeared by their feet, wagging his tail hopefully, lured by the aroma of freshly baked cakes. His cute little face did nothing to calm Oliver's mood.

Oliver flinched, lifting the tins slightly higher as if Simon Le Bon might leap up and snatch one out of his hands. "Is that dog allowed in here?"

"Well, we are a dog charity," Fiona replied. Normally she wouldn't tolerate such ill will towards her beloved pet, but Oliver did them a big favour every day. "Are you sure you want to keep doing this, Oliver?" she asked.

"A promise is a promise." He put the tins on the table and popped the lid off one to reveal a moist, bulging, round cake, as big and bright as a bouncy castle. "Got a lemon drizzle for you today."

Everyone surrounded the table, cooing with wonder as Oliver laid the cake onto an awaiting plate.

"I am partial to a bit of lemon drizzle," said Partial Sue.

"Me too." Daisy whipped out her phone to take a picture to upload onto various social media platforms.

From under the table, Simon Le Bon whined, feeling left out and worried that no one would give him any.

Oliver's grouchiness hid the fact that deep down he had a kind heart. Aggressive but kind. When Fiona first had the idea for Tuesday mornings, she had gingerly approached him, tentatively asking if he might donate any leftover, bordering-on-stale cakes to serve with the tea and coffee. He'd glared at her, his face growing scarlet. "Why the hell do you want to serve stale cakes!" Fiona had apologised and had been about to make a tactical retreat when Oliver had said, "I'll bake you a fresh one, free of charge." But he had gone even further and started baking cakes every day to donate to all the charity shops along Southbourne Grove so they could sell slices to raise money for their respective causes. They had all jumped at the chance except Sophie from the Cats Alliance, who, after sampling one that Stewart had made, commented that it was "delicious" but "lacked poise", whatever that meant.

"I've been run off my feet," Oliver said. "And these charity cakes don't help matters."

Fiona reached for her purse. "Let me give you some money." Oliver had a knack for guilt-tripping people.

"No, I won't hear of it. Now me and Stewart have got more deliveries, so we'll be on our way." He picked up the stack of cake tins, as if they were his cross to bear.

As they were leaving, the Wicker Man was about to enter, as he always did this time, lured by a slice of free cake. He stood back and opened the door. "Greetings, Ollie," he said joyfully.

"My name's Oliver." The baker pushed past him.

He got a warmer reception from Stewart. "Ah, greetings, Sir Wicker Man of Wickershire." Stewart's geekiness dovetailed nicely with Trevor's theatricals.

The Wicker Man doffed an imaginary hat. "Stew-art in heaven."

"Hello be my claim," Stewart replied.

The unlikely pair chuckled at their exchange, while barely audible groans came from everyone else. Though Stewart was only in his late twenties, it appeared, like the Wicker Man, that he'd been born in the wrong era. "'Tis always an honour to greet thee."

"The honour is all mine."

They stood in the doorway, continuing their verbal joust. A double act of back-and-forth ye olde greetings, until Oliver cut it short. "Stewart! Come on! We've got cakes to deliver!"

"Alas, I must cease my dilly-dallying, for I must bustle. Good day, ladies and gentlemen." Moving his unathletic body, Stewart waddled after his father, nearly sending cake tins toppling.

"Fare thee well," the Wicker Man replied. Entering the shop, he eyed the lemon drizzle. "Any of that cake going gratis?"

"It's for our coffee-morning guests, but if there's some left over, you're welcome to have a slice. Only a pound."

"Ah," said Trevor. "No, it's okay. Do they know about Sarah's demise?"

"Not sure," Partial Sue replied.

"My guess is probably not," Fiona added. "Today's the day when they catch up on all the news."

"Maybe we shouldn't tell them," Daisy suggested.

Fiona shook her head. "I don't think that would be right. They should know."

"Oh, okay," said the Wicker Man. "Then I shall make myself scarce, bid you good day and wish you luck on your task of being bearers of bad news."

"We'll save you some cake." Fiona saw him out, closed the door, then turned to her friends. "Well, they'll be here soon."

"What shall we do?"

"Make tea. Lots of it. Our guests are going to need it."

They headed towards the storeroom to get everything ready. From behind, they heard the tinkle of the bell above the front door. Glancing over their shoulders they saw not Sarah's friends, as expected, but the formidable silhouette of the smartly dressed young police detective from yesterday. Wearing a different outfit but still immaculately dressed in a well-cut double-breasted trouser suit, her hair was slick and glossy, pulled back into a tight ponytail. She was followed into the shop by her tall colleague, decked out in sportswear.

"Hello." She held up a warrant card in one hand. "I'm DI Fincher and this is DS Thomas. I was wondering if we could have a word with you about Sarah Brown."

CHAPTER 8

Fiona placed a steaming cup of herbal tea in front of the DI before joining the others around the table. DS Thomas had declined the offer of a hot drink and stood silently by the door, arms folded.

"Thank you." DI Fincher spoke in a smooth, soft contralto voice.

Daisy pushed the unsliced lemon drizzle towards her. "Cake?"

"No thanks. I don't think I could manage a whole one."

Partial Sue laughed a little too enthusiastically, clearly starstruck by the presence of two police detectives. "Sorry, I've never met a real DI or a DS before. It's very exciting. Oh, and serious, as well, of course." She stopped short of calling her "Your Highness".

Daisy approached DS Thomas to offer him some cake. He raised a hand to silently decline.

"Have you ever shot anyone?" Partial Sue blurted out.

"You need special training to use firearms." From her jacket DI Fincher produced a phone, a black police notebook and a pen. She placed all three side by side on the table with fastidious precision, each object perfectly parallel to the other and equidistant apart. "Do you mind if I record our conversation?"

"We're allowed a copy of the recording if we request it, aren't we?" asked Partial Sue, sitting down.

"You are indeed." DI Fincher smiled.

"I read that in a crime novel."

"Do you want me to send you a recording?" asked the DI.

Partial Sue waved the question away, merely wanting to show off her police knowledge for the DI's benefit. "No, it's fine."

DI Fincher thumbed a few buttons on her phone. Activating the recording app, she spoke the date, time and location.

Fiona swung the conversation back to the real reason the DI was here. "Do you have any leads?"

"I can't divulge matters about an ongoing case."

"Yes, yes, of course."

DI Fincher cleared her throat. "First, an apology. I understand you reported to the officers at the crime scene yesterday about finding a knife with blood on it."

"That's correct," Fiona replied.

"They should have brought that to my attention immediately."

"Was Sarah Brown stabbed then?" Partial Sue jumped in with both feet, talking rapid-fire. "Did the blood on the knife match Sarah's blood? It did, didn't it? Otherwise, you wouldn't be here."

"I'm sorry, as I said, I can't divulge information about an ongoing case. I understand you found the knife in a box left outside your shop."

Fiona took a deep breath. "It came from the shop over the road, the Cats Alliance. I saw Sophie Haverford, she's the manager."

"Dresses like a Scottish widow," Daisy interjected.

"She took it from her pile and dropped it onto mine."

"Pile?" questioned the detective.

Fiona explained the nuisance of donations being left outside charity shops and how she'd seen Sophie dump one of her boxes on their pile.

"And what time was this?"

"About ten past eight."

"And you're sure it was this Sophie Haverford?"

"Positive."

"Okay, then I'll need to question her about this matter."

Inside her head, Fiona shouted, "*Yes!*" Slippery Sophie Haverford was not going to wriggle out of this one.

"How would you describe Sarah Brown's relationship with Sophie Haverford? Did they have any disagreements?"

The three charity volunteers exchanged blank looks.

"Sarah Brown didn't know Sophie Haverford," Fiona explained. "She never went in the Cats Alliance."

"Did she not like it?" asked the detective.

Fiona shook her head. "No, I don't think it ever crossed her mind."

"One of the officers you spoke to also told me Sarah Brown was a regular customer here."

"That's right." Fiona filled her in about Sarah Brown struggling to get to the community centre because of the minibus being scrapped, and the subsequent idea to let her and her friends meet here.

"And who cut the minibus budget?" asked DI Fincher.

"That would be Malorie Granger," said Partial Sue. "She runs the community centre."

DI Fincher scribbled the name in her notebook. "Was there any animosity against Malorie from the older folk, after the minibus stopped running?"

"Oh, yes. Lots," Partial Sue stated.

"Tell me about that."

"Well, they all hated her for it—"

"Hate is too strong a word," Fiona interrupted. "They weren't happy, as you can imagine."

"Did they blame Malorie?"

"Yes," Partial Sue replied. "But it wasn't her fault. Malorie didn't have a choice. Something had to go, or the community centre would've closed completely, but they didn't see it that way."

"They started calling her Malfunction," Daisy pointed out.

"Including Sarah Brown?" asked the DI.

"I'm not sure," said Fiona.

"And how did Malorie take it, being called Malfunction?"

Fiona shrugged. "Don't know. I don't know her personally, but not very well, I'm guessing."

"I wouldn't want to be called Malfunction," Daisy stated.

Fiona leaned in. "Er, you don't think Malorie did it, do you?"

DI Fincher remained poker-faced. "I'm keeping an open mind. Just trying to get a complete picture, information gathering. Can I ask what Sarah was like as a person?"

"She was a stalwart," Partial Sue declared.

"What do you mean by that?"

"Made of stern stuff," Fiona answered.

"Strong?"

"Yes, absolutely."

DI Fincher scribbled something in her notebook. "Being strong can sometimes be taken as bolshie or bullish."

Fiona was quick to clarify. "No, no. Not at all. She was spirited and positive, wouldn't let things get her down, and she was very generous."

"She would let the local kids into her garden after school," said Daisy, "so they could help themselves to her raspberries and apples, well up until about ten years ago."

"What happened ten years ago?"

"I think they all got iPads."

The detective made more notes. "Apart from being irritated at Malorie for cancelling the minibus, did she have any enemies?"

There were collective "Oh, no's" from around the table.

"Sarah was popular," said Fiona. "Everyone liked her. Had time for everyone. That's why it's such a shock that anyone would do this."

"Okay. What about her family?"

"None, as far as I know," Fiona replied. "Eddie, her husband, died about twenty-six years ago. She had a son who moved to Australia, but he was killed about ten years ago in a car accident. Steven, I think his name was."

DI Fincher noted it down, then closed her notebook. "Well, thank you very much, ladies." She turned to her partner. "Do you have anything you want to ask, DS Thomas?"

He shook his head, maintaining his strong, silent-type persona.

DI Fincher turned back to the three ladies. "You've been most helpful and thank you for the tea." She hadn't drunk any. She got to her feet and retrieved three business cards from her pocket and slid them across the table. "If you think of anything else, let me know."

"We will, DI Fincher. We will." Partial Sue snatched up her card and read every detail, then held it to her chest as if she'd just been given a John Lewis gift card topped up to a grand. "If we think of anything else, we'll let you know. You can be sure of that. Yes, indeed. Information will be forthcoming in the detail department . . ."

Partial Sue continued rambling until Fiona cut her off. "How did Sarah die? Was she stabbed with that knife?"

DI Fincher sighed. "I'm sorry, as I said before, I can't talk about that at this moment in time."

Fiona wasn't deterred. "Thing is, in about five minutes this shop is going to be full of her friends. We'll have to break the news to them that Sarah Brown is dead. They'll all want to know how she died."

DI Fincher tried her best to look sympathetic. "All I can say at the moment is what's been released to the press, that a Tesco delivery driver found a woman's body early yesterday morning. However, I would like to speak to her friends."

"I don't think today would be a good time," Fiona said.

"No, of course not. But maybe you could give me their contact details — do you have them?"

Fiona nodded.

"Would you mind emailing them to me? I really need to talk to them. All of them."

"You don't think one of them did it, do you?" Daisy twiddled one of her grey curls nervously. "They were all very close, I can tell you."

Another sympathetic look from DI Fincher. "At this stage we have to keep an open mind. Explore all avenues."

"I can email you their names and contact numbers," Fiona offered.

"That would be great, thank you. Look, if you want me to break the news to Sarah's friends, to save you the distress, I'd be happy to do that."

"That's very kind of you," said Fiona. "But I think it would be better coming from us."

"Okay, if you're sure."

Fiona held the door open for the officers. Before stepping through, DS Thomas spoke for the first time. "Does the name Ian Richard mean anything to you?" He had a deep, calm timbre to his voice.

The three ladies looked at one another. "Never heard of him."

"Okay, no matter," he replied.

The two police officers gave them the briefest of smiles, which would hardly have registered on the glee scale if there was such a thing, and then they were gone.

CHAPTER 9

Partial Sue held up the detective's business card. "I like her."

"We could tell," Fiona replied.

Partial Sue stowed the card away in her pocket. "Do you think she liked me?"

"I'm sure she did."

"She was nice, though, wasn't she? I mean, if I had my time again, I'd like to be just like her. A smart female police detective. Working cases and collaring nonces."

"What's a nonce?" asked Daisy.

"You don't want to know," Fiona warned.

Daisy got out her phone and googled it, wincing as she read the online definition.

"Well, I think they're both a credit to the force," said Partial Sue.

"Bit difficult to tell," Fiona said. "DS Thomas hardly uttered a word."

"That's the good cop, quiet cop routine," Partial Sue remarked. "Must be the new, updated version of good cop, bad cop."

Daisy cleared away the detective's untouched herbal tea. "Well, at least neither of them smelled of alcohol."

The other two stopped what they were doing and stared at Daisy with incredulous expressions.

"Why would they smell of alcohol?" Fiona asked.

"Don't all police detectives have hang-ups?" Daisy replied. "Drink problems or messy divorces. Never talk to their kids. They seemed quite normal, apart from DS Thomas being a bit quiet."

"Not all police detectives have hang-ups, Daisy," Fiona replied. "Not in the real world."

"It's to make them more interesting characters," Partial Sue explained. "Backstory and all that. Fighting the bad guys while fighting their own demons. Classic trope. But not DI Fincher. I think she's great."

"She hasn't caught Sarah's murderer yet," Fiona pointed out.

Partial Sue did a half eye roll. "Give her a chance. It only happened yesterday."

"We don't know the exact time of death. Could've been the night before."

Daisy shivered. "Well, I couldn't do what she does. I don't like being near dead things. I once had a dead fox at the end of my garden. I had to get a special team to come and remove it. Once they'd taken it away, I couldn't go to the end of the garden again. Not for ages."

"Why not?" Partial Sue asked.

"Well, for the obvious reason."

"What's the obvious reason?"

Daisy steadied herself, then spoke in a hushed tone. "The fox's ghost. I'm even more terrified of ghosts than I am of dead things."

Partial Sue planted both hands on her skinny hips. "Isn't that kind of the same thing?"

"Not really. Nothing more terrifying than the ghost of a fox. You don't want one of them haunting you. They make that horrible squawking sound in the middle of the night. Bloodcurdling." Daisy proceeded to produce a fair approximation of a fox's bark.

"Er, you know living ones do that as well," Fiona pointed out.

Partial Sue nodded in agreement.

Daisy's glance shifted between the two other women, attempting to detect if they were winding her up. "Don't be daft. You're having me on."

"We're not. That's just normal for foxes."

"Really?" Daisy still wasn't convinced.

Partial Sue changed the subject back to the matter in hand. "I'd love to be there when they question Sophie, to see her squirm."

"I don't think she's ever squirmed in her life," Fiona replied. "She makes everyone else squirm."

Before any of them could continue predicting how Sophie would attempt to wrap the young DI and the older DS around her well-manicured little finger, the door opened and the first coffee-morning guests arrived. Fiona felt her heart tighten as she braced herself to be the bearer of bad news.

CHAPTER 10

Two hours later, after the last of them had left, a worse gloom lingered over the shop. Sarah's friends had not taken it well. Did anyone take it well after hearing a friend had passed? There'd been tears, disbelief and anger, of course. They'd all been inconsolable, and no amount of tea or cake or coffee had alleviated their shock and grief. The shop, once a haven of friendly joy, had become a place of sorrow and mourning. One of their number had passed and her big personality would leave an even bigger hole in their close-knit little group.

To spare them additional distress, Fiona had held back on telling them that Sarah had been murdered and was now regretting it, wondering if it had been the right thing to do. Had withholding this grisly detail helped or hindered matters? Had she just made it worse, prolonging and adding injury to their pain when they finally found out the morbid truth?

"I wish there was something we could do," Fiona said, helping Partial Sue clear away the cups and plates. Daisy stood at the sink in the storeroom, filling it with soapy water.

"I know," Partial Sue added. "Saying 'I'm sorry for your loss' doesn't really cut it, does it?"

"Maybe smashing something would help," Daisy called out, rather randomly. "I'll clear up the mess. I don't mind."

"Don't tempt me." Fiona ran a cloth over the table while Partial Sue moved a tray of cups and saucers into the storeroom, out of harm's way, just in case Fiona gave into temptation.

"What shall we do with this cake?" Fiona asked. "No one's touched it. Does anyone want any?"

The other two shook their heads. "I'm not partial to cake right this minute," Partial Sue replied, depositing crockery at the sink for Daisy to wash up.

"We can save it for later," Daisy suggested.

Fiona stretched clingfilm over it and continued wiping down the table a little too aggressively. "You know what's getting me? The person who did this is still out there swanning around, thinking they've got away with it."

Partial Sue came out of the storeroom and started tucking in the chairs. "Don't worry. DI Fincher and DS Thomas are on the case. I have a good feeling about those two."

"Yeah, I know, but I just wish there was something *we* could do. I hope the killer doesn't slip through the net."

Partial Sue sighed. "Yep, I feel useless too."

Daisy ceased washing up, letting the water settle. She dried her hands and came out from the storeroom. "Why don't you two try to find the killer?"

Partial Sue and Fiona halted what they were doing. Never usually lost for words, Daisy had silenced them both.

"You know loads about crime," Daisy continued. "You read all them novels. You're always talking about murders and clues and CGI." They were sure she meant CSI, but they didn't correct her. "You must've picked up a thing or two."

Fiona looked doubtful. "Reading crime novels and doing it for real are two different things."

Partial Sue nodded. "Armchair policing, they call it. It's frowned upon."

"So what? Wouldn't it be better to at least try, rather than have it eat away at you?"

Fiona stared at Partial Sue. "She's right, you know."

42

Partial Sue's eyes lit up. "Become amateur sleuths, like Miss Marple in *The Murder at the Vicarage*. I'd love a crack at that. Imagine if we caught Sarah's killer!"

"You know what, I think I would too," said Fiona. "That's a brilliant suggestion, Daisy."

"Why, thank you." Daisy had become all smiles, chuffed that one of her ideas was a good one.

"And you can help us," Fiona added.

Daisy's smile evaporated. "What? Me? I don't know anything about crime. I didn't even know what a nonce is. I told you, dead bodies give me the willies. And I'm not the sharpest tool in the box."

Some cruel customer had once called her that. Fiona had wasted no time marching them out of the shop. Daisy wasn't stupid — scatty maybe, but not stupid. She didn't recall information like others and sometimes she got her words confused. People were always surprised to hear that she had been a primary school teaching assistant before she'd retired. Perhaps not the best educator in the world, but her school had been loath to get rid of her. Always enthusiastic and encouraging, the children adored her, and whenever one of them got angry or upset, it was always Daisy they fled to for comfort.

"You're a lateral thinker," Fiona said. "Unconventional, you don't think in straight lines. That's extremely valuable in crime solving."

"She's right, Daisy," Partial Sue said. "We need your right-angled brain. Besides, I wouldn't want to do this unless we're all in it together."

"Me neither," Fiona said.

Daisy became bashful. "Well, only if you're sure."

"Never been surer of anything."

The three of them met in the middle of the shop, joining one another in a three-way hug. Simon Le Bon wandered out of his bed to see what all the fuss was about. Scooping him up in her arms, Fiona added him to the ensemble, turning it into a four-way embrace, where he proceeded to lick everyone's faces.

Daisy abruptly broke the moment of affection. "We need a name, like Charlie's Angels or something."

"The Charity Shop Angels!" Partial Sue suggested.

Daisy looked unconvinced. "That sounds like a reality TV show where they fix up rundown charity shops."

Fiona put Simon Le Bon back on the floor. "I don't think I have the figure to be an angel."

"Me neither," said Daisy. "My body's definitely not a temple."

"Mine's more like an old garden shed that needs Ronsealing." Partial Sue giggled.

The three of them pondered on the name, wringing their minds, hoping for a drip of inspiration to issue forth.

Fiona clicked her fingers. "How about something simple — the Charity Shop Detective Agency."

"I like that," said Partial Sue.

Daisy smiled. "Perfect."

Fiona straightened up, becoming all officious. "Right, that's settled. From henceforth we shall be known as the Charity Shop Detective Agency."

The three of them jigged with excitement, toasting with invisible champagne flutes.

"Hey, we should get some merch," Daisy suggested.

"What's merch?" Partial Sue asked.

"It's what the young people call merchandise — you know, get some embroidered fleeces made."

Fiona didn't like the sound of this. "We'd look like an elderly hen party. Plus, I'd rather keep this on the QT. Now, first order of business: find Sarah Brown's killer."

Daisy's expression became serious rather quickly. "But where do we start? How do we start?"

"We start with Sophie. She had the knife and she tried to hide it in our pile." Partial Sue was stern.

Fiona shook her head. "As I've said before, much as I'd like Sophie to be the villain in all this, firstly, I don't think she knew the knife was there, she was just being a cow dumping her junk on our doorstep. Secondly, we should let the detectives question her first."

"That may take time," Partial Sue said. "They may need to find more evidence against her."

"That's true," Fiona replied. "However, thirdly, and most importantly, Sophie wouldn't have had any motivation to kill Sarah Brown. The pair never crossed paths. They didn't know each other. What reason would Sophie have had to kill Sarah?"

"That's what we need to find out. But we don't know any details. We haven't seen the body."

Fiona grinned. "But I know someone who has."

CHAPTER 11

"Do you mean asking DI Fincher?" Partial Sue asked. "Because she seemed pretty tight-lipped to me, and DS Thomas's lips hardly moved at all."

"Not DS Thomas or DI Fincher," Fiona replied. "But she's not nearly as tight-lipped as you think. She let something slip. Fairly innocuous but enough to get us going."

"Come on, spill the beans." Daisy was shaking with impatience.

Fiona pulled out her credit card. "Beans are right. Because I feel a Tesco delivery coming on."

They parked themselves at the table, eager to hear more. Partial Sue got it straight away, that quick brain sifting through everything the DI had said. "Aha! She let it slip that the delivery driver was from Tesco's. They didn't say that in the news. They just said a delivery driver found a body."

"Correct."

"But how does that help us?" Daisy asked. "We don't know who he or she is."

"You saw the police cordon when you were on your way to work. What time was that?"

"About nine thirty. I was already late. Apologies."

"Like I said, doesn't matter. Police were already there, tape across the road. Sounds like they'd been there a while. Tesco's earliest delivery slot is between eight and nine in the morning. That must have been the slot Sarah booked when the delivery driver discovered her. We book the same slot, as soon as possible. We're in the same neighbourhood, so hopefully we'll get the same driver. Then we question him or her."

"What if it's not the same driver?" Partial Sue asked.

"Then we keep on booking deliveries until we get the right one."

Daisy beamed. "Let's go shopping."

Fiona pulled out her phone and went online. The other two gathered round the little screen, each taking it in turn to add items to the basket, killing two birds with one stone — get their weekly bits and solve a murder. Possibly the first time that these two activities had been combined. They managed to secure a slot for two days later.

"Oh, I forgot Scotch eggs," Daisy said. "Is it too late to add Scotch eggs?"

"Are you allowed to call them Scotch eggs?" Partial Sue asked. "Don't they have to come from Scotland?"

Fiona stabbed away at the screen. "I think I can still amend the order. As long as it helps us catch the killer. Scotch eggs or Scotch-inspired eggs have now been added to the basket. Total is now forty-seven pounds and eighty-five pence."

Partial Sue sucked in air through her teeth. "I hope we get the right driver, or this is going to get expensive."

"Don't worry. I'm paying," Fiona said.

"Oh, no," Daisy protested. "We've all ordered things. We should all chip in. Split it three equal ways."

"Er, I think I might have ordered a tad less than you two." Partial Sue shifted uneasily. She wasn't hard up and had more money than Daisy and Fiona put together, but chose to live a life of frugality. Before she'd retired, Partial Sue had been a talented, in-demand accountant — brutal, some might say. Ledgers had been known to tremble in her presence. Mercilessly cutting costs, she'd saved many a small business from going bust, and often waived her fee if she knew they were in dire straits. However, her legacy had followed her into retired life, and she lived in a tiny house, where pennies were pinched and fists were tight.

Daisy's normally soft face hardened as she gave her the harshest of looks.

A humbled Partial Sue said, "I'm sure three ways will be fine."

Fiona's finger hovered above a big blue button on the screen. "Okay, I'm hitting buy. Done. Now we wait."

CHAPTER 12

Thursday came around slower than a dishevelled, untucked schoolboy wandering home from school, dragging his feet and bag along the pavement. This was not helped by the fact that customers were thin on the ground. There was not a jot that the Charity Shop Detective Agency could do until they spoke to the person who found the body. With time to kill, Fiona and Partial Sue took it in turns reading alternate chapters of the Val McDermid novel. Gradually they became more impatient that the other person wasn't reading fast enough.

"You standing over me is only going to make me slower," Fiona said, not looking up from the pages of the book. "It's like going to the loo. You can't do it if someone's watching."

"Sorry." Partial Sue backed away. "I'm just dying to find out what happens next."

"Yeah, so am I."

Daisy kept out of it. After she'd exhausted the things she could clean, she thumbed through pages of the *Southbourne Monitor*, a freebie that came every month. The sedate magazine didn't offer much in the way of editorial. It was mostly a vehicle for tradespeople's ads — firms that replaced misted windows or cleaned out gutters. However, one section,

"Bygone Southbourne," had been given over to local residents who were invited to send in their pictures from the past. Sometimes the section would run to three or four spreads, full of faded photographs of yesteryear. Images ranged from sepia shots when Southbourne Grove was little more than a dirt track, right up to the late nineties.

Daisy chuckled to herself. She held up the little magazine for the other two to see. "Look, it's a picture of Malorie with the mayor."

The picture showed a slightly younger Malorie standing outside the community centre with the mayor, who'd just tugged a sash to reveal a plaque to commemorate the new flat roof, of all things.

They were distracted by the front door opening. Like meerkats, their heads spun in its direction, even Simon Le Bon's, the women hoping it was the Tesco delivery.

It wasn't. A middle-aged lady in a crumpled raincoat poked her head in and scowled. "You open?" A fair question seeing that it was only ten past eight. They'd all come in early to catch the delivery slot.

"No," Partial Sue replied.

"Yes," Fiona corrected. She couldn't turn away a customer who had the potential to buy something, thereby raising money for homeless dogs. Fiona smiled. "Please come in, feel free to browse."

The lady didn't return the smile but came in anyway. Simon Le Bon growled at her. She threw him a filthy look, almost baring her teeth, then edged around the outside of the shop, picking things up, examining them with disdainful beady eyes, then putting them down again. Strangely, she had a knack for alighting on objects without a price tag. "How much is this?" She held up a pale blue glass vase.

"Er, three pounds," Fiona estimated.

She grimaced, thrusting it back down as if it were burning her hand, the princely sum of three pounds clearly far too extravagant. She moved on, eyeing a small shoe rack on the floor. "And this?" She tapped it with her foot, again managing to home in on an unpriced item.

"That's five pounds."

The woman tutted, shuffled towards the rotary hat rack. She spun it several times then plucked off a wax flat cap, turning it over in her hands, seeking out a price tag. "This hasn't got a price either. How much is it?"

Fiona forced a reluctant smile. "Six pounds."

"Six pounds! For a cap!"

"It is a genuine Barbour," Partial Sue informed her.

The woman shook her head and mumbled something incoherent but by her tone, Fiona could tell it wasn't good.

They all knew the type. This woman was an enthusiastic moaner, trolling her way around charity shops to complain about the price of everything, being of the mind that everything in a charity shop should be pennies not pounds. Fiona had had enough.

"How much is this?" The woman held up a tacky-looking mug with a slogan printed on the outside: *Putting The Bad Into Badminton*. Underneath this it read, *Southbourne Badminton Club*.

"That's one pound fifty," Fiona replied, still managing a gracious smile.

"But it's got a chip in it," came her harsh reply.

"It's extra if you want chips," Fiona said wryly.

Partial Sue snorted.

The woman did not look the least bit impressed with Fiona's deep-fried pun. "I can get this for half the price at Oxfam."

A shadow came over the front of the shop as a bright blue delivery van pulled up outside. This woman had just outstayed her welcome. Fiona came out from behind the till, approaching her at a rate of knots. "Well, I suggest you go to Oxfam then." She swept past her and held the front door open. The woman stood dumbfounded. "Chop, chop," Fiona said, "before we sell the bargain of the century to someone else."

"I still haven't made up my mind yet," the woman grumbled.

"That's okay. Because we have." Partial Sue shooed the woman out of the shop, as if she were a youngster who'd been indoors over the summer holidays and needed a good dose of fresh air. First awkward customer of the day ousted, they didn't have time to feel pleased with themselves. They needed to switch into detective mode.

Two bare, muscular, tattooed arms carried three plastic crates of bagged groceries to the front door. The delivery driver they belonged to had a wide, weather-beaten face but not an unfriendly one. He wore a blue polo shirt with a Tesco name badge, informing them that his name was Ted.

"Morning, ladies. Would you like me to unload it for you?" Ted asked.

"Yes please. On the table there." Fiona pointed.

"Right you are." He stepped inside and deftly manoeuvred the crates through the shop without bumping into anything and avoiding stepping on Simon Le Bon, who followed him like a little furry shadow. Ted began offloading the shopping, carefully placing the bags on the table.

They would have helped him, but they needed to string this out. Keep him here to answer their questions.

"Do you normally deliver around here?" Partial Sue asked.

He was unloading the groceries at a blistering speed. "Oh, yes, this is my regular patch."

"Has it been a long week?" Fiona made small talk.

"Started on Monday, but I've got tomorrow off." He'd finished one crate and started on the next one. He'd be out the door and onto the next delivery in no time.

Fiona needed to speed things up. "Say, you didn't deliver to that poor lady who died, did you?"

Up to that point Ted's demeanour had been bright and sunny. In the blink of an eye, it turned dark and arctic. "Er, yes. I did."

"Can we ask you some questions?" Partial Sue said.

"I'd rather you didn't. Besides, the coppers said I'm not supposed to talk to no one."

"Please," Fiona said. "She was our friend."

"I'm sorry, I can't." He emptied the last crate, stacked them up, and was on his way out.

"We can make it worth your while," Partial Sue barked.

Shocked, Fiona shot her a look, not entirely sure what she was proposing. The guy halted, then did a half-turn. Partial Sue snatched a smart grey suit off a nearby rack and draped it across one arm seductively.

Fiona relaxed.

Partial Sue turned on the sales patter. "You'd look good in this. Bet it's just your size."

Ted looked it up and down. "I don't need a suit. What else you got?"

Fiona darted over to the DVDs, desperately seeking out something to the guy's taste. She snatched one from the shelf and read out the blurb. "'Jeremy Clarkson Unleashed — everything he can't do on TV".' The cover showed a bouffanted Clarkson from twenty years ago, his hair nearly adding another foot to his stature.

"Urgh." He grimaced.

Fiona put it back. Daisy joined her, aiming for the books this time. Bizarrely, she selected *Twilight*. Fiona couldn't tell how her logic had led her to that choice. She waved it in front of him.

The guy shook his head. "Definitely not. Hundred-year-old bloke who hangs around schools? No thanks."

Frantically the three women scanned the contents of the shop, hoping for something, anything, that would tempt the Tesco driver to stay. The more they looked, the more they became snow-blind. Nothing seemed appropriate for a guy with tattoos and thick arms.

"What about that?" He pointed to the till.

All three of them swung their gaze to where his finger was indicating. Following its direction, they converged on the book beside the till.

"Is that the new Val McDermid?" he asked.

"Oh," said Partial Sue. "That's not for sale."

Fiona shook her head. "Yes, it is." She made her way over to the till, picked up the book and dropped it in the upper-most crate. "It's yours now. If you answer our questions."

He put down the crates. "Okay, if you're quick."

"Don't worry." Partial Sue pulled a small notebook from her pocket. "We've already got our questions worked out."

They all sat around the table. Partial Sue rattled off the questions quick-fire, in chronological order.

"Had the door to her house been forced open?"

"No. It was unlocked."

"When you went in, were there signs of a struggle?"

"Not that I could see."

"How was the body positioned?"

"Face down, in the hallway."

"How far from the door?" Fiona asked.

"About three metres, facing away from the door."

"Could you see any injuries?"

"Yes, she had a gash in her back."

"A stab wound?"

He nodded. They all gasped.

"Definitely a stab wound?" Fiona asked.

"Well, I guess so. I've never seen a stab wound before but it looked like one."

"How big?" asked Partial Sue.

He thought for a moment. "Maybe an inch."

The blade of the paring knife Fiona had found had been an inch wide. "How deep?"

"Couldn't tell."

"Whereabouts was the stab wound on her back?" Partial Sue asked.

"On the right, below her shoulder blade."

"Any other injuries?"

"Not that I could see."

"And she was dead when you found her?"

"Yes."

"How could you tell?"

"I felt for a pulse. There wasn't one."

"Was anything taken?" Daisy asked.

"Don't know. Didn't look like it. She keeps the place very tidy. Although it does smell faintly of roast dinners — always makes me hungry." Ted glanced at the time on his phone. "Look, I really need to get going." The guy rose to his feet and turned to retrieve his crates.

Flummoxed, they'd run out of questions but desperately wanted to know more, except they couldn't figure out what else to ask. Fiona didn't know about the other two, but she felt a wave of amateurishness crash over her. They should have thought harder and longer about what they needed to know. They had the key witness on the hook. A gift horse who was about to leave.

"Can we have your number, in case we need to ask you something else?" asked Fiona.

"I'd rather not. This is a one-time deal. Sorry for your loss and all that, and thanks for the book." He headed for the door, then stopped. "There is one thing that was a bit weird, but I probably shouldn't tell you."

"You can't not tell us now." Fiona took a step to block his path and gave him a beseeching look.

He paused.

"Please," Daisy cried.

Ted's shoulders slumped. "She had a domino in her hand."

"A domino?" Fiona frowned.

"Yeah, it dropped out when I felt for a pulse. She'd been holding on to it with her left hand."

"What number did it have on it?" Partial Sue asked.

"A two and a one, I think. It was wooden and black, and had a name scratched on it."

"A name?" Fiona repeated.

All three women leaned forward, waiting for him to continue.

"Yes. Ian Richard."

CHAPTER 13

Partial Sue couldn't contain herself. "Ian Richard. That's the name DS Thomas mentioned."

"I know," replied Fiona. "But what's it doing scratched on a domino?"

"Do you think it's the name of the murderer?" Daisy asked.

Fiona went over to the till and rang up an imaginary sale.

"What are you doing?" asked Partial Sue.

"We exchanged that book for information. It was a donation and we need to reimburse the charity for it."

Daisy got to her feet. "It's only right. Come on, Sue."

Reluctantly, Partial Sue got to her feet and joined them at the till, huffing. "We only had a few more chapters to go."

"One pound each," Fiona stated. They each dropped pound coins in the tray, then went back to their seats.

Daisy's bottom lip began to tremble. "Poor Sarah. Stabbed in the back. Who would do such a thing?"

"I think we all need a cup of tea." Fiona went into the storeroom to put the kettle on. "I know it's early, but there's some leftover cake from yesterday. Anyone want a piece?"

Two hands shot in the air. It had been one of those mornings when only tea and cake could help.

Partial Sue's eyes became fiercely determined. "We need to find this Ian Richard and give him what for." She sank her teeth into the soft sponge, almost signifying what she'd like to do to the killer.

Daisy took a slurp from her cup. "Do you think he's the murderer?"

"Has to be," Partial Sue said with her mouth full. "Who else would it be? It's classic. Victim knew the killer. Opened the door to him. In her dying breaths, leaves us a clue. More than a clue — she's told us who he is."

Fiona cleared her throat. "There are a couple of problems I have with that. Are we saying that after being stabbed in the back, Sarah had the energy to grab a domino, rather than a scrap of paper and a pen, then proceeded to scratch her killer's name onto it?"

"Maybe it was the only thing to hand."

"What about the phone?" added Daisy. "If she could've picked up a domino, she could've picked up the phone. Why scratch a name when you can just call the police or an ambulance?"

Partial Sue frowned. "You're right. It's a bit of a leap. She'd also have needed something sharp, like a pin, to scratch the name."

"Or a protractor," said Daisy.

Fiona and Partial Sue looked bewildered.

Daisy attempted to elaborate. "You know, they draw circles?"

"You mean a compass."

"I thought that was a protractor."

"A protractor measures angles," Fiona said.

"Ah, is that the one that looks like a plastic sunrise?"

The other two nodded their heads.

"I like those." Daisy smiled. "I always used to get those two muddled up at school in my pencil case." Quite how something sharp, metal and pointy could be confused with something flat, clear and blunt was a mystery hidden in the deep recesses of Daisy's brain that might never be fathomed.

57

"Anyway," continued Fiona, "whatever it was, she'd have had to muster the energy to scratch his name on the side of a domino."

"Rather than calling someone for help," Partial Sue said. "It doesn't make sense."

"It makes no sense whatsoever."

Daisy disagreed. "I'm not so sure. We don't know what happened in that house before she was killed. Say, Sarah is having a tidy up. She liked to keep her place clean. And the driver did say the place was tidy, apart from smelling of Sunday roast. Imagine she's dusting under the furniture — I find all sorts of things under my furniture when I clean. She finds a stray domino and a pin, and maybe a few other bits and bobs. She's from the make-do-and-mend generation, so she puts them in her pocket rather than throwing them away. This happens just before the killer arrives, this Ian Richard. He does the horrible deed. Poor Sarah is dying on the floor, she can't move."

"And she can't cry out," Partial Sue added. "Not if she's been stabbed in her upper back. Knife would've gone into her lung."

"Maybe that's why she didn't try to grab the phone, she couldn't speak."

Daisy winced. "If it were me, I'd just lie there feeling sorry for myself, waiting to die."

"But this is Sarah we're talking about," Fiona said. "Survived Nazi air raids. She's a tough one, determined the killer's not going to get away with it. She remembers the objects in her pocket. With her last ounces of energy, she scratches his name into it."

"The driver didn't say anything about finding a pin," Partial Sue pointed out.

Fiona cast her eyes down at the floor. "Would you notice a pin down there? I wouldn't and even if I did, it's not the sort of thing that would stand out as significant. I think Daisy makes a good point about Sarah. She wouldn't have wanted the killer to get away with it, even if it was the last thing she did. We have to follow the logic through. Assume Ian Richard is the killer."

The front door opened. The Wicker Man popped his head in. "Any cake going gratis?"

The three of them were deep in thought with brows rucked up like unkempt rugs. He read their expressions as sad and disappointed. "Was it something I said?"

"Oh, hello," Fiona greeted. "Sorry, we're just in the middle of something."

The Wicker Man stepped into the shop, not concealing his nosiness. "Oh, anything exciting?"

Fiona thought fast, attempting to conjure up a reason that would get him out of their hair quickly without offending him, so they could get back to what they were doing. She didn't want him interrupting the momentum they'd built up, not when they were making progress.

"It's a stocktake," Partial Sue explained.

"Do charity shops have stocktakes?" he asked.

"This one does," replied Fiona. "Pull up a chair and we'll tell you all about it."

He retreated, edging backwards towards the door. "No, no, I graciously decline."

The Wicker Man was about to exit the shop, much to the relief of all three, when Stewart appeared in the doorway, a stack of cake tins in his hand, his eyes glued to his phone, until he looked up and saw the Wicker Man. "Good sir. How art thou?"

"Stew-art in heaven," the Wicker Man responded with a medieval bow. "Never better on this blessed day."

Fiona looked at the other two, pained expressions on their faces. This could take some time. If left unchecked, their Shakespearian shenanigans could go on indefinitely. Time to nip this in the bud. "Gentlemen," Fiona announced. "Wouldst thou conduct thine affairs elsewhere?"

Rather than having the desired effect and sending them out of the shop, this only seemed to encourage them. A new addition to their Dickensian duo.

"Good madam, we shall oblige." Stewart approached the table and dropped off their complimentary cake for the day. "May I bequeath this small token. Made by my fair hands." He pulled the lid off the tin to reveal a fragrant and spicy fruit cake. Daisy fetched a plate and immediately transferred it, hoping to move things along. Dark and dense, and weighing the same as a small moon, the cake thudded onto the plate. Stewart was a fairly good baker, but he had a tendency to over-egg things, both metaphorically and literally, hence the heft of this particular creation. Fiona wondered if a knife would actually pierce its black, tarred crust, or whether she'd need to invest in a motor-driven cutting device. She'd have a problem shifting slices of this. Customers didn't mind buying a bit of Victoria sponge or lemon drizzle for a pound, a little light indulgence on the go, whereas fruit cake, though delicious, was more of a feet-up-by-the-fire kind of cake, best served in a bowl drenched in hot custard or brandy pouring cream.

Daisy took a photo of it. The Wicker Man made a bee-line for the table, going in completely the wrong direction. "Why, that looks positively divine!" He licked his lips.

Stewart dropped his archaic banter momentarily. "If you think that's good, check this out." He held up his phone. "I made an app. Turns your face into a pizza. Gonna make a mint from selling it. Get my own place." He clicked off a shot of the Wicker Man, then flipped it round to show him.

The Wicker Man guffawed at his face transformed into bread, mozzarella and tomato. "What fun! Do the three of them." He gestured to the three ladies at the table.

Stewart raised his phone to take shots of them. Fiona held up her hand like someone famous blocking a paparazzi shot. "Sorry, Stewart, we've got a ton of things to get on with. Thank you for the cake, it's much appreciated."

"You're very welcome, my fair lady." Stewart picked up his other tins and headed out of the shop, the Wicker Man by his side, mesmerised by the pointless app. "Such wizardry they have these days." Their annoying banter resumed, it was some relief when the front door closed behind them.

"I'm wondering if this table will hold the weight of this fruit cake." Daisy tested the table's stability. "It's like a cannon ball."

"It'll be fine," said Fiona. "Now, where were we?"

"Ian Richard. Suspect," Partial Sue stated.

"We need to investigate whether Sarah Brown knew anyone called Ian Richard," Fiona suggested.

Daisy looked up from her phone screen. "There are twenty-four Ian Richards in the Bournemouth, Poole and Christchurch area, according to this online directory."

"That's a lot of Ians. Which one do we start with?" asked Partial Sue.

"We investigate them one by one," Fiona said. "A process of elimination."

Daisy showed them the red dot on the online map. "This one only lives five streets away from Sarah Brown."

Fiona clapped her hands together. "Good work, Daisy. Did you know that serial killers are defined by the area in which they kill, rather than how they kill? I read that in . . ." She clicked her fingers trying to recall the novel she'd absorbed that information from.

"This isn't a serial killer," Partial Sue corrected.

"No, but what I'm trying to say is that a local killer makes more sense."

Daisy looked uncomfortable, as if she'd sat on something sharp. "I know I'm new to this crime-solving lark, and I don't want to sound stupid, but wouldn't the police already be looking into all these Ian Richards, this one especially?"

Fiona smiled. "That's not stupid at all. In fact, you make an excellent point, Daisy. He may have had an alibi already worked out beforehand to get the police off his back. But we can do something the police can't." She let the statement hang in the air for effect.

Neither Partial Sue nor Daisy looked enlightened. They appeared confused.

"What's Jack Reacher's greatest virtue?" asked Fiona.

Partial Sue's eyes lit up. "Are we going to beat a confession out of him with a broken chair?"

"What? No."

"Jack Reacher's really good at beating up bad guys, that's what he's known for."

"Yes, true, but what else is he known for?"

"Drinking coffee," Partial Sue suggested.

"Yes, apart from that."

Partial Sue thought hard. "Being a drifter?"

Fiona could tell her example of Jack Reacher wasn't the most appropriate one. Time to cut her losses. "His patience," she said.

Partial Sue screwed up her face. "That's not the first thing that springs to mind with Jack Reacher."

"Okay, maybe not the first thing. But he plays the waiting game. Watches his suspects. Learns everything about them, then *bam*!"

"He hits them with a broken chair!" Partial Sue enthused.

"No, that's not what we're going to do. Police would've already questioned him. If he's the killer, he'd have denied it. They can't watch him all the time, but we can."

Partial Sue looked gleeful. Daisy, worried.

"We're going on a stake-out," Fiona announced.

CHAPTER 14

The squeegee shrieked as it was dragged across the inside of the fogged-up windscreen for the umpteenth time.

"This never happens in TV stake-outs." Partial Sue's Fiat Uno had been commandeered for surveillance duties. "Windows of police cars never ever steam up."

"Well, there are three of us in here," said Daisy, who was working her way through a packet of Jaffa cakes.

Fiona had left Simon Le Bon at home because she knew he'd whine the whole time, wanting to be let out. It wasn't fair on him, and it would drive the other two crazy — although they seemed to be doing a pretty good job of that themselves.

Daisy yawned. "I'm bored."

They'd been there since five forty-five, after closing up the charity shop and dropping Simon Le Bon back at Fiona's. It was now ten thirty and between then and now, precisely nothing had happened. Outside it was dark, damp and quiet. Apart from the inside of the car continually misting up, they had a strategic, uninterrupted view of Ian Richard's house from where they were parked across the street. A big, solid property — possibly four bedrooms, judging by its generous proportions — it had red brick reaching halfway, then white-painted render took over, stretching all the way up to the eaves. A tall hipped roof topped it off and would have made an excellent candidate for a loft conversion with all that space up there going begging.

Daisy squirmed in the back. "Nothing's happening. Is this really worth it?"

"That's the nature of surveillance," Partial Sue said. "Nothing ever happens until something happens."

Daisy scratched her head. "But isn't that the same with anything?"

Fiona twisted around in the passenger seat to face her. "It means we just have to wait. It's like a David Attenborough programme. Those cameramen sit for weeks just to catch ten seconds of footage of a snow leopard. But when they do, it's worth it."

"I don't think I can sit here for weeks, not even for a snow leopard. The back of this car's not built for someone with my girth, and my bum's gone numb. Plus, what happens when we're at work, and not here to check up on him?"

"That's a good point," Partial Sue said. "We might have to take it in turns. Do shifts."

Daisy shook her head. "Oh, no. I can't do that. I need my sleep. I need my creature comforts, and when will I get time to get my bits from M & S?"

"When you're not on your surveillance duties," Fiona suggested.

"But I'll be sleeping then or at work. We've got a charity shop to run. And what is it we're expecting to happen here? Because he's not going to reveal himself as the killer right outside his own house."

Fiona could feel her confidence waning. Daisy's logic was right. Nothing was going to happen outside his house. The best they could hope for was that Ian Richard would emerge at some point and they could follow him, but to where? The Co-op? The Post Office? The newsagent? This surveillance project could take weeks, even months of tedium. And if they did discover who Ian Richard hung around with, would it help at all? If he'd acted alone, which was highly likely, would knowing where he went and whom he met provide strong evidence of his guilt?

Maybe Fiona had jumped the gun on this one, got swept up in her own enthusiasm to play amateur detective. She'd made a rookie error, embarking on a stake-out and not thinking it through. Sitting in a Fiat Uno watching a rather nice suburban detached house was not the best use of their time. They'd only just started their investigation, and it was already going nowhere.

"Why don't we just knock on his door and ask him?" Daisy suggested.

"He's hardly going to confess to a murder on his own doorstep at ten thirty at night."

"No, of course not," Daisy replied. "I mean just to get his reaction."

"That's not a bad idea," Fiona said.

Partial Sue rolled her eyes. "You can't be serious."

"Maybe not as blatant as that. But what if we knock on his door? It's late. It'll catch him off guard. We say we're lost, looking for a local hotel or something. Bit of misdirection. Then out of the blue, one of us says, 'Oh, do you know Sarah Brown?' If he hesitates or is stumped or stunned, we'll know he's hiding something. If he shrugs it off and says, 'Nope, never heard of her,' we cross him off our list and move on to the next Ian Richard."

"I like that idea," Daisy said.

Partial Sue agreed. "I have to admit, it's better than sitting here, watching the car mist up, and it does get the ball rolling."

Fiona lowered her tone. "A word of caution. We need to be prepared. If this is our killer, he could be a nasty piece of work. He might try something."

Daisy gave a whimper. "I'm not sure I'm so keen on this plan anymore. I don't do conflict. I can't even watch *Question Time*."

Fiona placed a reassuring hand on her arm. "Don't worry, Daisy. There are three of us and one of him. Safety in numbers. But if he does try something, we need to defend ourselves."

"I have a can of WD40 in the boot," Partial Sue said.

"Yes, grab it. If he tries anything, douse him with it. Daisy, you have your mobile ready to call the police."

"O-okay." Daisy's voice wobbled.

"Listen, Daisy, you don't have to do this," Partial Sue reassured her. "You can always wait in the car."

She sniffed back a breath and straightened up, as much as she could in the back of a Fiat Uno. "No. We go together. Let's do this."

The three women exited the vehicle. Partial Sue armed herself with the spray lubricant, slotting it into the pocket of her coat but keeping her finger firmly on the nozzle, ready to deploy if things went pear-shaped.

They approached the front step. "Let me do the talking," Fiona said. "If he gets nasty, Daisy, call the police. Sue, spray him with the WD40 to incapacitate him, before he realises it's not pepper spray. That should give us time to get back to the car and get out of here. Remember, this Ian Richard is a potential killer. A dangerous individual. The kind the police warn the public not to approach."

Partial Sue and Daisy nervously nodded their heads. They had never looked more serious, or more scared.

"Ready?" Fiona felt a surge of adrenalin.

They nodded again, widening their stances, ready for action.

Fiona rang the doorbell. They waited.

It took a while, but eventually the door unlocked. A tiny man in a wheelchair awkwardly opened it, holding onto the handle and slowly reversing. In his late eighties or possibly early nineties, he was about the size of a scrawny ten-year-old boy. His striped pyjamas drowned him, giving him a deflated look. He had a small, fluffy, silver-haired head, reminding Fiona of a tennis ball that had been left outside for too long.

He stared at them through two watery eyes. "Are you here to put me to bed?"

CHAPTER 15

The three of them exchanged shocked glances. Certainly not what they were expecting, Ian Richard didn't fit the bill of vicious, psychopathic killer. With his sparrow-like frame, it was doubtful he had the strength to lift a spoon, let alone stab someone in the back with a knife.

Partial Sue whispered in Fiona's ear, "I don't think we'll be needing the WD40."

"What's that? What did you say?" He blinked several times. "So, have you come to put me to bed or not? The nurse from the agency is usually here by now. Are you his replacements?"

"Er, no," Fiona said.

"No?" Ian Richard reversed his wheelchair slightly. "But I want to go to bed. I can't get up them stairs on my own. I need to sleep."

"Have you tried calling your nurse?"

"He's not answering, which means one of his other clients — they call us clients now, not patients, probably because they charge a fortune — has fallen over, and he's had to wait for an ambulance, which means I can't go to bed yet."

"Oh, er, well, I hope they're okay," Daisy said, concerned.

"Who?" asked Ian.

"The person who fell over."

Ian Richard harrumphed. "Well, if you haven't come to put me to bed, what are you here for?"

Fiona's backstory about getting lost and asking for hotel directions had become redundant after seeing Ian Richard in the flesh. Partial Sue leaned over and whispered in Fiona's ear again, "I think we should just be straight with him."

"What's that? What are you saying?"

Fiona smiled at the diminutive gentleman. "We're sorry to bother you. We were friends with someone called Sarah Brown. Did you know her?"

"I might, I might not."

"What does that mean?"

"I'll tell you if you put me to bed."

"Really?"

"Have the police talked to you about this?" asked Partial Sue.

"Get me up them stairs and I'll tell you whatever you want."

"Done," Fiona said.

He reversed his wheelchair all the way back into the vast hallway, which had a churchlike feel, all dark wood and stone floors. They stepped in and Daisy closed the door behind her. Turning around, he wheeled himself to the bottom of the impressively wide wooden staircase and nodded to the galleried landing above, hung with rich oil paintings of a bygone Britain. In fact, all wall space was covered in traditional art of countryside scenes, each one surrounded by a thick, ornate picture frame.

"My bedroom's the first on the right," Ian Richard said.

"What's the best way to lift you?" Partial Sue asked.

He pointed at Fiona and Daisy. "You two stand either side of my wheelchair. Scoop one arm under my knees. Put your other arm around my back. I'll put my arms around your shoulders. Then lift. Keep your backs straight; I don't want to call the ambulance for you two, or I won't get to sleep until midnight."

Fiona and Daisy obliged, following his instructions. Once in place, they both lifted Ian Richard, who weighed less than a balloon.

"This isn't so bad," Daisy said.

"I'm light, aren't I?" Ian Richard proclaimed proudly. "Like a baby bird, I've been told."

Carefully, they ascended the stairs, one step at a time with Partial Sue in tow. About halfway up, Ian said, "You know what, I've forgotten my reading glasses. Can we go back down?"

"Tell me where they are," Partial Sue said. "I'll grab them for you."

"No, no. I can't remember where I left them. Be quicker if I look myself. Just carry me back down."

They reversed direction, cautiously retreating down the stairs. When they got to the bottom step, Daisy asked, "Shall we put you back in your wheelchair?"

"No, might as well just take me into the lounge like this. Be quicker."

"Fair enough." So they carried him into the lounge, a vast high-ceilinged room containing two brown leather sofas that had seen better days.

After several circuits of the room, Ian said, "You know what, I might have left them in the kitchen, it's just at the end of the hallway. Would you be so kind?"

Daisy and Fiona ferried him out of the lounge and into a kitchen that had survived from the seventies, decorated in faded oranges and browns.

Partial Sue whizzed around the room seeking out the glasses, ahead of Daisy and Fiona, with Ian still supported between their arms as if he was a pharaoh of old being regally carried around his property and Partial Sue was his herald.

"No glasses here," she said.

"Let's try the study," Ian suggested.

"I think it'd be easier if we just put you back in your wheelchair," Fiona said, impatience creeping into her voice.

Ian was quick to respond. "No. You know what? I think I might have left them in the bedroom, so if you could take me back up the stairs?"

"Right you are," said Fiona through gritted teeth. Although not physically taxing, the carrying lark was wearing a bit thin. She was hoping the information they'd glean from Ian Richard would be worth it all.

For a second time, they ascended the stairs, lifting the small man towards the promised land of nod. As they reached the upstairs hallway, they heard a key turn in the lock.

Below them, the front door opened and in stepped a large man with a beard and a shaved head, wearing a navy-blue nurse's smock buttoned on one shoulder. "Hello," he called out in a thick and cheerful Polish accent. "Sorry, I'm late, Ian, I was just—" His sunny demeanour disappeared abruptly when he noticed the scene above him. His hands made fists, which he planted on both hips. "What the hell is this?"

"I'm very sorry," Fiona apologised. "We were just . . ."

"Not you, madam. I was talking to Ian. What are you doing?"

"Nothing," Ian replied. Never in the history of the English language did that word ever sound convincing when used to answer that question.

The nurse climbed the stairs and joined them on the wide landing. He had a kind, doughy face with widely spaced eyes. A name tag informed them he was Stef from Cherry Tree Nursing Agency. "What did he ask you to do?"

"He asked us to carry him up to bed," Daisy explained.

Stef shook his head. "You can put him down. He doesn't need carrying up to bed. He's quite capable of walking, he just needs a bit of support getting up the stairs. And the wheelchair isn't really necessary."

Daisy and Fiona gently relinquished their grip on Ian, who reluctantly stretched his legs out until his feet touched the carpet. "Why did you ask us to carry you?" Fiona asked.

Ian Richard ignored the question.

"He has a thing for being carried," Stef said.

"No, I don't," Ian snapped.

"Did he make you take him around the house?" Stef asked.

"Well, only to find his glasses," Partial Sue said.

Stef shook his head. "He doesn't wear glasses. What did he promise you in return?"

"Information about our friend, Sarah Brown."

Stef glared at Ian. "Do you know anyone called Sarah Brown?"

Ian cast his head down. "No."

"You don't know Sarah?" Fiona asked, her patience now worn through.

"No. Never heard of her."

"So you lied to us, just so we'd be your slaves for the evening?"

"Well, if you're stupid enough to believe everything you're told, that's your own fault."

The nurse stepped between them. "Okay, that's enough, Ian. I think you should apologise."

"Sorry," he said defiantly.

CHAPTER 16

A few days later, enthusiasm for finding Sarah's killer had not improved. In fact, it had dwindled with every passing second. As they sat around the table in Dogs Need Nice Homes, muted into silence by their failure, their first outing as the Charity Shop Detective Agency had not been one they wanted to remember.

Firstly, their choice of suspect had shown up massive flaws in their investigation technique. If they'd actually *had* an investigation technique. They'd picked on that particular Ian Richard merely because of geography, that he happened to live nearby. They hadn't looked into his background — they'd hadn't looked into anything. If they had, it would have at least revealed that this particular Ian Richard, with bones as light as balsa wood, would have had a job overpowering the far sturdier Sarah Brown. Not impossible but highly improbable.

Secondly, rather than being super-sleuths, outsmarting and outmanoeuvring him with their intellect and guile, he had run rings round them, even though he wasn't great on his feet. They'd gullibly fallen for his ruse, carrying him around his house as if he were some South American deity adorned in baggy pyjamas.

Some detectives they had turned out to be. It was extremely doubtful that they were cut out for this. Their value and self-worth as investigators, though they had barely started, was nosediving into negative equity and looked unlikely to recover.

Fiona gripped the edge of the chair she was sitting on, digging her nails into the hard plastic. She could feel *It*, the thing she dared not mention, starting to cast a deep shadow over her mind and thoughts. She realised she hadn't felt *It* for a while. Not since the day they'd decided to embark on their investigation. Usually, she could sense its tendrils stretching out, trying to ensnare her. Just out of reach but always there, threatening to pull her down.

She'd first encountered *It* when she had retired and moved down from London. Not straight away. *It*'s rise to power had been a gradual one, festering and growing. The ivy creeping up around the oak tree.

After being married to her career, retirement had felt like a divorce from a selfish partner who took more than they gave. Parting was sad, but she had gained the freedom she'd once craved. The most taxing decision she had faced every day was what to do with her time. A nice problem to have, she'd mooch around, walking on the beach or losing herself in the vast and ancient New Forest. Some days she'd just read in Christchurch Gardens in the shade of the lichen-encrusted priory, or head into nearby Bournemouth for a movie or a show.

She had luxuriated in her new lifestyle, and couldn't believe it could be so good. Strange then, that a mote of discontentment began to float around in her brain, looking for somewhere to land. At first, she had ignored it, putting it down to a period of adjustment, maybe a sadistic longing for her old, demanding life in London. She had known that wasn't true. As the weeks went on, the mote grew. It became a splinter and lodged itself in her brain, pricking away at her, getting larger and more uncomfortable all the time.

She had known she was depressed but wouldn't dare admit it or seek help. So she had ignored it and started calling this feeling *It*. Her depression was only matched by her confusion. Why the hell was she feeling like this? Her life was perfect, wasn't it?

She had delved deep into her mind, soul-searching for the answer. She found nothing. Fiona treated her life like she treated work. A brief that needed to be fulfilled with a list of deliverables at the end. They were all present and correct, yet something was still missing.

Trouble was, she knew life was an emotional journey, not an intellectual one, and sometimes what she thought she wanted wasn't always what she needed. Equally, throughout her life she had stumbled on happiness in the strangest places. She had been happy when she was in London. Stressed, yes. Overworked, yes. Tired, oh yes, but despite all these things, she had been happy. It didn't take a genius to figure out that the crucial element missing from her life was work.

Surely not? People work all their lives to get away from the world's worst four-letter word, don't they? To get to the point where they could have what she had — endless time on their hands to do all those things that work prevented them from doing.

Fiona wasn't stupid. She'd outlived her usefulness. She'd become shapeless. Directionless. Her life had become the same pitch and tone. All her time was free time. She needed a thing. Something. *Anything*.

Dogs Need Nice Homes had come to her rescue. As soon as she started volunteering, her depression retreated. She'd had purpose again. Although her depression didn't evaporate completely. She could still sense it at the periphery of her mind, stretching out its tentacles, hoping to coil them around her once more. *It* was still there, but had become more manageable.

However, in the past couple of days, *It* had fled, had been completely absent and she hadn't even noticed. Of course, it was starting to creep back now. But something about investigating Sarah Brown's murder had made it melt away.

Oliver and Stewart entered the shop, dropping off their regular daily cake donations.

"You look how I feel," Oliver said, revealing a rich and seductive coffee cake, its irresistible tang instantly filling the air. Normally the three women would be fawning over his creation, but today all that Fiona, Daisy and Partial Sue could manage was a weak, collective, "Thank you." Daisy couldn't even muster the energy to pop off a shot of the magnificent cake and post it somewhere.

Oliver nodded, while Stewart performed a bow, nearly knocking over the hatstand and toppling the cake tins while still managing to clutch his phone. "Come on," Oliver commanded. "Before you wreck the place."

A minute later, the Wicker Man popped his head in to say good morning, lured by the possibility of a free slice of cake to have with his coffee. He swiftly retracted his head, spotting the ladies' downcast faces, offering to come back later.

Worst of all, the failure had made the three women stand-offish. Nobody blamed anyone. It had been no one's fault. However, when they looked at one another, it reminded them of their foolishness and failure, so they simply didn't speak about it — or anything else for that matter. The shop, once filled with friendly banter, had become a cold, uninviting place.

Simon Le Bon sensed something was up and had taken to lying in his bed with his head angled awkwardly, pretending to be relaxed but clearly not relaxed at all.

The would-be Miss Marples had been more comedy caper than crime thriller, and they all knew it, putting them off amateur sleuthing for good. Better to stay in their lane and keep the crime solving where it belonged, in the pages of the books they read and in the TV shows they watched. Though none of them had said this, it was what they were all thinking.

However, the world of crime had other ideas and was not finished with them just yet.

The bell above the door tinkled. The first customer of the day. Except it wasn't a customer. It was DI Fincher and DS Thomas. Neither of them looked very happy.

DI Fincher stepped in, followed by DS Thomas, who shut the door behind him and turned the "Open" sign around to "Closed". "Do you mind if I do this?" he asked.

"Looks like you already have." Fiona sensed that the police officers' appearance was not a good sign. As if to confirm this, her tinnitus squealed. Simon Le Bon gave the officers a lacklustre tail wag from the safety of his bed.

Still with a fan-girl police crush on the officers, Partial Sue snatched up the coffee cake and waved it around. "Would you like some cake, Detectives?"

"No, thank you," DI Fincher answered for the both of them.

"Tea?"

"No, thanks."

"Coffee?"

"No, thanks."

"Herbal tea. You like herbal tea, I remember." Partial Sue sounded pleased with herself for remembering the officer's favourite tipple.

"Just had a cup."

"Orange squash?" Partial Sue asked DS Thomas directly, as if he were a five-year-old. "I think we have a bottle under the sink somewhere." Not the most enticing offer of a beverage.

DS Thomas shook his head and took up his usual spot by the door, arms folded. DI Fincher gestured to the table. "Would you all mind taking a seat? I'd like to ask you a few questions."

They did as they were told, exchanging bewildered looks. By the tone of DI Fincher's voice, they could tell it wasn't good.

She cleared her throat. "This is not a formal police interview, but I have to warn you, it might become one depending on how you answer the following question. Are you investigating the death of Sarah Brown?"

Silence.

"Are you investigating the death of Sarah Brown?" DI Fincher repeated.

"We are," Partial Sue said.

"We *were*," Fiona corrected. "I think we've abandoned it." She looked at the others for their consent. Fiona and Daisy nodded half-heartedly in agreement. "We'll leave it up to you professionals from now on."

"That's what I thought. Glad to hear it." DI Fincher sounded slightly relieved, but they weren't out of the woods yet. "What form did your investigation take? You're not in any trouble. Not yet, anyway."

"There's no law against performing our own investigation," Fiona pointed out.

"You're quite right, but I would still like you to tell me what you did to investigate Sarah's death. Please answer honestly and in detail. Start at the beginning."

Fiona began. "We tracked down the Tesco delivery driver, Ted. Asked him some questions."

"A Ted talk," Partial Sue said to lighten the mood and impress the two police officers. Nobody laughed.

Fiona continued. "He told us about the name scratched on the domino: Ian Richard. Don't worry, we haven't mentioned this to anyone. So we checked online for all the Ian Richards around here, and the surrounding area. We picked the nearest one to start with. I know from what I've read about serial killers that it's area that defines them most. Not necessarily the pattern of their killing, as everyone thinks."

"What made you think it was a serial killer?"

"Oh, we didn't think that," Partial Sue said. "We were just using what little knowledge we had to form a strategy."

Fiona nodded. "It seemed like the logical place to start."

"I would probably agree with that," DI Fincher said.

The three women looked shocked. "Really?" Fiona said. Perhaps their technique wasn't as awful as they'd thought.

DI Fincher gave a fleeting smile. "Although, I would have done a thorough background check on Ian Richard, plus all the other Ians, before prioritising that particular one. But you're right, geography is one of the strongest factors in a murder case, that and whether the killer knew the victim." She gave a twitchy, dismissive shake of the head, annoyed that she'd allowed herself to digress. "Okay, then what?"

"We decided to observe Ian Richard," Fiona continued. "But we gave up and decided to knock on his door, ask him directly if he knew Sarah Brown."

DI Fincher didn't comment.

Fiona carried on. "When he opened the door, we realised we'd been . . ." She struggled for the right words.

"Slipshod," Partial Sue stepped in.

"Yes, slipshod, I suppose," Fiona agreed.

"How so?" DI Fincher asked.

"Well, I'm sure you've seen him, questioned him," Fiona replied.

"He looks like an evacuee," Daisy said, "that hasn't been fed."

"Then he asked us to carry him up to bed, as his nurse hadn't turned up and then—"

DI Fincher held up a hand, signalling for Fiona to stop. "Okay, I've heard enough. Your story checks out. His nurse told us that three women matching your descriptions were in Ian's house at around quarter to eleven two nights ago. He said he was late getting to Ian's house and found the three of you there."

"That's right."

DI Fincher rose from her chair, ready to leave. "Okay, I think we have enough."

Fiona also got to her feet. "Can I ask what this is all about?"

DI Fincher didn't respond. Didn't look at them. Her eyes were fixed on an invisible spot at the back of the shop. She appeared to be deep in thought. She took a large breath. "Your methods weren't slipshod. Well, a few of them. But you got a lot right, some of them by accident, but that doesn't matter in detective work. A win is a win."

Fiona, Partial Sue and Daisy had no idea what she was talking about.

"You had the right Ian Richard," DI Fincher continued. "But he wasn't the murderer. He was the victim."

CHAPTER 17

"Wait. *What?*" Fiona's eyes widened.

DI Fincher sat back down and laced her fingers together. "Yesterday, Ian Richard's nurse came to put him to bed like he always does at ten o'clock in the evening. He found him in the hallway, face down, stabbed in the back. Domino in his hand."

The three ladies all gasped, clamped their hands over their mouths.

"After questioning the nurse at length, he mentioned finding three older women in Ian's house two nights earlier. I had a hunch it was you three embarking on your own investigation."

Fiona wanted to say something, could feel her lips itching to form words. None came forth. She was too shocked.

"How would you describe Ian Richard?" the detective asked. "Did he seem scared?"

They all shook their heads.

"He was unconventional," Daisy said. "Probably an Aquarius."

"But harmless," Partial Sue added.

"Unconventional in what way?" DS Thomas asked.

"More eccentric," Partial Sue replied. "He asked us to carry him up to bed under false pretences."

DI Fincher nodded. "Yes, his nurse told me he was fond of that. Anything else?"

"Not really," Partial Sue said. "Perhaps a bit cantankerous, but nothing extreme. Not enough for him to get stabbed."

"Depends on who's doing the stabbing," Daisy said. "Maybe he conned someone into carrying him around and they didn't like it. They got annoyed."

"Annoyed enough to stab him in the back?" DI Fincher asked.

Daisy backtracked. "I'm not saying that's what happened. It seems a little harsh for something so childish."

"Did Sarah Brown ever get up to anything like that?" DI Fincher asked.

Fiona appeared shocked at the mere suggestion. "Oh my gosh, no. She was as straight as they came. Why do you ask?"

"Just looking for patterns. Things that may have linked the two victims. Anything else you can think of? Anything you noticed?"

The three ladies went silent, their minds sifting over the night they were in Ian Richard's house. Nothing significant came to the fore. One by one, they all shook their heads.

"Okay. If you do think of anything, call me. I'd better get going. I have two murders to solve."

"But this means it *is* a serial killer," Fiona exclaimed. "Two identical murders."

DS Thomas piped up. "Strictly speaking, it has to be three or more murders to be classed as a serial killer."

DI Fincher nodded in agreement. "Between you and me, I'm ninety-nine per cent sure it's heading that way, and that's what worries me. There are more murders to come. Your thoughts of a serial killer, though unintentional, were correct. Bit of intuition, I'd say. Remember, you have my number — call me with any information."

Partial Sue waved her phone around. "I've already added it to my list of contacts."

"Good. Thank you, ladies." DI Fincher got to her feet.

Before she could make it to the door, Fiona asked, "Was there a name scratched on the domino?"

The police detective halted. She didn't answer.

"Please," Fiona said. "We just want to find Sarah's killer. Any crumbs you could give us would really help."

"We won't take any credit," Daisy promised. "I don't like being in the spotlight."

DI Fincher gave the thinnest of smiles. "You certainly didn't hear the name Sharon Miller from me, understood?"

They nodded.

"Or the numbers one and one," DS Thomas added.

"What's one and one got to do with it?" whispered Daisy.

"The numbers on the last domino, I'm guessing," Partial Sue whispered back.

"Oh," Daisy said.

DI Fincher's tiny smile departed. "The information we've given you is on the understanding that you tell no one, and I mean no one. No friends and certainly no press. I want to keep this Domino Killer quiet. If I do hear about it on the news, I'll know where it came from. The next chat we have won't be so friendly, and it won't be in here. It'll be in a police interview room. Deal?"

"Deal." The three ladies nodded simultaneously.

DI Fincher hesitated one more time. "Oh, just to put your minds at rest, we've interviewed all of Sarah Brown's friends and cleared them from our inquiries."

"And Sophie Haverford?" Fiona asked.

"Her too," replied DI Fincher.

Fiona, like everyone else at Dogs Need Nice Homes, had a sliver of hope in their minds, secretly and somewhat sadistically devoted to witnessing the day when the cape-wearing narcissist would be slapped in handcuffs and arrested.

DI Fincher and DS Thomas left the shop. Fiona closed the door behind them, turning the sign around back to "Open".

"The Domino Killer," Partial Sue said dramatically. "The Domino Murders, that's what they'll call them. One murder leads to the next. A domino effect. Toppling people instead of pieces. Which means, like the detective said, there are more to come."

Fiona glanced at her two friends. "More bodies are about to pile up. Are we all in agreement that the Charity Shop Detective Agency is back in business?"

"Oh, yes," they both replied.

"We should do that thing where we all put our hands in the middle," Partial Sue proposed. "Like they do in American TV shows."

"I'd rather not," Fiona replied.

CHAPTER 18

Partial Sue and Fiona were back on the road where Ian Richard lived. Last time they were here it had been damp, dark and empty, and Ian Richard had been alive. Odd and eccentric, they'd carried him around like the Queen of Sheba. Not the fondest of memories of a person, but the strange fellow hadn't deserved to be murdered. It sent a numbness through Fiona's bones. At least the sun peeked out now and again, and *It* had retreated completely. Her mind felt free and unfettered. Something about investigating the murders sent her depression packing, she was certain of it now. The worthier the cause, the further it fled. After all, what could be more important than bringing a killer to justice?

The road itself was impenetrable, sealed off at either end by police tape in the same manner as it had when Sarah Brown had been found. Still classed as a crime scene, it would probably remain that way for a few more days until the police had got what they needed, which meant Partial Sue and Fiona couldn't get what they wanted — to chat with Ian Richard's neighbours.

Daisy had fancied coming too, not wanting to miss out on any drama. She hadn't hidden her disappointment when Fiona and Partial Sue had nominated her to stay and look after the shop. She wasn't missing out on much. There didn't seem to be anything significant happening here today, only a single uniformed officer standing guard outside the house. A few people had gathered by the tape, doing little else but gawping and taking selfies. Simon Le Bon pulled on his lead, not liking the atmosphere of the place at all.

"Damn it," Fiona cursed. "It hadn't occurred to me that the police would still be here."

"Don't be too hard on yourself," Partial Sue tried to reassure her. "It slipped my mind too. How are we going to talk to Ian Richard's neighbours?"

"Don't know," Fiona replied. "We'll think of something."

They stood at the end of the road waiting to think of what that *something* was, not uttering a word. But that *something* proved elusive. Simon Le Bon whined at Fiona's feet, not approving of the sedentary nature of this particular walk.

Eventually, Partial Sue broke the silence. "What do you think the dominoes mean? Killer's obviously leaving them on the body as some sort of sign, and he's scratching the next victim's name on them, but I wonder if there's a deeper meaning."

"It could be as simple as a visual cue. Like you said, the killer wants us to know that this is a domino effect. One murder leads to the next."

"That seems the most likely explanation, but what if we're missing the obvious. Did Sarah Brown play dominoes? Maybe she was in a club, and she was killed by a jealous rival."

"No, her game was bingo. Another reason she was so annoyed at Malorie scrapping the minibus to the community centre. It was the only place she got to play."

Partial Sue looked disappointed, then brightened a little. "What about the numbers on the dominoes? Maybe they're part of a code."

"Good thinking," Fiona replied. "Like the Zodiac Killer. He used to send codes to the police to taunt them. Trouble is, we've only got two dominoes and four numbers. You're good with figures. Is that enough to make a code?"

"I'm good at accounting and balancing books, but I'm no Alan Turing."

"Aren't there sites for that sort of thing on the internet?"

"Gosh, I don't know."

Fiona got on her phone, stabbing away at a Google search page. "Ah, here we are, a codebreaking site. What were the numbers again?"

"First domino was a two and a one, second was one and one. Two, one, one, one."

She fed the numbers into the site and hit return. It all came back a meaningless jumble, apart from one. A crude, childlike code where each number corresponds to a letter of the alphabet: one equals A, two equals B, three equals C, and so on. It resulted in the word 'BAAA'.

Partial Sue screwed her face up. "Baaa? Like a sheep? What the hell does that mean?"

Fiona shrugged. "Farming? Wool? Counting sheep? Who knows? But it's a bit of a simple code, don't you think? The sort of thing you get in a children's spy kit along with invisible ink. Not exactly a challenge to break."

"I'm going to do a straightforward Google search of the number," said Partial Sue. "See if it's an area code for somewhere or something."

She gasped when the result came back.

"What is it?"

"Two, one, one, one is symbolic in numerology. Extremely symbolic. It's a so-called 'angel number'. That's got to be it. The victims are dead. Killer's turned them into angels."

Fiona Googled it too. "Hmm, I'm not so sure. It's not that kind of meaning. Says here if you see the angel number 2111, it means you need to think about your future and start realising your potential. Not that you don't have a future and are going to wind up as an angel."

"Yes, but if you take the literal meaning of angel, most people will say it means you've gone to heaven. He's sending us a message. The Domino Killer is also the Angel Maker."

"Really? Do you think he needs to send us a message that he's killing people? I thought stabbing his victims made that pretty clear."

The debate would have continued but the *something* Fiona and Partial Sue had been waiting for appeared. Two women approached the caution tape. One was wearing a headscarf, the other carrying a bag of shopping. They stopped by the strip of thin police tape, shifting nervously on their feet, wanting but not having the nerve to duck under it. Not sure what to do with themselves, they stared desperately at the policeman outside Ian Richard's house.

"Those two look promising," Fiona remarked. She sidled along the tape, followed by Partial Sue, until they were both standing beside them.

"Excuse me?" Fiona asked.

The woman closest jumped, nearly throwing her shopping everywhere.

"Sorry, didn't mean to alarm you."

The woman shuddered. "That's okay. I'm not feeling myself today."

"Sorry to hear that," Fiona replied. "Is everything okay?"

"We were supposed to deliver groceries to that house, with the policeman outside," said her companion.

"Do you know what's happening?" asked Partial Sue.

"It doesn't look like anything good."

Fiona bit her lower lip, in case she accidentally let it slip that she knew a man had been murdered in that house. "Do you know who lives there?"

"He's a friend of ours," said the woman with the shopping. "A member of our church."

"Church?" Partial Sue exclaimed a little too loudly, surprised that Ian Richard had been a person of faith.

Fiona got a jolt of adrenalin. Is this what the coded sheep sound meant? Sheep references were heavily used in church scenarios. Congregations were often referred to as flocks, and the angel number connection went without saying. Was the pattern to do with religion or belief?

"Yes, Ian goes to our church, Southbourne Brethren. It's very small. Just the three of us, plus Samuel, our elder. We don't believe in ministers or priests."

"Do you believe in angels?" Partial Sue said without a moment's hesitation.

With a trembling lip the woman in the headscarf said, "Yes, of course. But our church is getting smaller all the time, and now it looks like something terrible might have happened to him."

Normally, Fiona and Partial Sue were the kind of people who'd offer support and comfort to anyone in distress. However, they didn't want to lie and offer false hope when they knew the truth: that one of the congregation had been murdered. Simon Le Bon tugged on his lead, harder this time, sensing their awkwardness, or perhaps trying to get closer to the contents of the woman's shopping bags.

"The three of us is all we have," the head-scarfed woman said.

"What about Samuel, the elder?" Fiona asked.

"He's not local. He comes down alternate weeks from another brethren church in Swindon to take our service."

The other woman lifted her shopping-bagged hand to cuff a tear. "Our church won't survive without Ian."

Fiona wanted to be sympathetic, but she was desperate for information, and she couldn't squander the opportunity. She needed a gentle segue to steer the conversation towards their investigation. Partial Sue stepped in to provide it, although it was about as subtle as a baseball bat embedded with nails.

"Does he ever play dominoes?"

The question startled the two women, snapping them out of their distress. "Dominoes?" the one with the headscarf questioned.

Partial Sue prodded the air repeatedly. "Yes, you know, with all the little dots."

The two women dismissed the idea, shaking their heads.

"Oh, he never has time for games."

"He's too busy with his charity work."

"Charity work?" Now it was Fiona and Partial Sue's turn to be startled. Ian Richard was turning out to be a bit of a dark horse, although he had preferred it when other people were the horse.

"He's such a generous man," said the woman in the headscarf.

"He gives money to lots of good causes," the other woman added.

"He donates to the Samaritans, Julia's House, Great Ormond Street, English Heritage, RNLI, Cancer Research . . ."

The other woman rapidly nodded her head. "He's as generous as the day is long. He gives money to the community centre, even though he never goes there. Said he doesn't like the smell of it. But he knows how important it is to the folks around here."

"Do you know, he gave a thousand pounds to keep their minibus going?"

Now they had Fiona and Partial Sue's attention. Finally, a link with Sarah Brown, albeit a tenuous one.

"But didn't the minibus get scrapped?" asked Fiona.

The woman adjusted her headscarf. "That's right. He wasn't very happy about that. He'd only donated the money a month before. Of course, he complained to the manager — what's her name?"

"Malorie," Partial Sue said.

"That's the one. He was very cross with her. Told her he wanted the money back so he could give it to a cause that would use it properly. She said there was nothing she could do."

"And how did he take that?" Fiona asked.

"Not well, not well at all. Made sure that anyone who'd listen knew what Malorie had done. Thievery, if you ask me."

"Thievery," agreed the other woman. "He didn't want her to get away with it. Complained to her boss, to the local council. Nothing happened, of course."

Fiona and Partial Sue looked at each other, reading each other's mind.

Fiona turned to both women. "Sorry, we have to go."

CHAPTER 19

Ten minutes later they were back at the charity shop sharing their findings with Daisy, who still looked more than a little put out that she'd had to stay behind.

"Was Sarah Brown religious at all?" Fiona asked. "Ian Richard was a big churchgoer, apparently."

Daisy shook her head. "Not really. Apart from Christmas."

"Yes, she was partial to a candlelit carol service, as we all are," said Partial Sue. "What about sheep? Do you ever remember her mentioning sheep? We've racked our brains and can't remember anything. But did she ever mention them to you?"

Consternation at this strange request dominated Daisy's face. She appeared frightened that she might give the wrong answer.

Fiona clarified. "A code that emerged from the dominoes spells out 'baaa'."

"Baaa?"

"Baaa."

Daisy didn't look any more enlightened after this bleated exchange. "Erm, her favourite animals were dolphins. I don't think she particularly liked or disliked sheep. Although, she did enjoy shopping at the Edinburgh Woollen Mill. Practically lived in one of their cardies."

"Doesn't matter. We have a stronger connection between the two victims," Fiona announced, her shoulders hunched with the enthusiasm of it all.

Partial Sue rubbed her hands. "Better than that, we have a motive."

"But Ian Richard didn't know Sarah Brown," Daisy replied.

Partial Sue grabbed a slice of coffee cake meant for the customers. "That's right. But they were both connected to the community centre. Ian Richard didn't go there but he regularly gave to good causes. One cause he gave to very generously was the minibus. He donated a thousand pounds." She bit into the soft sponge sandwich, causing the cream filling to spill out of the sides. "Mm, I am partial to a bit of coffee cake."

"Cake is a pound a slice," Fiona reminded her. "We're not a charity. Well, we are a charity, but you know what I mean."

Reluctantly, Partial Sue put the cake down, dragged her feet all the way to the till and dropped in a pound, then joined Fiona and Daisy back at the table.

Fiona continued, "When the minibus got scrapped, Ian Richard, like Sarah, was none too pleased. He'd donated a grand to keep it going. Though they didn't know each other, they were both very outspoken about Malorie. Extremely vocal about how unhappy they were about her actions."

"But so were a lot of people," Daisy remarked.

Partial Sue swallowed hard, emptying her mouth of cake. "Not like these two. Sarah didn't suffer fools lightly and Ian Richard thought he'd been ripped off. He even went as far as reporting her to the local council."

Fiona became serious. "And now we have two victims and one very powerful motive. Malorie wanted to shut them up. Seek revenge for being bad-mouthed."

Daisy frowned. "I know Malorie can be a handful, but I don't think she's got it in her to kill two people just because they talked about her behind her back."

"People have killed for less," Partial Sue said.

Daisy shook her head. "But she shops at Marks & Spencer's."

Fiona and Partial Sue stared at Daisy, awaiting her logic to fill them in and banish their confused looks.

Daisy attempted to clarify. "Criminals don't shop at Marks & Spencer's. It's not that sort of place. Can you imagine Peter Sutcliffe browsing their 'Dine in for ten pounds' offers on a Friday? It's impossible."

"You've heard of Peter Sutcliffe?" Partial Sue asked. "I thought you didn't know anything about crime."

"Everyone's heard of the Yorkshire Ripper, and I bet he didn't carry a Sparks card."

"Look," Fiona said, "when you first met Ian Richard, would you have said he was a great philanthropist who gave all his money to charity?"

"Not really."

"Well, there you go. Don't judge a book by its cover."

"I always judge books by their covers." Partial Sue brushed crumbs off her lap. "If it has a man with his shirt open, flashing a bronzed six-pack, I avoid it like the plague. And if he's sitting on a horse, and it has 'forbidden' in the title, that's a definite no-no."

"How did you get on searching for our next potential victim — Sharon Miller?" Fiona asked Daisy.

Daisy picked up her phone and began scrolling. "I followed your instructions. Checked with directory enquiries online. It's a common name. There are forty-four Sharon Millers in the area. Five in Southbourne, eight in Christchurch, seven more in Boscombe, nine in Bournemouth and a whopping thirteen in Poole."

"Good work, Daisy."

"It didn't take long. So I did some other digging. Looked all over the internet for mentions of our Sarah and this Ian Richard fellow, you know, any Facebook posts, anything on forums they belonged to, things they might have posted that would have made them enemies."

Fiona and Partial Sue stared at Daisy warmly, not hiding the surprise at her initiative. Although, Daisy was playing to her strengths. Never one to be off social media, she knew her way around it better than the other two, who could never understand Daisy's compulsion to take pictures of whatever food or drink was put in front of her. Whether it was a salad, a prawn sandwich or one of Oliver's and Stewart's cakes, all of it had to be digitally documented for social media. Apparently, it was the done thing, the etiquette to keep one's followers happy and prevent every social media enthusiast's worst nightmare — being unfollowed.

Daisy clocked the expressions on her co-workers' faces. "What?"

"Oh, nothing," Fiona replied, grinning. "We're impressed. That was a smart thing to do."

"I just remember DI Fincher saying about making enemies." Daisy scrolled through her phone. "Lots of people say nasty things on the internet, trolls, so I thought it was a good place to start. Guess what I found?"

"What?" Fiona and Partial Sue chorused, eager to hear what Daisy had uncovered.

"Nothing. Not a dickie bird. No trace of either Sarah Brown or Ian Richard online anywhere."

Their optimism was short-lived. "Well, a lot of older and retired people aren't on social media or the internet," Fiona remarked.

"Last time I looked, we're older and retired, and we're on it," Partial Sue pointed out.

"I know, but we're in our seventies."

"Er, excuse me, I'm still only in my sixties," Daisy was quick to point out.

"Ian and Sarah were in their late eighties," Fiona said.

Partial Sue had a wry smile playing on her lips. "Are you being ageist?"

"As a seventy-six-year-old, I'm not sure that's possible," Fiona replied. "I'm just stating a fact. A lot of people older than us never got to grips with the digital revolution. I'm not saying all of them, but the majority of them still use landlines, write letters and buy newspapers. I can't remember Sarah ever saying she had broadband or Wi-Fi. All the folks that come to our coffee morning don't have a mobile number or email address among them."

"Then how did Sarah Brown get her shopping delivered?" Partial Sue asked. "You need to be online to order Tesco deliveries."

"That's true," Fiona replied. "How did she do online grocery shopping if she wasn't online?"

"I think her neighbour did it for her," Daisy said. "Lovely woman, apparently. Now what was her name? Sarah used to call her Saint something . . ." Daisy clicked her fingers. "I've got it. It's June, Sarah used to call her Saint June, because she was a really good neighbour. Even put her bins out for her."

"We should pay this June a visit," Partial Sue said. "Just to check that's true."

Daisy thumbed her phone screen. "I think I've found her. She's definitely online. And she's got loads of numbers after her profile name — June2111."

"Sorry, did you just say two, one, one, one?" asked Fiona. Daisy nodded.

Fiona and Partial Sue's mouths dropped open.

CHAPTER 20

"What?" Daisy asked, noticing that she'd managed to shock her co-workers again.

"Are you sure it's the same June?" Fiona asked.

"I think so," Daisy replied. "Can't see any pictures of her, but it's got Southbourne down as her location."

"Let me see." Fiona peered into the screen, Partial Sue beside her.

Daisy became worried. "What? What is it?"

Fiona swallowed hard. "The name she uses online is June2111. The number sequence of the dominoes found on the dead bodies. Same as that angel number."

"Angel number?"

Fiona explained it to her. Dropping her phone on the table in front of her as if it had suddenly become white hot, Daisy clamped her hand over her mouth. Her breathing became intense and laboured, not helped by the fact she had her mouth covered.

"Take your inhaler," Fiona suggested.

Daisy obeyed, reaching into her bag to pull out her grey inhaler and took two deep puffs. Gasping and wafting air into her face by flapping both hands, she took several strangled breaths and then said, "Oh my gosh. Do you think she's the killer? Turning people into angels?"

"Domino Killer and Angel Maker," Partial Sue said with some relish. Realising she was being a bit melodramatic and unnecessarily adding to Daisy's worries, she quickly countered it. "Although it could just be a coincidence."

"That's no coincidence," Fiona replied. "As numbers go, two, one, one, one is pretty specific. It's not like having one, two, three, four as your PIN number."

"I don't know," said Daisy, still breathless. "Two, one, one, one would make a good PIN number. Easy to remember. It's not mine, by the way. Mine starts with a zero."

Fiona halted Daisy with her hand. "You're not supposed to tell people your PIN."

"It's only the first number."

Partial Sue frowned. "But isn't that a bit sloppy? Using the same numbers in her profile name as the ones she's left on the dead bodies?"

"Unless she's doing a Zodiac Killer and taunting the police," Fiona said.

Partial Sue shook her head. "But his letters were highly encoded, almost impossible to crack. This is hardly the height of sophisticated encryption. It's more like pointing the finger at yourself, saying, 'Here I am'."

"Yes, but didn't the Zodiac Killer sign all his letters with a sort of cross-hair symbol, same as the logo on the watch he wore."

Partial Sue shook her head. "That was Arthur Leigh Allen, and he was just one possible suspect. A cold-case team now think it was Gary Francis Poste—"

Daisy cut her off, before it turned into a debate about the Zodiac Killer. "So what do we do now? We've got two people who could be murderers."

"We need to be systematic about this," Fiona said. "First, we visit the community centre, see if they have a member called Sharon Miller. If they have, we need to know if she's made an enemy of Malorie and given her a motive to kill her. Then we visit June2111 and do the same. Establish if she knows Ian Richard and anyone called Sharon Miller, and if she has a motive to kill them as well as her neighbour, Sarah Brown. Daisy, you up for a little investigative trip with me?" She expected Daisy to jump at the chance after being snubbed last time.

Daisy shook her head like it might come off. "Malorie makes me nervous, and it's not because she might be a serial killer. Whenever I go shopping in Southbourne, she always appears out of nowhere, trying to rope me into doing things. Volunteering and the like. I always tell her I'm already volunteering here, but she never takes no for an answer. Classic Aries."

Though she'd never met her, Fiona had heard of Malorie's knack for bulldozing people. It bordered on being downright aggressive. It was no wonder she'd been bad-mouthed up and down Southbourne. Would this Sharon Miller be another in a long list of people who Malorie had rubbed up the wrong way? Perhaps that was all it was, and maybe Sarah Brown's neighbour June was the real killer, hiding behind her saintly persona. In Fiona's mind, whenever she read a crime novel and a character appeared to be too nice, she instantly assumed they were the murderer using their niceness as camouflage. Nine times out of ten she was right. But now she was in her own detective agency, of a sort, her theories needed to be backed up, solidified by hard evidence. Otherwise they were just opinions, flimsy and paper-thin. Fiona didn't want to fall into that trap. They'd certainly be accountable for their actions if they began pointing fingers at would-be suspects and informing DI Fincher. They had to be sure, as far as possible, beyond reasonable doubt, and for that they needed to carefully gather evidence and build a case, not throw their opinions around with wild abandon. You never knew who might get hit. She would never forgive herself if she accused the wrong person.

"Daisy," Fiona said. "Go online and see if you can find those forty-four Sharon Millers. All the victims have been older, so maybe narrow it down to only those who are sixty or over. It might be tricky as some of them won't have an online presence, but it's worth a try."

Daisy nodded and smiled. This was much more up her street.

"Come on," Fiona said to Partial Sue. "Let's pay Malorie a visit and then June. See what we can find out."

CHAPTER 21

If Kevin McCloud from *Grand Designs* were to cast a critical eye over the Southbourne community centre, he might say that it had the ambience of a flat-roofed pub, and was just as uninviting — and that would be on one of his more generous days. Pretty, it was not. Practical, well, possibly. Adequate would be closer to the truth. It was a building in the loosest sense of the word, having more in common with underpasses and multistorey car parks than with the traditional buildings around it that were far easier on the eye. Wrapped in seventies' salmon-pink brick — which should have no place in a civilised society — it was a landmark for all the wrong reasons. A bland and plain post-war box only fit for dereliction.

The cold aluminium doors put up a fight as Fiona tried to open them. Metal scuffed against metal, leaving her to wonder how the community centre's more fragile visitors made it in. At least they'd added a ramp. Inside, the ambience wasn't much better. Though the place was packed and resonated with chatter, the disinfectant-laced air smelled of schools. Essentially it was a large hall with a suspended ceiling, a little too low for Fiona's liking, the white polystyrene tiles hiding a multitude of sins, no doubt. It put Fiona in mind of the type of place where a murderer would stash a

99

body. She always thought a suspended ceiling would make a terrible hiding place, as it would make such a mess, especially if it came crashing down in the middle of an important meeting where some committee or other were discussing the colour of what highlighter pens they should order. Cracked lino covered the floor and had strips of blue tape, also worn and broken in places, running this way and that, presumably to mark out a badminton court. Fiona pictured the shuttlecock rebounding off that low ceiling and annoying the players.

Despite her reservations about the interior that had seen better days, it had no effect on the atmosphere. For those who lived alone, who craved a bit of company, it was beloved and cherished. A little haven of tea and chat, there was warmth and friendship here. Tables were arranged in no particular order — organically, you could say. Some had just a couple of people around them, while others teemed with ten or more people of pensionable age parked around the edge, cups and saucers in their hands. Some played board games, others just enjoyed one another's company, giggling and laughing.

An elbow nudged Fiona gently in the ribs. Partial Sue nodded towards a rather smartly dressed gentleman clad in brogues and tweed. He sat alone, engrossed in a large slab of an iPhone. Partial Sue gave Fiona a look, as if attempting to prove a point: the gentleman appeared to be well into his eighties, using both thumbs to rapidly craft a message with the deftness of a teenager.

Partial Sue edged closer. "Excuse me, is that the new iPhone?"

He broke off from whatever he was doing online and smiled proudly. "Oh, yes." He held it up for her to see. "Got a twelve-megapixel camera on this bad boy. It's a doddle for posting on Instagram."

Surreptitiously, Partial Sue turned to Fiona and gave her an I-told-you-so look.

Fiona stepped forward. "That's a nice phone."

"Thank you." The man pulled out a cloth and gave the screen a clean, as if he were polishing his two-seater MG sports car on a Sunday morning.

"Have you been coming here long?" Partial Sue asked.

The man stopped cleaning his phone and regarded Fiona, perhaps wondering if this was his lucky day and some sort of chat-up line.

Fiona cottoned on and brought the conversation back on track. "We were wondering if you might know our friend, Sharon Miller. Have you heard of her?"

The man's wrinkled forehead wrinkled some more. "Can't say I have. Still, I don't know that many people here. Your best bet would be to ask Malorie. Oh, look, here she comes now."

Through the throng of people and plastic chairs, came the striding, determined and intimidating shape of Malorie. Red-headed, rosy-cheeked and heavy-breasted, she wore a horsey, green quilted vest over a checked shirt, the sleeves of which were rolled up, revealing two freckled forearms. She looked as if she should be organising grouse shoots on an estate rather than running a community centre.

"Which is it?" she blustered.

"I'm sorry?" Fiona said.

"Which is it? Member or volunteer? Can't come in here unless you're one or the other. So, what shall I sign you up for? New membership or some jolly helpful volunteering? Could really do with some help in the tea-making department. My girls are good, but they can't keep up with this lot. They go through it like billy-o."

"Er, neither," Fiona replied.

Malorie recoiled theatrically. "Ah, I can see I have my work cut out for me with you two. Need the old sales pitch, eh? Well, come on, follow me."

Reports of Malorie's bullishness had not been exaggerated. Fiona and Partial Sue followed her, chicaning past the various tables, each one adorned with a plate of Family Circle biscuits, judging by the selection.

Malorie pointed out activities happening at each table. "This is our knitting group, the Yarn Birds."

Five ladies looked up and chorused, "Hello," while continuing to clack, click and purl, the interruption not breaking the incessant rhythm of their needles. A man knitting on the end gave Malorie a harsh stare.

"Sorry, Harold. Yarn Birds and Boys, I should say." His grimace transformed into a grin. As they moved away from them, Malorie whispered, "Lucky I came up with that name. Otherwise they wanted to call themselves the Needle Exchange."

The next few tables had been given over to board games. "Mind my presumptuousness but you two look like Scrabble aficionados. Am I right?" Malorie wasn't wrong. Being both crossword fans, Scrabble was Fiona's and Partial Sue's natural go-to board game.

"We are partial to a bit of Scrabble," Partial Sue answered.

"Well, there's a cracking little Scrabble club here. You could see if you can knock Dickie off his perch. He's the reigning champion."

Ears burning, a rotund gentleman in a chunky-knit cardigan hunched over a handful of lettered tiles slowly turned and smiled at them. "Yesterday, I scored fifteen points with just three letters."

"Really?" asked a shocked Fiona. "What was the word?"

"Fizz."

"Doesn't fizz have four letters?" Partial Sue asked.

"Yes, but it's a little-known fact that you can also spell it with one 'Z'," Dickie informed her, as if he were discussing an important legal issue. "It's lawful and permitted. Would you like to join us for a game?"

"No can do, Dickie." Malorie wagged a finger at him. "Only members of the community centre are allowed to play." She winked. "Good news is, I can sign you up right now." Almost as if she had anticipated this moment, Malorie reached inside her quilted vest and whipped out a ream of folded forms. She unfurled them and slapped them on the table, interrupting the game. From another pocket she retrieved a ballpoint pen, clicking the top of it purposefully. "Right, who's going first? You, I think." She pointed at Fiona with the nib. "What's your name?"

"Er, we'd like some more time to think about it," Fiona replied.

Malorie harrumphed. "More time! Nonsense! What is there to think about? What's not to like, as the young people say these days. Now come on, don't be a wet blanket."

"No, really. We just came in to have a look around."

"And you've done that, so it's time to sign on the dotted line."

Fiona's tinnitus rose like a kettle approaching boiling point. One time when she was on holiday in Magaluf, she'd been followed down the street by a man and woman trying to sell her a timeshare. They had flanked her and wouldn't leave her alone, banging out their well-rehearsed sales pitch as they followed her back to her accommodation. They would have continued had she not had the bright idea of heading into the local police station.

This felt similar. That dogged, not-taking-no-for-an-answer attitude. Fiona feared if she signed up, she'd never hear the last of it and would have Malorie hounding her for the rest of her life, demanding to know why she hadn't been back to the community centre. She and Partial Sue were here strictly on a fact-finding mission and had to stick to that.

"No, thank you," Fiona said as sweetly as she could.

"We're good," Partial Sue added.

"Well, this is utterly unbelievable. Why don't you want to join? I'm sure everyone here would like to know." Malorie folded her arms. Her last question had gained her quite an audience. Anyone within earshot had swivelled around to observe Malorie guilt-shaming and browbeating two people into joining when they clearly didn't want to.

Was this why the place was so busy? Had all these people once stood where Fiona and Partial Sue were? Put on the spot, bullied into joining, and from then on afraid that if they didn't keep up their attendance, Malorie would be on them, following them home, badgering them to come back. The people seemed happy enough, but she knew how easy it was to put a brave face on things. Daisy had said she didn't think Malorie had it in her to kill. That was yet to be proved. However, Malorie was clearly a bully. Used to getting her own way, and she certainly didn't like being challenged.

"Why on earth would you not want to join our happy brood?" Malorie was laying it on thick, more for the benefit of those around her, wanting to garner support and draw attention to the pair who weren't complying. "Come on, give me one good reason."

Fiona had had enough. She wouldn't let anyone bully her or Partial Sue, and her tinnitus was playing up something atrocious. Time to shut it and Malorie up.

"What can you tell me about Ian Richard?" she asked.

CHAPTER 22

It wasn't exactly like the saloon going quiet when the stranger walks in, but it was near enough. The curious faces that had a moment ago swung around to witness Malorie's bullish behaviour, now pivoted back to what they were doing. Although Malorie's expression remained poker-faced, the comment had gagged that motormouth of hers. She had the look of someone who wanted to be anywhere else but there. Fiona had rattled her. However, as soon as Fiona had said it, it had occurred to her that she had annoyed a possible serial killer. Would she now be added to that list that included Sarah Brown, Ian Richard and new addition Sharon Miller, and possibly many others who had earned Malorie's disapproval? Fiona had to be careful, or she might seal their fate for herself.

"Follow me," Malorie said in an altogether more subdued tone.

They headed to the back of the hall, towards a wide rectangular serving hatch, its shutter up and its counter laid out with rows of avocado-coloured cups and saucers that had somehow, along with the salmon-coloured brick outside, survived from the seventies.

They passed through a door beside the hatch into a hectic kitchen, dominated by a vast metallic boiler puffing and grumbling away, struggling to keep up with the demand for tea refills from an orderly queue positioned outside. A small woman with a pageboy haircut darted back and forth filling up teabagged cups. On the counter, an unsliced Bakewell tart and chocolate cake waited beneath a fly-proof wire mesh. These weren't Oliver's and Stewart's handiwork, but a pair of shop-bought cakes. Tasty-looking but factory-made, they lacked the girth, heft and handmade magnificence of the bakers' creations. Fiona noticed many of the people in the queue had plates in their hands, rotating them slowly as if they were the steering wheels of imaginary cars.

"Excuse me, Malorie," said a small mousey woman, heading up the queue. She swallowed self-consciously. "We were wondering if we could have some cake."

Malorie halted and turned to face them, planting two palms on the counter in a wide, dominant stance. "You know very well that we don't serve cakes until eleven. Otherwise, it wouldn't be elevenses, it'd be ten to elevenses, twenty to elevenses, and so on."

"I think elevenses is only a rough guide," said a man behind. "Like brunch, it can be pretty much any time between breakfast and lunchtime."

"Depends on when you have your lunch," someone else said. "My granddaughter doesn't have lunch until four in the afternoon sometimes. Can you believe it?"

There were gasps from around them at the granddaughter's cavalier attitude to lunch.

"Surely that's afternoon tea," the man said.

The mousey woman interrupted before it turned into a debate about meal-timing etiquette. "I suppose what we're saying is, can we be a bit more flexible?"

Malorie glared. She had an uprising on her hands, fuelled by cake, or the lack thereof. Fiona was interested in how she'd respond, how she'd handle them and put down the rebellion. Heavy-handedly, Fiona assumed, just like moments earlier, when she'd tried to sign the two of them up.

Malorie gave a sly glance in Fiona's direction, conscious that her behaviour was being observed. Her scowl transformed into a forced smile at the assembled plate-holders before her. She sighed. "You know, I would love to break out the cake. But there are people still eating Family Circle. If I served cake now, the biscuits would be neglected, and I'd be left with a load of stale ones. They'd go to waste, and we all hate waste, don't we?" Malorie was attempting contrition, putting a lid on her bubbling pot of bullishness.

"I miss the pink wafer," a gentleman at the back declared. "Why doesn't Family Circle have the pink wafer anymore?"

Malorie threw Fiona and Partial Sue a pained look that could roughly be interpreted as: "Welcome to my world".

"You could put them in a tin," the woman at the front suggested. "Stop them going stale, then have them later." She was accompanied by copious heads nodding in agreement.

Patience frayed, Malorie barked, "Cake is served at eleven. Always has been, always will be. Now, if you'll excuse me, I have some business to attend to."

Malorie marched towards a door at the end of the kitchen, sidestepping a couple of volunteers standing over an open dishwasher, its top tray extended. They were having a heated discussion about the correct way to load it. One of them kept repositioning the plates that the other one had just inserted into the rack.

"Malorie, small plates go on the top, don't they?" asked one volunteer.

"They always go on the bottom," insisted the other.

Malorie had no intention of getting involved and held up a hand. "Not now!"

Malorie unlocked and entered a cramped office, followed by Fiona and Partial Sue. Rounding a large, handsome wooden desk strewn with letters and papers and hastily scribbled to-do lists, Malorie collapsed into a tatty, high-backed, leather swivel chair. Closing her eyes, she rubbed the bridge of her nose.

Fiona and Partial Sue stood in front of the desk. There were no other chairs. Perhaps Malorie made all her visitors stand in front of her to make them uncomfortable and give her the psychological advantage. Not today, though. Malorie seemed to have reached breaking point. Her eyes suddenly snapped open, a rage behind them. "Do you see what I have to deal with? People trying to bend the rules. If I don't keep them in line, they'd run riot."

Fiona couldn't see what the fuss was all about. If it were up to her, she'd let people have cake whenever they wanted.

"Thankless task this is. See all this?" Malorie gestured to the mess of paperwork in front of her. "It's mostly invoices. People who want paying. Each year it costs more money to run this place and I get less budget."

Being a manager herself, albeit a volunteer, Fiona did have sympathy for Malorie's plight — the continual struggle of wrestling overheads to the ground and keeping them in a headlock, knowing from experience they had a nasty habit of wriggling out and clobbering you back. However, she had to be careful not to be taken in. Her rant could possibly be a smokescreen to distract them from the fact that she had killed Sarah Brown and Ian Richard because they had criticised her, very publicly.

Fiona steadied herself. "Ian Richard gave a thousand pounds to keep the minibus going, didn't he?"

"Oh, I see," Malorie snarled. "So that's what this is all about."

"Yes, it is."

"What's he been telling you?"

Reminding herself that Ian Richard's death wasn't common knowledge, Fiona chose not to answer.

Malorie filled the silence, seizing the opportunity to tell her side of the story. "Yes, he gave us that money for the minibus, and that's exactly what I spent it on. Regardless of me telling him it'd be throwing good money after bad. The minibus was on its way out. Had it. The big end had gone. But he wouldn't listen. Insisted on me spending the money on getting it fixed. So that's what I did, even though the mechanic said it'd be a waste of time. When the new budget came through, we didn't have enough money to run the minibus, let alone replace it. Cutting it was a no-brainer. However, Ian had it in his head that I'd pocketed the money for myself. He dragged my name through the mud up and down Southbourne Grove. I tell you, I could have had him for slander."

"Do you have the invoice from the mechanics?" Partial Sue asked.

Malorie glared. "I don't have to justify myself to you."

"How did it make you feel?" asked Fiona. "When Ian Richard said those things?"

Malorie's eyebrows knitted together. "What are you insinuating? How would you feel if someone made up lies about you?"

"Why didn't you just show him the invoice? Prove where the money went," Partial Sue said.

"As I said, I don't have to justify myself. This is starting to feel like an interrogation. Now, if you'd like to join or volunteer, I'd be happy to oblige. Otherwise, please leave."

They weren't going to get any further with Malorie, but they had all they needed. Partial Sue and Fiona looked at each other, as if reading each other's minds and confirming what they both knew. Malorie was hiding something.

The pair of them got up to go. Before they opened the door, Fiona asked, "Do you know anyone called Sharon Miller?"

Malorie screwed up her face. "Who? Never heard of her."

CHAPTER 23

On her way out, to be sure Malorie wasn't lying, Fiona stopped at several tables, striking up brief conversations and asking if anyone knew a Sharon Miller. All she got back were shakes of the head and blank looks. Sharon Miller was not a member of the Southbourne community centre. While Fiona was sweet-talking its members, Partial Sue edged around the outside of the hall, snooping here and there, sifting through leaflets and generally having an innocuous nose around.

They regrouped outside on the pavement, unpicking what they'd learned.

"I don't know about you, but Malorie is still our number-one suspect," Fiona said. "Only thing that doesn't add up is Sharon Miller. There's no link with her and the community centre."

Partial Sue nodded. "Trouble is, we don't know which Sharon Miller it is, and by the time we do, it'll be too late. Maybe there's a connection with Malorie and our unknown Sharon, but it's not related to the community centre. I'm sure Malorie's rubbed people up the wrong way in other walks of life."

Partial Sue and Fiona headed back down Southbourne Grove towards Sarah Brown's road, weaving through clusters of people on the pavement, not really looking where they were going.

"One thing we do know," Fiona said, sidestepping a mother and toddler, "Malorie's not telling us the whole story. She got very shirty when I mentioned the mechanic's invoice. I think she's spinning us a yarn. A cover story for the missing money." A middle-aged couple tutted as they nearly shunted into the back of her. Fiona had stopped in her tracks. Something had caught her attention.

"What?" Partial Sue asked. "What is it?"

Fiona pointed to a narrow, scruffy, gravel-ridden alley-way. A dented and rusting notice had been screwed to the wall, pointing out a garage hidden at the end of it called AAA Garage. "Aren't there two garages in Southbourne?"

"That's right," said Partial Sue. "The other one is ABC Garage."

Both names had probably been conceived back in the day when people relied on the *Yellow Pages* to look for things. Every business wanted to be listed first alphabetically under their designated category — a pre-Google equivalent of being top of a search page. AAA Garage would have had nudged ahead of its rival ABC Garage with an alphabetically superior name, and therefore was more likely to get picked first when anyone needed their brakes seen to. Fiona mused that some bright spark should have opened another one back in the day, economically and frankly called A Garage.

Partial Sue nodded to the sign. "That one's the cheapest. That's where I take my car for its MOT. They're a little bit more lenient, if you know what I mean."

Judging by the state of her car, Fiona would have said *very* lenient. "If Malorie wanted to save money, that's where she'd have taken the minibus. Come on, follow me."

Fiona and Partial Sue negotiated the pothole-ridden track until they reached a small, cracked square of scruffy concrete, jammed with waiting cars. Behind it was a small hutlike building topped with a pitched corrugated roof, damp with moss.

They wandered in through two wide-open doors to the workshop, buzzing and clattering with the cacophony of engines being pulled apart. A man in overalls bent over the bonnet of a car called out, "Be with you in a second."

A moment later he straightened his burly frame and turned to face them. He was bearded and ruddy-cheeked. Fiona couldn't tell if it was from necking too much cider or because he'd had his head inverted in a car engine and the blood had rushed to it.

Fiona smiled. "Hello. I was wondering if this was the same garage that did work on the community centre minibus."

He looked sheepish and swallowed hard. "Er, what's this about? You're not from the Inland Revenue, are you? You have to tell me if you are by law."

"I think that's only police officers," Partial Sue said.

Fiona took a step forward. "We're not tax inspectors or the police. Someone donated some money for the minibus. We were just checking up on it. Making sure the money went to the right place."

He shifted uneasily. "Are you sure you're nothing to do with the Inland Revenue?"

"Positive."

"Well, I don't know about any donations, but I remember telling Malorie that the cost of fixing it was more than the thing was worth. Should've been scrapped there and then."

"What happened?" Fiona asked.

"She insisted on getting the work done. Asked if I could bring the price down to a grand. I said we could if it didn't go through the books. She paid in cash. Probably shouldn't be telling you that."

"I see," Fiona replied. "Well, that's all we needed to know. Thank you, you've been most helpful."

Fiona and Partial Sue were about to leave when the man said, "Don't tell Malorie I've been talking to you." He looked genuinely worried. "It was supposed to be kept between the two of us, something about going against council regulations."

Fiona pretended to zip her mouth. "Your secret's safe with us."

Back out on the main road, the pavement thronged with people seeking lunch. As they dodged hurrying workers seeking wraps, bagels and sandwiches, Partial Sue said, "What is it about Malorie? She's got everyone scared, including that beefy mechanic."

"I know, she's intimidating, but it sounds like she was telling the truth. She spent Ian Richard's money on the minibus, even though it was a waste of time. She kept her word."

Partial Sue stepped off the kerb to avoid a group of giggling and gangly sixth-formers munching on Subway sandwiches. "She could still be the killer." She hopped back onto the pavement.

"True, but it muddies the waters. I mean, would a serial killer also have impeccable integrity when it comes to money? It just makes our case against her a little harder."

Partial Sue shook her head. "It doesn't change anything. I'm sure Harold Shipman continued paying his mortgage and his car tax while he killed his patients. We still have a motive. A strong motive."

"Yes, but it's hearsay at the moment. We need more meat on the bones. Come on, let's visit Sarah's neighbour June. See what else we can find out."

Partial Sue had an odd look on her face, as if she were in desperate need of the loo.

"Are you okay?"

"Never better. Come on, let's go and see Saint June."

CHAPTER 24

The police tape had disappeared from the end of the road but was still stretched tightly across Sarah Brown's front door, barring entry.

Fiona and Partial Sue stood outside on the pavement staring at the house, wondering on which side her neighbour June lived. Both homes were strong red-brick houses with large windows and mature, well-tended front gardens, that had never succumbed to the urge to be block paved and were all the better for it, in Fiona's opinion.

In the end, Fiona and Partial Sue decided to try both, figuring it wouldn't hurt to question the neighbours each side. There was no answer from the first house they tried, the one on the right, so they trooped around to the left-hand side.

Before Fiona slammed the strong brass knocker against the heavy wooden door, she prepped Partial Sue on her theory about nice people in crime fiction. "If people call her Saint June, don't be fooled by her kindness. If she's the killer, she'll really overdo the Mother Theresa act to throw us off and distract us, especially if she thinks she's some sort of angel with that number in her profile. We need to stay focused and see through all that, stay cynical."

Partial Sue nodded. "Don't worry, I'm as cynical as they come."

"Of course, I might be jumping to conclusions and all her niceness might be completely genuine." Fiona thumped the huge metal knocker once more.

A curtain twitched to the side of them, then a few seconds later, a shrill voice came through the door. "Are you Jehovah's Witnesses?"

"No," Fiona called out.

"Mormons?"

"No."

"Seventh Day Adventists?"

"No."

"Christadelphians?"

"No."

"Episcopalians then?"

"Epissy-what?" Partial Sue muttered.

Fiona feared that they might have to trawl through the full list of Christian denominations before moving on to other world religions, which could take a very long time.

"Excuse me, are you June?" Fiona asked.

"Who wants to know? I don't need my double glazing replaced for free. Please take my name off your marketing list and leave me alone."

"We've not been sent by anyone," Partial Sue informed her. "We're friends of Sarah Brown."

There was a pause. "Does she owe you money?"

"Er, no."

"You know she's dead, don't you?"

For someone Sarah Brown had referred to as Saint June, the woman's blunt responses were currently putting her divine, angelic status in jeopardy.

"Can we speak to you?" Fiona asked.

"That's what we're doing now, isn't it?"

"I mean, with the door open."

"Oh, no. I know that trick. You get me to open my door, then I end up dead like my neighbour."

Fiona looked at her friend. She hadn't considered that June's curt replies might be coming purely out of fear and shock over what had happened just a few feet from her door. They needed to be more sensitive. Attempting to reassure her, Fiona softened her voice. "Please, we're friends of Sarah's. We work at the Dogs Need Nice Homes charity shop. Sarah used to come to our coffee mornings."

A few seconds later, numerous locks and security mechanisms clunked, jangled and slid back. The door swung open to reveal a sixty-something woman, roughly the same age as Daisy, but as thin as a strip of Sellotape with short-cropped silver hair and a haggard face. A large navy-blue fisherman's smock hung off her small frame.

With a sympathetic smile, Fiona offered her condolences. "I'm sorry to hear about your neighbour passing away."

Without making eye contact, June said, "She didn't pass away. She was murdered."

"That must have been horrifying for you. Were you in at the time?" Partial Sue asked.

"I was out, running around after people." June spat out her words, like a mouthful of venom she'd sucked from a wound. "Look, the police told me I'm not supposed to talk about it."

"Yes, of course," Fiona said. "What about Sarah's neighbours on the other side. Did they see anything?"

"Nope. Sylvie is *still* away on a cruise." June spoke with more than a modicum of bitterness. Fiona couldn't tell if she was jealous, annoyed, or both.

"She's definitely away?" Partial Sue asked.

"Yes," June snapped. "Got me watering her garden, taking her post in, mowing her lawn. I think I'd know if she was back."

Her grumpy attitude had wrong-footed Fiona and Partial Sue. Saint June seemed to be the patron saint of irritable neighbours. The conversation faltered, leaving an awkward, pointed silence.

Saint June broke the deadlock. "I suppose I should thank you for those coffee mornings you organised."

Fiona couldn't hide the confusion in her reply. "Oh, er, that's okay."

"Yes, I was a big fan of your coffee mornings. Only time I got a minute's peace."

"Sorry?" said Partial Sue.

"Well, I know you're not supposed to speak ill of the dead, but when Sarah was at your coffee mornings, she wasn't pestering me. I didn't have to go running around after her. Usually it was: June, do this, June, do that. June, put the bins out. June, pull up the weeds in the crazy paving. June, put up a curtain hook for me. June, do my online shop."

"Sarah wasn't online then?"

"Oh God, no. It was always up to muggins here. Lucky I don't drive, otherwise I'd have been taxiing her to the community centre every day. She was a nightmare when the minibus got scrapped. Moping around, never stopped complaining. Gave me earache, that did. Told everyone about how Malorie was the Antichrist. Started calling her Malfunction, she did."

June described a Sarah Brown that was alien to Fiona. Generous and fiercely independent, the Sarah Brown she knew wasn't the complaining type, except when it came to Malorie and the minibus. Maybe Fiona had got her all wrong. Did Sarah Brown reserve a cantankerous version of herself for her neighbour and another more reasonable one for everyone else? Or could June be exaggerating, playing the hard-done-by victim for effect?

Across the road, the front door of an elegant Georgian house, complete with thick ivy clinging to its walls, opened. A man in his eighties gradually emerged, not being the quickest on his feet.

June groaned and her face gurned. "Oh, what now?" she muttered under her breath.

With painfully flat feet and a crooked wooden walking stick, the man shuffled to the end of his pathway, clutching

117

a slip of paper as if his life depended on it. "June! June!" he called out dramatically.

Like the abrupt end of a solar eclipse, June the Miserable became June the Joyful, the saint that they had heard so much about. She left her house and hurried across the road to meet him. "Are you okay, Kenneth?"

"I need a prescription, June. My ankles are giving me gyp. I hate being a burden on you, but I need this urgently. Would you mind?"

"Not at all, Kenneth." June took the prescription note from him. "Now, do you need anything else?"

"Well, now that you ask, I could do with some Alka-Seltzer for the old tum-tum. Last night's shepherd's pie is repeating on me."

"Not a problem. We've got to look after you." She touched him lightly on the wrist to signify all was well.

"Thank you, June. I don't know what I would do without you."

"It's my pleasure."

She turned to go but was halted by Kenneth, issuing her one more task. "Oh, and when you've got a minute, would you mind retuning my digital box? It's all over the shop."

"Yes, of course. I'll be over later," she said sweetly, but her shoulders, hunched with pent-up frustration, betrayed her.

As she came back across the road, all trace of Saint June disappeared, replaced by a very unhappy bunny, a bunny about to go into meltdown. Her eyes burning with annoyance, she almost crushed the prescription note into non-existence, leaving Fiona to wonder how the pharmacist would read the thing.

"Never a minute's peace," she said as she rejoined Fiona and Partial Sue. Huffing and puffing, she pulled a pen from her pocket and straightened out the crumpled prescription. Using a dried-up birdbath to lean on, she filled in the back, scratching the pen hard, almost going through the paper. "You know, before Sarah passed away, I had three of them all pestering me every minute of the flaming day. Sylvie, Sarah and Kenneth. It was like living in a geriatric Bermuda triangle. All of them rattling around in great big houses they're too old to look after." She waved the prescription paper around like an angry Neville Chamberlain.

Fiona realised that June was one of those people whose British politeness prevented her from saying no. She'd set a subservient precedent for herself and had gone so far with it that she couldn't back out. Trapped herself in a self-made loop of agreeableness. A prison of niceness. Constantly saying yes to everything had cultivated an underlying bitterness, spilling out like toxic waste buried in a barrel that had corroded. Did that make her a killer? That was what they needed to find out.

"Excuse me, ladies," June said through a pair of tight lips. "I've got a prescription to collect."

"We'll get it for you," Fiona suggested.

June nearly toppled over with shock. "What?"

"I said, we'll get it for you."

June steadied herself. "You will?"

"Of course, why not?"

"Kenneth doesn't trust anyone to get his prescriptions. Only me."

Partial Sue drew closer and tapped the side of her nose. "Kenneth doesn't need to know. We'll collect it and pop it through your letter box. No harm done."

A playful smile dared to dance on June's lips, not quite believing her luck. "What if there's a problem at the chemist's? It's got my name on the back and not yours."

"What's your number?" Fiona took her phone out. "I'm sure it'll be fine, but just in case."

June didn't need to be asked twice and gave it to her.

"Maybe give me your email too," said Fiona. "Just to be on the safe side. Belts and braces."

June was not about to look this pharmaceutical gift horse in the mouth. "It's June2111@simbian.net."

Playing into Fiona's hands, this gave her the opportunity to delve into the numbers. "Oh, what do the two, one, one, one stand for?"

"That's my dad's birthday. Born in 1921 in November."

"Were they local, your parents?" Partial Sue asked.

"Oh, yes. Southbourne born and bred, like me."

"Right, let's leave you in peace and get this prescription for you. I'm Fiona and this is Sue, by the way."

"Thank you. Both of you. That's very kind of you. Nobody ever offers to do anything for me. I can see why Sarah spoke so highly of all of you." June had that pre-tears look in her eyes and was genuinely touched.

Fiona rested a hand on her arm. "It's really not a problem. I was going to ask, do you know anyone called Ian Richard or Sharon Miller?"

June sniffed back an oncoming tear. "I can't say I do. Were they friends of Sarah?"

Fiona ignored her question. "No problem. We'll be back in a jiffy with this prescription."

As they walked away from a far more contented June than the one they had met, Fiona's mind was whirring. "What do you think?"

Partial Sue snorted. "She's possibly the most miserable person I've ever met. Wound up tighter than a bad facelift. Not an ounce of sorrow over Sarah's death. She's certainly got a motive to kill her."

"Yes, my thoughts exactly. But there are two problems with her being the killer. One, she's making no attempt to hide her motives. She's pretty open about her dislike of running around after her neighbours, which she's definitely exaggerating for our sake. Following the logic, I can see she has a motive to kill Sarah, but surely she'd want to kill her other two neighbours for the same reason, rather than Ian Richard and this Sharon Miller, whom she says she doesn't know."

"Do you think she was lying?" Partial Sue slowed her pace for a moment.

"Not really. I mean, she's a good actor, good at deceiving people. But it's more of a polite putting-on-a-brave-face, suffer-in-silence type of lying, rather than lying through her teeth."

They emerged back onto Southbourne Grove. Filtering between all the hurrying pedestrians, Fiona said, "But if she's not the killer, I still can't understand this two, one, one, one business with her online profile and how it ties in with the dominoes."

"A coincidence?"

"Jack Reacher says he doesn't believe in coincidence, and neither do I."

Partial Sue gently elbowed Fiona. "Have you got a crush on Jack Reacher?"

"No."

"You keep mentioning him."

"He says a lot of smart things."

"Unless Reacher says nothing."

Fiona gave Partial Sue a half-smile at the bookish reference. "I see what you did there. Very clever. Well, if it's not a coincidence, then what's the significance of the numbers? Do we believe her story about her dad's birthday?"

"Can I look at that prescription?" Partial Sue took it from Fiona and read the back. "June had to fill in her details. Her second name is Haricot. I think we can check her story right now. Look at her birth records online." She handed Fiona back the piece of paper. They found a nearby bench and sat down. Partial Sue got on her phone, pulling up the public records website. "We've got her full name and her place of birth, plus we know her parents were born in Southbourne too."

"I wondered why you asked her that."

"Ah, here we go — only one entry under June Haricot, born 1955 in Southbourne. Parents Adrian Haricot and Olivia Haricot, maiden name Atkinson. Now we cross-reference her dad's birth." She thumbed her phone some more. "Adrian Haricot, born Southbourne, November 1921. Her story checks out. Unless she's an extremely sloppy serial killer who's left random dominoes on her victims that she hasn't noticed coincide with her dad's birthday, and therefore her online profile name."

"That does seem a bit of a stretch," Fiona said. "There is one other explanation."

"What's that?"

"Someone is setting her up."

CHAPTER 25

"Malorie!" Partial Sue jumped out of her seat, earning lots of curious sideways glances. "She's trying to set up June as a patsy!"

"It's possible," Fiona replied from the bench. "Malorie's disagreements with both Sarah Brown and Ian Richard are well known. Everyone we speak to seems to know about one or the other. She could do with someone to take the heat off her. Bit of misdirection."

Partial Sue wriggled with the thrill of this new possibility. "So she sets June up as a possible suspect. Finds out about June's dislike for running around after Sarah. Then leaves dominoes on the bodies matching the numbers in her online profile."

"It makes sense. But why haven't the police figured this out too?"

"Police might not know. We should go to DI Fincher, tell her about it."

"I don't think we have enough evidence."

"Oh, I think we do." Partial Sue sat back down and rummaged inside her coat, retrieving something loosely wrapped in tissues. Carefully, she pulled the tissues back one by one to reveal a small, scuffed-up rectangular wooden box. A box of dominoes.

"Where did you get that?" Fiona asked, dreading the answer.

"From the community centre."

"You stole it."

"*Borrowed* it."

Fiona shifted along the bench, closing the distance between them, shielding the evidence from view of passers-by. In a whisper that really wanted to be a shout, she hissed, "You need to put them back, right now."

"Not until I've had a peek inside." Partial Sue used a pen to slide back the top, exposing a well-used black wooden domino set. The pieces were packed in tight with no room to spare, apart from the row on the top, which slid around loosely. It was clear that some pieces were absent.

Partial Sue gasped. "Two dominoes are missing."

CHAPTER 26

After collecting Kenneth's prescription and popping it through June's letter box, Fiona and Partial Sue hurried back to the charity shop, bursting through the door and startling Daisy, who happened to be serving a customer at the till. The woman, buying a garish red satin blouse, swung around, scowling at the cacophonous interruption of her purchase.

Fiona and Partial Sue attempted to be calmer and more sedate, although this was scuppered by Simon Le Bon. He scurried out of his bed and hurled himself at Fiona's legs, bouncing around, tail wagging. Fiona made a fuss of him, bending over to let him lick her face.

The customer tutted her disapproval then left. The three of them gathered around the coffee table.

"How did it go with Malorie and June?" Daisy asked.

"June's an outside possibility, but we've got something on Malorie." Partial Sue opened the box, still wrapped in tissue paper and slowly upended it, letting the dominoes gently tumble out onto the table. Daisy reached out a hand to pick one up.

"Don't touch them!" Partial Sue commanded. "Sorry, but that's evidence, that is."

"We should be wearing gloves for this," Fiona said.

"Good idea." Partial Sue disappeared into the storeroom at the back.

"Where did you get these?" Daisy asked, keeping her hands firmly by her sides.

"From the community centre," Fiona replied.

"What? They gave them to you?"

Fiona winced. "Not exactly. Sue may have, er, borrowed them. No one knows we have them."

"You mean you took them." With a disgusted look on her face, Daisy folded her arms, clearly not approving of their methods.

"Sometimes the end justifies the means," Fiona said weakly. "I know it's a bit dodgy but there are two pieces missing. Domino sets normally have twenty-eight pieces. This one only has twenty-six. If the two pieces that are missing match the two found on the bodies, we've got evidence against Malorie."

Partial Sue emerged from the storeroom, holding up a couple of packets of Marigolds. "Pink or yellow?"

"I don't think it really matters," Fiona replied.

"Let's go with yellow." Partial Sue handed Fiona the gloves. They snapped them on and began turning the dominoes over, revealing their numbered sides.

When they'd finished, Daisy asked, "What dominoes were found on the bodies again?"

"A two and a one, and a one and a one," Partial Sue informed her.

The three women scanned every domino on the table desperately seeking a match, or more precisely, a lack of one.

"I can't see a two and a one," Daisy said.

"Neither can I," Partial Sue replied.

"And there's no one and one either." Fiona got an effervescent hit of adrenalin. For the first time since embarking on this investigation, they had something concrete that firmly pointed the finger in Malorie's direction. Fiona would never high-five anyone, but she could have slapped her co-workers' palms right now until they stung. "Oh my," she said. "The missing pieces match the ones found on the bodies. I think we have her."

Partial Sue thrust two hands straight into the air, as if she'd scored against Germany. Thankfully, she didn't attempt a knee slide. "I knew it. I bloody knew it. We've got the Domino Killer. I can't wait to tell DI Fincher. She'll want to sign us up as part of PIP."

"PIP?" Daisy asked.

"Professionalising Investigation Programme," Partial Sue replied. "The police hire members of the public to assist them on hard cases. She's going to be so chuffed with us, she'll want us on the team, helping her solve murders and the like."

Holding her tongue, Fiona couldn't quite imagine that the young DI would be happy that three retirees had found the killer before she had. "Hold on a second. Let's be realistic. This evidence is inadmissible," Fiona pointed out. "We can't use this, and neither can DI Fincher. It's been taken from the community centre."

"Stolen," Daisy corrected.

"Which makes it as good as useless to get a conviction."

Partial Sue looked offended. "I didn't steal it. I borrowed it. I'll sneak it back in there. Send DI Fincher an anonymous tip-off. Nobody will have even noticed it's gone. I mean, who's going to notice a missing domino set?"

The door flew open, slamming against one of the displays. In stomped Malorie, her face red all over and ready to roar, followed by Sophie, whose stupid velvet cape swooshed along behind her as if she were the Charity Shop Inquisition. Gail brought up the rear, timid as a dormouse.

Simon Le Bon growled at them from the safety of his bed. The adrenalised excitement pumping around Fiona's body turned to dread and shame.

Reaching the back of the shop, Malorie extended an accusing finger at the three ladies seated around the table. "Thieves!" she snarled. "Thieves! That domino set belongs to the community centre. How dare you steal it?" She barged forward, scooping up the pieces and stuffing them back into the box. "You'll be lucky if I don't press charges."

When the pieces were safely back inside, she snatched up the lid and slid it on the box, then marched back out of the shop, briefly stopping to thank Sophie and Gail. "I really appreciate your help. You're both upstanding members of the community, unlike this lot of reprobates." She gestured over her shoulder.

Sophie gave a saccharine smile. "Just doing our duty, aren't we, Gail?"

"'S'right," said Gail, not looking totally sure what she was agreeing to.

Malorie spun around and glared at Fiona, Partial Sue and Daisy. "You three — all of you are banned from the community centre! For life!" She slammed the door behind her, making the bell above wobble wildly, adding to the ringing already rising in Fiona's ears.

Sophie approached them, taking long, slow, deliberate steps. She cast a pitying eye over the three women assembled around the table. "Well, well, well. The staff of Dogs Need Nice Homes resorting to common thievery, and from a community centre of all places. This must be a new low. What has become of you?" She held up a hand just in case any of them had the audacity to answer. "I'll let you work that out for yourselves. However, I will be keeping hold of this little gem of gossip to wield at a later date, when the need arises. You can be sure of that."

She turned to go and then looked back. "Oh, I suppose you're wondering how I knew about your light-fingeredness. Well, it's all thanks to Gail here." Sophie gripped Gail's shoulders and thrust her forward, parading her almost like a child prodigy, the discomfort on her face intensifying. "Gail saw you in Southbourne Grove on a bench, huddled around a scruffy domino set. Of course, she didn't know they were stolen until I received a curious call from Malorie, asking if I had a spare domino set in the shop because theirs had gone missing. Gail told me how she'd seen you two waving a box of dominoes around in broad daylight. Not the best look if you've just stolen them. Naturally, being a concerned law-abiding citizen, I felt it was my duty to inform Malorie about the misdemeanour. Malorie wanted to confront you by herself, but I said no. Not on my watch. You need backup if you're dealing with lowlife criminals. Who knows what those three are capable of? So we accompanied Malorie just in case things turned nasty. Isn't that right, Gail?"

"'S'right," Gail replied with more than her usual reluctance, clearly uncomfortable at being portrayed as Sophie's unwitting snitch.

Sophie's self-satisfied grin beamed brighter than phosphorus. "So, now you're all caught up. I do like the rubber gloves, by the way, gives you a very subservient look. Oh, and I had a visit from that ethnic policewoman the other day."

Partial Sue spoke through gritted teeth. "Her name is Detective Inspector Fincher."

"Whatever, dear. Anyway, please don't spin any more of your lies about me leaving bloody knives outside your shop. The policewoman saw right through it. What with that and stealing domino sets, instead of Dogs Need Nice Homes, you might have to rename this shop OAPs Need Arresting. Come on, Gail. Our work is done here. Toodle-oo."

They watched Sophie saunter towards the door, clutching the edge of her cape so it didn't catch on anything. Just before she left, Sophie swept around theatrically, sending it billowing out and swatting Gail in the face. With a curious expression, Sophie regarded the interior of their shop. "I do love what you *haven't* done with the place. But tell me, why do you have a table in here? You don't sell furniture, do you?"

Fiona and Partial Sue were too angry to answer. Daisy stepped in. "It's for coffee mornings. For the folk who can't make it to the community centre."

Sophie sniggered smugly to herself, then swished out of the shop, followed by Gail.

CHAPTER 27

Silence hung in the air as heavy as iron. The three women sat around the table, staring at their hands, neither of them daring to catch one another's eye or shift position. Humiliation rooted them to the spot, dragging them down. In the awkward minutes that followed, no customers came in to create a distraction from their despondency. They could have really done with one, a diversion from the embarrassment of what had happened.

The stinging silence continued until Daisy spoke. "We're not very good at this, are we?"

The heads of the other two women bowed slightly, a physical affirmation of what she had uttered. She was right. They weren't very good at this. The initial enthusiasm of forming the Charity Shop Detective Agency in a bid to find Sarah Brown's killer had given them gusto and bravado, sweeping them up and carrying them along. A self-righteous crusade to bring about justice. However, it was becoming brutally clear that gusto and bravado were little more than a couple of brash, overconfident brothers who promised a lot but delivered very little. The three women had stumbled and fumbled through a fledgling investigation, and now that fledgling was gasping its last few breaths.

Fiona's self-confidence had fled, evaporating like cheap perfume. She couldn't tell whether this was because of their amateurishness or being caught red-handed with stolen goods. A bit of both probably, but mostly the latter. They were supposed to be fighting crime, not being accused of it.

"Sorry," Partial Sue apologised. "This is all my fault. I stole the dominoes, and now I've brought the whole thing crashing down on our heads. Buggered it up, good and proper."

Fiona gave her a reassuring, sympathetic smile. "I don't think any of us knew what we were doing."

"I never know what I'm doing," Daisy remarked. "Whether it's investigating murders or doing a direct debit."

The other two smiled.

"I think that goes for all three of us," Fiona said. "Question is, do we want to keep going? I don't know about you two, but this all seems a bit of a farce. Like we're kids dressing up."

Partial Sue peeled off her rubber gloves, tossing them onto the table with abandon. "But we have a solid suspect in Malorie."

"I know you two are the crime experts," Daisy said, "but would Malorie really come in here making a fuss over stolen dominoes if she was also leaving them on dead pensioners? I certainly wouldn't. Plus, how many people have access to those dominoes? It's not just Malorie. Dozens of people go to that community centre. Any one of them could've swiped a couple of dominoes and stuck the knife in Sarah's back. God rest her soul."

Partial Sue shook her head and looked doubtful. "No one at that community centre has the strength to put a knife in someone's back — they're all too fragile, apart from someone sturdy like Malorie. It's a lot harder than you think to drive a knife into a body, especially if it's protected by the ribcage." She made an imaginary stabbing motion in the air. "Body puts up resistance, knife comes to an abrupt halt. That's why kitchen knives used in stabbings end up injuring the attacker. Their hand slips forward onto the blade, cutting their fingers. Unless you've got good grip strength, like Andy Murray."

"Hey, they have a badminton club at the community centre," Daisy said. "Could be one of them. I was going to join but I don't like shuttlecocks, they give me the creeps. They look like mistreated dreamcatchers."

Partial Sue released a sigh. "A badminton player wouldn't have the same grip strength as a tennis player. That's like comparing gravy with curry sauce. It's not the same."

"Daisy has a point, though," Fiona said. "That community centre is used by hundreds of people, not just OAPs. And would Malorie really make such a big deal of her missing dominoes if she was the killer? We have to be careful that we're not making Malorie a suspect because we want her to be one."

"But she's got a motive."

"Yes, but so could somebody else who goes to that community centre. We'd have to interview every member to be sure. One by one."

Partial Sue became fierce. "Go on, say it."

"Say what?" Fiona asked, perplexed at her sudden mood change.

"What you're dying to say. That I've ruined the chance of that happening because I've got us all banned."

"I didn't mean that."

"Well, it sounds like you did." Partial Sue folded her arms. "I was going to put the dominoes back."

Fiona pulled off her gloves and slapped them on the table. "So you keep saying."

"At least I moved the investigation forward."

"Until Malorie came in here, accusing us of being thieves," Fiona replied. "Now we're back to square one. Worse than that, we're all banned from the community centre, the most probable link to the killer."

Partial Sue stared Fiona in the eye. "I wish you'd just say it was my fault and be done with it."

"Stop it!" Daisy cried. "Please can you stop arguing and blaming each other. It's horrible and it's getting us nowhere. And it's a complete waste of time if we're going to give up the investigation. Let's just forget about it and go back to how we were before. Being nice to one another and having cups of tea and eating cake and holding coffee mornings."

Before either Partial Sue or Fiona could answer, the bell above the door tinkled, breaking the heated conversation. A rather red-faced, smartly dressed gentleman with thinning, slicked-back grey hair and no chin of which to speak popped his head inside the door. "I need a new watch battery fitted."

"Sorry," Fiona replied. "This isn't a jeweller's anymore, it's a charity shop for homeless dogs." This was an occupational hazard of working in a charity shop. People would refuse to believe that the original shop had ceased to be and had been commandeered for charitable purposes, despite the visual evidence all around them — in this case, the fact that the watches, rings and necklaces had disappeared and been replaced by musty-smelling clothes, books and knick-knacks, as well as the large sign above the door that didn't feature the word 'jeweller' anywhere.

"Oh." He cast his eyes around the shop, taking in its contents. "That's a pity. Well, can you take some links out of this for me?" He thrust his arm out and did a little shimmy with his wrist, jiggling off the chunky, tasteless gold watch. "Been on that paleo diet and now I'm worried the damn thing might fall off."

Fiona was about to explain to him that their status as a charity shop hadn't changed in the last few seconds when Daisy interrupted, "I could probably give it a go. I think I've got some little screwdrivers out the back."

"How much would it cost?"

"Nothing," Daisy replied.

Fiona cleared her throat. "Maybe just a small donation to help the homeless dogs."

"Done," the man said.

Fiona and Partial Sue watched on in amazed silence as Daisy fiddled with the man's watch with the dexterity of an elf, extracting mouse-sized screws from the strap, which was big enough to replace the tracks on a tiger tank. When she'd relieved it of two of its links, the man tried it on for size. "Ah, perfect. Thank you. That's much better." He reached into his back pocket, slipped out his wallet and placed a twenty on the table. "For the poor little homeless doggies."

"That's very kind of you," Fiona said.

When the man had gone, Partial Sue nudged Daisy. "You're full of surprises. Where did you learn to do that?"

"I'm a miniaturist."

"Like the book?" Fiona offered.

"Yes, I love doll's houses and fiddling with little objects. Making little rocking horses and furniture."

"You know," Partial Sue said with plenty of enthusiasm, "you'd be good at picking locks. Getting us into the community centre to snoop around."

Fiona glared at her. "We're not going down that path again, are we?"

Partial Sue raised her hands in a surrender. "I'm just saying."

Fiona snapped up the twenty and took it over to the till. She surveyed the buttons, trying to figure out which category to cash it under. Nothing really fitted the bill, so she decided to ring it in under clothes and jewellery.

Her finger hovered over the button. She looked up. They had to remain positive. Fiona knew that more than anyone else. Stay busy, keep your mind and body occupied — that was her mantra for banishing negative thoughts and keeping *It* away. She just needed to convince the other two of it, gee them up. "We should carry on trying to find Sarah's killer."

Partial Sue shrugged. "I'm not really feeling very motivated at the moment."

"Me neither," Daisy agreed.

Fiona stepped out from behind the till. "But look how far we've come. We can't give up now. We can't let one little setback put us off. Besides, I've just thought of something. Something the police will have missed."

CHAPTER 28

Partial Sue rocked back and forth in her seat with childlike excitement. "Come on, come on. Spill the beans. Tell us."

Fiona joined them at the table. "Throughout this, I've been trying to channel Jane Tennison."

"Who?" Daisy asked.

Partial Sue became animated. "You know, played by the great Helen Mirren."

"Oh, I know," Daisy grinned. "She's really funny."

"Funny?" Fiona questioned.

"Yeah, she gets her jugs out for charity with all those other women."

Partial Sue groaned. "That's *Calendar Girls*. We're talking about *Prime Suspect*, DCI Jane Tennison. One of the best TV detectives ever." Partial Sue leaped out of her seat and scuttled over to the DVDs. Running her finger along the shelf, she alighted on a second-hand copy of the ground-breaking crime drama. She slid it out and returned holding it aloft as if it were the Holy Grail, then placed it in front of Daisy.

Daisy read the back. "'Detective Chief Inspector Jane Tennison investigates the murder of a young woman found dead in a seedy bedsit while battling to prove herself in a male-dominated world'."

"It's a masterclass in police investigation," Fiona said. "In the face of rampant sexism."

"She's our role model," Partial Sue said. "Watch and learn. That's the first one, there are seven seasons in total, plus *Prime Suspect 1973*, when Jane Tennison was a young copper."

Daisy smiled politely, in the way that most people do when a recommendation is foisted upon them. "Okay. I'll give it a go, but I'm not promising anything."

Partial Sue stared at Fiona and lightly tapped the table impatiently. "Come on, you were about to make a revelation."

"Oh, yes. Throughout this I've been thinking, 'What would Jane Tennison do?' So when I rang that donation into the till, it made me think of something. Jane Tennison would want a list of every domino set sold in the last six months."

Partial Sue nodded her head, eager to hear more. "Yep, I bet DI Fincher has done that already."

"And we know that line of enquiry didn't work because they haven't arrested anyone yet."

"Correct."

"Shops and online retailers keep a record of every single sale," Fiona continued. "It's impossible to buy anything these days without knowing where and when it was purchased. Even our systems log sales, but they only do it generically, under very broad categories: books, clothes, household items, toys and games. The purchase of a domino set from a charity shop wouldn't show up."

Partial Sue shook her head. "But I still think it's Malorie. She's already got a domino set at the community centre."

Sensing the debate circling back around to where they were a few moments ago, Fiona quickly nipped it in the bud. "Let's just assume for a second it's not Malorie or anyone else at the community centre, for the reasons we just discussed. That line of enquiry is closed to us at the moment so there's no point going there. Plus, my gut is telling me otherwise. There's something fishy about it. It feels like a red herring, excuse the pun. I can't see a smart killer using dominoes from a set where it's obvious that everyone's going to notice that two pieces are missing — ones that match those on the bodies. I think we're being played, misdirected. So let's just assume it's someone else. The killer would need to get hold of an untraceable domino set. Best place to do that would be at a charity shop."

"Couldn't they just use one they already had at home?" Daisy asked.

"True," Fiona replied, "but it'd be covered in their DNA, and you really don't want to leave DNA on the victim's body, or anything that could identify you."

"You can get rid of DNA with bleach and UV," Partial Sue pointed out.

"Nothing's a hundred per cent," Fiona said. "There's still a chance some would be left behind. Why take the risk when you could buy a second-hand, untraceable domino set covered in someone else's DNA and fingerprints? Much easier and no record of the purchase."

Partial Sue blew out through her teeth. "But if there's no record of their purchase, how are we going to track them down?"

Fiona pulled her phone out of her bag and placed it on the table. "We pull in favours and play to our strengths. We call up our fellow charity shops in Southbourne, Bournemouth, Poole and Christchurch. Ask if anyone's sold a set of dominoes recently."

"That could take ages," Partial Sue said.

"Well, then, we'd better get started."

Daisy raised a hand as if she were in class. "Not to duck out of hard work or anything, but I'm not so great at talking on the phone."

"How did you get on looking into Sharon Miller?"

"Still working on it."

"Okay," Fiona said. "You continue looking. Try to narrow the Sharon Millers down to those who fit the victim profile."

Daisy stared back at Fiona. "Victim what?"

136

"Sharons who are older," Partial Sue clarified. "In their eighties."

"Sue and I will hit the phones."

Partial Sue got up and headed for the storeroom. "We're going to need tea, and lots of it."

"And cake," Daisy added.

CHAPTER 29

One by one, they worked through every contact they knew in the charity shop world, as well as the ones they didn't. They rang so many that their phone banter fell into a natural pattern, repeating the same patter, as if they were working off a script. Same opening, same greeting, same enquiry, and sadly, the same negative response, time and time again.

Light began to fade outside the shop, as did their hopes of finding anything useful. What little renewed enthusiasm they'd initially had was spent, sucked into the tiny black hole of their phone receivers. No one could remember selling a domino set in the last few months or even in the last year. By charity shop standards it was not a popular item, and not the sort of thing that people wanted to donate or to buy. One manager of a charity shop went to great lengths to explain this to Fiona, treating the call as an opportunity to retail-shame her, lecturing Fiona about what she should be selling, which did not include dusty old domino sets. Charity shop one-upmanship was rife, and not just between her and Sophie, as she had first thought.

Partial Sue blew out through her teeth again, after another dead-end call.

Tinnitus buzzed in Fiona's ear, a dentist's drill that had been whining louder and louder as the hopes of tracking down a domino set had become fewer and fewer. She grinned, wishing the act of smiling would banish the growing pessimism and stifle the noise.

"How are you doing?" she asked Partial Sue.

"Not a dickie bird. You?"

"Nothing concrete yet." Fiona had to keep up the optimism. The Charity Shop Detective Agency might not recover from another hit of bad luck. "A few shops have offered to ask around their volunteers and get back to me."

Partial Sue grunted.

Fiona turned her attention to Daisy, who was nose deep in her phone. "How are you getting on?"

"Hmm," Daisy said, emerging from a stint in cyberspace and coming back to reality. "Oh, yes, good. I think I've narrowed down our older Sharons. Not to be ageist or anything, but assuming like Sarah Brown and Ian Richard they aren't online, especially not social media, by a process of illumination—"

"Elimination," Partial Sue corrected.

"Sorry, by a process of elimination, I've found six Sharons who are on phone directory enquiries sites, but have no online presence at all. No Facebook, Instagram or Twitter, leading me to believe that these would be older Sharons, probably be in their eighties or more."

"Well done, Daisy." Fiona was managing to maintain her smile through the whistling in her ears. "A few Sharons will have slipped through the cracks — a lot of people are ex-directory — but it gives us something to work with."

"So, what do we do now? How do we use this information?"

Fiona hadn't thought that far ahead. That was a very good question. Without anything forthcoming from charity shops about the domino set, they were back to good old-fashioned knocking on doors. "Well, I think we need to call on each of these Sharon Millers one by one. Try to tease some information out of them. See if there's a connection with Sarah Brown and Ian Richard."

"Won't the police have already done that?" Daisy asked.

"Yes," Partial Sue replied. "But they don't know about the connection with Malorie and the community centre. We've got the jump on them there."

Fiona's tinnitus rose in pitch, stinging her ears. Partial Sue was still refusing to put her theory to one side that Malorie was the killer. She was about to wade in and tell her to give it a rest for the moment so they could at least investigate other avenues when her phone rang. "Oh, I bet this is a charity shop calling back with information about the dominoes." She slapped the phone to her ear, eager to hear if one of the shops had a lead.

In the background, Partial Sue persisted with her murder theories, aiming them at a reluctant Daisy. The two conversations going on in Fiona's head meant she had to ask the caller to repeat themselves several times. Their words wouldn't lodge in her brain. They slid and slipped out of her reach as soon as they were uttered. Partly because of the distraction, but mostly because Fiona wanted to confirm the incredible information passing into her frontal cortex. News like this had to be heard at least three times before it would take root.

As she hung up, Fiona caught the tail end of Partial Sue's argument. "Until we have solid evidence to the contrary, Malorie is still our number-one suspect."

"It's not Malorie," said Fiona.

"See, I disagree with you—"

Fiona raised her voice, stopping short of banging her fists on the table. "I said it's not Malorie. That was DI Fincher on the phone. They've found another body. A Sharon Miller in Poole."

Daisy and Partial Sue both gasped.

"DI Fincher said the time of death was around lunchtime, when we left the community centre and were on our way to see June. Poole is easily half an hour away."

"More like forty minutes with lunchtime traffic," Daisy added.

Fiona nodded. "Malorie can't be the killer, and neither is June."

"Oh my God," Partial Sue breathed. "Did the police tell you anything else, anything about the murder?"

Fiona had to clutch hold of both her hands to stop them shaking. Her voice wavered and her lips trembled. "They found another domino on the body."

"Was there a name on it?" Daisy asked.

Fiona nodded.

"What was it?" said Partial Sue.

"Mine."

CHAPTER 30

DI Fincher had strongly urged Fiona to take up her offer of staying in a police safe house for the next few days. Though she was terrified and in shock at the thought that someone could be out to murder her, Fiona didn't want any special treatment. She declined the offer and told DI Fincher to give it to one of the other twenty-two Fiona Sharps that lived in the area. The detective was not happy about this act of reckless selflessness. She had tried to persuade Fiona to at least stay in a hotel, at the force's expense. Again, Fiona refused. In the end, they came to a compromise. Fiona would stay with Partial Sue, but before that could happen, DI Fincher would have to inspect the security of Partial Sue's house to make sure it was up to scratch. Safety Planning had to be satisfied before the detective would sign off on Fiona staying there, which meant going around the house, checking it for any weak points.

Having proudly showed off her window locks, Partial Sue moved on to her smart, composite front door that she'd had fitted last year. Holding it wide open, letting in all the cold night air, she began taking the detective through its sophisticated features, including the less important ones, such as pointing out that its subtle shade of blue-grey was referred to as "pebble" in the sales brochure, leaving Fiona to deduce that there might be a point when the detective would have to include that in her report, should it get kicked in by the Domino Killer. Hopefully with Partial Sue's level of security it wouldn't come to that, plus the Domino Killer had never needed to kick in any doors. They'd all opened like magic without a struggle.

A metallic wrenching sound dragged Fiona from her uneasy thoughts. Partial Sue repeatedly yanked the door handle up and down to show off its sturdy five-point locking mechanism. Three chunky deadbolts snapped in and out, along with two rather savage-looking hooks top and bottom that were designed to grip the door frame and never let go.

"Nothing's coming through that," Partial Sue boasted.

"Another one ticked off the list," DI Fincher noted.

Hugging herself, Fiona watched the two of them, her skin growing colder, and not because of the chilly night air blasting in from outside. Her whole body had been enshrouded in shock ever since DI Fincher had informed her that the name Fiona Sharp was scratched into the domino found on the last victim. Up until that point, crime had been an abstract thing that only existed in the pages of the books she'd read and in the box sets she'd watched. Or it happened to other people. Now it was tangible and terrifying and, worst of all, on her doorstep. Fiona wondered if she was making the right decision staying here instead of a police safe house, where her protection would be guaranteed. She knew she'd feel guilty about taking up a spot that another Fiona Sharp might need. Plus, she'd prefer being somewhere familiar, somewhere she felt at home. Fiona had protested when Partial Sue had first suggested staying with her, worried that she might be putting both their lives at risk. But her hardy friend, who had never had a day off work sick and had been known to come into work with broken toes and a dislocated thumb, had waved her concerns away as twaddlish nonsense.

She'd been to Partial Sue's house on many occasions and knew it well. The compact two-bedroom mid-terrace was huddled on a tight, congested Southbourne Road with residents-only parking out front, another handy deterrent. Anyone with murder on their mind would have one hell of a job finding a spot. Unless they opted for the park 'n' ride scheme — hardly likely to be the chosen getaway vehicle for fiendish killers.

Inside, an organised clutter ensued, not unlike the storeroom in the charity shop. Newspapers were stacked everywhere, jostling for space with dog-eared, half-finished sudoku and crossword puzzle books. Her staircase had been commandeered as storage for all her hardback crime novels, which formed a trail up the stairs, piled on the left-hand edge of each tread.

When DI Fincher had arrived, Partial Sue had apologised profusely that she had not had time to clear up since this morning — a little white lie, as it always looked in this state, whatever the time of day. Hoping to distract the detective from her muddle of a house, Partial Sue had been quick to mention that it only had one point of entry, a great benefit from a security perspective. She was also hoping the DI would be impressed, as she had referred to it as a "point of entry", rather than a front door as everyone else did. To a self-confessed crime geek, having a real-life detective in her humble abode giving her security advice was all her birthdays rolled into one and covered in glitter, or icing sugar if that option were available. From the moment DI Fincher had set foot in her property, Partial Sue had hung off her every word.

"Okay, you can close the front door now," DI Fincher said. "I'm satisfied with your home security. The overall level is good."

Partial Sue obeyed. "Oh, thank you, Detective."

"One suggestion I would make to improve it—"

"Yes, yes." Partial Sue couldn't wait to hear.

"Install a doorbell camera, as soon as you can."

"Right you are. Excellent idea. Duly noted."

DI Fincher turned her attentions to Fiona. "How are you doing?"

Fiona forced out a reluctant smile. "As good as anyone who has a serial killer after them."

"Don't worry. This is a good place to stay. The police safe house would be better, but I'm satisfied with the setup here. There's two of you. Plus, you have your dog. A dog is a great deterrent." After a beat she asked, "Can we sit down somewhere?"

Partial Sue darted towards the lounge. "Follow me." She quickly did a round of the whole room, tidying and shifting books and newspapers out of the way so all three of them could sit.

DI Fincher perched on the edge of an easy chair, teetering piles of books beside her. "Fiona, I have to ask you the same question I did when I first spoke to you about Sarah Brown's death. Do you have any enemies? Anyone who would want to threaten your life?"

Fiona wanted to say Malorie, after she'd given her and Partial Sue lifetime bans from the community centre, but she wasn't relevant anymore, not after the last victim had been killed around the same time that they had left her little disinfectant-smelling flat-roofed kingdom. She shook her head.

"I need you to think hard about this. None of the other victims had anything in common, but you knew Sarah Brown. Is there anyone who may have had a problem with either of you?"

Fiona foraged through her fear-addled brain, desperate to make a connection with someone, anyone who might have had it in for the two of them. "I'm sorry. I can't think of anyone. I usually get on well with everybody."

"Well, not everybody," Partial Sue muttered. "What about Sophie Haverford?"

DI Fincher shot her a questioning look. "This is the manager from the Cats Alliance across the road."

"Yes," Fiona replied. "Although I wouldn't say we're enemies. It's more like an unfriendly rivalry. She's irritating and annoying, but that's it."

DI Fincher thought for a moment. "When I questioned her, she said the box containing the knife had been outside your shop, not hers."

Fiona shook her head. "Not true. I saw her carry it across the road and dump it outside mine."

"Why would she do that?"

"Because she's a cow," Partial Sue replied.

DI Fincher, having met and questioned Sophie Haverford, appeared to be suppressing a knowing smile. "Go on, Fiona."

"I don't know if she knew the knife was in there or not. If I'm honest, I'd say she was being cheeky."

"That's putting it mildly," Partial Sue interrupted.

"Cheeky?" DI Fincher asked.

"You know, like sneaking rubbish into a neighbour's bin when yours is full. It's rude but not serious."

"I see. And does she do this a lot, dump her unwanted donations outside yours?"

Fiona shrugged. "Who knows? Maybe she's been doing it for years and that's the first time I've caught her."

DI Fincher began scribbling in her notebook. Both Fiona and Partial Sue craned their necks, almost cricking them, keen to spy any conclusions the detective was making about their nemesis. The second DI Fincher looked up, they snapped them back as if they had been doing nothing. The detective moved on to a different matter. "Last time we spoke, you were doing your own little investigation of Sarah Brown's murder."

"That's right."

"Have you told anyone about what you were doing?"

"Er, no, not really," Fiona stuttered.

"Have you mentioned her murder, or any of the murders to anyone? Given them details?"

"We've been very discreet," Partial Sue said.

"Haven't mentioned any murder," added Fiona. "Not that I can remember."

"Are you sure?"

146

"Positive," Fiona replied. "Why?"

"I didn't want to mention this because I didn't want to add to your fears, but as you've declined the offer of the safe house, I feel I must. There's a slim chance that you may have made yourself a target by investigating Sarah Brown's murder."

The blood drained from Fiona's face.

CHAPTER 31

Fiona shivered, cold sweat forming in the gap between her shoulder blades. She hadn't thought of this. Had she inadvertently put herself on the killer's radar? Fired a flare saying, "I've decided to poke my nose into things that don't concern me; you should kill me next."

Partial Sue fidgeted in her seat. "If that's the case, why can't we have an officer outside to guard Fiona?"

"Firstly, we don't know if the killer is targeting Fiona specifically," DI Fincher replied. "Like I said, it's only a slim possibility, especially if no one knows about your investigation. Secondly, I have a list of twenty-two Fiona Sharps that need protecting, some more vulnerable than others, but far too many to protect with the limited resources at my disposal. I do not have the option nor the authority to take officers off the street to guard them. What I do have is space in a safe house. That means I have to prioritise my list of Fionas. Right now, you are the top of that list, which is why I strongly recommend you take the offer of the safe house."

Fiona shook her head. Though she was still trembling with fear, there was an obstinate and stubborn side of her that refused to let this idiot with his dominoes dictate how she lived her life. She'd stay at Partial Sue's, but that was as far as she was prepared to go.

Fatigue came over DI Fincher's face. "Fiona, once I leave, the offer of the safe house will go to the next Fiona on the list."

"Give it to her," said Fiona. "I'll be fine."

"If you're sure."

"The only reason Fiona would be top of the killer's list is if we were getting close," Partial Sue remarked.

"That's correct," DI Fincher replied. "Which leads me on to my next important question. Have you made any breakthroughs that you haven't told me about? Something that may have made the killer take notice?"

Fiona swallowed hard, hoping to mask the new terror she felt, and squash the unbearable idea that she could have brought this on herself. "But that's just it, we haven't found anything. We thought we had, but it turned out to be a dead end."

"Tell me about that," DI Fincher said.

Fiona gave the detective a condensed version of their investigation into Malorie, her motivation and the missing dominoes from the community centre — leaving out the part where Partial Sue stole them, of course — and how June's online name also matched the numbers on the dominoes.

"Trouble is, it all came to nothing," Partial Sue finished. "Sharon Miller's time of death put the kibosh on them being suspects. We were with them roughly around that time, give or take ten minutes. Certainly not enough time for either of them to have popped off to Poole and back and do the dirty deed."

"Okay, that's good," DI Fincher said.

"It is?" Fiona spluttered.

"Yes. I'd already dismissed Malorie and June from our initial inquiries. Neither of them was in the area when Sarah Brown was murdered. But I'll admit I did not know about June's online profile name matching the numbers on the dominoes, though that's probably because I also ruled her out at a very early stage."

Partial Sue uttered a disappointed, "Oh."

Fiona had never felt more like an amateur. The police had removed Malorie and June from their inquiries early, simply by verifying their whereabouts at the times of the murders. Something they should have done from the out-set, instead of their clumsy, toe-stubbing investigation of the community centre. A rookie error. Before Fiona could wal-low in the self-pity of her own incompetence, DI Fincher pulled her out of it. "However, you've just given me some-thing that I wasn't aware of, something quite crucial that puts a different complexion on things."

"We have?" Partial Sue said.

"The killer has possibly tried to set up two different peo-ple as the murderer, June and Malorie. It's too much of a coincidence otherwise. So I need to look at who Malorie and June may have annoyed."

"Good luck with that," Partial Sue remarked.

"What do you mean?"

"Well, I can't speak for June — she's miserable, but everyone loves her, thinks she's a saint. However, Malorie manages to annoy everyone."

"How come?"

"She's bolshie and bullish," Partial Sue said. "A bull-dozer in Barbour. Doesn't take no for an answer. Everyone's scared of her."

"I see. And what about June? You said everyone loves her."

"June's sort of the same but the opposite," Fiona replied. "She can't say no to anyone. Suffers in silence. Resents run-ning around after her neighbours but won't show it to their faces."

"I see. I will look into these two further, might be a lead in there somewhere." DI Fincher scribbled away in her notebook again then snapped it shut. "Okay, I have all of your phone numbers including the landline to this property. Make sure your mobiles are fully charged and there's plenty of credit on them. If not, I can provide credit. I can't stress how important it is that all your phones are in good working order. They could save your life."

"We're both on contracts," Partial Sue informed her. "And my landline is all paid up every month by direct debit."

"Good. They are literally your lifeline. Now I've put an electronic flag on this address and your mobile numbers, so any 999 calls you make will be given top priority, and I'll be instantly notified. If you do call, just make sure it is urgent. We've had people in your position calling 999 to say they've run out of milk for their tea. I know some people would consider that an emergency, but please only call if you believe your life is threatened, otherwise it could reduce the chance of another Fiona Sharp getting the help she needs."

"Understood," Fiona said.

"One other thing." DI Fincher pulled a device from her pocket that appeared to be an old-style mobile phone, except a little smaller and fatter, and it had a large button in the centre. She handed it to Fiona, who regarded it with grim curiosity. "That is a personal GPS alarm. Keep it on you at all times. If you get any trouble, hit the button. It'll ping us your whereabouts so we can respond. Again, like the phones, only use it for a real emergency. Not if you need a lift back from the supermarket." DI Fincher produced a sheet of paper and handed it to Fiona. "I also need you to sign this official threat-to-life document. It's called an Osman warning."

"Like Richard Osman?" Partial Sue said. "I like him. *Thursday Murder Club* and *Pointless*."

"Not that Osman," DI Fincher replied. "Ahmet Osman was shot dead by Paul Paget-Lewis in 1988. Police had information that Paget-Lewis was a danger to Osman but didn't warn him. Now we issue Osman warnings whenever we can to stop it happening again. Fiona, you need to sign it, please. Just to say that you've listened and understood my suggestions to keep you safe while your life is possibly in danger."

Fiona shuddered at those last six words. The most trouble she'd ever been in was attending a safe driver course after being caught by a speed camera. Compared to that, this seemed like she'd fallen into a parallel universe. It was all unreal and uncomfortable, jarring with the genteel life she'd built for herself. She took the document and tried to read it but couldn't get past the first sentence. She'd been having trouble concentrating since she'd first heard that someone had scratched her name on a domino and left it on a corpse.

"I don't have a pen."

Before Fiona could blink, DI Fincher had handed her the pen she had been writing with. Fiona took it, signed the form and handed the two items back.

DI Fincher slotted them both into her bag. "I'd better get going. I've got five more homes to check tonight. DI Thomas and the rest of my team are out doing the others."

Before she could get up, Partial Sue asked, "Is there anything significant you can tell us about the case?"

The detective hesitated. Clearly there was.

CHAPTER 32

DI Fincher flashed a sympathetic smile. "I can't tell you anything, I'm afraid, especially after what we've just discussed about possibly flagging yourself up to the killer. It would be irresponsible of me to give you any more details. I've already told you too much, something I totally regret doing. You should cease investigations of any kind."

Partial Sue wasn't about to let DI Fincher off the hook that easily. "If Fiona's already on the killer's radar, it's not going to make any difference what you tell us now. She's already a target. Nothing's going to change that."

DI Fincher took a deep breath. "I will say, we are looking for one very dangerous individual."

Partial Sue didn't look too impressed. "Not to sound ungrateful or anything, but we sort of knew that already, what with all the people he's killed."

DI Fincher allowed herself the smallest and most fleeting of smiles. "Okay, I've never come across a killer so self-confident. Most of them go out of their way to hide what they're up to. This one's handing it to us on a plate, telling us who the next victim will be. The pressure is exhausting. My boss is on me twenty-four-seven demanding a result seeing as we've been given the ultimate heads-up — the killer's next victim."

"You think he wants to be caught?" Partial Sue asked.

DI Fincher shook her head.

"Then he's taunting you," Fiona said.

"Yes, I think so. Fits the typical profile of an individual who wants to prove he or she is smarter than us, better than us. It's like a footballer taking a penalty and telling the goalkeeper where they're going to kick the ball, and then scoring. It's all designed to humiliate."

Partial Sue had managed to loosen the DI's tongue and wasn't going to stop now. "What was the number on the domino the killer left on Sharon Miller?"

"A one on its own. The other half was blank."

"Any luck cracking the pattern of the numbers?" Fiona asked.

"My tech officers are still working on it. That's all I can say."

"Can you tell us anything about Sharon Miller?"

"I'd rather not. Only that, like all the other victims, she was older and wasn't online."

"Why is the killer targeting people who aren't online?" Fiona asked.

DI Fincher thought for a moment. "Don't know. But it bodes well for you, Fiona — you're fully digital. But don't get too complacent. This could be coincidence. It might be that the killer is targeting older people, and that's just the law of averages coming into play, that people in their eighties are less likely to be online. So we have to keep an open mind."

Partial Sue opened her mouth, desperate to get another question in. "Can I just ask—"

DI Fincher got to her feet. "I'm sorry, I really must go." She made her way out of the lounge and into the hallway, followed by Partial Sue, Fiona and Simon Le Bon, who hoped that a walk was in the offing since they all appeared to be heading out. The detective grasped the handle of the door and looked back at Fiona. "Last chance to take the safe house."

"I'll be fine here."

"Okay, then. I can't force you. Lock this door up tight once I've gone. No opening the door to anyone unless they're expected. If you need to go out to work or to the shops, you go together, everywhere. Keep the GPS with you at all times, as well as your mobile. Belt and braces. Make sure it's always fully charged and stay off the landline if you can, just in case we need to call you."

"Understood."

The door slammed shut and the detective was gone. Partial Sue flipped the handle up, engaging all five of the locking points and turned the key. She gave it several rattles just to be on the safe side.

Fiona stood as stiff as a statue in the middle of the narrow hall, feeling water pooling in the corners of her eyes, the terror rising up to ensnare her like rampant weeds coiling around her legs.

Her friend rushed to her side and locked her thin arms around her. "Don't worry, everything is going to be fine."

"I'm scared, Sue."

"I know you are, but you're not alone. I'm here. Are you sure you wouldn't rather be in the safe house? I'm sure we could grab DI Fincher before she leaves."

Fiona shook her head. "I'd rather stay here."

"Stay as long as you like. I'm not leaving your side until this is all over."

"You're a good friend, Sue."

Partial Sue relinquished her embrace and waved away the compliment. "Ah, you'd do the same for me. But there's nothing to worry about. We're all locked in, safe and sound."

"But I can't help thinking all the victims opened their door willingly to the killer. What if we fall for the same trap?"

"But we're not going to open the door to anyone, are we? We're smarter than that." Partial Sue thought for a moment. "Let's make an early-warning system."

"What?"

"An early-warning system." She bustled off to the kitchen at the back of the house and started rooting around in the cupboard under the sink.

Reluctantly, Fiona followed. "What are you doing?"

On her knees, Partial Sue's head was deep in the back of a cupboard. "Looking for light bulbs," came her muffled reply. She shuffled back out and got to her feet, proudly holding up a couple of old-style bayonet light bulbs. "I knew I still had some of these left over. I switched to low-energy ones years ago, but you know me, never throw anything away."

"What are you going to do with them?"

"I read in a spy novel — I think it might have been a Ken Follet, or was it Robert Ludlum? — where the spy smashes a couple of light bulbs and leaves broken glass on the front doorstep. Anyone sneaks up to the front door and they'll step in the glass, making it crunch and alerting us to their presence."

Fiona whipped up Simon Le Bon off the floor and hugged him. "I'd rather we don't do that. It might get into Simon Le Bon's paws."

"Ah, yes, I didn't think of that." Partial Sue put the light bulbs back and looked around the kitchen.

Fiona spied a bright red tube perched on the counter. "What about using Pringles, they're really crunchy."

Partial Sue recoiled in horror. "That's a waste of good snack food. I am partial to a Pringle or two of an evening. I tell you what I do have." She crossed the tiny kitchen and swung open both cupboard doors above the sink. Inside it was a mess of bags for life, stuffed in every available space. She plunged her hand in and rummaged around. "Got it. I knew I still had them." As she retracted her hand, sending a few bags falling into the sink, she presented a half-opened packet of biscuits. Going by the imagery on the front, they looked like custard creams but were something very different.

"Custard-inspired creams?" Fiona read.

"Yeah, for some reason they're not allowed to be called custard creams by the Food Standards Agency. I got them from the twenty pence shop."

Fiona had been past the twenty pence shop but had never dared venture inside. She'd been in pound shops, ninety-nine pence shops and even a fifty pence shop, but Fiona drew the line at the twenty pence shop, figuring that food that cost less than a second-class postage stamp might not actually be edible. "How do they taste?"

"Strange, like budgie food."

"I've never tasted budgie food."

"I did once by accident. My nan gave it to me thinking it was muesli when I was little. I've had these for ages. They'll be as hard as rocks by now."

"Don't biscuits go soft when they go stale?"

Partial Sue pulled one out of the packet and snapped it in half, revealing the filling. "Not these little fellows. You could lay a patio with them, a patio for Action Man, admittedly. Come on, let's spread them outside."

Fiona followed Partial Sue to the front door, still holding onto Simon Le Bon, who struggled in her arms, lured by the scent of the custard cream imposters. Cautiously unlocking the door, Partial Sue poked her head out and did a quick recce.

"All clear."

Standing in the doorway, clutching Simon Le Bon for security, Fiona wouldn't explore any further. She watched as Partial Sue scattered stale biscuits over the doorstep, beneath the two ground-floor windows and around her compact driveway. She returned, dusting her hands triumphantly, then accidentally trod on a biscuit as she made her way back inside. It crunched loudly. "Whoops!" She smiled. "Well, at least we know they work."

The pair went back inside. Partial Sue relocked the door, testing it several times to make sure it wouldn't open. "Now, are you hungry?"

Fiona put Simon Le Bon back down and shook her head. "I don't think I'll be able to eat tonight."

"What about a nice cup of tea?"

"That would be good."

After Partial Sue had made their drinks, they took them into the lounge, where they sat in silence. Simon Le Bon leaped up on the sofa next to Fiona. He turned several circles then snuggled down beside her, sighing contently. Fiona wished she felt as relaxed.

"What would you like to do?" Partial Sue asked. "We could watch a TV show, a movie, play some games . . ."

"I don't think I can concentrate on anything at the moment, but thank you."

"Sure, sure, no problem. Just say if there's anything you need or want to do."

Fiona gave her a weak smile. "I just feel so helpless, you know. I'm used to taking control of situations. With this, I just have to wait until something does or doesn't happen. I'm sort of angry and scared at the same time, and infuriated that I'm being put through all this."

Partial Sue gave her a sympathetic look. In this most extreme of situations, Fiona knew there was not a lot anyone could say or do to improve her dilemma.

"Well—" Partial Sue squared her shoulders — "there is one thing we could do that might make you feel better."

Fiona was all ears.

CHAPTER 33

Partial Sue became sheepish, almost reluctant to say. "We keep our minds busy."

"How?"

"We keep investigating."

Fiona squirmed uncomfortably on the sofa, nearly spilling her tea and disturbing Simon Le Bon, who'd been drifting off into a snooze. "I'm not sure I want to do that. Not after what DI Fincher said. I've probably put myself in this position, and the other Fionas, by investigating the murders in the first place."

"We don't know that for sure, and like *I* said, that doesn't make any difference now. If you're on the killer's radar, nothing can change that, but we can still catch them. Get back on the horse and all that. Or we could just sit here and worry. But doing something is always better than doing nothing."

"That's easy for you to say. Your name's not been scratched on a domino. And what are we going to do that we haven't done already?" Fiona knew Partial Sue was right, but she didn't want to admit it. Keeping busy and staying occupied was always the right course of action — now more than ever.

Partial Sue scooched forward until she perched on the edge of her seat. "We have new information. Another domino left on the last victim. Another number, a one. That's got to be worth putting into a codebreaking website to see what happens. Aren't you curious?"

Slowly rotating her cup of tea with both hands, Fiona mulled it over. She knew it made sense. Sitting around feeling sorry for herself was only going to make her feel worse. The downward spiral loomed, where the only thing waiting for her at the bottom was *It*. Besides, she was dying to know what the new set of numbers would throw up. "Let's do it."

"That's the spirit." Partial Sue grabbed her phone. "I've got the codebreaking sites saved on my favourites. Here goes." She typed in the numbers. Two, one, one, one, one. Her face dropped.

Fiona came over and sat beside her, much to the annoyance of Simon Le Bon, who was none too pleased that their snuggling had ceased without warning.

"Nothing," said Partial Sue. "Apart from what we had before. Just a longer version of 'baaaa'. I don't understand it."

"What about doing a general Google search for the number?" Fiona suggested.

Partial Sue typed the numbers into the search engine. The results were an eclectic collection of meaningless hits, ranging from a zip code for an area in Baltimore in Maryland, to an industrial code of practice for oil extraction. They investigated them all, digging deep into the details of each one. Nothing seemed relevant and no matter how hard they tried or what theory they concocted, any connection, no matter how tenuous, refused to link itself to older people who happened to be offline being murdered in Southbourne.

Fiona couldn't think of anything to say, apart from an unhelpful, "Well, at least it's not the angel number thing anymore. Maybe there's no code to be broken."

"Then why go to all the trouble of leaving a domino on each victim's body?"

"To give us the name of the next victim?"

"Could've done that with a Post-it Note. Although, the Post-it Note Killer doesn't have the same ring to it."

The initial enthusiasm from moments earlier popped and deflated. At least the distraction of disappointment had taken Fiona's mind off being murdered. It had also cleared it, allowing her to think straight. "I have a better idea," she said. "Websites and Google searches are never going to be as good as a human being. My great-nephew Dan is studying Further Maths at Surrey University. He's always loved puzzles, even as a little boy. Why don't I phone him? Set him this as a little task."

Partial Sue jiggled with excitement. "That's a great idea." Her jiggling ended abruptly. "Oh, wait. What time is it?"

"Five past nine."

"That's not too late to call, is it? I have a strict no-calls-after-nine-o-clock policy, both for making them and answering them. Well, apart from the present situation we're in."

"He's a student. It's never too late for anything."

"DI Fincher told us to stay off the landline."

"We'll be quick, and we've got our mobiles if she really needs to contact us."

"Okay, do it."

Fiona called Dan and asked him if he could examine the domino numbers. Thrilled at the challenge and the welcome break from coursework, he accepted and promised to call straight back as soon as he had something.

"What shall we do while we wait?" Partial Sue asked.

"How about looking into the game of dominoes itself? We haven't touched on that."

"I can't imagine there's much to it. It's not exactly a complicated game."

Twenty minutes later and they realised how wrong they were. Like chess, it had its own vast terminology, opening plays and finishing strategies.

"Well, for a serial killer, dominoes is a rich vein for sinister names," Partial Sue remarked. "Listen to this. Putting two matching dominoes together is called a hook, and dominoes not in play are called sleepers. And if you play on your own without a partner, you're called a cut-throat."

"How about this," Fiona replied. "Dominoes are also called bones because they were originally made from bone. And the pile you pick your dominoes from is called the boneyard."

Partial Sue winced. "That is sinister. Perhaps the killer is creating his own boneyard. A domino set made out of dead people, sleepers. Three so far, another twenty-five to go."

Fiona looked up. "Jeez. I didn't think of it like that. What a terrifying thought. Have you found anything else?"

"A few things. The last domino, a one with a blank, is called an ace, and there are names for every type of move. For instance, the first double put down is called a spinner."

"Sounds like a folk trio," Fiona remarked.

"You're thinking of The Spinners, and they were a quartet."

"Weren't they on *Morecombe & Wise* once?"

"Don't think so. I remember seeing The Beatles on there, way back in the sixties."

"I used to love *Morecombe & Wise*."

"Wasn't Christmas without them."

"Oh my gosh, yes! Sitting on the sofa, Christmas evening, the whole family in a food coma and *Morecombe & Wise* on TV. Proper telly."

Before either of them had the chance to be enveloped by that softest of comfort blankets, nostalgia, Fiona's phone rang, making them jump. She was relieved to see that it was her great-nephew calling her back.

"Hi, Dan, I've put you on speakerphone. My friend Sue is with me."

"Hello, Dan," Partial Sue said loudly, worried that he wouldn't hear her. "Thank you for helping us."

"How did you get on with the numbers?"

Dan cleared his throat. "Well, firstly, thing is with numbers is that any given bunch can have a pattern to them. That's the beauty of maths, you can find patterns everywhere if you play with the numbers in different ways — adding, subtracting, square roots, et cetera. Even with this small set, you can get tons of patterns."

"That's good, right?"

"Yes and no. It's a case of quantity not quality. I can make the numbers do lots of things but getting any meaning out of them is a different matter, apart from the most obvious pattern, which I'm sure you've already spotted."

Partial Sue and Fiona stared at each other. Maybe he was referring to the angel number, although that wasn't exactly a pattern of numbers, more of a numerological symbol. Plus, it wasn't relevant anymore, not since the last domino had been added. "Er, what's that then?" Fiona asked.

Dan cleared his throat. "Okay, so if you add together the two numbers on each domino, you get a sequence of three numbers. First domino has two and a one on it. Add them together, it gives you three. If I do the same with the second domino, add one and one together, that gives you two. And the third domino is one and a blank. If we assume the blank is zero, that gives us just one. You get a sequence of three, two, one — a countdown."

Fiona felt the floor drop away from her and her head spin. How did they miss this? It was so simple, so obvious and so terrifying. She had been scared before but now her heart and her head had been ensnared by absolute panic. A countdown? To what? Countdowns always ended in something big and spectacular — or in this case, diabolical. Would this be the killer's crescendo, rounding off their killing spree with something imaginative and inventive with Fiona at the centre of it? The fear of what was in store petrified her. She couldn't move or speak.

Dan broke the silence. "I'll keep trying. Test out lots of different things, but it's 'how long is a piece of string?' And if I do find something, there's no guarantee it'll make any sense. Is that okay?"

Fiona remained silent, eyes wide with shock. Partial Sue had to speak for her. "That's great, Dan. Thank you so much."

"You're welcome, Sue. Bye, Auntie."

"B-bye," Fiona managed to croak. As soon as she'd hung up, she shook her head rapidly from side to side, a metronome of oncoming madness. "This is bad. Very bad. Countdowns always lead to something big. Domino Killer's got something big and nasty in store for me. I just know it."

Partial Sue tried to soothe and calm her friend as best she could. Not her greatest strength. "It could just mean our killer's winding things down. To their last victim, I mean."

"That would be me."

"We don't know that, Fiona."

Simon Le Bon gave an impromptu grumble, as if he disagreed with them.

They ignored him and were about to continue when he raised his head, all alert and vigilant. He grumbled again, louder this time. Both his ears pricked up and he let out a long, low growl.

From outside they heard a noise. A biscuit being squished had never sounded so menacing.

CHAPTER 34

Partial Sue leaped across the room and slapped the light off.

"Why did you do that?" Fiona hissed.

"Don't know. That's what people do."

In the gloom, Fiona could hear Partial Sue making her way across the floor, occasionally bumping into the stacks of books and other things piled everywhere. So much for stealth.

Simon Le Bon continued his low growls. Reaching the window, Partial Sue cautiously edged back the curtain to get a glimpse at who or what was outside. A chink of dull light appeared supplied by a street light out on the pavement.

Hands shaking, Fiona held onto her phone, desperate to call 999. She had her GPS alarm in the other. She recalled DI Fincher's strict instructions about only contacting them if it was urgent. She didn't think the police would be too happy if she alerted them only to report a broken biscuit. "What can you see?" she whispered.

From outside came another crunch underfoot. Partial Sue's baked early-warning system had worked well. "There's someone out there. Call 999."

Fiona stabbed at the numbers on the screen. Before she hit the last one, there was a knock at the door.

She dropped her phone and swore.

Partial Sue continued her commentary. "He's bending over, looking through the letter box. Hurry up! Call the police!"

Fiona didn't bother retrieving her phone from the floor. Instead, she was about to hit the button on her GPS alarm when she heard the dull thud of flesh hitting hard concrete and a howl of pain, followed by copious cursing.

Simon Le Bon jumped off the sofa and barked at the lounge door.

"Wait!" Partial Sue shouted. "I know that voice! It's the Wicker Man."

Fiona hesitated, her index finger hovering over the device. "Are you sure? What's he doing out there?"

"Don't know. But I'm going to find out." She marched towards the lounge door, stubbing her foot several times on the way, then turned the light on, blinding them both.

Fiona didn't like this one bit. "Wait! You can't open the door. What if he's the killer?"

"It's just the Wicker Man. He's out there, flat on his back, writhing in agony."

On cue, another groan came from outside.

"I still don't think we should open the door."

"Fiona! Sue! Anyone!" the Wicker Man called. "I think I've done me back in, good and proper."

"That could be a ruse," Fiona proposed. "To get us to open the door. He pretends to be hurt, we open the door, then the next second we're stabbed in the back with dominoes in our hands."

"The Good Samaritan scam."

"Exactly."

More complaints emanated from the Wicker Man. "I'm in agony . . . I think I might have broken something."

Fiona shook her head. "Don't listen to him. He's laying it on thick. Appealing to our good side."

The wails and moans became more beseeching. In response, Simon Le Bon's barking had been replaced by concerned whimpering at the torment going on outside.

Partial Sue became worried. "He seems to be in a lot of pain. Sounds like a whale dying out there."

Fiona couldn't deny that the complaints sounded genuine. Mentally, she pinched herself. This was the Wicker Man they were talking about. Never one to shy away from the chance to be theatrical, he was quite the actor. If anyone could fake it, he could.

"I really think we should go out there," Partial Sue said.

A stalemate rooted Fiona to the spot. The Wicker Man could have truly injured himself, or it could all be a pantomime, and one that would end in her death and possibly Partial Sue's too. The only way to be truly sure was to open the door, but by then it would be too late.

A third, more uncomfortable solution presented itself. She could call the police. Get them here and let them sort it out, while she and Partial Sue stayed safely inside. But DI Fincher would be none too pleased if she mobilised her forces for a furniture salesman with a slipped disc. Fiona couldn't see any other way out. Reluctantly, she retrieved her phone and dialled 999.

"What are you doing?" Partial Sue asked.

"Calling the police. It's the only way to help the Wicker Man and ensure we don't get murdered."

Fiona was about to get connected when Partial Sue, for the second time that night, shouted, "Wait!"

CHAPTER 35

A column of light flashed at the chink in the curtains. Engine noise outside signalled a vehicle pulling up. Fiona joined Partial Sue at the window, where they saw the unmistakable silhouette of Daisy emerging from her car. The second she noticed the Wicker Man, squirming beside the front doorstep, she rushed over to his aid, kneeling beside him. Fiona gasped, fearing the worst. She had half-expected him to make a miraculous recovery and do something awful to her. Instead, he was lying flat on his back, like someone who'd fallen over and done themselves a mischief.

Partial Sue made for the front door followed by Fiona. She unlocked it, but before she could open it wide, a furry shadow whizzed past her legs and darted out of the house.

"No!" shrieked Fiona, worrying that Simon Le Bon was about to sink his teeth into the Wicker Man, adding injury to injury. Simon Le Bon did no such thing. He ignored both him and Daisy and went straight for the faux custard creams scattered everywhere, sucking them down one after the other. Before Fiona could protest, he'd snaffled them all, even the crushed-up broken ones. She couldn't worry about his eating habits at that particular moment or his laissez-faire approach to guard-dog duty.

"Why wouldn't you open the door?" the Wicker Man protested, grimacing as he did so. The fake Dickensian dialogue had fled since the fall, replaced by his native Essex twang. "I'm in pain."

"We didn't know who you were," Partial Sue said. "We thought you were a prowler."

"We were scared," Fiona added. "What are you doing here?"

"That would be my fault," Daisy answered. "I tried phoning you to see if you were both okay, but I couldn't get through. I was worried so I called him to ask if he would check on you. I didn't want to come on my own in case . . ." Daisy trailed off, realising she'd already said too much.

"We've been in all night," Partial Sue said. "The phone didn't ring."

"We were on the phone to my nephew for a bit," Fiona pointed out. "What time did you call?"

"About eight-ish."

"That was when DI Fincher was here."

"We would have still heard the phone. Are you sure you called us?" Fiona asked.

"Positive," Daisy replied. "Maybe I called the wrong number. You know what I'm like with technology."

Fiona disagreed. Out of the three of them, Daisy was the most proficient with technology. "Did you try calling after that?"

Daisy shook her head. "I was driving. On my way here."

"Try calling again," Partial Sue suggested. "Make sure your phone is working."

One by one, Daisy called their mobiles and Partial Sue's landline. All three worked perfectly, ringing loudly and efficiently.

"Sorry to interrupt your telecoms tittle-tattle," said the Wicker Man, who had regained some of his dramatic delivery, "but I'm still lying here on terra firma. Could the three of you possibly assist? If it's not too much trouble."

"Are we sure we should move him?" Partial Sue asked.

"I think that's just for dead bodies," Fiona replied.

"Or motorbike accidents," Daisy added. "You're supposed to leave their helmets on, I've been told."

"Have you broken anything?" asked Fiona. "Should we call an ambulance?"

"No and no," replied the Wicker Man. "I slipped on something dastardly and crunchy."

"That would be a custard-inspired cream," Partial Sue said.

"What the hell's that? And what were they doing all over the place?"

"We dropped them earlier," Fiona quickly replied. "With the shopping." She wasn't sure how much Daisy had told him about their current predicament. Nothing, she hoped, in which case, she didn't want to let it slip out that they'd scattered dodgy biscuits everywhere to alert themselves to any domino-wielding murderers. Even if she did tell the Wicker Man, she doubted he would believe them because it sounded so utterly bizarre.

"We meant to clear them up, but it completely slipped our minds," Partial Sue said.

From down on the ground the Wicker Man craned his neck. "Looks like Simon Le Bon's done that for you."

Hearing his name, Simon Le Bon trotted back, looking extremely pleased with himself, ears pert, tail wagging and tongue licking his muzzle.

"How did you slip on a custard cream?" asked Daisy.

"Custard-inspired cream," Partial Sue corrected.

"Maybe one broke open and he slipped on the filling," Daisy suggested.

"I would have thought the filling would be sticky," Fiona said.

"Look," said the Wicker Man, still flat on his back. "Could we discuss the adhesive qualities of sandwich-style biscuits some other time? Just grab me by the hands and hoist me up."

The three ladies obeyed, gripping him by his wrists and heaving him up. When his body reached a forty-five-degree angle, he cried out in pain, then gasped with relief once he got upright.

Daisy held him by the elbow, reluctant to relinquish her grip. "Can you walk?"

He staggered forward, taking baby steps, wincing with each one. "Well, there's no way I'm driving or walking home tonight."

"Do you think you can make it inside?" Daisy asked.

"Let's hope so, otherwise I'm going to be sleeping on the doorstep."

Fiona took hold of his other elbow. Together, they shuffled him over the threshold and into the house. Partial Sue went ahead, shoving books and other obstacles out of the way to clear a path. Manoeuvring him around the corner, they managed to get him into the lounge and seated on the sofa. The sitting position not doing him any favours, he shrieked in agony. "It's no good, this body's not meant for bending at the moment. I'm going to have to go horizontal." Painfully and with much complaining, they managed to get his legs up at one end of the sofa and his head on the arm at the other. They removed his shoes, revealing two odd socks. "Do you have any painkillers?" he asked.

Partial Sue nodded and returned with a small box of paracetamol, the graphics of which put it at circa 1990s. Fiona was horrified at the ancient packet. "How old are those?"

"They're fine. They work long after their sell-by dates, they're just not as strong."

Daisy turned her nose up. "I won't touch chicken if its use-by date is today. Just isn't worth the risk."

"I'll take anything at the moment," the Wicker Man said, desperate for relief.

Pushing a couple of pills out of the cracked and faded blister pack, Partial Sue handed them to him with a glass of water.

"Thank you."

"Shall we all have a nice cup of tea?" Fiona suggested.

"Splendid. That would be most agreeable." The Wicker Man was edging back to his full-fat Dickensian spiel, a good indicator that he was feeling better.

"Would you like something to eat?" Partial Sue asked. "Some cheese and crackers perhaps?"

"No, thanks. Never seen the point in crackers. A frivolous and fiddly food. They fall apart as soon as you bite into them. What's the point in that?"

"Don't biscuits do that too?" Daisy asked.

"Sort of," the Wicker Man replied. "But I'd wager that their structural integrity is far superior. You can dunk them for a start. Can't do that with a cracker."

"Digestives can be biscuits or crackers," Partial Sue stated. "They're the intersection of the baked provisions Venn diagram."

Fiona wanted to cut the crackers-versus-biscuits debate short before it got out of hand. "Ladies, let's pop into the kitchen and get the kettle on."

"Does it take all three of you?" the Wicker Man asked.

"I'll stay here," Daisy said.

Fiona glared at her and nodded her head in the direction of the door.

Daisy changed her mind. "Oh, er, on second thoughts, I might come and give you a hand."

The Wicker Man harrumphed as the three women rose to their feet and made their way into the kitchen followed by Simon Le Bon, hoping to snag a few more stray treats. Fiona closed the door behind them. Partial Sue put the kettle on.

"Does he know about the murders?" Fiona asked Daisy.

Daisy shook her head. "Not a jot. I just said I was worried about you both, as I couldn't get hold of you. He didn't want to come at first, said he'd got to a juicy bit in *Outlander*, which I didn't think would be his sort of thing. You know, romantic drama."

Partial Sue set about putting teabags in each mug. "It's set in the eighteenth century. He probably likes the way they talk."

"Or the how's-your-father," added Daisy. "There's quite a bit of it."

"Then what happened?" Fiona asked.

"I persuaded him to come here, to check on you. I was really worried about you both. Did I do the wrong thing?"

"No," Fiona replied. "That was very thoughtful of you, but we were fine."

"Yes, but I didn't know that. I couldn't get hold of you. Feared the worst had happened."

It all made sense, but a tiny part of Fiona wasn't convinced, despite all evidence to the contrary. She knew that Daisy had instigated the Wicker Man's visitation, but fear and paranoia overwhelmed her common sense. She had an uncomfortable and unfounded sliver of a suspicion that the Wicker Man was the killer and was biding his time.

They quickly brought Daisy up to speed, regarding the dominoes and how Dan had deciphered them with a simple code, revealing that they could be a countdown.

"A countdown to what?" asked Daisy.

Fiona shuddered. "Something like this. He's got all three of us here at once. Maybe it's a murdering job lot."

Daisy balked at this. "The Wicker Man? The killer? Don't be daft. He wouldn't hurt a fly."

She was right. The Wicker Man was as gentle as they came. But Fiona's logic was currently offline thanks to her overwhelming paranoia and fear. "Did you arrange to meet him here?"

"No," Daisy replied. "But after I called him, I thought I'd better come too. Just in case."

So, Fiona thought, he could've still been playing the injured man and might have capitalised on the situation had Daisy not shown up. Fiona conveniently ignored the fact that Daisy had called him in the first place. Instead, she focused on something else Daisy had said earlier. How do you slip on a biscuit, of all things? They weren't exactly a trip hazard. She wasn't buying it. If he was the killer, then he'd got what he wanted — to get in Partial Sue's house without a struggle. Unless you counted him struggling through the door, but that could've all been part of the act. Faking it. Should she

173

flag up her concerns to the other two? They might not believe her. Unless she could catch him out.

The three women regrouped in the lounge with a tray of tea and biscuits, not custard-inspired ones, but reliable and dependable Rich Teas. With a few hisses of pain, Daisy helped the Wicker Man up to an angle where he could sip his tea and dunk a biscuit or two without spilling them all down himself.

"Sorry for the imposition and all," he said. "But I don't believe this mortal coil shall be shuffling off anywhere soon."

Partial Sue plumped up a cushion behind his head. "That's okay. I'll get you some blankets. You can stay on the sofa until you feel up to moving."

Fiona bit the inside of her lip. This was not what she wanted, not by a long chalk. Not only had he got in the house, he was also staying the night. Locked in with them. "Are you sure that's a good idea?" she said. "Wouldn't you be more comfortable in your own bed?"

The Wicker Man took a slurp of tea. "I dare say I would. It's just getting there that's the conundrum."

Half an hour later, Daisy left. Fiona wanted to go to bed so Partial Sue showed her to the spare room. Similar to the rooms downstairs, it had become a makeshift storeroom, stacked with books and piles of household objects she never used but would never throw away. Partial Sue's obsessive hoarding had started soon after she'd lost her partner Kate to cancer. The two of them had been inseparable, and she still couldn't really talk about Kate. Partial Sue had lost the most precious person in her life and now couldn't dispose of anything because she didn't want to risk losing something else. Though she would never admit it, she clung to objects to give herself comfort.

Fiona helped her clear a space to allow her access to the bed, which also needed to be unearthed. "Do you buy it?" she asked.

"Buy what?" Partial Sue replied, her arms full of old issues of *Heavy Horse Times*. She also had an affection for shire horses and odd corners of her home were littered with horse brasses, giving the place the feel of a small country pub. Although a spot of Brasso wouldn't have gone amiss now and again.

"The Wicker Man. His backstory, excuse the pun. He's got in your house without raising a finger."

Partial Sue straightened up and laughed. "Oh, Fiona. You don't seriously think he's the killer? Daisy told us she phoned him and asked him to come over, remember?"

"What if it was a coincidence? What if he was already coming over? To kill me and possibly you too. The climax to his domino countdown."

"That's one hell of a coincidence, and this is the Wicker Man we're talking about. We've known Trevor for years. Sells furniture nobody wants, talks like a Lannister and comes round to scrounge cake. You know what I think? That brain of yours is on high alert. Imagination running wild. Completely understandable given the circumstances. Fear will do that to you. I'd get some sleep, and if you're worried, lock your door."

"You lock yours too," Fiona said.

"If it makes you feel better, I will."

"Please make sure you do."

"I will. I promise. But the Wicker Man is not the killer. You have nothing to worry about."

Partial Sue reassured her again and wished her good night. As soon as she was gone, Fiona locked the door and shoved a chair up against it for good measure.

She climbed into the bed. It was narrow and sagged in the middle, far too soft for her liking. Simon Le Bon jumped up and slept next to her. In one hand she gripped her phone and the GPS alarm, the other hand wrapped around a tarnished trophy that Partial Sue had been awarded for cricket in her school days, in case she needed to defend herself from a knife-wielding furniture salesman.

While she lay there, sleep eluding her, Fiona started to regret not taking up DI Fincher's offer of the safe house.

Fear had her well and truly in its frigid embrace. But fear was not alone and had brought along a friend, a plus-one for the evening. Fiona shouldn't have been surprised, the two of them complemented each other perfectly. *It* was back and stronger than ever.

Fiona rolled over on her other side, hoping to shrug off the hold *It* currently had over her mind. A futile exercise. As she lay there in the darkness, staring up at the ceiling, she realised that the dynamics of the situation had now changed. Before, she'd been the one on the hunt tracking down the killer. Now she was the victim, and that gave her depression the leverage it needed to bring her down and drive out all her self-worth.

Fragile and frightened, she gripped the trophy tightly in her shaking hand, keeping her eyes on the darkened bedroom door, willing the salvation of the morning to come.

CHAPTER 36

Next day, they were all back in the charity shop. Fiona had bypassed her usual tea and gone straight for coffee. She was on her third cup, having not slept a wink last night. Despite her terror and firm grip on the makeshift weapon, there had been no sinister footfalls in the night, no terrifying creaks of the floorboards and no ominous tries of the door handle.

She sat at the table with Partial Sue, who was sipping her tea and kept reassuring her that everything would be all right. Ever the optimist, her reasoning went along the lines that Fiona had made it through the night without being murdered, therefore the glass was half full. Not being killed had been a good outcome and should be celebrated as a victory.

Fiona couldn't see the positive side of remaining unmurdered for one night. She wanted to stay unmurdered, preferably for the rest of her life. None of what Partial Sue said calmed her mind whatsoever. Nothing had changed. Fiona was still on the killer's hit list. Her hands wouldn't stop shaking, no matter what she did with them or where she placed them, not helped by the jitter-inducing caffeine.

"You need to take your mind off it somehow," suggested Partial Sue. "Think nice thoughts. Go to your happy place."

"This is my happy place. Here in Southbourne with you, Simon Le Bon, Daisy and the shop."

"Where is Daisy, by the way? I know she's always late but she's never *this* late."

The little bell above the door tinkled sweetly, heralding the first customer of the day. A woman wearing a smart double-breasted jacket with matching skirt and a white blouse stepped in and smiled. Her hair was straight and grey, cut in a long pageboy style, parted to one side.

Partial Sue rose from her seat and was about to greet her good morning when recognition dawned on her. This wasn't a customer.

"Daisy?" she choked. Fiona did a double take.

"Morning team," Daisy said.

Simon Le Bon, who'd been feeling the worse for wear since they arrived, mainly because he'd ingested half a packet of stale custard-inspired creams the night before, raised his head and gave a half-hearted grumble.

Fiona had needed a distraction and she'd got it. How or why Daisy had abandoned her maxi dress and unkempt curls in favour of business attire and salon-straight hair was anyone's guess. "Daisy, I didn't recognise you. What's brought this on?"

"What? Nothing."

Partial Sue slowly circled Daisy, taking in every angle of her new outfit. "Looking sharp, Daisy. Come on, what's the big occasion? Is it a fella?"

"No, no reason. Just fancied a change."

"Well, I think you look marvellous," said Fiona, not realising that some happiness had sneaked back into her fearful head. "It really suits you."

"She's right," Partial Sue agreed. "I like it."

Daisy made herself a tea and joined them at the table. "What happened to the Wicker Man? How's his back?"

Partial Sue took a sip from her mug. "He felt a bit better this morning. I offered to give him a lift home, but he said he couldn't bend enough to get into my little car. I dosed him up with painkillers and he decided to walk home instead — very slowly, I might add. Said it would be better for his back. I doubt he'll be in today."

"How are you doing, Fiona?" Daisy asked.

"Same, really. Problem hasn't gone away. Just got to stay cautious." She didn't mention that she felt a whole lot better the further away she was from the Wicker Man. It would just come across as paranoid and delusional, but she couldn't help the feeling her gut was sending her.

An awkward silence ensued until Daisy cleared her throat. "Let's carry on investigating," she suggested.

"That's a good idea," Partial Sue agreed. "What do you say, Fiona?"

Fiona squirmed awkwardly in her chair. Truth be told she didn't really want to do anything except find a very large rock somewhere the killer couldn't find her and hide under it. She knew the smart thing to do would be to call DI Fincher and ask if she could be put in the safe house tonight. But she felt like she didn't deserve it. If the killer was indeed targeting various Fiona Sharps because of her investigative actions, then she was to blame for putting them all at risk. She sighed. "Er, okay."

"Right, I've had an idea," Daisy said with authority. Fiona and Partial Sue still weren't used to the new, assertive Daisy 2.0. "Last night got me thinking. We need to look at how the killer gets in. We haven't done that yet. This may open up some new avenues of investigation. I got inspired after watching an episode of *Prime Suspect* last night—"

As if she'd been electrocuted, Partial Sue leaped out of her seat and snapped her fingers. "That's it! Your new look! It's DCI Jane Tennison! It is, isn't it?"

Daisy blushed a little. "What? No, don't be silly."

"Fiona, back me up. She's dressed like Helen Mirren in *Prime Suspect*."

Fiona eyed Daisy up and down. "You know, I think you're right. That's definitely her to a 'T'."

"The hair, the business suit. It's her."

179

Daisy shrunk in her seat. "I don't know what you're talking about."

"You've pulled it off, Daisy," Fiona said.

"Look, can we just move on and concentrate on thinking about how the killer gets in?"

Partial Sue's smile dropped from her face. "Yes, of course, DCI Tennison."

Daisy's skin glowed red. Whether with embarrassment or rage, they couldn't tell.

Fiona began to feel better. Daisy's doppelganging of their favourite TV detective had brought some light back into her darkened mind. "Let's brainstorm some ideas. What person would you open a door to and let into your house quite happily? We'll make a list — anything goes — then we'll sift through them later."

"Wait a second." Partial Sue disappeared into the storeroom. After clattering about and shifting boxes around, she emerged with a slightly battered whiteboard someone had donated. Fiddling with the legs for a minute or two, she managed to stand it upright, albeit a little crookedly. She grabbed a marker pen and stood poised beside it, as if she were a presenter on *Countdown*. Simon Le Bon waddled over, curious to see what all the fuss was about, his tummy still making strange gurgling noises.

"A vicar?" suggested Fiona.

The pen squeaked as Partial Sue wrote the first suggestion at the top of the board.

"Avon lady," Daisy blurted out.

"Do they still have them?" Fiona asked.

"Oh, yes," Daisy replied. "Mine's called Kim."

After this, the suggestions came thick and fast.

"Doctor."

"Meter reader."

"Plumber."

"Personal trainer."

"Painter and decorator."

"Electrician."

"Carpenter."

"Drain cleaner."

"Police officer."

"Fireman."

"Removal man."

"Beautician."

"Financial advisor."

"Jehovah's Witness."

"Door-to-door salesman."

"Charity collector."

Partial Sue struggled to keep up, the pen scrawling rapidly across the whiteboard.

"What about someone who desperately needed the toilet?" Daisy offered.

Fiona and Partial Sue stared at her.

"What? I let someone in to use my toilet. They had their legs crossed and everything. Eyes watering."

"You shouldn't let random strangers in your house," Partial Sue said.

"The man was desperate. I thought he was about to pee everywhere."

They continued brainstorming and Partial Sue continued scrawling until there was no more room left on the board.

The bell tinkled above the door. The trio were about to get up from the table and switch into retail mode until they realised it was Sophie, minus her cape for once, followed by Gail subserviently shambling along behind.

Sophie grinned with the full force of her expensive veneers. "Morning, ladies. I have some wonderful news to share."

Fiona shuddered. Whenever Sophie came across to flaunt good news it always meant bad news for Dogs Need Nice Homes.

CHAPTER 37

Simon Le Bon mustered enough energy to get up onto his paws and growl.

"Such a charming dog." Sophie caught sight of Daisy. "I'm loving your new look."

"Thank you," Daisy replied.

"My nanna used to dress like that in the eighties."

Before Daisy or any of them could retaliate, Sophie turned her attention to the whiteboard. "What's this I see? Fiona, are you thinking of a new career? Let's have a look. Definitely not a beautician, so many reasons why that wouldn't work." She scanned the list. "Ah, yes, drain cleaner. We've found a suitable match." She giggled. "I'm only joking, of course."

Fiona had had enough of her passive-aggressive cheek. "What do you want, Sophie?"

"Oh, why so hostile?"

"Probably because you've come in and insulted us," Partial Sue sneered.

"No, no. Just being honest. So many people are fake these days, and I simply refuse to be one of them."

Three perfectly choreographed and simultaneous eye-rolls occurred around the table. Even Gail's eyes spun into the back of her head.

Sophie produced three glossy flyers and placed them on the table. Fiona picked one up and read the headline, "'Grand opening with celebrity guest'."

Partial Sue read the subheading. "'Join us for the launch of our new coffee bar at the Cats Alliance charity shop'."

Sophie clapped her hands together with glee. "Yes. One corner of our charity shop is now a charming little café. I've sourced genuine French bistro chairs and tables, and I have a real Gaggia espresso machine. We'll be making the finest coffee this end of Southbourne, complimentary for all Cats Alliance customers, I might add. What inspired this great idea, I hear you ask? Well, I realised now that the community centre minibus isn't running, and a lot of the OAPs down this end have nowhere to meet up. So, I thought why not bring the mountain to Mohammed, so to speak? Give them a place where they can meet that's closer to where they live."

"Hey!" Partial Sue shouted. "That was Fiona's idea. We already have a coffee morning here for that. And it's very popular, thank you very much."

Sophie scoffed. "What? A chipped old table and some crusty coffee from a jar, oh please. I think our older folk deserve better than that."

"You stole Fiona's idea," Daisy said.

"Does it matter who had the idea first? Great minds and all that. What matters is that our dear octogenarians and nonagenarians have a nice place to meet, and now they have a choice."

Fiona didn't spare the anger in her voice. "This isn't about them, is it, Sophie? This is about you showing off and getting one over on us. Trying to outdo us. For what reason, I have no idea. It's not supposed to be a competition."

Sophie spoke as if she were giving an acceptance speech at the Oscars. "You know, I just do what my heart tells me. I'm doing it for the community, for the people. That's what matters most to me."

Partial Sue muttered several swear words under her breath.

Sophie continued her monologue. "I'd dearly love you all to be there and I've got a wonderful celebrity to open it. A household name, literally. I must confess, I did pull in a few PR strings. Guilty."

"Who's the celebrity?" Daisy asked.

"It's a surprise."

Now it was Fiona's turn to scoff. "That means they haven't confirmed yet."

"No, it means it's a surprise. Anyway, our grand opening is next Tuesday morning."

"Tuesday morning!" Fiona roared. "That's when we have our coffee mornings."

Sophie contorted her face into fake shock. "Oh, really? What a coincidence. I had no idea."

"Course you knew. You did that on purpose to lure our customers away."

"Heavens no! I wouldn't do a thing like that. But, having said that, it will be interesting to see which one they prefer."

"Our customers are loyal to us. You'll see," Partial Sue said.

"Mm, I wonder which one they'll choose. Somewhere modern and stylish, offering free, freshly ground gourmet coffee, made to my exacting standards, or boiling water poured onto something out of a jar, served in a dusty old place with all the charm of a Victorian morgue."

Partial Sue stood up. She was about to unleash a torrent of abuse when unholy, guttural moans emanated from Simon Le Bon. He began to retch and was sick over the floor with last night's ill-gotten gains.

"Oh, look," Sophie said. "Simon Le Bon's throwing up custard creams. I rest my case." She turned on her heel. "You know, this is one of those occasions when I desperately wish I was wearing my cape."

She strutted out of the shop. Gail looked apologetic, then followed her.

CHAPTER 38

Standing shoulder to shoulder, Partial Sue and Daisy stood in front of Fiona like a Saxon shield wall. Not a particularly wide shield wall, granted. However, their two-person phalanx only had to bar her from leaving and doing something she would later regret to Sophie Haverford and her pretentious establishment.

Fiona had never lost her temper before because she didn't have a temper to lose. Level-headed with the smarts to back it up, she preferred rationalising and reasoning her way out of problems rather than throwing her toys out of the pram. She could tell Partial Sue and Daisy were scared by the unprecedented rage that currently had Fiona in its spikey grip.

It hadn't surfaced straight away. After Sophie and Gail had left and Fiona had cleared up the mess Simon Le Bon had made, she had sat at the table clutching her coffee cup as if she wanted to squeeze the life out of it. Partial Sue had retaken her position by the whiteboard, attempting to put Sophie's rude interruption behind them by resuming their brainstorming session. It hadn't worked. While Partial Sue and Daisy had contributed suggestions, Fiona had not. Instead, she had brooded silently, her simmering, hissing anger threatening to bubble over. They'd asked if she was okay. Fiona had stood up, eyes burning as she'd looked out of the window to the Cats Alliance across the street. Someone had left a shopping trolley out on the road nearby.

Fiona calmly but through gritted teeth had said, "See that shopping trolley? I'm going to hurl it through Sophie's window."

Hence the impromptu shield wall to stop her.

"Let me through!" demanded Fiona. "Get out of my way."

Partial Sue had her skinny arms planted firmly on Fiona's shoulders. "No way. You're not going over there and giving her what she wants."

"Yes, I am! And what she wants is a shopping trolley through the window."

"Please," Daisy said. "Don't do this. Think about it."

"I have thought about it, and the solution is a trolley in her window."

"She's a rubbish human being," Partial Sue said. "But don't stoop to her level."

Fiona barged forward. "I don't mind stooping to her level. Honestly, I don't."

The pair stood firm, two against one. Partial Sue's attempt to calm her was a bit like attempting to reason with an angry sea. "This is not you, Fiona. Think about what's happening to you at the moment. Your life's being threatened. You've got a lot of fear in you right now. It's making you do rash things."

"I'm not frightened. Far from it." Fiona attempted to prise both women out of the way, as if she were pulling apart a pair of jammed lift doors.

"Remember what Yoda said," Daisy remarked.

Fiona stopped struggling and regarded her curiously. Partial Sue did too. "Yoda?"

Thankfully, she didn't attempt to do the voice. "Fear leads to anger, anger leads to hate, hate leads to something or other. I can't remember the rest."

186

"Yoda's right. I mean, Daisy's right," Partial Sue corrected. "Fear is making you do this. It's morphed into anger, and it needs an outlet. You need someone to lash out at, and because you don't know who, you've got Sophie in your sights."

"Yes, but—"

Partial Sue held her hand up to signify that she'd like to finish. "Usually, Sophie annoys you, winds you up. This isn't anything new. You always rise above it because you're more dignified than her. You're a better human being than she is. Now she's got you wanting to vandalise her shop, not because you really want to but because of the stress you're under. These are not normal circumstances. Having a murderer after you will do that to a person. That's what's causing you to act like this, not that show-off Sophie Haverford."

Fiona's shoulders slumped. She turned and dawdled back to the table and collapsed down in her chair. A large sigh escaped from her lungs.

Daisy and Partial Sue waited a beat, hanging around by the door. Fiona presumed they did this because they thought her actions were a ruse and the second they relinquished their supervision of the door, she would bolt and fulfil her mission.

She didn't. She just sat there breathing heavily, all the fight gone out of her. Sensing her hurt, Simon Le Bon hopped up and snuggled into her lap. She didn't mind that he smelled vaguely ripe and sickly. A dog can be a calming presence, preferably after it's finished throwing up.

They joined her at the table, no one wanting to speak first. After a while Fiona said, "You're right, of course."

The other two didn't respond. Cast their eyes down.

"I would have regretted doing it. That would have been the end of my days with Dogs Need Nice Homes. The end of my days as a volunteer with any charity for that matter. Staving in windows is frowned upon in the voluntary sector."

"No, it wouldn't have been a good idea," Daisy said. "Not a good idea at all."

The three of them went silent again. Partial Sue broke the quiet. "Still, I would've loved to have seen it."

"Me too." Daisy giggled.

Fiona smiled devilishly. "I can still make it happen."

"No!" they chorused, standing up, ready to resume their posts.

Fiona held up her hands in surrender. "I'm joking. Don't worry. I'm fine. I'm not going to do anything. Much as I'd like to."

Slowly and tentatively, they both sat back down.

"The sheer cheek of the woman though," said Partial Sue. "Stealing your idea and our customers. What is her problem?"

"Let's change the subject, shall we?" Fiona suggested.

"How about a nice cup of tea?" Daisy asked.

The tea came out and everyone felt a whole lot calmer. Only tea can do that. They drained their cups and decided to have a second one because it was that kind of day, then turned their attentions back to the whiteboard. After squeezing out a few more suggestions, they set about whittling down the list. The majority could be ruled out easily. People such as doctors, tradespeople and even the dear old vicar would only be invited into a house if they had an appointment or had called ahead first. Appointments and phone calls left a trail — evidence of logged calls and diary entries. Far too risky. So they had to assume it would be someone who had turned up unannounced. But no one in their right mind would open the door and just let in anyone who'd randomly appeared on their doorstep. This left only two plausible candidates.

"Police officer and meter reader," Daisy read off the whiteboard.

"I hate it when the killer turns out to be a police officer," grumbled Partial Sue.

Fiona agreed. "I know what you mean. It's always a bit of a let-down. Bit too convenient. However, we shouldn't rule it out. We shouldn't rule out any of these. We should put them on the back-burner."

"Our back-burner's a little overcrowded, like a stove on Christmas Day."

"That just leaves a meter reader," Daisy said. "But everyone knows you don't let meter readers in your house without the proper identification. They used to ram it down our throats with all those public information ads in the seventies. Do you remember them?"

Partial Sue made a face. "Urgh, they used to give me the willies. Some of them were more terrifying than watching *The Shining*. Do you remember that one with the spirit of dark water, with the guy in the hood?"

"Oh, yes," Daisy replied. "That gave me nightmares. Worked, though. I never went swimming in a disused tip."

"And I never put a rug on a highly polished floor or climbed an electricity pylon to get a kite."

Partial Sue and Daisy loved to take a stroll down memory lane, which, had you believed the public information films in the seventies, was a dark and terrifying place full of unsuspecting dangers waiting to have your arm off. Fiona brought them both back to the matter in hand. "Speaking of electricity, when was the last time you had a meter reader in your house?"

Partial Sue racked her brain. "Can't remember. Not for ages, years."

"Mine's all done automatically," Daisy said. "A guy called Jeff came and fitted a smart meter three years ago. I remember because he had bad breath."

"Me too," Partial Sue agreed. "Not the bad breath bit, the meter bit. It's all online now. Everyone has smart meters round here. I saw the van going house to house fitting them. There's no need for meter readers. Either they don't exist or they're very rare."

Fiona gasped. "That's it! Everyone has smart meters because they're all online. It's just easier. All except our victims. None of them had the internet, which would mean—"

"They'd still rely on a traditional meter reader to come round and do it the old-fashioned way," Partial Sue jumped in. "They'd definitely open their door and invite them in without a struggle. I think we're onto something."

"Hold on," Daisy said. "Don't energy companies let you phone and email your reading if you don't have a smart meter, or post it?"

Fiona nodded. "That's true, but Ian Richard had trouble walking and Sarah Brown needed a walking frame. Meter cupboards in big old houses are sometimes in awkward places. If someone showed up asking to read the meter, our offline victims would've let them in."

"Really? Falling for the old meter-reader-at-the-door routine. You think it's that simple?"

"Why not?"

The bell above the door tinkled. In shuffled the portly shapes of Oliver and Stewart decked in their bakers' uniforms and carrying teetering towers of cake tins.

Oliver deftly edged his way around the shop displays while Stewart bumped and bounced off them like a pinball, distracted by the phone in his hand, which he managed to clutch while also gripping the column of cake tins that appeared in danger of toppling over at any second. Neither of them noticed Daisy's new look. Oliver offered no greeting and in his usual curt manner simply stated, "Red velvet cake here." He pulled off the uppermost tin and placed it on the table. "Get a plate for it sharpish because I need the tin back."

Partial Sue, who was nearest the storeroom, made a beeline for the plates drying on the draining board. She returned and expertly flipped the moist, luscious cake onto the plate. "Shall I wash the tin for you, Oliver?"

"Don't bother. I'll do it," Oliver said, as if he couldn't trust her to do it properly.

Stewart lifted his head from his screen. "Hey, where's the Wicker Man?"

Fiona stuttered, "Er, he hurt his back. He might not be in today."

Stewart looked disappointed. "Oh, I made a new app to show him. Makes your face into toast. Gonna make a mint from it. Get my own place."

Oliver shook his head dismissively. "Before you become the next Jeff Beeswax, you can help me deliver the rest of these cakes."

Stewart huffed. "It's Bezos, Dad. Jeff Bezos."

"Don't care." His dad turned to leave.

"Before you go," Fiona said, "do you know if there's still such a thing as meter readers around here?"

"Dunno, I've not seen one for ages. Pity the Wicker Man's not here."

"Why's that?"

"You should ask him. He used to be one."

CHAPTER 39

"I knew it! I knew it!"

After Oliver and his son had left, Fiona had said these same three words over and over. Partial Sue and Daisy watched from the table as Fiona paced frantically up and down the shop, taking four or five steps, then turning abruptly to march in the other direction, repeating the pattern again and again. The caffeine flooding her system had not helped matters. She spoke in short, fast, shrill sentences. "I told you it was the Wicker Man. It's so obvious. He worked for the electricity board. Got made redundant. This is revenge for being sacked. Killing their customers. Turns up pretending to read their meter then stabs them in the back."

Partial Sue wasn't convinced. "But if he wanted revenge on the electricity board, why would he go after their customers? Why not kill the people who gave him the sack?"

Fiona stopped pacing and regarded the other two sitting at the table. "I have to admit, his motive is a little unclear on that score. Maybe he hates customers for doing business with them."

"That doesn't make sense either," Daisy said. "It's not just the electricity board anymore. There are tons of different energy suppliers these days with all sorts of weird names. Mine's called Jelly Energy. I like saying that, Jelly Energy."

"Who knows?" Partial Sue replied. "I mean, if he's the serial killer, and I'm not saying he definitely is, his logic doesn't have to add up. He's not going to be thinking straight."

That last phrase caught Fiona's attention, rattled her. Was she actually thinking straight? Or was this just the product of a mixture of last night's fear, depression and caffeine-induced anxiety? "Do you think there's something in this? It's not me just being paranoid, trying to make things fit?"

Partial Sue sighed. "Reluctant as I am to admit it, everything seems to be pointing to him. Three victims open their door, three victims who weren't online, and therefore three victims who wouldn't have smart meters. And we have a suspect who used to be a meter reader in our midst."

Daisy's face became a mask of horror. "But that would mean last night he could've been coming to kill you. And I asked him to look in on you."

Fiona nodded. "Could've already been planning it when you called him."

Partial Sue agreed. "Or he was seizing the opportunity. He gets Daisy's call, which gives him the perfect alibi. He comes over and kills us, then claims he found us like that after Daisy asked him to check on us. However, Daisy shows up unexpectedly, so he has to abruptly call it off, hence the bad-back routine to throw us off the scent. You know, we should've checked him for a knife."

"And a domino," Daisy added.

"Dominoes," Partial Sue corrected. "There were two of us."

Fiona stopped short of slapping her forehead in exasperation. "Why didn't we think of that?"

"It was a stressful situation," Partial Sue replied. "It's easy now we have hindsight."

The bell above the door chimed as a couple of customers came in to browse. Fiona, Partial Sue and Daisy had to rapidly suppress the ugly revelation that the killer could be, and probably was, the Wicker Man. Fiona put on a brave face for the customers and became all sweetness and light, greeting them with cheery good mornings. She could've really done without the interruption and wanted them to leave so she could resume examination of the facts. She eyed them as they browsed the shop painfully slowly, not looking for anything in particular.

Nonchalantly, goods were picked up and put down again. Clothes were slid along the rails and occasionally lifted out to determine suitability, then hooked back on. Books were selected, flipped through, then replaced.

Fiona willed them to go. She had life-and-death matters to discuss with her colleagues and these two were time-wasting. In the end, neither customer bought anything, but one of them did splash out on a slice of Oliver's cake.

Finally, the charity shop ladies could resume their discussion. "We need evidence," Partial Sue said. "We could place a bug in his shop. I've got this catalogue at home full of spy equipment. Really clever stuff. I've always wanted to order some."

"Does it have night-vision goggles?" Daisy asked. "I've always fancied a pair of those."

"Why would you need night-vision goggles?" Fiona asked.

"In case I run out of bulbs. Or there's an apocalypse."

Fiona straightened a few items of clothing the previous customers had sifted through. "Bugging his shop is a good idea, but it might be weeks until he mentions anything, if he mentions anything at all. By which time he could've murdered more people, me included. He's in there alone. It's highly unlikely he's going to mutter anything incriminating himself."

Silence hung in the air. Minds cogitated.

Partial Sue raised her hands in a surrender. "Before you have a go at me, just listen to what I have to say. I think we have to face cold hard facts. The only way to be sure is to gain solid evidence. We need to get in his shop, search it for dominoes, knives and what have you."

Fiona's stomach lurched.

CHAPTER 40

Fiona shook her head and returned to pacing up and down the shop. "Oh no. We're definitely not doing that. Breaking the law. Look what happened last time."

Partial Sue attempted to calm the situation by pointing out how bad it was. "This is different, your life is at stake. We have what's called lawful excuse."

"I think that's only if you see a dog in a hot car and you break the window."

"Can't we just go to DI Fincher and tell her?" Daisy interrupted.

Partial Sue became agitated. "Tell her what? All we have is a whiteboard, a hunch and some broken biscuits outside my house. It's not enough. We need solid evidence before we accuse the Wicker Man. There's still a chance he's innocent."

Fiona stopped pacing. "But if we do find something, won't the evidence be inadmissible?"

Partial Sue smiled. "We do it properly this time. Get in, search the place and get out again without anyone seeing. If we find anything, we leave it untouched, then we send an anonymous tip-off, as we should have done with Malorie."

"Malorie had an alibi," Daisy said.

"Which is why we need to be totally sure."

Fiona slowly came round to the idea, mostly because she couldn't see any other option. "Okay, so how are we going to get in? His place is locked and we don't have a key."

Partial Sue swivelled around to face Daisy. "That's where you come in. How about it? Want to put those dexterous fingers to good use and learn how to pick a lock?"

"Oh, no. You can't ask Daisy to do that."

"Whyever not?"

A back-and-forth argument erupted between Fiona and Partial Sue. They talked over each other, attempting to take the moral high ground, neither side giving an inch.

"I'll do it," Daisy said.

The argument continued.

"I'll do it." Louder this time.

The two stopped. Fiona's heart was hammering. "Daisy, I really don't think—"

She waved Fiona's protests away. "It's my decision. No one's forcing me. I want to do it. We need to know. Remember, your life's at risk here. If there's a chance this will save it, then it needs to be done."

Fiona hadn't thought of it like that. She was more worried about whether it was lawful or not, stressing about getting herself and her friends into trouble. But there were more important issues at stake, like whether she'd actually make it out of this alive.

Partial Sue slapped the table triumphantly. "Then it's settled. Daisy, could you start watching YouTube videos on how to pick a lock? There are loads on there."

"There are?"

"Oh, sure. It's a lot easier than people think. I would have tried it myself but I'm too much of a jitterbug, hands too shaky." Partial Sue rose and shrugged on her coat.

"What are you going to do?" Fiona asked.

"I'm going to get Daisy what she needs to practise." She left the shop and headed purposefully up Southbourne Grove.

Fiona sat with Daisy huddled round the screen of her phone as they watched video after video, slightly shocked at how simple it was to pick a basic tumbler lock.

"What sort of locks has the Wicker Man got?" Daisy asked.

"I think he's just got the one if I remember rightly. A deadbolt, probably the minimum to qualify for insurance." Security wasn't much of an issue for the Wicker Man. Old seventies-style wicker furniture wasn't high on the list for career criminals breaking into shops, and would be harder to shift than second-hand copies of *Fifty Shades of Grey*, of which Dogs Need Nice Homes had more than they knew what to do with.

"Ta-da!" Partial Sue returned clutching a brown paper bag and a smaller plastic one. From the paper bag, she pulled out a shiny new mortice lock with a deadbolt. "Got this from the hardware store for Daisy to practise on. It's the same brand as the one on the Wicker Man's door."

Daisy clapped her hands excitedly and took the lock from Partial Sue. "I can't wait to get started." She took the small rectangular slab of pressed metal and headed for the storeroom.

"Wait! You'll need these." Partial Sue produced a packet of hairpins from the smaller plastic bag. "For picking the lock."

"Couldn't you get proper lock picks?" Fiona asked.

Partial Sue shook her head. "One, I don't think you can buy that sort of thing on Southbourne Grove, and two, putting a mortice lock and set of lock picks on my credit card on the same day isn't going to look good."

Daisy took the items to the storeroom and set herself up on a stool at the draining board with her phone propped against a bottle of washing-up liquid to follow the online tutorials. "Here goes." She closed the door.

Partial Sue and Fiona attempted to distract themselves by tidying and cleaning, straightening books and wiping the shelves. It didn't really work and all they could think about was what was going on in the storeroom.

Two hours passed and they hadn't heard a peep from Daisy.

"Should we go in and check on her?" Partial Sue asked.

"No, we should just leave her to it. She'll come out when she's good and ready."

"I'm also desperate for tea."

"Me too, but interrupting her now will only slow things down."

Five minutes later, Daisy emerged, beaming brighter than a supernova, the lock in her hand, the pins still sticking out of it. "I did it!" Daisy did a little dance, holding the lock aloft.

They crowded around her, jigging merrily. It was the first bit of good news they'd had in a long time.

CHAPTER 41

Gathering by the draining board, Daisy proudly showed off her newly acquired skills, walking them through it as if she were on *CBeebies* showing kids how to make a Mother's Day card. Partial Sue and Fiona watched, amazed and impressed at the unsuspecting talents of their gentle friend. Daisy held up the first hairpin, which she'd bent at the end to form a small right angle.

"Now, this little fellow is called your tension wrench. I pop it in here, like so." Carefully, with the seasoned skill of a safe-cracker, she inserted the hairpin into the bottom of the keyhole. "His job is to slightly turn the cylinder inside the lock but only a smidge. He has a friend called the pick." She held up another hairpin that she'd shaped like a hook. "He goes in above the first one. There are five tiny pins inside the lock. I have to use the hook to push each little pin up and out of the way."

Partial Sue leaned in closer. "That doesn't sound too hard."

Daisy gently fiddled with both hairpins, making micro movements. "The tricky part comes each time I push one out of the way, I have to apply a tiny bit more pressure to the tension wrench, turning the lock ever so slightly to hold them and stop them slipping back down again. Then I can move on to the next one. *Fiddlesticks!*"

"What happened?"

"First lock pin slipped back down. Too little pressure and the pins you've moved out of the way drop again. Too much and you won't be able to push the remaining pins up. It's a balancing act."

After twenty tension-filled minutes of watching Daisy prod and pick, wiggle and jiggle, the lock finally made a satisfying click, and the deadbolt slid back.

There were whoops of joy and Daisy got hugged from both sides.

"That is the cleverest thing I've ever seen," Fiona said.

"So clever," Partial Sue agreed. "You are, without a doubt, the most amazing member of the Charity Shop Detective Agency."

Daisy blushed. "I knew all those hours of making chests of drawers and wardrobes for my dolls' houses would come in handy for something."

Fiona grew serious. "This is an incredible achievement, Daisy, but do you think you can get it down to just a couple of minutes?"

"I can try."

"That's the spirit." Partial Sue patted her on the back.

"Keep practising," Fiona said. "Do you need anything from us?"

"Tea. Lots of it," Daisy replied. "And an obscene amount of cake."

* * *

Just before six o'clock, the three of them were waiting inside Dogs Need Nice Homes. Their coats were on, the lights were off, and the "Open" sign had been flipped to "Closed". Daisy sat clutching her trusty hairpins in her fist, pre-bent and ready for action, with a few spares for backup. Partial Sue and Fiona had their phones charged, ready to use the built-in torches for snooping around the Wicker Man's shop and to snap anything significant that would incriminate him.

Darkened and empty, the other shops had shut for the day. There was just one left that needed to close its doors: the Cats Alliance. Dead opposite, on the other side of the road, Sophie and Gail had a clear view of their comings and goings, and neither of them ever missed a thing. After being caught red-handed with the dominoes from the community centre, the last thing they wanted were these two witnessing them breaking and entering. They couldn't make a move until they were sure the pair were out of the picture.

Never taking their eyes off the front door of the rival shop, the three women sat quiet and still. The only movement came from Simon Le Bon, who was fidgeting by the door, figuring that if everyone had their coats on then a walk was definitely on the cards. Regretfully, they would have to leave him behind, locked in the shop until their mission was over. Maybe Fiona should have trained him to sniff out dominoes, then he could've come with them to help. His soft brown eyes bored into hers as if to say, *How could you do this to me?* Pleading, guilt-tripping her for a walk.

She'd take him out later. She would probably need a walk after this herself to calm down, judging by the rate at which her heart was knocking against her ribcage.

"They're going," Partial Sue hissed.

Outside, Sophie and Gail emerged from the Cats Alliance. Once she was out on the pavement and had room to manoeuvre, Sophie swung her ridiculous cape around her shoulders in a wide and unnecessarily dramatic arc, swatting Gail in the process. She supervised Gail as she locked up, then climbed into her vast, shiny, black Range Rover parked outside. In a cloud of oily diesel smoke, Sophie left the building.

Then Gail did something Fiona never would have expected. Unaware that anyone was watching, quiet, humble Gail gave a subtle V-sign to the back of Sophie's car. Then she zipped up her hi-vis yellow cycling jacket, plonked a wonky helmet on her head, unlocked her bike and rode for home.

"Well, I never," Daisy said. "She stuck two fingers up at Sophie."

"Can't say I'm surprised," Partial Sue replied. "The way Sophie treats her like a skivvy."

"Ready, everyone?" Fiona was unable to mask the small tremor in her voice.

Two nods came in response. They rose and left the charity shop, Fiona pausing briefly to lock the door and keep Simon Le Bon from escaping.

The name of the game was looking natural and not drawing attention to themselves. Most people usually lingered for a while after leaving work, stringing out their goodbyes. Fiona, Partial Sue and Daisy pulled this off with aplomb, appearing to dither and chatter, edging along the pavement as they did so until they reached the Wicker Man's door. Halting in front of it, they continued their trivial conversation. Fiona glanced around, making sure the coast was clear. She winked at Daisy, who immediately turned to face the door, stooping down so her eyes were level with the lock. With their backs to her, Partial Sue and Fiona closed in around her, obscuring her from view. It also helped that it was almost dark now, the blackening sky above them and dreary pavement below. Daisy got to work.

Seconds later they actually heard a pin drop. One of Daisy's tools had slipped out of her hand.

"Leave it," Fiona whispered. "Use the spare."

They dared not look at Daisy, worried it would draw attention to what they were doing or put her off. Gauging her progress, all they could go by were the huffs and puffs coming from behind them as Daisy's delicate battle against the lock continued. Back in the shop, practising all day, she'd got it down to a couple of minutes. Picking a lock in the safety of the storeroom was one thing, but doing it out in the real world on a damp, empty Southbourne street was quite another. To make matters worse, the one she'd practised on had been fresh and new, its mechanism slick and tight. The lock that currently challenged her was old and stiff, rattly and worn.

She had resorted to swearing under her breath now. Not a good sign. Daisy never swore.

"Take your time, Daisy," Fiona said, stifling the urge to shout, "*Hurry up!*" But that would only make Daisy panic and force more errors.

As seconds ticked into minutes, Partial Sue and Fiona were running out of light-hearted, nothing-to-see-here conversation, something they had no trouble doing in the confines of the shop. Yet outside, exposed and self-conscious, their chatter kept drying up. All talk abruptly stopped as a woman with a phone to her ear hurried towards them, a bag of shopping in one hand. Partial Sue and Fiona held their breath as she passed. Engrossed in her phone, she seemed to be interrogating someone in a call centre about why her car insurance had gone up. The woman didn't notice either woman, and certainly not Daisy hunched behind them.

Then they heard it.

The sweetest and most subtle of sounds.

The lock clicked open.

CHAPTER 42

As soon as they were inside and had closed the door to the Wicker Man's shop, Partial Sue had a coughing fit. "Doesn't he ever clean this place? It's so dusty."

"That's the drawback of wicker furniture," Daisy said. "Lots of places for dust to hide." She produced an antibacterial wipe from somewhere.

"Daisy, what are you doing?" Fiona asked.

"I was going to give the place a once-over."

"This is breaking and entering," Fiona reminded her. "Not *How Clean Is Your House?* We can't disturb anything. We need to search without leaving a trace."

Reluctantly, Daisy put the wipe away. Flashing their phone torches, they worked from the front of the shop to the back, carefully searching everywhere, hoping to discover a hidden domino set, a knife or anything that would point to the Wicker Man being the Domino Killer. Easier said than done. Furniture had been piled up haphazardly with no thought to presentation. The place was a hotchpotch of tangled chairs, tables, stools and wardrobes.

Partial Sue rifled through a chest of drawers. "No wonder he never sells anything. Place is a mess, more like a dumping ground."

"But perfect for hiding evidence," Fiona said.

Towards the back of the shop, the layout was similar to Dogs Need Nice Homes, except instead of a storeroom, it had an office-cum-kitchenette with a desk and filing cabinets, equally messy and scruffy.

"This looks more promising," Partial Sue remarked. Closing the storeroom door behind them, all three began searching the cluttered space, filtering through hanging files and dog-eared boxes stacked up in giddy piles. Like the showroom outside, if you could stretch to calling it a showroom, every available inch was full of useless junk.

Fiona attacked the desk, going from drawer to drawer. Stuffed with old bills and invoices, it yielded nothing except a couple of paper cuts. She reached the last drawer, a slender one on the top right-hand side. She tugged on the little brass handle. It wouldn't budge.

"Hey, this one's locked."

"That's suspicious," Partial Sue said.

"Step aside." Daisy made a beeline for the desk, brandishing her hairpins. Knee joints popping and cracking, she knelt down and went at it, inserting the tension wrench first, then the pick. "I'll only be a jiffy."

While she waited, Fiona turned her attention to the cupboard under the sink, which, rather than containing cleaning products and spare light bulbs, housed his drinks collection. There were several types of whisky, the bottles all half-drunk, and a slender bottle of something yellow and Greek that looked like a souvenir liqueur, its sealed lid intact. Several Frey Bentos steak-and-kidney pie tins kept the drinks company. She wondered how he cooked them, as they were no signs of an oven or even a microwave, just a battered kettle on top of the sink next to an opened bottle of milk swiftly turning into cheese.

Fiona suddenly froze, glancing at her companions, who had done the same. A noise was coming from the showroom. It sounded like the front door being opened and closed.

It was at that point that Fiona realised they'd made a terrible and unforgivable rookie mistake. They should've posted a lookout at the front of the shop to guard against this happening. They'd also left the front door unlocked, allowing anyone to walk in.

Too late now. In the torchlight, the three women stared at one another.

"What do we do?" Partial Sue whispered.

Fiona put her finger to her lips.

"Is anybody here?" asked a deep, well-spoken voice, and it wasn't the Wicker Man's.

Footsteps came closer. "Hello, anybody here?"

"I'm going out there," Fiona muttered.

"No, no, no," Partial Sue mouthed.

Fiona ignored her and left the office, shutting the door behind her.

In the gloom, a man in a sensible anorak and glasses stood before her. "Oh, sorry, the door was open. Are you still open? I wasn't sure. All the lights were off."

Fiona went mute. Rooted to the spot with nothing to say for herself, she must have looked like a simpleton. One thing she was sure of, she didn't want to turn the lights on and illuminate herself or this whole fiasco. "Power cut," she managed to say.

The door opened and in came a petite woman preceded by her rather large pregnancy bump. The man turned to her. "You should've stayed in the car. You'll be more comfortable."

Shuffling along, she said, "I wanted to see the furniture." She smiled at Fiona. "Sorry, I know it's after closing time, but we've just moved down from London to Hengistbury Head. Much nicer for raising kids. And we need a few bits. I absolutely adore old-school wicker, so natural and authentic."

Fiona's muteness refused to budge. She nodded slowly.

The couple looked awkward. "Would it be okay to buy something?" the woman asked.

It dawned on Fiona that in her current state of stupefied high alert, she must have come across as the oddball yokel, not used to strangers or speaking in complete sentences. More importantly, she realised she was off the hook. These two weren't a pair of concerned citizens. She hadn't been rumbled on the job. They were customers.

The woman turned and pointed to a piece in the window. "That wicker cot. I love it. I've never seen one before."

Thinking quick, Fiona realised this was her opportunity to get these two out of here by putting them off. They were health-and-safety-conscious millennials to whom everything and anything could be a potential threat to life itself.

"There's a reason for that," Fiona warned them. "It wouldn't pass health and safety standards these days. The baby's head could get stuck."

"I don't like the sound of that," the man trembled.

"It'll be fine," the woman reassured him. "We'll just put a padded cot liner in there. Lots of cots have them. How much is it?"

This was another chance to send them packing. Fiona pulled an outrageous price out of the air. "Five hundred pounds."

"We'll take it," the woman said gleefully. "And I need a chair to go with it, for those midnight feeds."

Fiona's strategy wasn't working. The woman was here to buy, and buy she would at any price. Fiona desperately tried to think of a new tactic to get them out. However, after volunteering in a shop for several years, she'd developed a natural instinct for sales that would kick in automatically whenever she sensed opportunity in the air. She couldn't resist the temptation to upsell. "Have you thought about a rocking chair?"

"No, why?"

Fiona led them over to a rocking chair that, thankfully, wasn't entangled with any other bits of furniture. "Well, getting in and out of a chair with a baby in your arms in the middle of the night plays havoc on the knees. A rocking chair really helps, much easier to get in and out of, plus the rocking motion helps soothe the baby back to sleep."

"I like the sound of that." The woman lowered herself into the rocking chair, using both arms for support. Toing and froing several times, she launched herself up and out of the chair in one smooth motion. "You're right, that is so easy. What do you think?" she asked her partner.

"Er, a rocking chair sounds nice."

In the end, Fiona sold them a cot, a rocking chair, a side table to go next to it and a toy box. She watched out of the window as the man slid most of it into the back of his sensible Audi estate with the back seats down, apart from the rocking chair, which had to be lashed to the roof with luggage straps.

After they'd driven away, Fiona returned to the office at the back.

"What happened?" Partial Sue hissed. "We were worried stiff. Was it the police, community officers?"

"No, it was a young couple."

"What did they want?"

"Furniture, so I sold them some."

"You did *what*?"

"I sold them some furniture."

"I thought you told us not to disturb anything," Daisy protested. "To leave no trace that anyone's been here."

"I know, you're right, but I couldn't think of what else to do to stop them getting suspicious. I couldn't exactly say, 'Sorry, this isn't actually my shop, I've broken into it because I think the owner is a serial killer.'"

"What did you sell?" Daisy asked.

"A cot, a rocking chair, a table and a toy box."

"How much did you get?" Partial Sue asked.

"A grand."

"A grand!" Partial Sue nearly collapsed. "Who pays a grand for a few bits of dusty old wicker furniture?"

"They were from Notting Hill."

"Oh, okay."

"How did they pay for it?" Daisy asked.

"They wanted to do a bank transfer, but I don't know the Wicker Man's account details or if he even has online banking. I told them to drop the cash in tomorrow. Hopefully, he'll be back in by then."

Partial Sue looked doubtful. "Won't he start asking questions?"

"What, about someone dropping a thousand pounds in his lap? I doubt it. Plus, it was really gloomy out there, you could hardly make out the furniture, let alone faces."

"You're quite the salesperson, Fiona," Daisy remarked. "Not everyone can sell furniture in the dark."

"And in someone else's shop," Partial Sue added. "While breaking and entering."

"Thank you. Did you find anything?"

Partial Sue shook her head. "We stopped when you went out there. We were worried about making a noise."

"Come on," Fiona said. "Let's finish what we started and get out of here before anybody else comes looking for overpriced wicker goods."

Daisy cracked open the locked drawer, which, rather than containing confidential documents or evidence of his guilt, was stuffed full of old betting slips and unpaid invoices. After a half an hour of more searching, they'd found no clues pointing to the Wicker Man's guilt. They had nothing to show for their evening's efforts apart from making their suspect a thousand pounds better off.

CHAPTER 43

Fiona and Simon Le Bon spent another night at Partial Sue's. Fiona didn't sleep a wink. Again, she had her phone and GPS alarm at the ready, and the cricket trophy firmly in her grasp as the uneventful night dragged on. At least she didn't have the Wicker Man stretched out on the couch below. Despite this, fear still circled like a hungry vulture. Thankfully, her depression had skulked back into the shadows since getting stuck back into the investigation, despite how fruitless their evening had been.

The next logical place to look would be the Wicker Man's home. But Fiona had to face facts — she really didn't have the stomach for any more breaking and entering, especially into someone's home. She'd broken the law twice already and had nothing to show for it. She didn't want to chance it a third time.

*　*　*

Coming into the shop the next morning, the mood was sombre. To make matters worse, they'd run out of milk. Denied her second cuppa of the day, she sat waiting at the table while Partial Sue nipped to the corner shop to stock up on milk and hopefully a packet of biscuits, although knowing her penchant for saving money, she'd return biscuitless, or at best, with custard-inspired creams from the twenty pence shop.

The tinkling of the doorbell tugged Fiona from her thoughts. The Wicker Man hobbled his way into the shop. He'd acquired a natty walking stick from somewhere to aid his ambling while his back healed. With his flair for the dramatic, the stick had a bulbous bejewelled top and clunked along the floor as he walked, slowly tapping out a slow rhythm.

"Greetings, my fair lady," he proclaimed.

It suddenly occurred to Fiona that she was on her own. Alone with their number-one suspect. DI Fincher's instructions had been clear and simple: while her life was threatened, she should never allow herself to be alone anywhere. It had never crossed her mind that this could happen while Partial Sue popped out for some milk — it seemed so innocent, and she'd only be gone for a minute or two. But a minute or two was all it took to be murdered.

"Are you okay?" he asked. "You look like you've seen a ghost."

She tried her best to appear unflustered. "I'm fine."

"Where is everyone?"

"Er, Sue's here. She's just gone to the shop to get some milk. She'll be back any second. And Oliver and Stewart will be popping in too, like they do every morning," she reminded him just for good measure. Safety in numbers.

"Oh good, I could do with cake and a cuppa. I was hoping to have one in my shop but the milk's gone off." He pulled up a chair and slowly lowered himself down, sharply wincing with every degree of movement.

Fiona needed to keep him talking, to buy herself some time so Partial Sue could get back. She reached into her pocket and wrapped her hand around the GPS alarm, ready to summon the police should the Wicker Man try anything. "How's your back?" she asked.

"Better, much better. Got some industrial-strength painkillers from a chap I know. I think they're from China.

Strong stuff, maybe a bit too strong. Made the old grey matter go a bit doolally."

"How so?"

"Well, I spent all of yesterday flat on my back at home. When I opened up first thing this morning, a chap pulls up in a car and hands me an envelope full of used readies. Not the first time that's happened," he said conspiratorially, out of the side of his mouth. "Anyway, this chap says it's for the cot and rocking chair and a few other bits they'd bought. He smiles, then jumps back in his posh car and takes off. Gave me a grand, he did. You know, I've got no recollection of selling anything like that. I would've remembered, I haven't sold anything in weeks. But sure enough, I get in the shop and the cot's gone, so's the rocking chair, toy box and a little table."

Fiona didn't know how to respond. Was her guilty conscience showing? Probably. Along with the fear that she could have a killer sitting across the table from her. She felt the colour evaporate from her face completely.

"Fiona, are you sure you're okay?"

She stared at the Wicker Man, not speaking, not moving, paralysed with grim thoughts filling her head like black mist. Would he attempt to kill her there and then? She was alone and there were no witnesses. How would he do it? In his present state, he'd find it a struggle, unless he was still faking. She glanced at the walking stick by his side. Maybe he'd bludgeon her to death with it, or maybe it contained a hidden blade that he'd plunge into her back when it was turned. That was more his style, something theatrical.

He stared at her as if trying to work out what was wrong. "I said, are you feeling okay?"

Fiona shook herself out of her stupor. "I'm fine, honestly. I just didn't sleep very well last night at Sue's."

"You stayed there again? How come you keep kipping at hers?" His Essex accent was back.

"Er." She'd let that slip without meaning to. She couldn't exactly tell him she'd stayed there because a murderer was threatening to kill her and she thought it was him.

She made a quick excuse. "I'm having some work done at home." Changing the subject, she said, "Tell me about when you used to work at the electricity board."

The Wicker Man appeared mystified. "Really, you want to know about that?"

"Yes, you've never told me about that part of your life."

"Oh, okay, well, it's rather dull. Not much to tell. I was an electrical engineer. Thought I'd be doing that until I retired. Then I got ACVD."

"What's that?" Fiona asked.

"It stands for Acquired Colour Vision Deficiency. I went colour-blind. You can't work with electrical wiring if you're colour-blind. Can't tell the wires apart. It's a bit of a disadvantage. Actually, it's downright dangerous."

That explained why he sometimes wore odd socks. Fiona had thought it was all part of his eccentric Englishman act. Now she realised it was because he couldn't pick out matching shades. "I'm sorry to hear that. Must have been a shock."

"Yes, it is when you've been used to recognising colours all your life."

"So did they make you redundant because of the colour-blindness?"

"Oh, no. That came later. They offered me another job, something that didn't need full colour vision. I became a meter reader, going from house to house."

Fiona felt a rush of adrenalin. She had to keep calm and use this as an opportunity for gathering evidence. "Did you feel resentful? Was it degrading after being an engineer?" Fiona fished for murderous motivation.

"No, I quite enjoyed it. Meeting lots of different folk. Plus, it was a lot less pressure than my last job. Biggest challenge was finding the meter cupboards. It's amazing how many people forget where they are."

"But then you got made redundant."

"Yes, they started bringing in these smart meters. They didn't need so many of us anymore."

"Did that make you angry?"

213

"Angry? Not a bit. Best thing that ever happened to me, and it was voluntary redundancy. Got a big wodge of spondulicks. Put it into the shop, which I regret doing. Should've just moved to Barbados and lived in a beach shack smoking cigars and sipping rum."

"Do you still have your equipment, for recording the readings?"

"Er, yeah. I think I've still got it somewhere. I don't know why I bothered keeping it."

For getting into people's home and killing them, thought Fiona. "Are there still meter readers around?"

"Yeah, a few."

"I suppose they need them for people who aren't online and can't have a smart meter." Fiona wanted to test out her theory.

"Oh no, you don't need to be online to have a smart meter."

"You don't?" Fiona's theory began to wobble.

The Wicker Man shook his head. "No, common misconception. Smart meters use a separate network. It's called the DCC network. It's all secure, sends the information from your smart meter to your energy company."

Fiona sensed her meter-reading murderer theory shuddering, like an old tower block about to be demolished. "So why are there still meter readers then? If you don't have a smart meter, surely you just phone in the reading or email it."

"That's true, but there are a few people who can't do that. People who are disabled or partially sighted. They still need a meter reader. What's got you so interested in this all of a sudden?"

Partial Sue burst through the door, clutching a bottle of milk in one hand and a red packet of what appeared to be Digestive biscuits in the other, although there was something odd about the branding, as if they'd been transported from a parallel universe.

Fiona gasped, relief flooding over her. She felt a whole lot safer now her friend was back.

"Morning!" Partial Sue said cheerfully until she realised who Fiona was talking to. Her eyes widened and her faced dropped momentarily. A possible killer in their midst had been left alone with Fiona. She managed to regain her composure before the Wicker Man noticed. His attention was on the biscuits in her hands. He tilted his head slightly, attempting to read the packet.

"*Suggestives*? What are they?" he asked.

"They're like Digestives but they're not allowed to be called that, probably for legal reasons."

"You've been to the twenty pence shop again, haven't you?" Fiona asked.

"I have. Now who'd like a cuppa?"

"Is the milk from there too?" asked Fiona.

"No, I got that from the newsagent's."

"Then, yes. I'll have a cup of tea, but I'll pass on the fake Digestives."

"I'll give them a taste drive," said the Wicker Man, chortling. "Get it, taste drive?"

"You won't be laughing or making puns after you've tried them, or broken your teeth."

Fiona's phone rang. She pulled it out of her pocket and regarded the screen. *Caller ID unknown*. Fiona was always reluctant to answer when that appeared. Usually, she'd get a recorded message telling her not to hang up and that she'd won a prize draw or had a mysterious package that she'd never ordered and needed to pick up. This time, curiosity got the better of her. "Hello?"

Fiona shushed the Wicker Man as she tried to listen to what the caller was saying. When she heard, she nearly dropped the phone.

CHAPTER 44

"Thanks for picking me up." Daisy squeezed into the back of Partial Sue's Fiat Uno, not helped by Simon Le Bon attempting to lick her face as she did so. Daisy lived in Christchurch in a house that was like her. Sweet and cutesy, it overlooked a stream beside a bridge and had window seats, one having been cleared of cushions to make way for her vast collection of Wade Whimsy figurines, at which very small children passing by would stare and coo over. With regimental regularity, she would clean each one to within an inch of its life, as she did with every inch of her house.

Daisy had lived alone ever since she'd split from her husband, and the less said about him the better. When her high-maintenance daughter had fled the nest to get married there had been nothing to distract Daisy from what a nasty man he was. The pair parted ways a year afterwards. Daisy got to keep the house, thanks to Partial Sue, who'd loosened her normally tight fists and dipped into her vast savings to help pay for the best divorce lawyer money could buy.

"I was just about to leave for work." Daisy had abandoned her DCI Tennison look. The business suit had been swapped for her usual maxi dress, a pink one, and her hair had gone back to its normal curly self.

"We're not going to work," Fiona said. "We're going to Westbourne."

Daisy became excited. "Oh, I do like Westbourne. They have some lovely tea rooms."

Westbourne was about the same size as Southbourne and had a similar genteel, Victorian vibe, except a shade posher. Its claims to fame were that JRR Tolkien had once lived nearby, as had Robert Louis Stevenson in a fittingly Gothic mansion. At the other end of the scale, Westbourne had a ridiculous number of cosy tea shops, easily outgunning Southbourne, which was no slouch either. Westbourne also boasted an M & S Foodhall, which Southbourne did not. If Southbourne residents wanted to flex their Sparks card, they had to travel a mile down the road to neighbouring Christchurch. However, Christchurch also had a Waitrose, which Westbourne did not, so, swings and roundabouts.

"We're not going there for tea," Partial Sue said. "We're going there to collect evidence."

"Evidence?" Daisy leaned forward between the gap in the two front seats. "Tell me more."

Fiona twisted around to face her. "Remember when we phoned around charity shops to ask if anyone had bought a set of dominoes?"

Daisy nodded eagerly.

"Well, one got back to me this morning, End Global Hunger in Westbourne. The manager Maureen said she's got something for us."

"Do they know who bought it?"

"That's what we're going to find out."

Daisy looked worried. "Oh, wait, who's looking after the shop?"

"No one," Fiona replied. "I thought we all needed to be here for this."

Half an hour later, Partial Sue orbited Westbourne's one-way system for the umpteenth time until she found a space. They parked up and headed to the shops, Daisy acting like an excited puppy. "Can we cut through the arcade? I love the arcade."

"Why not?" said Fiona.

They wandered through the storybook Victorian shopping arcade, its pretty barrel-vaulted glass ceiling tethered with delicate ironwork. At ground level it was lined with quirky and eccentric independent boutiques with hanging signs outside and white-painted sash windows above. The temptation to window-shop was overwhelming but they resisted, apart from Daisy, who had to be dragged away from one of the many gift shops selling carved dogs and picture frames made of driftwood.

They found the End Global Hunger charity shop almost opposite the entrance to the arcade.

"Great spot," Partial Sue remarked.

Led by Fiona, the three of them entered the posh charity shop that would easily give the Cats Alliance a run for its money. However, unlike the Cats Alliance it hadn't managed to eradicate the collective mustiness of all those second-hand clothes. Simon Le Bon's nose was going nineteen to the dozen sniffing all the wonderful new smells.

Fiona approached a jolly-looking lady behind the counter in a bright floral dress and whose peroxide hair contrasted sharply with her skin, which appeared to have recently seen a little too much sun. "You must be Maureen. I'm Fiona. We spoke on the phone."

"Ah, yes. Pleased to meet you."

Fiona turned to introduce her two colleagues, only to find they'd been distracted by the merchandise and were holding up garments against themselves to assess suitability.

"Ladies, can we remember why we're here?"

"Sorry," Daisy said. "You have some lovely stock."

"Oh, don't apologise," Maureen replied. "We are lucky being so close to Canford Cliffs and Sandbanks. Rich clientele go through fashion at a rate of knots, then they offload it here."

"Thank you so much for seeing us about our little matter," Fiona said.

"Well, I'm sorry it took so long. I only got back off holiday yesterday. A cruise around the Caribbean."

"Oh, how lovely," Daisy said. "I'd love to go to the Caribbean."

"You simply must. Anyway, I got back yesterday, and I saw the note someone had scribbled down, asking about dominoes."

"So do you remember someone buying a set?"

"No."

Fiona became crestfallen. "No?"

Maureen fiddled with her earring. "That's the puzzling thing. I know we had a domino set in a little wooden box. I have a good memory for all our stock. None of my staff remembers selling it, and neither do I."

Fiona struggled to work out how this helped them. If this was the case, then they'd just wasted a journey to Westbourne for information that could have easily been conveyed over the phone.

Maureen clearly read the disappointment in Fiona's face. "Well, that got me thinking," she continued. "Logically, if no one here sold it, then someone stole it."

Fiona tried to be as diplomatic as possible. "Oh, okay. So how does that help us?"

Maureen pointed to a corner of the ceiling. They all followed the line of her finger, directing their gaze to a compact CCTV camera at the back of the shop. She became serious. "We get a lot of shoplifters in here, lured by our second-hand designer clothes. They think we're easy pickings, a soft touch because we're a charity shop. Thing is, every time someone steals something, it's taking the food out of hungry mouths, and I'm not having that, I can tell you, so I had CCTV installed."

"Is it HD?" Partial Sue asked.

"I don't think so." Maureen reached into a drawer behind the counter and rooted around. "But I do know it keeps a record of everything for the last thirty-six days." She produced a USB drive and handed it to Fiona. "I took the

219

liberty of transferring it to a data stick. I would have emailed it to you but it's quite a big file. Didn't want to risk it."

Clutching the USB stick, Fiona beamed as if she were holding the answer to life itself. "Thank you, thank you so much. You don't realise how much of a help this will be. I'll return the stick to you afterwards."

"Well, I don't know if there will be anything useful on it. But can I ask — why all this trouble to track down a domino set? Is it valuable or something?"

"Yes,' Fiona replied. "It's very valuable."

* * *

Partial Sue tried every shortcut to get them back to Dogs Need Nice Homes as fast as automotively possible. The traffic was terrible whichever route they took. Fiona was still holding the USB stick aloft in front of her, not daring to let it out of her tight grasp. All she wanted to do was fire up the shop's laptop, shove the USB into the appropriate slot and start reviewing the footage.

"How long do you think it will take to watch thirty-six days of footage?" Daisy asked.

"There's a clue in your question," said Partial Sue.

"I don't understand," Daisy replied.

Partial Sue waited.

Realisation dawned as bright as a summer sun. "Oh, right, yes, silly me. Thirty-six days."

"I'm sure there will be bits we can fast-forward," Fiona said.

After they got back to the shop, they went straight to the laptop on the counter, not even stopping to make tea. Gathering around the screen, the black-and-white footage was fairly clear and gave them a direct view of a low shelf holding a stack of large board games. It was too far away to tell what each one was, however, sandwiched in between them was a distinctive rectangular wooden box, just the right dimensions to be a domino set. It also helped that a few hours into the footage, someone browsing pulled the wooden box off the shelf and put it back with the top facing out, revealing the word *DOMINO* in big, block letters. Now they had a positive lock on the target, as Partial Sue dramatically put it, they could speed up the footage, only slowing it down when someone came near it.

After a while they came to the conclusion that it didn't need all three of them to do this. With hours and hours of mostly monotonous footage of people lazily browsing in a shop, it only took one of them to review it, so they took it in turns.

"Oh my gosh," Daisy blurted out. It was her turn on screen duty. Fiona and Partial Sue darted over from opposite ends of the shop. Fiona nearly knocked over a bin of soft toys, each one only a pound (or three for two pounds), on her way to the counter where Daisy was hunched over the laptop.

"Have you found something?"

"That women's just stolen a handbag! Bold as brass!"

"Where?" Partial Sue asked.

Daisy rolled back the footage. A woman in her forties was casually perusing the racks. She examined what appeared to be a neat brown Radley bag, judging by the little leather dog logo. She glanced over her shoulder, once then twice. After the third time, when she thought no one was watching her, she hooked the handbag over her arm and made for the door, unchallenged.

"Well, I never," Partial Sue said. "Makes you wonder if we get shoplifters in here. I mean, I've never caught any."

"We don't sell anything designer. Besides, our stuff's so cheap, what would be the point?"

Daisy resumed her search, then half an hour later she screamed again, waking up Simon Le Bon, who had been chuntering and running in his sleep in his basket by her feet.

Once more, Fiona and Partial Sue made a beeline for the counter.

"I think I've got something." Daisy wound the footage back and pressed play. From what they could tell, it had been raining outside because people were piled into the shop, water dripping off their clothes. The place was busier than usual. Typically British, they were pretending to browse the shop, not wanting to be accused of merely using it as a place to shelter. From one corner of the footage, a figure in a soggy and baggy black anorak with the hood up appeared, their face obscured. They mingled with the other customers meandering around the shop, randomly dawdling here and there. When they passed the shelf with the board games, the figure suddenly sped up and left the shop.

"There, did you see it?" Daisy exclaimed.

"Play it again," Fiona asked.

Daisy obliged, slowly rewinding the footage just a few seconds and pausing it at the point just before the figure approached the shelf. The dominoes could be clearly seen. She let the footage play again until the hooded figure had swept past the shelf and hit pause again. The dominoes were gone.

"We have a thief in an anorak," Fiona said. "But who are they?"

"Excuse me." Partial Sue leaned forward and hit the play button for just a second or two and hit pause as the figure exited the shop. She rewound and forwarded it several times until she had it in just the right position. The screen showed only the briefest paused glimpse, the frozen footage shimmying away, but that was all they needed. It was the only full-length image of the thief unobstructed by racks or displays. The "anorak" nearly reached to the floor.

"That's not an anorak, that's a cape."

Three mouths fell open at once and then blurted out, "Sophie Haverford!"

CHAPTER 45

Partial Sue stared out of the window, not taking her gaze off the Cats Alliance. "She's still over there. Prancing around outside, free as a bird. Why haven't the police arrested her yet?"

As soon as they'd seen the cape on the CCTV footage, Fiona had put a call through to DI Fincher to tell her they had found something. DI Fincher had patiently listened with interest and asked Fiona to email her the clip immediately. Then it had all gone quiet. Time had passed and they hadn't heard or seen anything.

Today was the grand opening of the new coffee bar at the Cats Alliance and Sophie was still there, flaunting it, strutting about on the pavement outside the shop, her cape billowing behind her, almost as if she were goading Fiona and her colleagues. In her element, Sophie was luxuriating in loudly directing the people she had hired to put on her big event. So far this included: caterers (who weren't local, which would not go down well with the Southbourne Chamber of Commerce); a team attempting to wrangle a balloon arch over the front of the shop, which appeared to be making an escape thanks to a stiff sea breeze; a trilby-wearing saxophonist to create that smoky, laid-back New York café vibe (although Fiona had heard that he wasn't actually from the Big Apple but from down the road in Lyndhurst); a couple of carpet-fitters, who had supplied a red carpet and velvet rope to keep the crowd back, as if it were a Hollywood bash; and two beefy security guards in black suits and shades to keep out the hoi polloi, as the Wicker Man had described it when he had popped in earlier. All this brouhaha (another one of the Wicker Man's phrases) just to announce they were now serving hot drinks. How the hell could she afford it all? There's no way a charity could stretch to such extravagances. Surely that was worth looking into as a side investigation. Money laundering perhaps, as well as serial murder? Wishful thinking.

The answer was probably a little more straightforward. Being an ex-PR maven, as she liked to call herself, Sophie had a silver tongue and would have leveraged all this for free, promising media exposure for all involved, neglecting to mention it would amount to no more than a few minuscule column inches in the *Southbourne Monitor*.

Fiona and Daisy joined Partial Sue at the window to watch the spectacle unfold. Fiona had to give it to Sophie, she certainly knew how to put on a show. A large crowd had gathered on both sides of the pavement behind the velvet ropes. Phones were out, snapping away. This was a big deal for Southbourne. In the crowd she recognised a cluster of people accompanied by wheelchairs, walking frames and sticks.

"That's our Tuesday morning coffee club! Have they no loyalty?" Partial Sue complained.

"You can't blame them," Fiona replied. "Things like this don't happen very often around here." Secretly, Fiona had hoped they would have bypassed the shiny shenanigans across the road in favour of the warm and genuine atmosphere of Dogs Need Nice Homes. No such luck. The shop remained empty.

"As long as they don't make a habit of it," Sue replied.

Fiona couldn't see that happening. Everything at the Cats Alliance was better than they had to offer. Who wouldn't want free barista coffee and saxophonists? She couldn't compete with Sophie, nor did she want to. She didn't have the energy or the budget.

As if reading her mind, Sophie threw a look over in their direction. A gloating, self-satisfied grin settled on her face. It said, *I've won, I'm better than you.*

Fine, thought Fiona. *You can have it all, if that's what's important to you.*

"I don't see Gail over there," Daisy remarked.

"No, Sophie always gives her the day off when she has events like this. Gets her out the way. Doesn't fit with her 'aesthetic'." Partial Sue did air quotes. "She always hires a couple of glamorous temps to help out."

"That's a bit mean."

"That's Sophie for you."

At that point, a white stretch limo pulled up in front of the red carpet. A familiar and distinctive face appeared. From the crowd rose a sea of phones, capturing the celebrity.

"Is that Laurence Llewelyn-Bowen?" Daisy asked.

The limo pulled away, revealing the famous TV interior designer in his full glory. He looked rather dapper in a well-tailored, mint-green, double-breasted suit.

"It is!" Fiona said.

Melodramatically, Sophie cavorted towards him, beaming with her arms outstretched. Many air kisses were exchanged — too many to count.

They watched Sophie's smugness rise to radioactive levels as she posed for shots on the red carpet with the interior designer, fawning all over him. Fiona could feel the bile rising up her throat, burning everything in its path like a rampant forest fire. She was about to turn away, unable to watch anymore, when a strange thing happened.

Another car pulled up beside the red carpet, a plain navy-blue BMW. Sophie tried to ignore it, playing to the crowd, but the car didn't move. She kept glancing over at it, her grin slipping intermittently. She clearly wasn't happy with it parked there as it wasn't part of the script — probably some ignorant member of the public getting in the way. She slipped over to one of the security guards and had a word in his ear, likely something along the lines of "Get that car out of here". The security guard immediately obeyed. An intimidating figure, he strode over to the driver, ready to flex his muscles.

Just as he reached the door, the guard halted and backed away, almost scared. The reason became clear. From out of the car, the sharp, businesslike figure of DI Fincher arose, holding up what they presumed was her warrant card. A second later, DS Thomas emerged, also holding aloft his warrant card, his baggy sportswear reducing Sophie's overall aesthetic by several degrees. A regular police car pulled up behind them and two uniformed officers stepped out.

Partial Sue gasped, nudging Fiona in the ribs. "Are you seeing this?"

"I can't look anywhere else," Fiona replied.

"It's better than telly," Daisy commented.

At first, Sophie was all smiles, perfectly cool-headed, welcoming the detectives as if it were all part of the show. They couldn't hear what was being said, but from her body language, Sophie appeared to be ushering them into the Cats Alliance, keen to get them out of sight under the guise of offering them free coffee. DI Fincher shook her head and took Sophie over to one side, quietly having a word with her, with DS Thomas and the two uniformed officers standing behind her. Sophie began gesticulating wildly, her hands pointing out that she was in the middle of something important. DS Thomas and the uniformed officers edged forward. DI Fincher turned and gestured for them to give her some space. The detective had another quiet word with her, except this time her expression was firmer. Sophie's shoulders slumped, defeated.

"I wonder if she's just threatened to put her in cuffs," Partial Sue said.

Fiona had never seen Sophie downcast. Her perma-smile defeated, she almost felt sorry for her. It didn't last long.

Her expression switched and she regained her composure, addressing the crowd in a confident, booming voice. "Ladies, gentlemen, esteemed friends, good people of Southbourne. Thank you all so much for coming. The grand opening will continue shortly. Alas, I must make a momentary exit, but I will be back soon to greet you, one and all. As many of you may know, I'm a legendary supporter of the police, and they need my help with an urgent case and, in my book, keeping the streets of Southbourne safe is my priority. So I must bid you farewell for the time being." She blew a multitude of kisses to the crowd, and with a swish of her cape, attempted to get into DI Fincher's BMW. DI Fincher pointed to the police car behind. Reluctantly, she got into the back of it, the top of her head guided in by one of the officers. It was perhaps the first time anyone had been allowed to touch Sophie's head who wasn't employed by Toni & Guy.

"Oh my God," Partial Sue said. "I think she's just been arrested."

CHAPTER 46

By late afternoon, the red carpet had been rolled up and taken away. The balloon arch had partially deflated and was sagging at a drunken angle. The crowds had dispersed and discarded disposable coffee cups rolled around on the pavement. It had been six hours since the police had taken Sophie away for questioning.

"I'd love to be a fly on the wall in the interview room," Partial Sue said, "watching Sophie squirm and try to sweet-talk her way out of it."

"Do you think she really killed all those people?" Daisy asked.

"We saw what we saw," Partial Sue replied. "And she had the knife in her box of donations. Who else could it be?"

"It's still circumstantial," Fiona pointed out. "We'll leave the police to come to their own conclusions."

Partial Sue glanced out of the window. "Speak of the devil."

A taxi pulled up across the road and out stepped Sophie, still swamped by her cape and a face like bubbling lava. She bypassed her own shop and stormed straight towards Dogs Need Nice Homes. The door flung open so hard, she nearly dislodged the little bell above from its moorings.

Simon Le Bon gave a whimper of fear.

"How dare you?" Sophie snarled. "You planned this, didn't you?"

"Planned what?" Fiona asked.

"You knew about my grand opening, which I kindly invited you to, but you were jealous, weren't you? Had to ruin my day. Decided to sabotage it in cahoots with that ethnic policewoman."

"Her name is Detective Inspector Fincher," Partial Sue reminded her.

"I don't care what she's called. You ruined my day on purpose. Made up some cock-and-bull story about me stealing some dominoes in Westbourne, so the police would turn up. Oh, yes, I saw the footage. I bet that was one of you dressed in a cape, pretending to be me."

"We did no such thing."

"Oh, please, it's so obviously not me. Which one of you was it, eh? Pretending to be me, just so you could set me up."

"Were you arrested?" Daisy asked.

"No, they questioned me. Kept asking me if I knew all these dead people, over and over, and where was I on this date and that date. And the coffee was terrible, worse than the stuff you serve. I don't know how you could do this to me." Almost instantly, Sophie's emotions shifted from anger to melodramatic sadness. Her eyes teared up. "All I've ever been is nice to you. I thought we were friends. How could you do such a thing? Me, an innocent, beautiful person who has vowed never to do harm, who has so much to give and whose only crime is to make life better for everyone."

Before Daisy, Partial Sue and Fiona had time to be sick, Sophie's emotions switched back. The tears miraculously disappeared, dried by the fire in her eyes. "Well, let me tell you, the gloves are off. You're going to regret this. There is such a thing as wasting police time. And defamation of character, slander, wrongful arrest—"

"You weren't arrested," Fiona pointed out.

"That's beside the point. You'll now need to worry about my solicitor, whom I will be contacting the second I've finished here."

"I don't think so," said Fiona.

"Well, I do."

Fiona snorted derisively. "Well, I don't. We didn't know about the footage until Maureen from End Global Hunger got in touch. She called us. We merely passed it on to the police, who, like us, thought it was you. It was their decision to act, not ours. You may know about PR and be best friends with TV celebrities, but we know about crime. If you're saying that it's one of us in disguise, then you'd better have some concrete evidence. Otherwise it's known as a false accusation. There's a law against that too. It's called perverting the course of justice."

"Average sentence is between four and thirty-six months," Partial Sue added. "Or sometimes a hefty fine."

Sophie's features wobbled slightly.

Fiona continued, "You must have proof that it's us, which I'm sure you have, otherwise you wouldn't be making this allegation. So by all means, call your solicitor. Let's get the ball rolling."

Sophie stood silent. Possibly a first. Her mind was chewing over the schooling she'd just received, which had shoved her well and truly out of her depth.

"Well?" Fiona asked.

"Well, what?"

"Have you got evidence?"

"Well, no, not at the—"

Fiona got to her feet. "Then don't come in here threatening me and my friends, accusing us of things we didn't do. You can leave our shop now, if you please."

Sophie didn't leave. She stood there defiant, jaw jutting out. "You think you're so clever, don't you, reading all those dreary crime stories. Here's one you might remember. Two women from Dogs Need Nice Homes visit the community centre to have a nose around. Then steal a set of dominoes, for what petty reason I cannot imagine. However, if falsely being accused of taking dominoes is enough to get me hauled in by the police for questioning, then I'm sure they'd be interested in a pair of thieves who have actually done it for real. And yes, I have concrete evidence, because we caught you red-handed with the stolen goods, right here in this shop. I'll get Malorie to back me up." She sucked in hard through her teeth. "Oh dear. It doesn't look good for you. I think I'd better put a call into DI Fincher right this second." Sophie turned and made a dramatic exit.

Fiona swore.

"She's bluffing," Partial Sue said. "She won't call DI Fincher."

"I bet she will," Fiona replied. "She believes she's been scorned. She'll grass us up and probably lay it on thick."

"I took the dominoes. I'll take the blame."

"We're all in this together," Daisy said.

"Agreed. We should call DI Fincher first, before Sophie does, and confess. It'll look better." Before Fiona could dial the detective's number, it rang. The name of the caller appeared on-screen.

DI Fincher.

Not giving the detective a chance to speak, Fiona rammed her confession down the receiver while Daisy and Partial Sue listened in. "I'm sorry. We stole some dominoes from the community centre. We were going to put them back. We thought they might be evidence—"

"Fiona, Fiona." DI Fincher attempted to halt her confession. "Look, I'm really not bothered about that. I've got bigger things on my plate. I'm just calling to give you an update."

"You are?" Normally, Fiona had to verbally twist DI Fincher's arm to get any sort of progress report.

"Yes. Firstly, you may or may not be aware that we released Sophie Haverford without charge, for reasons that will become clear."

Did Fiona detect a slight edge in her voice? If she didn't know better, she would say the detective sounded annoyed or perhaps tired, or maybe both. That would be no surprise if the last six hours spent questioning Sophie had led to a dead end. The information they'd given the police had amounted to nothing.

"Anyway, this next bit concerns you."

Fiona got a hit of adrenalin, both terrified and excited at what was coming next.

"While we were questioning Sophie, another murder took place," DI Fincher continued. "A Fiona Sharp was found dead."

The phone fell to the floor.

CHAPTER 47

The shock and relief had made Fiona lose control of her body for a brief moment. She snapped up her phone and put it to her ear.

"Fiona? Are you still there?" barked DI Fincher.

"Yes, yes. Please go on."

"Firstly, this means you are off the Osman warning list. Officially, your life is not under threat. Unofficially, the killer is still out there. Exercise caution and be vigilant. Do not take any unnecessary risks, stay in public places and do not open the door to anyone you're not expecting. Secondly, it means Sophie Haverford could not have committed the crime because she was with us."

Partial Sue, who'd been eavesdropping, wanted to know more. "Ask her about the murdered Fiona Sharp."

"It's okay, I heard that," DI Fincher said. "I cannot give any exact details at this point about the deceased."

"Please." Partial Sue leaned in closer. "It would really help us."

"I don't think it would be a good idea."

"You don't have any suspects yet," Partial Sue replied. "What harm could it do?"

The irritation in DI Fincher's voice turned up a notch. "No, we don't. Not after the last suspect we questioned for six hours."

Fiona apologised. "We thought we were doing the right thing by passing that footage on to you. Okay, the killer isn't Sophie, but how do you know it's not the killer in the footage trying to frame her? The killer seems to be making a habit of setting up different people. Sophie, Malorie and June. I'd say they've got a grudge. You can't say that's nothing."

The line went quiet. DI Fincher cleared her throat. "Okay, but this is all I'm giving you. The latest victim was a divorcée called Fiona Sharp who lived alone. She was killed in the same way — stab wound in the back. However, she didn't fit the pattern of the previous murders of being older and offline. She was in her early fifties, had broadband and worked part-time. That's all I can tell you."

"Was a domino left behind?" Daisy asked.

The line went quiet again. "A domino was found in her hand with the name Barry Taylor scratched into it. The number on the domino was the same as the victim before: a one on its own with a blank at the other end. Remember, what I've told you is all strictly between us. Now Fiona, you can go back to your house, but stay vigilant, okay?"

"Okay, thank you."

"You can keep your GPS alarm for the next couple of weeks, just to be on the safe side. Take it with you everywhere."

"I will."

The call ended.

"I can't believe another person is dead," Daisy said. "This is terrible. I thought the killer might have lost interest. That poor woman."

Fiona felt the floor drop away from her. Relief flooded her body, but the guilt crushed heavy as a planet. She'd been spared but another Fiona Sharp had died. Tears pricked at her eyes.

As if reading her mind, Partial Sue said, "We should be thankful it wasn't our Fiona they killed. You're safe." She gave Fiona a reassuring shoulder squeeze.

Fiona returned a weak smile. She didn't feel safe. Shocked would be more accurate. The bullet had been dodged, sidestepped, but it had hit someone else.

"Are you okay?" Daisy asked.

No, she wasn't okay. Perched at the top of the helter-skelter, she needed distraction to stop her from plunging down the spiral, or she might never claw her way back up. Her mind needed occupying.

"I'm fine," she lied. "Let's carry on investigating. It's clear the killer is showing no signs of stopping. We have to catch him, or people will keep dying, like this next guy. Barry Taylor."

"So much for the countdown code," muttered Partial Sue. "Another number one has been added to the sequence: 3,2,1,1 — what does that mean?"

"Countdown is on pause," Daisy ventured. "Or if we use the simple 'one equals A, two equals B' code, we've now got 'baaaaa'. Just a longer sheep sound than we had before. Maybe it's something to do with noisy sheep?"

Fiona frowned. No point in them speculating. She contacted her nephew, texting to tell him that the new domino in the sequence was another number one and a blank, to see if it might help him to extract any hidden codes or patterns. She jumped when he phoned her straight back.

"Hello, Dan." She put the call on speakerphone.

"That's the Fibonacci sequence," he said triumphantly. "Well, it's the Fibonacci sequence backwards, to be precise."

"I've heard of the Fibonacci sequence," Partial Sue said. "It's famous, isn't it? You add two numbers to get the next number or something."

"That's right," Dan replied. "Basically, each number is the sum of the two before it. So it goes 0,1,1, 2, 3, 5, 8, 13, 21 and so on. The combined value of each of your individual dominoes are a part of that sequence, but backwards: 3, 2, 1, 1."

Fiona's mind raced. "What does the Fibonacci sequence mean?"

"Well, the numbers grow bigger exponentially. Best example is an ammonite shell. As the shell grows out in a spiral, that spiral continually increases in size and proportion. It's a perfect real-world representation of Fibonacci."

"So it's all about dinosaur shells?" Daisy asked. Technically ammonites weren't dinosaurs, but everyone knew what she meant.

"Oh, no," Dan said. "That's just one example. The Fibonacci sequence is a repeating pattern in everything and anything — nature, science, computer programming, genetics, art, architecture, engineering — you name it, the Fibonacci sequence will be in there somewhere."

After Fiona had hung up, the three ladies threw themselves into Google, delving into the subject, hoping to find a connection that would link the murder victims with the famous mathematical series. Rather like the sequence itself, the deeper they delved, the more their results grew, to overwhelming proportions. With thousands of pages of hits, the Fibonacci sequence seemed to touch every aspect of life, was part of the DNA of the entire world.

"There's too much information here. Can't we narrow it down?" Daisy put her phone on the table, taking a break from the screen. "How about this? Fibonacci was an Italian mathematician. Pizza is Italian. Dominoes is a make of pizza. There, cracked it."

The other two ladies laughed at Daisy's thin-crust logic.

"Oh, if only it were that easy," Fiona remarked.

Partial Sue jerked upright after being hunched over her own phone. "Maybe it is. Maybe it's a pizza delivery guy. People open their doors to pizza delivery drivers. We didn't have that on the list."

Fiona wasn't so sure. "You don't let pizza delivery guys in your house, that's why it wasn't on the list. But also, Sarah Brown never ordered pizza in her life. She had a problem with mozzarella. Said it was like cheese-flavoured chewing gum, and I can't imagine Ian Richard was a pizza fan either."

"I bet he was more a cheese on toast man," Daisy remarked.

Silence descended as the possible connection dried up in front of them. Reluctantly, Daisy began thumbing her phone screen again. For such a rich clue, full of endless possibilities, Fibonacci was offering them very little in terms of practical, usable information.

Partial Sue folded her arms. "What I don't get is this Fibonacci sequence is all about things getting bigger. But in the case of our dominoes, it's backwards. Numbers are getting smaller. Maybe Barry Taylor is to be the last victim and the next domino we'll find on him will be completely blank to represent zero — the first number in the sequence."

They all considered this for a moment. Was that the message the killer was trying to send them? Previously, they had all thought the numbers had been a countdown — a build-up to a gruesome crescendo. But now with this new information, perhaps it was the opposite. The sequence was winding down, about to end.

"Doesn't matter," Fiona said. "We still have to catch the killer. Stop this Barry Taylor from being the last victim, if that happens to be the case. But we shouldn't assume any-thing." Fiona paused, thought for a beat. "Maybe we should change tack. We're not getting anywhere at the moment. Let's stick a pin in it for now. How about we look into this bloke Barry?"

This change in direction gave Daisy a renewed energy. Her thumbs moved in a blur. "Online directory has seventeen Barry Taylors in the Bournemouth, Poole and Christchurch area. Two of them are right here in Southbourne."

"We need to find what links this latest victim and all the other victims," Partial Sue said eagerly. "Then see if we can apply it to one of the Barry Taylors Daisy's just found."

"We've lost the only link the killer gave us," Fiona pointed out. "Unlike the other victims, the latest one was middle-aged, online and worked. She doesn't fit the pattern."

"But she still lived alone," Partial Sue reminded them.

"There is another link between all the victims, sort of," Daisy said.

Partial Sue and Fiona regarded Daisy, eager for her new revelation. "What?" Fiona asked.

"Well, their names are all a bit dull, aren't they? Sarah Brown, Ian Richard, Sharon Miller, Barry Taylor—"

"Fiona Sharp." The victim's namesake smirked.

"Yeah. I mean, no." Daisy blushed. "Oh, gosh, sorry. But do you know what I mean? There's nothing really exotic in there like, I don't know . . . Jemima Glockenspiel."

"You know someone called Jemima Glockenspiel?" Partial Sue asked.

"No," Daisy replied. "But I'd love a name like that. Something you can really wrap your tongue around. Jemima Glockenspiel. No one's going to forget that name."

"Dull or not, let's hope DI Fincher's budget stretches to police guards for all the Barry Taylors. Seventeen is still quite a lot of people to protect, and that's just the ones we've found."

Fiona nodded in agreement as despondency filled the air, the mood bleak and hopeless with the prospect of more bodies piling up before they could catch a break. The killer was getting away with it, and this didn't seem likely to change for the foreseeable future, unless the reverse Fibonacci sequence meant the killing spree was about to end abruptly. Neither DI Fincher nor the charity shop detectives were any closer to catching them than when they had started.

Partial Sue broke the silence. "That was a smart observation you made about the killer's habit of setting people up, holding a grudge. Who do we know who has a grudge against Sophie?"

"Us," Fiona replied. "Everyone else round here seems to love her. We're the only ones who don't like her, and she knows it. Probably why she thought it was us in the footage."

Partial Sue gasped. "The Wicker Man! He could have a grudge against her."

Daisy's eyebrows raised. "Really? I would have thought her theatrics would be right up his street."

"Exactly," Partial Sue replied. "I can remember when Sophie first came to Southbourne. Before either of your time.

He was besotted by her. Loved all that flamboyant nonsense. Lapped it up. Smitten, he was. Unfortunately, she wasn't into him. Snubbed his offers of affection. The Wicker Man put a brave face on it, laughed it off, but I could tell he was hurt."

"But if he's trying to set up Sophie for the murders, why set up Malorie and June?" Daisy asked.

"As decoys," Partial Sue explained. "If he targeted Sophie alone, it would look too obvious with his history of unrequited love. It would point the finger at him. But with three of them it blurs the lines of motivation."

Fiona straightened up and took a large, confident breath. "Okay, that only strengthens our case against the Wicker Man. He's back to being our number-one suspect."

Daisy pulled a puzzled face. "Makes it trickier to prove, though. I mean, DI Fincher said this latest victim was online, probably had a smart meter. How's he going to do his meter-reading trick to get in the house?"

"You don't need to be online to have a smart meter," Partial Sue replied. "Isn't that what he said to you?"

"I think it's irrelevant," Fiona pointed out. "If she hasn't got a smart meter, he just flashes a fake ID and says, 'I'm here to read the meter.' If she does have a smart meter, he could say something like, 'Your smart meter's malfunctioning and I need to recalibrate it, otherwise you'll be overcharged.' I'm sure most people would let him in. No one wants to be overcharged."

"I've heard that some of them go on the blink now and again," Partial Sue agreed. "Do we know where he was yesterday?"

Daisy thought hard. "He was in here first thing, I remember. To scrounge some of Oliver's cake. Then he went back to his shop, I presume."

Partial Sue became excitable. "His back's better now. He could've popped out for an hour, done the dirty deed and nobody would be any the wiser."

Fiona shook her head. "That's not good enough. We have a serviceable theory but it's worthless if we have no proof."

Silence descended again. Three minds cogitated on how they would gather evidence of the Wicker Man's guilt, preferably without breaking the law again.

Daisy clicked her fingers. "Wait, what was the date on the CCTV footage?"

"Twenty-seventh of September," Partial Sue answered.

Fiona leaned in. "A rainy day. I remember it. The Wicker Man's birthday. We got Oliver to bake him a cake with candles. Oliver complained about getting soaking wet. He left the moment we started singing 'Happy Birthday'. Joyful occasions always get Oliver's back up."

"Wasn't that just in the morning?" Partial Sue asked. "Did we know where the Wicker Man was for the rest of the time?"

"Er, no. He took the day off."

"He could still have done it." Partial Sue rocked back and forth, unable to contain her swelling excitement. "Plenty of time to get over to Westbourne and pretend to be Sophie to set her up."

"Classic Libra trait," Daisy added, as if she wasn't surprised. "Affectionate but self-pitying. Holds a grudge."

Fiona held up both her hands. "Okay, let's not get carried away. It might be him in the footage, it might not. Could be anyone. It's going to be tricky to find out. We can't exactly ask him, and before anyone suggests it, we are not breaking into his house to see if he owns a cape."

Partial Sue ignored the last comment, which was clearly meant for her. "If he's smart, he'd have destroyed the evidence. We need to establish his whereabouts on the twenty-seventh of September. We can't do that, but DI Fincher could. She could check traffic cameras, phone towers, establish where he went."

Fiona blew out through her teeth. "I'd be reluctant to give her any more leads after the last one. Not until we have more, but I don't know how we're going to get them."

The Catch-22 situation sent them into a deadlocked silence. They had a promising lead but no way of proving it without police help. But to get police help they would need to point the finger at the Wicker Man with nothing but a theory. A very good theory, but if it turned out to be wrong, they could very well repeat the Sophie debacle, tipping off the police about someone completely innocent. Without strong evidence, they would earn a reputation as three busybodies recklessly accusing those around them. What glimmer of credibility they had left with DI Fincher, if any at all, would be snuffed out for good.

CHAPTER 48

After work, Fiona wandered home in the dusky light, Simon Le Bon obediently trotting by her side. This was the first time she had done this in over a week. The front door scraped as she pushed it open against all the mail that had gathered on the floor in her absence. She stepped over the small pile on the doormat, not having the energy nor the inclination to pick it up, let alone open any of it. She could deal with that later.

As she wandered into the hall switching on the lights, the place felt unfamiliar and un-lived-in. What was it about the absence of a person, even for a few days, that turned the air stale? Fiona sighed and stooped to unclip Simon Le Bon's lead. He wasted no time in doing several circuits of the downstairs, sniffing his way around every room to check all was as it should be.

It felt good to be home. Even better to be alive. But as she drifted into the kitchen, with its rustic painted-wood cupboards, her surroundings appeared alien and strange. She felt like a ghost in her own house. The debilitating thoughts that had threatened to occupy her head earlier came slithering back.

Strictly speaking, back at the shop, they should have been investigating the latest victim, her namesake. Fiona had

242

managed to subtly steer the conversation away from this. Truth be told, she didn't have the stomach to pry into the woman's life, to discover the intimate details of a person who could have been her lying dead on a slab. It was too close to home. It made her shudder, made her nauseous that she'd come so close to being killed. *Why her and not me?* she asked herself. A large shard of guilt speared her mind. How had the killer decided that she lived while the fifty-something divorcée had to die? By what mechanism had he made that choice?

She poured herself a large gin and tonic, and would've added ice and a slice of lemon, but she didn't have any lemon and she'd neglected to fill up the ice tray before hastily moving into Partial Sue's — it hadn't been high on her list of priorities.

She took her drink into the lounge and sank into the soft, slightly battered brown leather sofa. It moulded around her familiar shape. She should have really lit a fire, but she couldn't be bothered. Simon Le Bon hopped up and snuggled beside her, offering her warmth in dog form instead.

It was the first time she had been alone in a while. Since the issue of the Osman warning, she'd always been in the presence of others, either at the shop or at Partial Sue's. Though she dearly loved her friends, she had also longed for the sanctuary of her own space. For peace and quiet.

Careful what you wish for.

The silence that she'd craved now hung about her, oppressive and threatening. She felt isolated, alone and vulnerable, but strangely not depressed. Survivor's guilt had overshadowed everything. There was something to be said for safety in numbers. She instinctively reached for her canine companion, stroking his fur for comfort. He sighed contentedly. At least one of them was relieved to be home.

After a few sips of her drink, all the strength it had taken to hold it together while her life had been under threat began to wane. All that nervous, adrenalin-laced energy departed her body. Nothing remained except exhaustion, leaving her hollow. She would have afforded herself a tear or two, but she was too tired even to cry.

Her eyelids began to descend. She kept flicking them open, but it got to the point where she couldn't prevent them from closing. She let herself be taken by sleep.

* * *

Fiona awoke to a tap-tap-tapping, erratic and irregular. She listened harder. The tapping sound wasn't on its own. There was some scraping in there too. Dozily, she glanced around. Somehow, she had made it up the stairs and into bed last night after dozing on the sofa. In the dim morning light, through sleepy, half-lidded eyes, she took in the familiar surroundings of her bedroom: the low pitch of the roof beams casting awkward shadows; her curtained dormer windows; and the tall, stately figure of her carved armoire. Simon Le Bon was curled up on the bed next to her, his nose tucked into his tail, fast asleep and oblivious to anything. Oddly he didn't seem bothered by the noise.

Fiona flinched and drew the covers closer as the sound came again. Scratchy and abrasive, it was coming from one of the windows. DI Fincher's warning thundered through her head like a freight train. *The killer is still out there. Exercise caution and be vigilant.*

Was someone trying to break in? Was it the Domino Killer adding another Fiona Sharp to the list, because this one specifically was too much of a meddler?

The noise ceased abruptly. Maybe the killer had given up. She didn't have time for relief. It came again. The scraping switched to the other dormer window. Clearly, the killer had had no luck with opening the first one and had moved on to try his hand with the second. Fiona reached for the GPS alarm and her phone.

She glanced across at her alarm clock. It was twenty to nine. She'd overslept and today was the first Wednesday of the month. It wasn't a killer outside her house scratching his fingernails to get in, it was Martin the window cleaner.

She clutched her beating heart. It was throbbing hard enough to pump blood into outer space.

Normally, by this time she'd be up and leaving the house for work, handing Martin his twenty quid (he preferred cash in hand) and, more importantly, a cup of tea. How had she overslept? She never overslept. Perhaps, after several nights of consistent insomnia at Partial Sue's, it was no surprise. The seductive comfort of being in her own bed had lulled her into the deepest of slumbers. Her body had taken full advantage of its surroundings, getting recompense for the deficit of sleep that had racked up.

Fiona swung her legs out of bed and threw on some clothes. Leaving Simon Le Bon snoring on the covers, she hurried downstairs and made Martin a quick cup of tea. While she waited for it to brew, she checked her purse. Empty. She had no cash to give him.

Throwing on her coat and pushing her feet into a pair of blue Crocs, Fiona stepped outside into the crisp autumn air. She found Martin still working on the front of the house with a brush on a stick, long enough for Olympic pole-vaulting. It reached up to Fiona's uppermost windows, while the other end had a thin yellow hose snaking its way to the van parked out on the road, on which was emblazoned a huge graphic of Martin's red-bearded head photoshopped onto the bronzed torso of a Californian lifeguard, to go with the name of his window-cleaning business: Bay Wash. It used to be called Fire and Water, which Fiona had preferred, because Martin was also a local firefighter and did this as a sideline to make a bit of extra cash. Previously, his van had been airbrushed with two mighty dragons, one breathing fire, the other water. But he'd never got any work from it as no one had understood what his business did. People had thought he supplied role-playing game equipment and would often phone the number on the side asking if he had the latest edition of Warhammer.

"Morning, Fiona," he called.

"Morning, Martin. Here's a nice cup of tea for you. I'll leave it on the windowsill. You look like you've got your hands full." Still delirious with sleep, Fiona wasn't quite sure how she was managing to arrange her words in the right order. Coherency was hard to come by without that first cup of tea in her hand. Why had she made the window cleaner one and not herself? "I'm just popping to the cashpoint so I can pay you."

"Right you are," Martin said.

"Won't be a minute."

As she made the short walk along Grand Avenue, drowsy thoughts swam through her head. Everything seemed surreal. Even her own road, the houses, the trees and front gardens, all usually so familiar, felt peculiar. At least her state of mind had improved since last night.

Crossing Southbourne Grove without incident, she saw with dismay that a queue had formed outside Southbourne's one and only bank and, therefore, its one and only cashpoint. There had been several major banks in Southbourne but they had all closed, replaced by apps. She joined the end of the queue, yawning several times, hoping that inhaling extra oxygen might help clear her head.

With her mind still wandering, she glanced around, idly reading the signage everywhere to try to stimulate her groggy brain. Posters in the bank window offered mortgage rates together with meaningless lifestyle shots: a parent swinging a little child around in the park; two pensioners looking lovingly into each other's eyes; and a young couple laughing while painting a wall. There were more serious notices, mostly above the cashpoint, telling you to shield your PIN and look over your shoulder to make sure no one was watching while you punched in your number. Beside the cashpoint was a little box for putting out cigarette butts, offset with a cautionary message telling you how many people died of lung cancer every day.

Fiona's eyes drifted to a telephone cabinet next to the cashpoint, which stood neatly against the wall. Painted in racing green, the box was about the size of a very narrow sideboard. It too had not escaped being commandeered as a medium for shouting out instructions. A large sticker with block writing told her to call an 0800 number if she saw this cabinet open or damaged. An instruction, in Fiona's experience, that would mostly be ignored. When she'd worked in London, she had passed one of these on her daily commute and, seeing its doors hanging open, had caught a peek at the wriggling mess of telephone wires within. Despite her calling the number several times, it had remained that way for well over a week, until one day she had found the doors closed and locked. Her mind drifted back to her old life in London, the bustle and hecticness of living and working in the capital. Never a dull moment and every day on fast-forward. Things were different now, slower and more sedate.

What was she thinking? There was nothing slow or sedate about having a serial killer after you. She had never had to contend with *that* in London. The closest she'd ever come to a crime was reporting that a telephone cabinet had been broken into. Not exactly urgent, judging by how long it had taken for the problem to be rectified.

The person in front of her took one step forward as the queue moved closer to the cashpoint. Fiona didn't respond. She just stood there, held by an invisible force. She didn't register the grumpy harrumphs uttered by the people queuing behind her. Something weird was happening to her brain. If there was such a thing as a mental slap in the face, Fiona had just got one.

CHAPTER 49

She was having an epiphany. Not a complete one, but she had all the right parts. They were jumbled up in her head, she just had to put them together, like the Ikea of epiphanies. A self-assembly revelation, except there were no instructions to follow.

After extracting some money from the cashpoint and paying Martin, Fiona started up the garden path to head to work, her mind still muddled and preoccupied. She'd barely reached the pavement when she was startled from her reverie to hear Simon Le Bon barking his disapproval from inside the house. She put a hand to her chest and hurried back to get him.

"Oh, I'm so sorry," she soothed, kissing his scruffy head and clipping his lead to his collar. As she walked back along Grand Avenue, stopping now and then to let Simon Le Bon do his "wants" (her word for the doggie call of nature), her head felt awfully strange. Epiphanies do that to a person, even flatpack ones. Transformed from its state of lethargy, her brain was now fizzing and popping with ideas, not fully formed but getting there with every step. Synapses lit up erratically, dots joined, unrelated ideas met in the middle, and thoughts began to rearrange themselves into something more coherent, resembling a theory of sorts, by no means watertight or rigorous but full of possibility.

When she pushed open the door to Dogs Need Nice Homes, Partial Sue and Daisy stopped what they were doing.

Partial Sue's concerned face greeted her. "There you are. We were getting worried. I was just about to ring you."

"Are you okay?" Daisy asked. "You look a little confused."

She ignored them both. Fiona didn't have time for niceties. All her energies had been rerouted, diverted to fuelling what was happening in her head. And what was happening was extremely fragile and precarious, being held together with the mental equivalent of chewing gum and bits of string. Fiona dropped Simon Le Bon's lead and he dragged it around the floor. She then marched straight to the till, snatched up a pen and paper, bent over and began scratching her thoughts down, trapping them before they could take flight.

Daisy and Partial Sue moved closer, standing behind her, gazing over her shoulder at the illegible mess of ink now filling up the paper. Random words were flung together with a doodle of arrows, strange symbols and phrases that ended in bold question marks.

Fiona kept this up for a good minute or two, until she raised her head and surfaced from her stream of consciousness. "Sorry, I just had to get that down before it left my head."

"Get what down?" Partial Sue asked.

"I think I know how the killer is getting into people's houses. Getting them to open the door."

"You do?" Daisy asked.

Fiona frowned. "Maybe 'know' is too strong a word. I have a passable — no, plausible — theory. It does rely on quite a lot of things to line up, though."

Partial Sue clapped her hands together. "Come on, come on, don't keep us in suspense."

Fiona sagged from her mental exertions. "First, I need tea. I haven't had one yet."

Daisy gasped, horrified. What madness was this? "You haven't had your first cup of the day? This is serious. I'll put the kettle on."

After Daisy had made them each a cuppa, the three of them sat at the table. Partial Sue and Daisy gazed at Fiona expectantly, like a couple of hungry chicks that needed feeding. Fiona took a deep breath, trying to decide where to start. After several gulps of deliciously calming tea, she began. "I believe we've already been visited by the killer."

Partial Sue and Daisy exchanged confounded glances.

"What?" Partial Sue asked.

"When?" Daisy asked.

"That first night I stayed at Sue's."

"So the Wicker Man *is* the killer," Partial Sue replied.

"Not the Wicker Man. I have no idea who the killer is, but I think he was on his way to kill me that night. DI Fincher put him off."

"How do you know?"

"Your home phone went dead briefly and so did our mobile phones."

"I tried to call you both," Daisy said.

"That's right. You couldn't get through. But we only knew about it afterwards."

Partial Sue looked puzzled. "But the phones were working fine after Daisy and the Wicker Man turned up. I'm not sure I understand."

Fiona rubbed the sides of her temples. "Sorry, I'm not explaining this very well. I've only just put all the pieces together myself. I still haven't got it all figured out yet, a lot of this is conjecture. There are a few holes, but I've been through it in my head, and it makes sense, sort of. Let me start again. Maybe from the killer's point of view."

"Go on." Partial Sue leaned forward." I'm dying to hear this."

"Me too," Daisy added breathlessly.

Fiona grabbed her paper full of scribbles, analysing it for a logical place to start that would make more sense. "Okay, it's all about landlines. The killer is using them to get in people's houses."

"Aren't they a bit small?" Daisy said, only half-joking.

"Not like that," replied Fiona. "I think he targets his victims by going to the telephone cabinet in the street, where all the landlines meet before they go off to the exchange. He breaks into the cabinet, identifies the landline of his intended victim, then disconnects it."

"How does that help him get in?"

"I think he knocks on the door and poses as an engineer from the phone company."

Daisy looked unconvinced. "But they'd only let him in if they were expecting him or if he had an appointment. We did this before on the whiteboard, remember? People are savvy to that sort of thing nowadays. They don't let anyone in who turns up unannounced."

"Not if their phone wasn't working," Fiona explained. "I don't know, maybe he shows up and says there's been reports of phone lines being down and could you check yours. Victim picks up their phone and finds the line is dead. Our generation relies on their landlines more than the younger ones. Even our fifty-something victim Fiona Sharp would have had one. The victim then panics when they find their phone is dead. They'd ask him if he could fix it there and then. I would if I had a phone engineer standing on my doorstep."

Partial Sue snapped her fingers. "That's right. When my home phone stopped working it took me a week to get an engineer out. I'd be practically dragging him inside if it were me."

"Bingo," Fiona said. "Our vampire's just been invited in. Once he's inside and the door is shut, he murders his victim, leaves the house, goes back to the cabinet and reconnects the victim's line. Probably takes him a second or two and he's out of there like nothing has happened."

Partial Sue raised her eyebrows so high they resembled two humpback bridges. "And phone cabinets are never in the

251

same street where you live. Mine was three streets away. Puts plenty of space between it and the crime scene."

"I didn't realise that. Even better for the killer."

Partial Sue slapped the table wildly with both hands. "This is a major breakthrough, Fiona!"

Fiona afforded herself the smallest of smiles.

Daisy had an uncomfortable, slightly constipated look on her face, as if she were trying to hold in an unpleasant thought that she didn't want people to hear.

"Daisy, you look perturbed," Partial Sue remarked. "This is good. This is progress."

Daisy looked hesitant about replying, picking at an imaginary thread on her dress. Without making eye contact, she said, "I know I'm new to this crime lark but don't things like that get checked by the police when there's a murder?"

"Yes," Fiona replied. "The phone records of the victim, certainly. But I've never heard of any police force checking a phone cabinet."

"But what about the fault?" Daisy asked. "Surely that would show up, the fact that the phone had been disconnected."

Partial Sue shook her head. "The phone company can test the line from their end, but if the fault is inside the cabinet it won't show up. That's what happened to me. They had to send an engineer out to open the doors and peek inside."

Fiona agreed. "Yes, those cabinets aren't monitored. They rely on the public to inform them of faults. You've seen the stickers on them, asking you to call them if you see them damaged or hanging open. I've seen them stay like that for days. Weeks, even."

Daisy still appeared unconvinced.

Partial Sue grabbed her mobile. "Look, why don't I check? Make sure. We know my phone went dead because you couldn't get through. Let's see if the phone company has any record of it."

They were treated for a long while to a repeating message about how important Partial Sue's call was to them, alternating with Barry Manilow's "Could it Be Magic" played on

252

Spanish guitar. Eventually someone answered. Partial Sue put it on speakerphone. She asked if there had been any faults on her line in the last month. They could hear the woman on the other end of the line typing away. Her reply was quick and to the point. According to their system, there had been no reports of faults or breaks in service on her line.

Partial Sue hung up. "We know that's not true. We got lucky. If you hadn't tried to call us, we wouldn't know any of this."

Fiona agreed. "I think the killer was out there. He'd already disconnected the phone."

"As I said, my phone cabinet is three streets away," Partial Sue said. "So he'd have been out of sight."

"Yes, then he's on his way there towards Sue's house, intending to knock on the door, but turns the corner and sees DI Fincher going in, which is when you tried to call us. He gets cold feet, backs off, returns to the cabinet and reconnects the phone. No harm done. No trace of him."

"But I couldn't get through on your mobiles either," Daisy said.

"That's not a problem for him," Partial Sue replied. "Not if he had a mobile phone signal jammer on him. I've seen them in my spy catalogue. They're about the size of a walkie-talkie. No calls or texts would make it in or out. Again, we'd have been unaware of it, and if we were, it would just have looked like our phones couldn't get a signal. Happens all the time."

Fiona shivered at the thought that the killer had been out there, targeting and stalking them.

Partial Sue's voice turned serious. "So our killer's got to be good with phones or electronics."

Fiona instantly thought back to the day when this had all begun. "When I found the knife in the box outside our shop, I went over to confront Sophie. Gail was in the back fixing a phone. One of those fancy-Nancy ones. I think it was a Bang & Olufsen."

"That sounds about right," Partial Sue said. "Gail is good with electrical stuff, that's for sure."

The shock on Daisy's face increased. "And she has a motive. Remember her giving Sophie the V-sign? I bet she hates working for her. She could be doing this to set her up as the murderer."

It had been a knee-jerk reaction for Fiona to mention Gail's name. Logic had spilled out: Gail fixed phones; Gail worked for Sophie; Gail hated Sophie; Gail could be the killer. But now Fiona was regretting blurting it out. She didn't like the way this was going. They were back to pointing fingers again, identifying suspects then trying to find evidence to make it fit their suspicions, latching onto the nearest person who fitted the bill. Was that how it was done? Maybe sometimes, but Fiona didn't like it one bit. Her fear returned that they would incriminate someone innocent again, just as they had with Sophie and the CCTV footage of the cape-wearer in the charity shop.

"Can't we go to DI Fincher with this?" Daisy asked.

Fiona took a thoughtful sip of her tea. "Not in the mood she's in, after we just wasted her time with the CCTV footage. We need to be sure. All we've got is someone who's good with a screwdriver and has poked two fingers up at Sophie."

"Okay, but what about the other bit, about the killer using the phone cabinets?"

"Again, it's a good theory, but we haven't got any evidence."

"How do we get evidence?" Partial Sue asked.

The room went silent. This was becoming a reoccurring theme for the Charity Shop Detective Agency. They abounded with theories but were a bit thin on the ground when it came to solid proof. If they were going to approach DI Fincher, they needed something as concrete as a multi-storey car park built in the sixties.

The silence lingered.

"I've just bought a new microwave," Daisy said out of the blue.

"Oh, er. That's nice." Fiona struggled to see where this was going.

"My old one used to ping once when it was ready, and that was enough. But this one goes off like a burglar alarm. It doesn't stop. Now every appliance in my kitchen buzzes when it's finished — the tumble dryer, the washing machine. Everything bleeps like there's no tomorrow. Drives me mad. Even the fridge beeps if you leave the doors open for too long. Which has got me thinking about the doors to these telephone cabinets. Seems like they're neglected, unnoticed. People can do what they like to them unless someone reports it or there's a fault. But mostly no one bats an eyelid. So what if we alarm them? Rig the doors so they go off if the killer tampers with them."

"Daisy, that's a genius idea!" Partial Sue yelled.

"Thank you," Daisy replied with a blush. "You can buy these little portable door alarms from Argos. They don't cost much. You stick them to the door and they go off when it's opened."

Fiona smiled. "I love your idea. But we'd need to be around to hear them. We have seventeen potential victims. That's seventeen alarms we'd need to monitor. Plus, wouldn't the killer see them if they were attached to the doors?"

Daisy slumped. "Oh, that's true. I didn't think of that."

"It's just given me another idea, though," Fiona said. "We can go one better than an alarm. We can get evidence. Better than that, we can ID the killer without them even knowing."

CHAPTER 50

All three of them hunched around the table, noses deep in online reviews. Star ratings were compared, features checked, and reviews pored over. But they weren't shopping for clothes or scatter cushions. This was far more fun. They were shopping for miniature spy cameras. They would have used Partial Sue's infamous spy catalogue, but they needed next-day delivery and the catalogue only promised three working days.

Daisy couldn't contain herself. "I feel like James Bond."

"Don't you mean Q?" replied Partial Sue. "He's the one who gives 007 the exploding pens and submarine cars."

Fiona enlarged the page on her phone. "Here's a good one. An HD wireless wide-angle stealth camera with night vision. It's magnetic so we wouldn't have to fiddle about attaching it, just stick it to the inside of the cabinet. Best of all, it's motion activated. Only starts recording when the motion sensor is tripped. Instantly sends an alert to your phone and streams the footage to its screen. Ninety days' battery life. That's more than enough."

The plan was simple. They would install a tiny spy camera inside every telephone cabinet that corresponded to each potential victim. Every Barry Taylor in the Bournemouth,

Poole and Christchurch area would be protected by a home-made surveillance network of seventeen spy cameras hidden among the wires in each one. The Barry Network they called it, or BarNet for short. If Fiona's theory was correct, they'd catch the killer in the act and be treated to a full view of his face the second he opened the cabinet, so long as it wasn't a genuine phone engineer come to fix a real fault. That was one drawback to their plan. There were a few others, the biggest one being that they'd need Daisy to pick the lock of each cabinet so they could slip a spy camera inside.

Daisy didn't want to break the law a second time and took a lot of persuading. Partial Sue's and Fiona's arguments were that, firstly, telephone cabinets didn't seem particularly high on the crime agenda for the police or the telephone company, so any illegal activity would be more likely considered a minor misdemeanour, especially since the cabinets were often happily left open, sometimes for weeks on end. Secondly, they could test out Fiona's theory without bothering DI Fincher. And, most importantly, they could save the life of a Barry Taylor and prevent anyone else from being murdered. All by performing a very small act of vandalism that would probably go unnoticed. It took a while, but eventually Daisy agreed and started scrolling through her phone to research what was involved.

However, there was another drawback to their plan, which only concerned one member of the Charity Shop Detective Agency but had led to her wanting to put the kibosh on the whole idea.

"How much?" demanded Partial Sue, her eyes narrowing.

"Forty-four pounds ninety-nine," Fiona replied. "Each."

"Each!" Partial Sue did a quick multiplication in her head. "That's over seven hundred and sixty quid for seventeen cameras!"

"It's two hundred and fifty quid split three ways," Fiona informed her. "But if we keep all the packaging, we can resell them afterwards and recoup most of the money."

Partial Sue grumbled.

"How big is each camera?" Daisy asked.

"It's a five-centimetre box," replied Fiona. "About the size of four Oxo cubes."

"That's tiny. No one's ever going to notice it. I think that's the one," Daisy said. "What do you reckon?"

They both looked at Partial Sue, who grumbled some more.

"We need to move fast on this," said Fiona. "Killer could strike again at any moment. We need to order these cameras and get them set up, toot sweet."

Partial Sue hesitated, her face stony. Finally, her shoulders sagged. "Go on then."

Fiona grabbed her credit card, entered her details and ordered seventeen spy cameras. "Done. That's part one of our plan. Daisy, how's part two coming along?"

"Okay, I suppose,' she replied, head down, studying the information on her phone. 'I'm working out what I'd need to do to pick the locks, but I'm still uneasy about it."

Fiona placed a reassuring hand on her knee. "If you don't feel comfortable doing this, honestly, it's fine. We don't want to force you to do something you don't want to."

"We could always install the cameras outside the cabinets," said Partial Sue. "But there's the risk they'll be seen, and the motion sensors will keep going off every time someone walks past."

Daisy sighed, weighing up her options. "I'll do it, but I'll need some more practise. I've been doing a little research into cabinets and they're different from the tumbler locks on a front door."

"What do you need?" Fiona asked.

"There are two types of lock," Daisy replied. "One is triangular, like the kind you use to drain a radiator but bigger. That one's fine. The other is circular, and trickier. I'll need to practise on that type but I'm not sure how, without actually going out and having a go."

Fiona became anxious. "I've seen some pretty big, modern-looking cabinets out on the street. They look armour-plated and impregnable. How are you going to get into those?"

Daisy smiled. "I know the ones you mean. Those are for broadband. We don't need to worry about them. It's the smaller, old-style telephone cabinets we're targeting. They look a bit forlorn next to the big new broadband ones."

Comparing the two types of cabinet, it was clear to see where the investment was going: definitely not into analogue landlines. The old system was being wound down, hence its neglect and shabbiness. Like everything else these days, it would soon disappear to be replaced by something shiny and digital. Was this why the killer had chosen now to strike, before the old system disappeared for good and they could no longer take advantage of its vulnerabilities?

"Did you say the lock on those old cabinets is circular?" Partial Sue asked.

"That's right. Takes a circular key, but I've never seen one before."

Partial Sue leaped up and disappeared into the storeroom. They heard boxes shifting followed by much rummaging around. She returned holding up a chunky, scuffed-up D-shaped black bike lock that had seen better days. "Like this?"

Daisy examined the lock. "This is perfect. I'll get started straight away." She took herself off to the storeroom and set herself up on a stool by the draining board, using a proper set of lock picks that she'd bought herself off the internet, rather than the makeshift hairpins from last time.

"You know, Fiona, if you're right about this telephone-cabinet theory, then the police are actually playing into the killer's hands," Partial Sue said.

"How so?"

Partial Sue leaned back in her chair. "Apart from the offer of a safe house, the police haven't got the resources to protect every potential victim, right? There are just too many. So they have to rely on their phones as a lifeline between them and the killer. Remember when DI Fincher issued you your Osman warning? She gave you a GPS alarm, but she couldn't emphasise enough how important it was to keep mobiles topped up and ensure landlines were working. Belts and braces, she said. With that in mind, if someone shows up posing as a phone engineer telling you your landline's down, you're going to panic after what the police have just told you. Especially if you check your mobile and that's got no signal either."

Fiona nodded. "The victim knows they need their land-line up and running. Keeping it working becomes their number-one priority. They'd probably forget all about opening the door to strangers."

"Exactly. The killer's using the police's own procedure against them."

"Very clever. But what about the GPS alarm? Could they jam the signal on that?"

"A decent mobile phone jammer will do that too. And disrupt your Wi-Fi, but it's all academic. The victim won't raise the alarm because they don't think they're at risk. They just think it's a telephone engineer come to fix the landline."

A chill snaked down Fiona's back. "We need to stop them. As soon as possible."

CHAPTER 51

Next day, the internet fulfilled its retail obligations and seventeen miniature spy cameras arrived at the shop. Fiona and the others wasted no time breaking all of them out of their boxes and having a play.

Each camera was a small black cube with a single beady-eyed lens on one side, giving it the appearance of a surreal, Picassoesque crow's head. With an entirely magnetic metal body, they clung limpet-like and with a satisfying clunk to any metal surface. Extremely simple to use, Partial Sue linked one up to her phone, took it out of the shop and plonked it onto the lamp post opposite. After she returned to the shop, they gathered around her phone screen and waited. A second later, someone walked past the shop, tripping the camera's motion sensor. An alert immediately popped up on her screen. Partial Sue tapped it. Her whole screen transformed into a high-definition view of the shop, seen from the camera. The detail was so good, they could see themselves through the window.

Whoops of joy came from all three ladies. Daisy waved back at her on-screen self. "There we are!"

"Hey, that's not bad quality, is that," Partial Sue remarked.

"I think we made a good choice," Fiona added. "We'd better test the others just to make sure they work as well."

Partial Sue repeated the process with all the other cameras. Discovering that they each worked perfectly, she set about sending links to everyone's phone so that if a camera fired off an alert, they'd all receive it. After testing all seventeen cameras, they found another unexpected bonus — they'd all come fully charged. Operation BarNet was officially launched.

Fiona made the difficult decision to close the shop for the day, hoping head office wouldn't find out, and set a deadline. The camera installations needed to be done and dusted in one day. An ambitious task, seeing as they had never done it before.

They'd found a handy website that provided them with the exact location of the nearest telephone cabinet for any given address. One by one, they had entered the addresses of each individual Barry Taylor they had found into the search box. They had located the exact position of every phone cabinet and had worked out the most efficient route to get around all the boxes within the time they had set.

They gathered up all the stealth camaras and placed them into bags for life as they would draw less attention, along with a few other important items to help them complete their mission: a generous flask of tea and a selection of Mr Kipling's finest — Bramley apple pies, fondant fancies and Bakewell slices.

"Are you ready, Daisy?" Fiona asked.

"As I'll ever be." She held up a fistful of lock picks, including two sets of spares, just in case. She'd been practising at every available moment in the storeroom, also doing a few dry runs on cabinets near her house. Her nimble fingers could now crack both types of lock in an impressive thirty seconds.

After Fiona locked up, all four of them, including Simon Le Bon (they figured having a dog with them would help with the nothing-to-see-here charade) crammed into Partial Sue's Fiat Uno.

"Operation BarNet is a go!" Partial Sue declared.

Simon Le Bon gave a single bark, sensing the importance of the occasion.

Christchurch was the first destination, down a pretty side road called Wick Lane, with picture-postcard cottages, a sweet little red-brick Victorian school and a traditional pub named after a local smuggler. One of the Barry Taylors lived in the neighbouring road, but his phone line found its way to a telephone cabinet tucked away against the chain-link fence of the school playground. Most people passed it by without a second thought. However, this innocuous shabby green cabinet had the potential to set up the murder of a Barry.

Not if the Charity Shop Detective Agency had anything to do with it. Partial Sue parked by the Quomps, a large stretch of green beside Christchurch quay. Flanked by the River Stour, where rowers glided past and sailboats bobbed at their moorings under the shade of grand oak trees, it simply begged to have a picnic blanket spread out upon it. Even more attractively, parking on the roadside was free for an hour, which pleased Partial Sue no end.

As they exited the car, Simon Le Bon strained on his lead, whining away to explore the grassy area.

"Er, I think I might have to let Simon Le Bon do his morning 'wants'," Fiona said, perhaps heralding the first moment when a mission of crucially important espionage had been halted by a small terrier's call of nature. But at least if they got it out of the way now, Simon Le Bon would be calmer for the rest of Operation BarNet.

The three of them watched impatiently as he took his sweet time, fussily sniffing around for the right spot. Just when it appeared as if he'd found one, he would abandon it and move on in favour of somewhere else. The pattern repeated itself for several minutes which felt like several hours. Jittery with adrenalin, the ladies were eager to get started, but as any dog owner will tell you, a dog's "wants" can't be rushed.

Finally, he went. Fiona bagged up his business and placed it in the nearest bin. Wasting no more time, they headed to the telephone cabinet.

A well-rehearsed manoeuvre followed, the same one they had employed when they broke into the Wicker Man's shop. Forming a human triangle, Partial Sue and Fiona stood in front of the cabinet at right angles to each other, using their bodies to shield Daisy, who had turned away from them and towards the cabinet, bent over as if she were tying her shoelaces. Gossiping away with Partial Sue, Fiona would drop the code words "apple crumble" into the conversation as soon as it was safe for Daisy to begin. Providing a double layer of security, Partial Sue would then concur that it was indeed safe from her point of view by adding "and custard".

As soon as she heard these two sweet phrases, Daisy whipped out her tools and got stuck in. While Daisy's delicate picks went at the lock, Fiona and Partial Sue continued to chat incessantly, but what they were really doing was surveying the street, their eyes flicking left and right, checking that no one was paying them any attention.

Everything was going well and the quiet street was deserted. Over thirty seconds had passed and Daisy would have the cabinet doors open any moment now. They dared not glance down as they didn't want to draw attention to what she was doing but they were acutely aware that Daisy had begun panting and huffing, and her lock picks, normally inaudible, had become scratchy and desperate.

Fiona spoke out of the side of her mouth without looking down. "What's happening?"

"The lock won't budge."

"Why not?"

"It's completely rusted up."

Fiona's heart sank. This was only cabinet number one. Maybe Operation BarNet wasn't a go after all.

CHAPTER 52

As a place to live, Christchurch was desirable for many reasons. It was historic, quaint and interesting, full of medieval ruins, ducking stools and sights that were achingly pretty. Two rivers, the Stour and the Avon met for the briefest of moments like a couple of star-crossed lovers, only to be swallowed by Christchurch Harbour. Watched over by the vast, aging priory, you wouldn't find a more charming town than Christchurch. However, what residents wouldn't tell you is that the relentless prevailing wind driven off the sea travelled on a direct collision course with the town, raking everything in its path with stinging, salt-laced air. Sooner or later, the corrosive mineral burned anything metal with rust unless it was well maintained. Telephone cabinets were not well maintained. Actually, they were not maintained at all, which meant the lock poor Daisy was currently attempting to crack didn't stand a chance, furred up as it was with legions of rust.

"Are you sure it won't budge?" Partial Sue muttered.

"Positive," Daisy replied. "What do we do?"

Fiona tried to think. This was supposed to be a quick, stealthy, in-and-out mission, and now they were standing around wondering, and possibly drawing suspicion. She hadn't anticipated this. "What do people do when metal is seized with rust?"

Partial Sue's sharp brain provided the answer. "WD40!" she answered a little too loudly. "It's still in the back of the car. I'll get it. We can spray it on the lock, loosen it up."

"Good thinking." Fiona watched Partial Sue dart back to the car with a fast walk that really wanted to be a run.

Simon Le Bon whined, concerned that one of them had left the pack, while Daisy got to her feet, her knees complaining with a snap, crackle and pop. She wiped the sweat from her top lip. "Let's hope this works."

"Me too." Fiona had no idea what they would do if it didn't.

Partial Sue returned and surreptitiously passed the can of WD40 to Daisy, who crouched down and doused the lock with spray lubricant. In one swift motion, Partial Sue took the can off her again and slid it out of sight into her coat pocket.

"Give it a moment or two," Partial Sue whispered. "For it to soak in."

Daisy obeyed and was about to insert her picks into the lock when the school bell rang, making them all jump. Five classroom doors burst open along the length of the playground. Bubbling with pent-up energy, dozens of little bodies came tumbling out for morning playtime. A chaotic mess of chatter and random movement, they spilled out in every direction. However, like a murmuration of starlings, one group simultaneously emerged and moved as one in the direction of the fence, lured by the sight of a cute, scruffy dog. The mass of little bodies squatted down and pushed their faces and hands through the fence, accompanied by a chorus of aahs. Simon Le Bon played right into their hands and began wagging his tail and licking their outstretched fingers.

One of the pupils giggled. "It tickles."

Fiona tugged Simon Le Bon back a little, figuring that this wasn't the most hygienic thing for small children to be doing.

A deluge of questions followed, generated by curious little minds.

"What's his name?"

"What sort of dog is he?"

"Can I stroke him?"

"What does he eat?"

"How old is he?"

"Does he bite?"

"Does he chase cats?"

"Can he do tricks?"

"What's his name?" This question got repeated more than the others.

"Simon Le Bon," Fiona replied.

"That's a funny name," a little girl said.

"Why is he called Simon Le Bon?" another asked.

"I bet he's French," a little boy answered.

Out of the corner of her eye, Fiona could see one of the playground monitors approaching to see what all the fuss was about.

"I think our cover is blown," Partial Sue whispered in Fiona's ear.

Fiona agreed. "Daisy, we need to get out of here."

"But I haven't—"

"Abort mission. Abort mission."

Daisy straightened up again, her knees complaining. There were sighs of disappointment from the children as the charity shop detectives made a swift exit with their tails between their legs, apart from Simon Le Bon's, which stood proud and pleased with itself thanks to all the attention.

CHAPTER 53

"This is going to be another Charity Shop Detective Agency disaster. I can feel it." Partial Sue's hands were clamped around the steering wheel as if she were trying to squeeze the life out of it. The crisis of confidence had started as soon as they had got back to the car. They hadn't actually gone anywhere and were sitting in the stationary vehicle, still parked beside the Quomps but out of sight of the school and Wick Lane. They really should have driven away, but they weren't sure what to do next. So they broke out the flask and sipped tea while they licked their wounds, in between bites of Mr Kipling's.

Fiona would have to turn this negativity around somehow, otherwise they'd be boxing up the spy cameras and sending them back for a refund. "We can't lose enthusiasm now. It's one little setback."

"I'm just facing facts is all," Partial Sue moaned. "Everything we do is a disaster. No wonder DI Fincher doesn't like us. We just muck everything up."

"Oh, thanks very much." Daisy was already on her second fondant fancy.

"No, but do you know what I mean?"

"Not really," Daisy replied. "Picking the lock was my responsibility and I couldn't do it. So what you're saying is, it's my fault."

Partial Sue became agitated. "I'm not saying that."

"You are, in a roundabout way."

"All I'm saying is we're making a habit of cocking things up."

"Yes, and the last one was my cock-up."

"Ladies, please!" Fiona shouted.

The car went quiet.

Fiona took a deep breath. "We stick to the plan. Continue with the next cabinet, and so on. We'll circle back to this one at the end of the day. The school will be closed, and it'll give the WD40 all day to really get to work."

"But what if they're all like that?" Partial Sue asked.

"There's only one way to find out. Onwards and upwards. Let's go. Next cabinet, quick as you like."

With a grumble, Partial Sue pulled away rather aggressively. No one spoke as they headed to the next location.

St Catherine's Hill was a quiet suburban area north of Christchurch populated with large, low-slung, pebble-dashed bungalows with generous front gardens and well-swept driveways. Though it was sedate and serene, with many roads ending in trouble-free cul-de-sacs, they had to be careful. This was a place where curtains twitched and windows boasted Neighbourhood Watch stickers.

They located the green cabinet easily. It squatted beside a neat front hedge that appeared to receive regular disciplining from a hedge trimmer. Partial Sue drove past it and parked several streets away, positioning them so it would look like the ladies were out on a ramble towards the wooded slopes of St Catherine's Hill, where they'd let Simon Le Bon off his lead.

The silence between the three of them continued as they made the short walk to the telephone cabinet. The effects of the little spat in the car had not evaporated. Not a good look for anyone who wanted to portray the deception of being out for an innocent jolly. The only one who seemed to be enjoying the current situation was Simon Le Bon, who couldn't believe his luck that he was getting yet another walk today.

Fiona knew just how to loosen their tongues. "Anyone see last night's *Bake Off*?"

From that point on, the conversation never ceased and Fiona found it hard to get a word in edgeways. She had to clear her throat rather forcibly when they reached the cabinet to remind the other two of the reason they were there. Still debating whether last night's contestant really deserved to go home, they went into autopilot forming the human triangle. When the coast was clear, Daisy got down to work.

After thirty seconds, Fiona heard the wondrous sound of a lock clicking open. Chancing a glance downwards, she saw the magnificent sight of both cabinet doors slightly ajar. Through the small vertical slit of an opening, she could make out several thick swirls of colourful cables intertwined like oversized DNA helixes.

Daisy selected two strands of cables and pushed them apart. Without looking, she reached an arm behind her back, where, in a well-choreographed move, Partial Sue pushed a spy camera into her hand. Daisy stuck it to the back of the cabinet with a pleasing metal thunk, then carefully arranged the wires so that the only thing that could be seen peeping through them was the camera's black lens. Partial Sue pulled out her phone to check the camera was sending her a clear, uninterrupted view. She gave a thumbs up and Daisy swiftly relocked the doors.

Estimating that the whole thing had taken less than a minute, Fiona couldn't help a smile forming on her lips. "Outstanding work," she whispered. One down, sixteen to go.

Confidence now boosted, they worked through the rest of the cabinets with military precision, driving from location to location, repeating the process over and over again. They were a well-oiled machine fuelled by an unquenchable thirst for justice, as well as tea and cake. By the time they'd installed the penultimate camera, they'd got the entire process down to under twenty seconds, from the lock picks going in, to the doors closing and the picks being extracted. This was mostly down to Daisy's rock-steady surgical fingers, but also due to Fiona and Partial Sue's ability to stand on a pavement in plain sight in the middle of the day giving off maximum ordinariness and acute nothing-to-see-hereness.

Now came the real test. As the daylight faded, they headed back to the Quomps once more to face their nemesis: the rusted lock. Would the WD40 have done the trick?

They parked in the same place and made their way down Wick Lane, past the school, now shadowy and locked up tight, the playground eerily empty. At least they would have the darkness of early evening to shroud their activities.

"Good luck, Daisy," whispered Fiona.

"You can do this," Partial Sue added. "And I'm sorry for the way I spoke to you today. We couldn't do any of this without you."

Daisy shook her head. "Stop apologising, and we're a team. I couldn't do this without either of you."

The inevitable three-way hug followed. Simon Le Bon wagged his tail, his enthusiasm for yet another walk having not diminished one bit.

"Come on," Fiona said. "Let's nail this last one."

Daisy spun around and crouched down, giving the lock another squirt of WD40, just to be on the safe side. She handed the can back to Partial Sue and then jabbed at the lock with her picks. Several seconds later, to everyone's relief, the mechanism yielded and the doors opened. Daisy placed the final camera inside.

Partial Sue did a quick test to make sure it worked. In the creeping darkness, the camera had automatically switched to black-and-white night vision. She gave a thumbs up. Daisy relocked the cabinet and BarNet was finally up and running.

Without fuss, they sidled past the school and out of Wick Lane. Once they were far enough away, there were no celebrations, no pats on the back or whoops of joy. Instead, there were the sloped shoulders of relief. The mission had been an ordeal, nerve-racking and exhausting for all of them except Simon Le Bon, whose incessant tail-wagging signalled that he was still up for more walking around unfamiliar places and sniffing out strange and wonderful new smells.

All they could do now was wait.

"Fancy a drink?" Fiona asked.

"Not really," Partial Sue replied.

"Me neither," Daisy added.

Fiona sagged with more relief. "I'm so glad you said that. I really feel like going to the M & S around the corner, getting some comfort food and putting my feet up in front of the telly."

"Me too," Daisy agreed.

"Now you're talking."

They put Simon Le Bon back in the car and made the short walk to the high street and the bright, inviting lights of the M & S Foodhall, filled to the brim with delectable delicacies. Once inside they each went their separate ways, seeking out their own personal guilty food pleasures. Careering down different aisles, they were spoilt for choice at the vast array, wondering what to take home tonight. Ten minutes later, after they had all passed through the tills, they regrouped outside on the pavement, curiously comparing the purchases residing in the bottom of their bags for life.

"What did you get, Daisy?" Fiona enquired.

"M & S Fish Pie. What about you?"

"Mm." Fiona now had food envy. Still, her choice was pretty high on the delectability scale. "Sausages, mash and gravy."

Daisy "Mm-ed" back at her.

"What about you, Sue?"

"Oh, I just got some eggs."

"Just eggs?" Fiona questioned, assuming that Partial Sue's tight-fistedness even stretched to auspicious occasions such as this. "Didn't you want to splash out on something more extravagant to celebrate our little triumph?"

"No, not really. See, I've got this lovely vintage Cheddar at home and some oven chips. If we're talking comfort food, I am partial to a freshly made vintage Cheddar cheese omelette and chips, dusted with sea salt."

Fiona changed her mind. Partial Sue had the best comfort food.

At that moment all three of their phones pinged. They couldn't get them out fast enough, already knowing what it was.

Partial Sue was the first to pull hers from her pocket. "It's a BarNet alert."

"Which one?"

"The one we've just come from. Wick Lane. Someone's opened the cabinet."

CHAPTER 54

With all three phones out, Fiona and her friends prodded at the link on the screen to pull up the view from the camera. This was it. This was what they'd been waiting for, although Fiona hadn't expected the wait to be so brief. Now they'd get their first view of the killer's face. The murderer had chosen tonight to take the life of another victim, Barry Taylor of Christchurch. The Domino Killer was in this very neighbourhood, standing where they had stood just minutes ago. They must have left moments before he'd arrived. A terrifying thought.

Fiona's adrenalin level was off the scale. She was certain the others felt the same. Her phone shook in her hand as she impatiently waited for the screen to load and unmask the murderer. It only took a second or two, but it felt like an era.

Confusion and disbelief threw a rather large bucket of ice water over Fiona. Her screen was completely fuzzy, like a TV with no signal. Nothing to see but snowy white noise.

Partial Sue peered at her phone. "I don't understand. I swear, it was working perfectly just a minute ago."

"Maybe something's wrong with the camera," Daisy said.

Fiona had to agree as she stared into her phone, willing a face to appear. Damn it. The camera had malfunctioned.

Were they all going to be like this? Perhaps it had sent out a false alarm, which was why their screens were now blank. Had something moved inside the cabinet? A stray wire perhaps had tripped the motion sensor. This made sense, as all they were seeing was nothing. Or had it lost connection and was sending them interference.

Something nagged at Fiona's brain. Something that didn't quite fit with either of these theories. If the motion sensor had been tripped by something moving inside, then surely the screen would be pitch black. She stared closer. The white noise wasn't entirely white, either. In the lower corners of the screen, tiny areas of definition appeared fleetingly. It was almost imperceptible. But she'd swear she could make out something faintly straight and vertical disappearing into the bottom of either side of the screen. She remembered seeing this before when Partial Sue did the test. The camera had picked up the edge of the open doors. But why was the rest of the image whited out and blurry?

Then it hit her. "He's wearing a head torch. The camera's night vision can't handle the brightness. It's whiting out the screen, which is why we can't see his face."

"Which means he's there now," barked Partial Sue. "Come on!"

They hurried back the way they came, almost tripping over their own feet with haste. Fiona rapidly debated in her head whether she should call the police or summon them with her GPS. They had to be one-hundred-per-cent sure this wasn't a false alarm, to get a look at whoever or whatever it was that had caused the alert before they did anything. If it turned out to be an engineer sitting on a folding stool fixing an emergency fault, they would look very silly indeed and would only confirm what DI Fincher already thought of them — that they were a trio of well-meaning amateurs with a habit of interfering and wasting police time.

They rounded the corner of Wick Lane. It was too dark to see. They had to get closer. Panting hard, the three ladies pushed on. Then out of the darkness, they saw a small cone of bright light. Fiona was right. It was coming from a head torch. The body it was attached to was certainly no phone engineer. From what they could tell, the shadowy figure crouched by the cabinet like a hooded Golem was dressed head to foot in black and there was no van in sight.

Fiona pulled out her GPS and hit the button. As they bundled closer, footsteps pounding, the head torch suddenly swung in their direction, illuminating the three of them and their bulging bags for life swinging by their sides.

They scared the life out of him. He leaped up and made a run for it.

"Hey!" Partial Sue shouted. "He's getting away!"

"Stop!" Fiona had no idea why she shouted this, as if any killer in the history of the world had ever obeyed the command to stay put and patiently await justice.

The ladies increased their speed, but they were no match for the man. He was running while they were performing more of a hasty power walk. Sprinting towards the end of Wick Lane, he effortlessly widened the gap between them.

"We'll never catch him," Daisy wheezed.

They got a full view of him under the street lights as he ran across the road that intersected with Wick Lane and headed towards the Quomps. Now in total darkness and with multiple exits, the Quomps would camouflage his escape. If he made it across the road, he'd be gone for ever.

"We need to do something," Fiona cried.

Without breaking her stride, Partial Sue delved into her bag for life and pulled out an egg. The best right arm at Wentworth Girls' School's under sixteen's cricket team, renowned for its power and killer accuracy, wound up and hurled the egg at him. It hit him square in the back, exploding everywhere. He stumbled forward, losing momentum only briefly.

Partial Sue loaded up another egg and let it fly. This one landed on the road, missing his right heel by a couple of inches. By the time she'd let a third one rip, he'd recovered his pace and slipped away into the night.

They gave chase into the Quomps, using the light of their phones to shine across the expanse. Three torches raked across the grass, hoping to catch a glimpse of the escaping killer or perhaps a trail of raw egg.

They found nothing. They'd lost him to the darkness.

CHAPTER 55

Fiona, Partial Sue and Daisy sat in the interview room sipping police coffee. It wasn't very nice, but then the force wasn't known for its barista skills. The room was bland but modern and surprisingly bright and cheerful, with yellow wood panelling and smart recessed lighting. Bournemouth police station, the main one in the area, was a fairly new construction, and felt light and airy. Maybe this was a psychological feature, worked into the design from the offset, to lull all who entered into a false sense of security. To gently suggest that you were somewhere more innocuous, a building society perhaps, for an appointment to discuss your mortgage with a cheerful advisor named Nigel, who enjoyed playing squash in the evenings. All with the intention of getting you to relax and drop your guard.

None of them had been in a police interview room before so they didn't know what to expect apart from what they'd seen on TV. Being brought up on cop shows like *The Sweeny*, all the interview rooms had been fifty shades of beige, that beige mainly a result of all the cigarettes the cops chain-smoked back in the day. This place was strictly no smoking, of course.

All in all, their surroundings would have been rather pleasant and relaxing had it not been for the situation they

278

found themselves in, exacerbated by the angry, radioactive stare of DI Fincher, which was strong enough to melt their faces off. She sat across the table from them next to the track-suited DS Thomas, his face its usual unreadable self.

"Why the hell didn't you come to me with this information?" DI Fincher's normally soft velvety voice had become a growl. She'd asked this question before, several times, but this was by far the fiercest.

"It was just a theory," Partial Sue explained. "We didn't know for sure."

"We had no proof. We didn't want to waste your time," Fiona added.

"You seemed really angry after the CCTV footage we gave you," Daisy said. "We didn't want to make you angry again."

DI Fincher leaned forward. "Yes, I was angry. Angry that it was a dead end. But I was angry in general. Angry at everyone. I'm under a lot of pressure to crack this case. However, that doesn't change the fact that at the start of this I did lay down a ground rule. I didn't have a problem with you carrying out your own investigation, but I clearly said that if you discovered any significant information that you were to bring it to me first."

"It wasn't information. It was just an idea," Fiona replied.

"Yes, an idea that has now turned out to be correct. If you had shared this with me, I could've done something about it. Got proper approval for surveillance. By the way, even if you had obtained clear footage of the killer, it would have been inadmissible."

"What?" Fiona didn't hide the shock in her voice.

"Those cabinets are private property. You need permission before you can use them." DI Fincher crossed her arms. "Plus, footage obtained from a covert camera is a huge legal headache for us."

"Oh dear." That was all Fiona could think to say, a weak and pathetic response. She didn't know how the others felt, but she was back to being six years old and getting scolded by a grown up. Their ingenious idea had been doomed from the start, naivety being the biggest factor. You couldn't just stick cameras willy-nilly and hope it would end in a conviction. There were procedures that had to be followed, legalities that had to be satisfied. She had sort of known this from her love of crime fiction but had somehow overlooked it. Perhaps because she was an amateur, she had thought it didn't apply. Or was it simply those two bumbling idiot brothers again, Bravado and Gusto, rearing their stupid but excitable heads, sweeping her along in their whirl of incompetent enthusiasm.

The room went quiet, the two officers letting them marinate in their shame.

DI Fincher broke the silence. "However, I do have to give you credit for figuring out the killer's technique — disconnecting phone lines — phone lines that we told potential victims in no uncertain terms to keep switched on. They'd have been only too happy to let this person in, thinking they were an engineer." DS Thomas nodded in agreement.

Fiona was surprised at the unexpected praise, the first positive thing the detective had said since they'd entered the room. It was short-lived.

DI Fincher leaned forward menacingly. "But you've blown it now. The killer knows their method has been compromised. You've spooked them. Forcing them to fade into the background."

Another shameful silence filled the room.

"Am I going to be arrested for breaking into telephone cabinets?" Daisy's voice trembled.

"You should, yes. All three of you should be charged. To be honest, I really don't know what to do with you. You've interfered with a police investigation and put me in a very difficult situation. But I blame myself. There's a reason why the police don't share information about cases with the public. I should have never told you about the dominoes or anything else."

"Well, to be fair," Partial Sue said, "you didn't tell us about the dominoes, not initially. We found that out from the delivery driver after we . . ." Her voice trailed off as she caught sight of the ever-increasing ferocity of DI Fincher's stare. The room went quiet again, guilt levels peaking on one side of the table.

DI Fincher leaned back, took a calming breath. "That said, you three have saved Barry Taylor's life. After Forensics had finished, a phone engineer inspected the cabinet and confirmed that Barry Taylor's line had been disconnected. And now we know how the killer works, you might have just saved the lives of any future victims."

"Did Forensics uncover anything?" Fiona asked.

"Not yet."

"Did you see the suspect's face at all?" DS Thomas asked.

"No, it was too dark," Fiona replied. "He had his hood up and a head torch. Not wearing any uniform. I suppose he changes into that once he's disconnected the line."

"He probably just throws on a hi-vis vest with the phone company logo on it," Partial Sue suggested. "He could fit it in his pocket—"

"How do you know it was a man?" DI Fincher interrupted.

"Er, we don't," Partial Sue replied.

"So it could've been a woman?"

"Yes, I suppose."

DI Fincher checked her notes. "And you said earlier you thought the person you saw was young, possibly twenties or thirties. What made you think that, if you couldn't see their face?"

"They were better at running than us," Daisy answered.

"Everyone's better at running than us," Partial Sue said.

"That wouldn't necessarily mean they were in their twenties or thirties." DI Fincher nodded towards her colleague. "DS Thomas here runs rings around me and how old are you?"

"Fifty-seven in November."

More silence.

DI Fincher placed her hands on the table in front of her, lacing them together. "So, we're still no closer to knowing the age or gender of our killer. Still no closer to knowing anything."

Fiona spoke. "Apart from he—"

"Or she," Daisy corrected.

"Or she is good with telecommunications."

DI Fincher finally agreed to something. "Yes, it would be more likely that the killer would have a background in that field, or at least electronics. However, I questioned the phone engineer who inspected the cabinet and he told me that disconnecting a phone line could easily be learned from a few dodgy internet sites. So I'm afraid we don't even have that."

The room went quiet again.

"Think, ladies. You are the only people to have seen our killer. Is there anything you can remember, anything useful or significant you can tell us?"

All three members of the Charity Shop Detective Agency exchanged searching glances, trawling their minds for any helpful sliver of information.

Partial Sue piped up. "I hit him with an egg."

CHAPTER 56

Autumn faded, duvets thickened and the mercury began its descent into winter. Fiona loved this time of year, when she could start lighting fires in the evening, getting all cosy and snuggling up with Simon Le Bon on the sofa, her hands wrapped around a mug of hot chocolate with a cheeky dash of brandy to warm her bones. But best of all, she loved the freewheel towards Christmas. The building excitement, when every day closer to the twenty-fifth seemed to fizz a little bit more than the last.

The charity shop ladies' advent calendars were already bought and paid for, poised to open behind the till. Fiona had gone for a classic Cadbury's, Daisy a Percy Pig, but Partial Sue had turned her back on confectionery this year, opting instead for something more controversial. A pork scratching advent calendar, which they were all keen to see opened to discover if each window contained a single pork scratching or a whole packet of the salty snack to which Sue was most partial.

Pulling on thick Christmas socks and a jumper, Fiona had been looking forward to today. A chance to do something happy and banish all the trauma and failure of the last few weeks. She headed out into the cold morning air towards the shop, her breath clouding in front of her and Simon Le Bon trotting by her side, looking extremely cute in his own Christmas jumper, a jolly red number adorned with white snowflakes. He would have received plenty of adoring oohs and aahs if there had been anyone around to see him. In the early morning darkness, Southbourne had not yet awoken, and the pair of them were the only ones wandering along Grand Avenue.

Every year at about this time, towards the end of November, Dogs Need Nice Homes had a tradition. The three ladies would come into the shop early on a Monday morning and spend the time transforming it into a seasonal wonderland. All of them being self-confessed Christmasoholics, their annual Deck the Halls Day would include cranking up the festive music, chain-eating mince pies and going completely overboard with the tinsel. Each year they'd acquire more and more of the glittery stuff, struggling to find places to store it for the rest of the year. However, it was worth it. By the time they'd finished, the shop would look splendid and enchanting in all its yuletide glory, the seasonal colours of red, green, gold and purple perfectly showcased against the rich dark-wood interior of the shop.

Of course, Sophie across the road would always outdo them but they didn't care. Everything she did always seemed a bit desperate, showy and contrived. One year she had hired one of those huge inflatable snow globes, which drew quite a crowd outside the shop, until it split and polystyrene flakes blew all the way down Southbourne Grove like giant dandruff. To this day, people were still finding it wedged into cracks and stuck in trees. By contrast, Fiona and her friends' approach to Christmas was more organic — chaotic and haphazard, to be more precise. Their philosophy was that as long as customers still had room to browse around, then they would try to fill the place with as many decorations as possible.

As she got closer to work, a merry sight warmed Fiona's heart. Partial Sue's Fiat Uno was parked outside almost buckling under the weight of a gargantuan Christmas tree strapped to the roof, just waiting to be brought inside, unfurled from its netting and decorated to within an inch of its life. As with everything, the three of them would split the cost of buying a tree for the shop, possibly the only time that Partial Sue didn't mind putting her hand in her pocket. This year, it seemed she had really pushed the festive boat out. In fact, you could probably carve a festive boat out of the tree that sat atop her car. It would take all three of them to manoeuvre it inside, which was probably why it was still on the roof.

Fiona found herself swaddled in seasonal joy as she pushed the door open. Carols filled the air and the warm spices of cinnamon and nutmeg and a citrus zest wafted over her. She was treated to the sight of her two friends similarly clad in Christmas jumpers and up to their necks in tinsel and baubles. Daisy had commandeered a rather large gold bauble and was wearing it as an earring.

"Merry Christmas," they happily chimed when they caught sight of Fiona.

"Merry Christmas!" Fiona beamed from ear to ear. She bent down and let Simon Le Bon off his lead. Sensing the happiness in the air, he scuttled towards Daisy and then Partial Sue, tail wagging like a rear windscreen wiper on the highest setting. Circling them affectionately, he received plenty of attention in return, the two of them cooing at the sight of his cute crimson jumper.

Thankfully, the murders had stopped. As DI Fincher had quite rightly predicted, the killer had slid into the shadows now that their technique had been exposed. Fiona took that as a win. And while she would have wanted to catch the killer more than anything, she was thankful for each day without incident, now that they had halted the murderous domino effect.

Consequently, the Charity Shop Detective Agency was on hiatus. One upside of this was that Christmas presents for all their friends and family had been sorted. They'd all be getting slightly used wireless spy cameras.

Daisy approached Fiona offering a plate of homemade mince pies, thick misshapen creations still warm from the oven. Fiona took one gladly.

"I hope you don't mind us starting without you."

"Not at all," replied Fiona. "It's the most wonderful time of the year, who can resist? Now, where shall I start?"

Partial Sue pointed outside. "Well, I think we need to get that tree off the top of my car before it crushes the suspension."

"Do you think it's big enough?" Fiona replied, gently sarcastic.

"Go for the biggest one possible, that's my philosophy."

"I think you succeeded," Daisy said. "If it will fit through the door."

"Well, only one way to find out. Shall we?" Partial Sue gestured towards the door.

"Let me just scoff this lovely mince pie," Fiona said.

"There's tea in the pot," Daisy added.

Fiona took a seat at the table, which was scattered with decorations, scissors and tape. She poured herself a cup of tea from a pot shaped like a giant Christmas pudding, reserved for use only at this time of year. She took a bite from Daisy's mince pie, sending pastry flakes everywhere. In a flash, Simon Le Bon was by her side, hoovering them up. Searching the table for something to use as a makeshift plate, Fiona came across the latest edition of the *Southbourne Monitor* among the festive paraphernalia. It was the Christmas edition, judging by the dubious use of seasonal clipart on the front cover. She couldn't resist having a quick flick, and went straight to the "Bygone Southbourne" section, which, if everyone was honest, was the only bit worth perusing. She giggled as she spotted a shot of several familiar faces. The bleached-out image was entitled "Local Southbourne Professionals of the Nineties".

Posing uncomfortably, not looking any happier thirty years ago even though he had a full head of hair, Oliver grimaced for the camera, dressed in a navy-blue polo. Next to him stood Malorie, who hadn't changed at all. Clad in a smart business suit, she had that same indomitable expression on her face. In front of them was Saint June, Sarah Brown's long-suffering neighbour, who had apparently been a nurse.

Her face appeared softer and rounder before the years of working double shifts on the wards and then running around like everyone's lackey must have turned it gaunt and bitter. Next to her stood Gail from the Cats Alliance, almost being nudged out of the picture by the others. She didn't look too happy about being there. A few other faces were in the shot but Fiona didn't recognise them. She called the other two over. "Hey, have you seen this? It's Oliver with hair."

"Let me see." Partial Sue couldn't get over there fast enough, and neither could Daisy. They abandoned the tangle of lights they were attempting to sort out, letting them drop to the floor.

"Oh my gosh! Oliver has actual *hair*," Daisy exclaimed.

"I didn't realise Saint June was a nurse," Partial Sue said. "And look at Malorie, she's still scary. I wonder what she used to do?"

"She was on the local council." Daisy peered closer at the picture. "What's that on Oliver's chest?"

Partial Sue squinted at the image. "Looks like one of them logos, you know, like a shark or a crocodile. They have them on polo shirts to make them cost more."

"Doesn't look like a shark or a crocodile." Daisy took a picture with her camera and enlarged it with her fingers.

There were three sharp intakes of breath, as it became clear that the logo did not belong to any fancy clothing brand.

It belonged to the telephone company.

CHAPTER 57

All decorating had ceased. The tinsel garlands lay idle, scattered across the carpet like flamboyant snakes. The baubles remained in their bubble wrap and Partial Sue's suspension suffered under the crush of the giant Christmas tree still residing horizontally on the roof.

The three ladies hadn't moved. They were sitting around the table, debating what to do with this information. It was common knowledge that Oliver had been an engineer in a previous life and had given it up due to stress to become a baker. He'd made no secret about that, but everyone had assumed he'd been a civil engineer or a mechanical engineer responsible for designing concrete flyovers or industrial machinery. It had never crossed their minds that he had been a telecoms engineer.

Daisy rung her hands nervously. "I don't want another telling off from DI Fincher. She said if we had any information, we were to tell her."

"Yes, it is information," Partial Sue said. "But is it relevant? It doesn't mean he's the killer. Remember, she said that you can learn to disconnect a phone line off the internet."

"It is relevant," Fiona remarked. "Oliver lives here. He's local. That's got to be relevant. Serial killers are defined by the area in which they kill, remember? Not necessarily by

288

the pattern of killing or the bizarre way they kill. That's a gimmicky Hollywood construct."

Partial Sue stuck out her jaw defiantly. "Well, I'd say this killer *is* defined by the way he kills — the dominoes, the sequence of numbers, the names scratched into them, the OAPs he kills. He's screaming something at us. I'm just not sure what it is."

"But the last victim wasn't an OAP," Daisy said. "She was in her fifties."

"Okay," Partial Sue conceded. "But they all lived alone. It's mostly older, widowed or divorced people who live alone. That's just the law of averages. It's easy to kill someone who lives on their own. It just happens that older people are more likely to live alone. That doesn't mean he's actively targeting them."

"He's got to be local. Think of the people he's set up and tried to frame: Malorie, Sophie, Saint June."

"Has Oliver got anything against those three?" asked Daisy.

Partial Sue nodded. "They're all in that photograph. That must have something to do with it."

"Sophie isn't. Sophie hadn't moved down here yet. She was still in London. Plus, there are other people in that photograph who we don't recognise. What's their story?"

They had been at it like this for nearly an hour. Going round the houses several times, abounding with theories, all of them unsubstantiated and flimsy, the arguments circling back to the same place but not achieving anything, and not actually getting any closer to the important question that really needed to be asked — probably because no one wanted to take responsibility for answering it: should they tell DI Fincher about Oliver being a phone engineer?

"What should we do, Fiona?" Daisy asked.

She took a deep breath. "I'm not sure that we have anything to tell DI Fincher. I'm pretty sure her and her team of officers would have investigated every phone engineer in a thirty-mile radius by now."

"Oliver stopped being a phone engineer twenty years ago. Would he have even been included in those interviews?"

Fiona mulled this over. What if he had slipped through the net? There was a strong possibility their inquiries had only included current or ex-phone engineers stretching back a decade.

"Surely it would be better to be on the safe side," Daisy said. "Even if he's innocent, the police need to know. So they can alienate him from their inquiries."

"Eliminate," corrected Partial Sue.

"Sorry, eliminate him from their inquiries. Why do I always have a problem with that word?"

Daisy had a good point. Even if they had their doubts or thought Oliver was innocent, it would be the responsible thing to tell the police. They needed to know all the facts. Plus, it would be much worse if it turned out he was the killer and they hadn't told them. Also, they didn't want to get on the wrong side of DI Fincher. They liked her, respected her. They'd be doing themselves no favours by withholding information from her a second time.

In her mind, Fiona knew all this but was still reluctant. She didn't want to point fingers. This detective work was hard. Your actions had consequences, so you had to be sure of what you were about to do. Fiona was normally a logical person, resolute and self-assured, but she'd never felt so wishy-washy or indecisive in her life.

The tinkling of the bell broke the deadlock. Speak of the devil. Oliver pushed his way into the shop carrying his usual towering stack of cake tins followed by Stewart, who was carrying a stack of his own, his head bowed, never taking his eyes off his screen.

Normally the ladies would offer the pair of them their warm collective hellos, but they became mute and froze. Their brains seized up with a single, all-consuming thought: was Oliver the killer?

He didn't notice their blank, pale faces shadowed with creeping fear. He seemed more concerned by the current state of the shop.

"What's happened in here?" he asked. "Looks like Father Christmas threw up."

Fiona went to speak, her voice getting caught in her throat. "Oh, er, yes. I think we overestimated how long it would take. Should've started earlier."

Oliver tutted. "Well, sitting around a table's not going to help. Where do you want this?" He slipped a tin off the top of his stack, scanning the table for space. Fiona got to her feet, nervously clearing an area by swiping decorations off the table with one forearm.

"You okay?" he asked. "You seem a little jumpy."

Fiona became tongue-tied. Partial Sue came to her rescue. "Not jumpy, excited. It's our annual Deck the Halls Day, as if you couldn't tell."

Oliver shrugged. "That's what I thought, which is why . . ."

He popped the lid off the tin to reveal a thick, hefty, sweet-smelling Christmas cake covered in pristine white icing with the words "Merry Christmas" written in swirls of red.

Fiona stared at the pretty cake, the whole situation bizarre and surreal. A minute ago they were debating Oliver's suitability as a bloodthirsty, psychotic serial killer and now he was bringing them a festive cake to thoughtfully coincide with this year's Deck the Halls Day. Did cold-hearted killers also have a place in their dark minds for such moments of baked benevolence? It seemed totally incongruous.

Part of her was grateful, the other half in shock, wondering if the cake had been created by hands that also ended lives. "Oh, Oliver, thank you."

"Not a problem." Oliver's expression was hard to read. Normally it was easy — just varying degrees of anger. However, at the moment, he was looking at Fiona with a mixture of confusion and curiosity. Oliver wasn't stupid. He knew something was up.

Daisy fetched a plate from the storeroom and transferred the cake onto it, then handed Oliver back the empty tin.

"Much obliged," he said. "We must be on our way. Come on, Stewart."

Stewart grunted and hadn't glanced up from his phone screen a single time since they'd been in the shop. Without looking or thinking, he clumsily moved forward and shunted into his father, who staggered forward, nearly sending cake tins everywhere.

"Stewart! Watch what you're doing!"

"Sorry, Dad."

"It'd do you good to take your eyes off that phone for once."

Stewart looked horrified at the idea.

Fiona spied a thick bunch of keys by Oliver's feet. "Oliver, I think you dropped your keys." She held them up and gave them back to him. That was when Fiona saw them. Just a brief glimpse but enough to send a spike of adrenalin through her system. Two strange-looking objects stood out from the jangle of regular keys.

"Oh, thanks." Oliver put the cake tins down and shoved the keys back into his pocket. "We'd better be off, before my son here causes any more damage."

Fiona clamped her mouth shut, clenching her jaws tight, in case words she might later regret came spilling out. She nodded rapidly.

Oliver noticed her muted response, as did the others around the table. He gave her one last peculiar look and headed for the door, Stewart trailing along behind him, eyes locked on his phone screen, not having learned his lesson.

Partial Sue got up and opened the door for them. When they were gone, she rushed back to the table. "Fiona, what is it?"

"I think Oliver is the killer."

CHAPTER 58

Daisy scooched her chair closer. "What did you see?"

Fiona took a large gulp of tea, then poured herself a refill. It was going to take a lot of Twinings English Breakfast to get her through this.

"I saw two keys on his key ring, among all the others," she said at last. "They stood out. They were shorter than the rest and weren't shaped like regular keys. One was round, a stubby cylinder, the other triangular. Perfect size for fitting both types of telephone cabinet lock."

"Are you sure?"

"Positive."

"Maybe it was a radiator key and a key for a bike lock," Daisy suggested.

Fiona shook her head. "Too large to be a radiator key. And when have you ever seen Oliver on a bike?"

Neither Partial Sue nor Daisy had a counter argument for that one. Oliver hated cyclists, as well as anyone on skateboards, electric scooters, mobility scooters, rollerblades and anything else on the streets that had wheels and wasn't a car.

Partial Sue brightened. "Maybe they were left on there from his engineering days and he hasn't got round to taking them off. I've got a key to an old suitcase on my key ring, but

I've lost the suitcase. Heaven knows why I still keep the key. Can't bear to part with it on the off chance that it shows up again. Highly unlikely, but there you go."

"That's right," Daisy agreed. "I have a shed door key on my key ring, and I don't have a shed. I've never had a shed, so I have no idea where it came from, but I'm loath to throw it away in case it fits some mysterious lock that I haven't found."

Fiona sighed. They made a good point. She had several redundant keys that still clung to her key ring for no reason whatsoever. Keys were hard things to throw away, even if the object that they fitted had long since disappeared. Parting with them was impossible, just in case there came a day when you would need them. "Yeah, you're right. That's probably what it is."

"There is a way to be sure," Daisy said. "When I was learning to pick the locks, I remember seeing something online about the triangular lock being introduced after the circular one. It's more modern."

"How modern?"

"Can't remember. But the circular key has been around longer."

"Are you sure Oliver stopped being an engineer twenty years ago?" Fiona asked.

"Definitely." Partial Sue replied. "His bakery opened at the end of October 2002, Halloween. I remember because I bought a spiced pumpkin tart. Lovely, it was."

"Can you remember the name of the website you read this on, about the triangular key?"

Daisy shook her head. "I went on so many."

Fiona became determined. "Okay, we have some research to do."

They all got their phones out and went online, searching for obscure, low-hit websites that appealed to people interested in the history of telephone cabinetry, the kind of people that even trainspotters looked down on.

"Got it!" Partial Sue announced. "Says here the triangular key was introduced in 2002, much to the annoyance of cabinet purists."

"What site is that?" asked Daisy.

"Lord of the Phone Rings."

"I'm on one called cabi.net. They say the same, 2002."

"When in 2002?" Fiona asked.

"This one says early 2002," Daisy replied.

"Mine too, February."

"So there's more than a strong chance he got issued with one of those keys before he left his job and never got round to taking it off."

"Looks that way."

"What should we do?" asked Daisy.

Conflicting thoughts were having a moral punch-up in Fiona's head. There was a perfectly logical and innocent reason Oliver had those two keys in his possession. However, the police needed to know about Oliver's employment history. It made him a suspect. Fiona knew full well they could be dropping a perfectly innocent person in the laps of the police, who'd go to town on him once they found out he'd been a telephone engineer. There was always the hope that they already knew about his past and had dismissed him from their list of possible suspects, which probably wasn't very long. But if they weren't aware of his background, then they needed to know, just in case there was an outside chance Oliver was the killer.

Reluctantly, Fiona put in the call to DI Fincher.

CHAPTER 59

Fiona sat at the table alone inside Dogs Need Nice Homes while Simon Le Bon snored contently in his bed. She wished she could be so peaceful, but her thoughts wouldn't give her a minute's rest.

Christmas had been and gone in a whirl of roast dinners and too much telly. The new year was barely a week old and her plan this morning had been to come in early to blitz the accounts while no one was around to distract her, and to avoid Partial Sue finding out. If she'd discovered Fiona was doing the books, she would have wanted to take over and wield her accountancy skills like a sharpened sabre. Once she'd had her way, they'd all be working by candlelight with the heating off to save money.

Despite her friends' absence, concentration was hard to come by. Her thoughts kept gravitating towards Oliver. He'd had no alibis for the times of the murders and had told the police he'd been at home or working in the bakery. His traumatised son, terrified and shocked at the accusations made against his father, had come to his defence. Stewart had been with him on every occasion. However, when the police pushed Stewart on this point, pressing him for details, he had caved in and confessed that he couldn't be sure. Sometimes his dad would slip out during the day to run errands, but he couldn't remember exact times or dates. And being a keen gamer, whenever he wasn't working, Stewart would spend all his evenings in his box bedroom with the door firmly closed, cramped among his consoles and computer equipment, escaping into cyberspace with his headphones on and his mind in gaming mode. When the police had checked his online gaming logs, they confirmed this. His hands were never off the keyboard. Reluctantly and tearfully, he had admitted he had no idea about what was happening outside the four walls of his room in the evening. His father could've been out dancing the samba for all he knew.

No traffic cameras had picked up Oliver's little white van during the times of the murders, although they wouldn't have been difficult to avoid. All the murders had taken place in suburban areas. He could have easily avoided detection if he had stayed off major roads and stuck to quiet back streets. And being in a plain white van with no graphics of which to speak, it wouldn't have raised any eyebrows.

But the real kicker came when they obtained a search warrant, scouring the tiny flat for evidence. They had peeled back the carpet and revealed a loose floorboard. Hidden in the dust, wrapped in a tea towel, they had found an assortment of dominoes that matched the ones found on the last two bodies, and a paring knife, wiped clean. However, testing had revealed tiny traces of the victims' blood — and Oliver's DNA. He had no defence. Only a weak and simple, "I've never seen those before in my life." As for the telephone cabinet keys, he claimed they'd been left on his key ring from his engineering days.

Oliver had been swiftly charged with the murder of all four victims. He denied all the charges, claiming he was innocent. But didn't every murderer?

The little cluster of businesses and residents around Southbourne Grove had gone into shock. One of their own, a trusted member of the community, albeit a very grumpy one, was a killer. There were equal amounts of disbelief and shock as there were I-told-you-so and I-always-knew-there-was-something-dodgy-about-him. Fiona kept out of the tittle-tattle, as did Partial Sue and Daisy.

Once his father had been taken away and locked up, Fiona had tried to support Stewart by making the effort to call on him several times to see how he was holding up and offer the poor lad some much needed comfort and a cup of tea. He wouldn't open the door or speak to anyone. She had even tried sending the Wicker Man round to call on him, knowing the pair shared a geeky rapport. Despite his best attempts, which in reality meant some truly awful wordplay spoken through the letter box, the door to the flat remained firmly closed.

Clearly and understandably upset and in shock at his father being revealed as a serial killer, he had holed himself up in the flat above the bakery for several weeks. The bakery below stood locked up tight, dark and cold. The press had camped outside for days, hoping for a glimpse and an opportunistic shot of "the Son of a Killer" and to bombard him with questions about his father, though they suddenly lost interest when a local MP was caught on CCTV in the early hours staggering along Poole Quay after leaving a party on a rather large luxury yacht. After making it a few hundred feet along the quayside, he had relieved himself up a statue of Lord Baden-Powell, founder of the Scout movement. The press immediately left Stewart alone and went after the shamed MP with plenty of urinary, Scout-based headlines, such as "MP Gets Woggle Out", "The Wee Small Hours", "Bob-A-Job Wee" and "Pee Prepared".

Apart from Stewart's obvious trauma, everyone else was happy — DI Fincher among the happiest. Although you wouldn't know it if you saw her. That cool, calm exterior remained intact, but Fiona was sure she had spotted a slight spring in the young detective's step. The Domino Killer had been caught and DI Fincher had brought him down, with a little help from three retired ladies who worked in a charity shop. Any animosity she had harboured against them had disappeared, transforming into delight and respect. She wanted to give them the credit for the lead that had resulted in the killer's arrest, even if it were to mention them anonymously in the press statements. Fiona, Daisy and Partial Sue had declined and wouldn't hear of it, refusing in no uncertain terms. That was not what they did it for. They'd achieved all they wanted and that was enough: to bring Sarah Brown's killer to justice, thank you very much.

It had all tied up rather nicely. Killer caught, plus plenty of evidence, all pointing in Oliver's direction. The police liked that. Boxes that needed to be ticked had been. Well, some of them had, anyway — more than enough for a conviction. There were a few boxes left empty, conveniently ignored, and that's what niggled Fiona. It irritated her but not enough for her to speak her mind. No one else seemed to be worried, so she kept her misgivings to herself. It reminded her of when she would go out with her walking group and an errant sock would slip down past her ankle and worm its way under her heel. She'd carry on walking rather than finding somewhere to sit and engage in sock maintenance, because it wasn't unbearable, just niggling, and she wouldn't want to hold everyone up. The killer had been caught and she didn't want to be the one to put the brakes on. They had started the new year on a high and the last thing she wanted to do was destroy the good mood in the shop. So she put up with the sock of doubt, which was slipping further and further down each day.

Firstly, a few things didn't tie up, like those dreadful hospital gowns that never do up properly at the back. The killer had been clever, very clever, bordering on arrogant. He was so confident that he wouldn't get caught, he'd been brazen enough to announce his next victim by scratching their name on a domino. As goads went, it was pretty much the goad standard. Almost as if he were saying, "Catch me if you can, I'm smarter than you. Here, I'll even give you a head start." Perhaps the ultimate head start, and they still hadn't caught him. If that weren't enough, he'd engaged in quite a bit of playful misdirection, setting up not one but three people as scapegoats. First, Sophie, then Malorie, followed by Saint June, and then Sophie again. He'd played games, juggled and set up multiple suspects, sent both the police and the Charity Shop Detective Agency off on several wild-goose chases that led up blind alleyways, and forced them to use mixed metaphors. And then there were the dominoes themselves. What the hell did they mean? Why dominoes and why the numbers? They still had no idea what the reverse Fibonacci numbers had to do with the murders. Oliver had denied any knowledge of what they meant. The killer had well and truly run rings round them and it was only sheer luck that Fiona had discovered his telephone-cabinet technique. If she hadn't stumbled on that by accident, he'd still be out there stabbing shuffling, slipper-wearing homeowners in the back.

This was one smart, self-assured killer who'd been giving them not just the runaround but had also hidden behind corners waiting to trip them up. So why, oh why had he made such basic, sloppy errors? Why hide the evidence in one of the most clichéd of hiding places, beneath a loose floorboard, one of the first places the police would look? In fact, why hide the murder weapon at all? Surely he would have had the sense to get rid of it, like he had with the first knife by dumping it in a box outside a charity shop. Though that was not the best way to dispose of a murder weapon. To be fair, he had done this to set up Sophie as a suspect, but he could have dumped the knife for each murder. Tossed it in the River Avon or Stour, where it would never be found, where all traces of DNA would have melted away after a week or two, severing any ties to him. Being a baker, Oliver could have easily justified the purchase of new knives.

Then there were the cabinet keys on Oliver's key ring. Why keep them on his person where there was the chance someone would see them? Maybe earlier in his killing spree it hadn't mattered. No one knew his technique, so it wasn't a problem. But once the cat was out of the bag and the phone-cabinet trick was common knowledge, logically he should have removed them. Why take the risk that some bright spark would recognise them, even if it were only a slim one? It didn't make sense.

Okay, some of this could be explained away. Maybe his slackness was the result of sheer arrogance — he believed he would never get caught, which had led him to being laissez-faire. But harder to explain away were the handy coincidences, and these never sat well with Fiona. How had the photo of Oliver in his telephone engineering days appeared in the *Southbourne Monitor* at just the right time? If she didn't know better, she'd say Oliver was being set up, and one thing that was consistent about this killer was that he liked setting people up, turning innocent people into suspects almost for fun. Luckily, all his previous targets had had alibis. The big difference this time was Oliver did not. He would go down for a very long time.

Most anomalous of all, Fiona thought, Oliver didn't have a motive. He had no reason for killing those people and, according to DI Fincher, he kept protesting his innocence, very loudly and with much banging of his fists on the interview table. Fiona had no trouble picturing that scenario. That was the drawback with having a temper. It didn't do him any favours. The police didn't need to find a motive for violence if Oliver behaved like someone who had the potential for it. Yes, he was hot-headed, but in all the years she'd known him she had never once seen his verbal aggression turn physical.

But if Oliver didn't do it, then who?

CHAPTER 60

Fiona had another stab at doing the books, but her head wouldn't stay in the lane marked "Accounts". It kept drifting into the one marked "Find the Real Killer". Every time she tried to get any work done, she couldn't help sneaking glimpses of an imaginary evidence board that had set itself up in a corner of her mind. Invariably, her glimpses turned into stares and before she knew it she was standing in front of it, examining pieces of evidence and trying to connect them with long bits of red string. The board was a mess and the string kept tangling. That was the problem with evidence boards that only existed in your mind, they became unkempt rather quickly. However, through the jumble of headshots, dates, times and location maps, she had a suspect, and it wasn't Oliver the baker.

Over the road, Fiona spotted Gail pushing her bike along the pavement. Although she was clad head to foot in garish hi-vis, she still managed to somehow fade into the buildings behind her. Fiona watched as she stopped beside a lamp post to lock up her bike outside the Cats Alliance, those nimble fingers making short work of attaching a big D-ring lock like the one Daisy had practised on. Was that significant? Had she been through a similar process learning how to pick locks so she could break into telephone cabinets? Gail had been the first person that came to mind when Fiona had discovered the killer's technique. They'd all thought it. She had technical know-how and knew her way around the inside of a phone and probably a telephone cabinet.

Okay, she remembered what DI Fincher had said, that anyone could learn this trick off the internet. But that wasn't the point. To conceive of such a dastardly plan in the first place, you'd need some basic working knowledge of phone systems. Otherwise where would you get the inspiration? Where would the idea originate without knowing the system had those flaws in the first place?

Gail was ticking boxes, and she ticked the most important box of all. She had motive. Fiona believed she wanted revenge. She wanted to frame people that she didn't like. The most obvious case in point was Sophie. Gail had framed her not once but twice, because her boss was a narcissistic bully who took advantage of Gail's quiet, humble nature, and would humiliate and belittle her at every opportunity. Maybe others had too. Perhaps Oliver, Malorie and Saint June had also wronged her in some way. They'd all appeared in that photograph together, elbowing Gail out of the picture. Still waters run deep but they also run bitter. Had all those years of being trampled on compelled her to take revenge, committing murders so she could set them up as suspects? Had they transformed her into a mild-mannered murderer in Velcro-fastening shoes?

Of course, some of her victims' setups had worked better than others. Malorie and Saint June had been eliminated from police inquiries at the beginning. Their accusation had barely registered with them. They'd had alibis, and weren't anywhere near the murders at the time. Sophie, however, had not escaped a good old-fashioned grilling from the police after being framed on CCTV. They had interrogated her for six hours, no less. She would regret wearing that cape for the rest of her life.

There was one little niggle with the Gail theory. On the day the police had questioned Sophie, she had given Gail the day off to get her out of the way for her café's grand opening. Gail had used that free time to go and murder the last victim. However, this had given Sophie a cast-iron alibi, more solid than the one she'd had before, because she had been in the company of the police. But maybe it was just bad timing. Gail would've had no idea that the police would show up on that day to question Sophie. She would have been completely unaware that was happening.

Oliver's setup had worked the best, though, mainly because he had no alibi. Not one that could be proved, thanks to his son's hermetic lifestyle. Was this by design or had Gail decided to really go to town on him in particular? Was he the main offender she'd wanted to take down? It wasn't difficult to imagine, going by the way he didn't mince his words and talked down to people he didn't respect, and Gail would have been at the very bottom.

Had she targeted him right from the start? Were the others just a warm-up? She would have known for decades that he'd been a phone engineer. The photo proved that. Her whole plan could have been built around him all along. She'd just thrown in a few red herrings along the way to even a few other scores.

For that theory to be true, Fiona would need to find real evidence that Gail was motivated by revenge. She would need to find out exactly how these people had wronged her. Sophie's was plain to see every day of the week, but she had no evidence for the other three.

From today she'd start subtly asking around, maybe using that picture as an icebreaker to get tongues wagging, innocently showing it to local people who were around when it was taken and gauge their reactions. Someone would know something.

And then there was the picture itself. Who'd sent it in? She would bet her life that it was Gail, anonymously of course. Fiona would call the *Southbourne Monitor* later to enquire about where it had come from, just to make sure.

If Gail had indeed set up Oliver, she would have also needed to break into his flat to plant evidence. Perhaps a bit of a stretch but not impossible. If Gail had picked the locks on phone cabinets, then just like Daisy, she could've transferred those skills to the lock on Oliver's flat, which had a separate entrance tucked away around the back of the bakery, out of sight of the main road. Fiona had been there before. Like the Wicker Man's shop, the front door was secured by a single tumbler lock. Not difficult to get past. Having a commanding view from across the road in the Cats Alliance, Gail would know when the flat was empty. It would have been easy to plant evidence.

Fiona got to her feet and looked out across the road to the Cats Alliance. She could see Gail frantically tidying the shop in readiness for Her Royal Highness Sophie. She felt sorry for the downtrodden woman. But being bullied was no excuse for murder.

Gail suddenly stopped as she caught sight of Fiona staring at her from across the road. The pair of them locked eyes in a sort of Mexican standoff. Did she know that Fiona was on to her?

Gail smiled. It sent a chill down Fiona's back. Neither she nor anyone else had seen her do that before. It was the smile of an assassin. Gail's eyes bore into hers like a couple of dark lasers. Fiona held her stare for a while, determined not to be intimidated, but it got too uncomfortable, and she turned away to see something far more inviting. A few doors up the road, the lights of the bakery were on.

CHAPTER 61

Stewart must have made the brave decision to go back to work, and that had to be a positive sign. Getting up and facing the world wouldn't be easy after his father had been arrested for murder. Fiona was going to try to put that right. But for now, she wanted to offer Stewart a bit of moral support, which she'd go and give him right this instant. She didn't want to smother the poor lad on his first day back, but she thought it was the right thing to do. She'd let him know she was there if he needed her.

She left Simon Le Bon in his bed, locked up the shop and headed up the road to the bakery. A delectable aroma of freshly baked bread wafted towards her, intensifying with every step. In the window, she could see Stewart carefully arranging trays of baked delicacies to tempt passers-by: French tarts; custard slices; hordes of brightly coloured iced doughnuts; and plenty of thick, round cakes made for slicing up and sharing — Victoria sponge, red velvet, coffee and walnut, too many to count. Stewart was back with a vengeance made of butter and icing sugar.

He smiled as he caught sight of Fiona. The poor lad had lost weight. His face was thinner and dark smudges underlined his eyes. She wasn't surprised after what he'd been through. Enthusiastically, he beckoned for her to come in. As she pushed open the doors, a triumphant wall of music struck her. A rousing score, epic and cinematic.

Stewart nipped around the back of the counter and turned it down. She noticed he wasn't wearing his usual baker's uniform and had instead decided to wear a baggy T-shirt tucked in at the waist, which said *Rick & Morty* on the front. Oliver wouldn't have approved of his civilian attire.

"The music's from one of my favourite games," Stewart said. "*The Elder Scrolls*. I find it comforting. Makes me happy. Dad would never let me play it in here . . ." His face dropped at the mere mention of his father.

Fiona smiled sympathetically. "How are you holding up? We've all been worried about you."

"As well as anyone who's found out their father's a serial killer."

Fiona cleared her throat. "I can't imagine what that's like."

"Dark, very dark. Spent a lot of time trying to work it out. That's why I didn't show my face. I wasn't ignoring you or the Wicker Man. Sorry about that, by the way."

"That's quite all right. No apology necessary."

"I just needed some alone time."

"Of course. Still a bit raw, I imagine."

"You could say that." Stewart grabbed a cloth and began wiping down the counter. "I've been over and over it in my head and it doesn't make any more sense than it did at the start. But I've come to the conclusion that I have two choices. I can let it rule my life and ruin it. Or I can put it behind me. Accept who he was and start a new life without him. As you can see, I've chosen the last one."

"Good for you, Stewart. That's the right thing to do."

"Thanks."

She dipped her head. "Glad to see you're in a good place. Well, a better place than you were before."

Stewart beamed. "I am. I really am. I feel more positive. I still have a life to live. I can run the bakery, earn a living.

I'm determined not to let this hold me back. I don't have to let what he did define me."

"That's the spirit. If there's anything you need, or you want to talk, I'm always here."

"That's good to know."

Fiona didn't want to push it. There were a million questions she was dying to ask him, but for now she held back. She figured that what he needed right now in his fragile state of precarious positivity was the offer of support without any strings attached. The last thing he needed was an interrogation by an amateur sleuth. Stewart just wanted to get on with his life and she didn't want to get in the way of that.

"Well, I'm happy you're back. I'd better be off, got to finish the accounts before opening time. But remember my offer," Fiona added. "My door's always open if you need a friend."

"Will do, Fiona."

She turned to leave, but then stopped and turned back. "Look, Stewart, between you and me and these four walls, I don't think your father did it. In fact, I'm pretty sure he's innocent."

Stewart ceased wiping down the counter. He looked up at her, his eyes widening in confusion. "What makes you say that?"

"I have my reasons. But I need to find out more." Fiona wondered if she should really have said anything. Maybe it wasn't fair to raise the boy's hopes.

"If it wasn't Dad, then who do you think did it?"

She tapped the side of her nose. "I'd rather not say until I have more to go on."

Stewart anxiously picked at the cloth in his hands. "But the evidence against him was overwhelming. They found the murder weapon in his room, and it was covered in his DNA and the victims' blood. I don't think you can come back from something like that."

"Yes, I'd heard about that. But evidence gets planted all the time. Now I'm not saying that is the case, but I think it's worth exploring. A sliver of hope."

Stewart didn't reply. This wasn't quite the reaction she had expected from him. She thought he might be happy that she believed his father was innocent. "Are you okay?"

"No. I mean, yes. I'm fine, honestly. I suppose I just got to the point where I'd got over the shock of who he really was and had started to move on. Not much, but a step in the right direction. Put it behind me. Now you're saying that there's a chance he didn't do it. That changes everything. Opens it all up again."

A prickly fire climbed its way up the back of Fiona's neck. The creeping sensation of regret and guilt. She should've kept her mouth shut until she knew more. Stewart had just got his life back on track and she'd derailed it. "I'm sorry. I shouldn't have said anything. Please ignore me."

Stewart attempted a weak smile, but he wasn't fooling anyone. Fledgling tears gathered at the corners of his eyes. "No, it's fine. It's a good thing. Just a shock. Another shock I need to get my head around. Do you have any evidence yet? Anything to tell the police?"

"No, not yet. It's just speculation. I shouldn't have raised your hopes. Please, just try to forget what I said."

"Can't really do that. If there's a chance he's innocent, I need to know."

Rather than encouraging him, Fiona had managed to upset him. She tried to downplay her theory. "Look, it's nothing more than a feeling, the hunch of a silly old woman. Don't give it a second thought. Focus on yourself from now on. You're what's important."

He nodded, his face downcast. "Okay, I will. But let me know what you find out, won't you?"

"Of course. I promise." Fiona swiftly changed the subject. She wanted to at least try and leave on a positive note. "Now, before I forget, I'd like that Victoria sponge in the window, if you don't mind. To sell in the shop."

"Oh, yes. But I won't be able to do that free-cake thing that Dad used to do. It's too much of a drain on profits."

Fiona waved away his concerns. "That's quite all right. I'm happy to pay."

"It's five pounds seventy-five for the whole thing. Let's just call it a fiver, shall we?"

"Perfect."

Stewart fetched a cardboard cake box from a stack behind the counter. He carefully lifted the Victoria sponge from the window display, transferred it into the box, closed the lid and placed it on the counter in front of Fiona. She delved into her purse.

"Ta-da," he announced, ringing the money into the till. "You're my first customer."

He was putting a brave face on things but she knew he was still hurting inside. Fiona had managed to reopen a wound that hadn't exactly healed, but had started to close over. She needed to leave — fast, before she made matters worse. "Right, must dash."

As Fiona closed the door behind her, she wanted to throw the Victoria sponge on the pavement, splattering buttercream and jam among the grit and grime. Disgusted with herself, she'd meddled in something that should have been left alone. Maybe Oliver *was* innocent. However, she should have kept that information to herself until she had something more concrete to offer. Instead, like the world's worst conspiracy theorist, she'd spouted her drivel about the murderer still being out there, without considering the effect it might have. Stewart was extremely vulnerable, and she'd gone wading in with her clumsy ideas, not thinking for one moment how that would affect his fragile state of mind. She felt utterly appalled by her behaviour. And who the hell said "must dash" anymore? It sounded like something from one of Joyce Grenfell's monologues.

CHAPTER 62

Fiona traipsed back to Dogs Need Nice Homes. Fumbling with the keys and dropping them several times, she managed to get back inside without cursing out loud at what an insensitive idiot she had been. *Must dash.* Her brain wouldn't let her forget her archaic choice of parting words, berating and embarrassing her.

Shutting the door firmly, she stood with her back pressed up against it. The shame that enveloped her like a cloying stench seemed unlikely to fade, not for a long while. How could she have been so stupid? *Must dash.*

She pleaded with her brain to stop those two irritating words from interrupting her thoughts. *Must dash.* It seemed it didn't want her to forget.

Simon Le Bon's tail wagged. He looked at her curiously from his bed, no doubt wondering what she was doing standing there, especially as she had cake in her hands. If she were honest, she wondered that too.

She felt like going home and crawling into bed. To abandon this day and start again. Put it behind her and hope that she wouldn't shove another foot in her mouth. She closed her eyes, concentrating on her breathing, attempting to still her mind. *Think calm thoughts, think calm thoughts.* She tried positive affirmations: *I am a good person, but I have a big mouth. I am a good person, but I have a big mouth.* They weren't completely positive affirmations. Half-positive. Half-firmations. But they began to work, gradually banishing her awful feelings.

Her mind had other ideas, however. *Must dash.* That phrase barred her from entering a more conducive state of mind, wrenching her back to where she had been. Fiona batted the side of her head with her palm like someone attempting to dislodge tomato ketchup from a bottle — the proper glass kind, not the squeezy one — hoping the phrase might pop out of her ear onto the floor, where she could crush it into non-existence.

Why on earth was her mind fixated on "must dash"? Maybe it was trying to tell her something.

Dashing. What had that got to do with anything? Handsome and dashing? Dashing through the snow?

Maybe not dash the verb. What about dash the noun? She knew all about different types of dashes from working in publishing: the em dash; the en dash; and the hyphen. Not much help here, unless the killer had some text he needed to punctuate properly.

What else had dashes? Morse code had dashes — dots and dashes.

She let out a short, almost manic hiccup of a snigger. Dominoes had dots. But they didn't have dashes . . . did they?

The blood in her veins almost stopped pumping. Froze right where it was, making her fingers numb. Fiona stumbled forward into the shop and put the cake down on the table. She pulled out her phone and fumbled with the screen, bringing up a fresh search page.

Scrolling through image after image of dominoes, Fiona gasped.

Each and every domino, no matter what style or colour, had a thin line across the middle that divided the top half from the bottom. She'd known they were there, but it had never registered with her as anything remotely significant.

That dividing line was a dash of sorts that had slipped under the radar. Dots and dashes. Could there be a message in Morse code, hidden in plain sight?

"No, surely it couldn't be." With trembling hand she reached for a scrap of paper and a pencil. With her other hand she entered another Google search for the Morse code alphabet. She knew the values on every domino found on the body of each individual victim off by heart now, she'd stared at them so much. The domino left on Sarah Brown was a two and a one. Two dots and one dot separated by a dash. Dot, dot, dash, dot.

Slowly her eyes scanned down the Morse code alphabet, and there it was. Dot, dot, dash, dot represented the letter F. Shakily, she wrote it down. The domino found on Ian Richard was a one and a one, or dot, dash, dot — an R in Morse code. The third domino on Sharon Miller was just a one with the other half blank. A dot and a dash. She thought this might be where her theory ended, but no. A dot and a dash represented A. She knew the fourth and last domino on Fiona Sharp had been the same, a one and a blank, another A. She had the word FRAA.

"FRAA?" It meant nothing to her. Maybe her theory meant nothing. Just her oddly wired brain seeing connections where there weren't any. Another dead end.

Before she put her phone away, she examined the Morse code alphabet one last time, to double-check that her deciphering had been correct. Then she noticed something. Morse code for the letter N was dash, dot. Spin the last domino upside down and you got a dash with a dot — the letter N. That made much more sense. She had a word. Better than that, she had a name: FRAN.

Was this the name of the killer?

CHAPTER 63

Fiona didn't have time to interrogate what this new revelation could mean. Fran, whoever Fran was, would have to wait. The doorbell tinkled. She slipped her phone back into her pocket and turned to see Stewart standing there, his face unreadable. Not happy or angry or sad, just blank.

"Stewart, are you okay?"

He entered silently, closed the door and took a couple of steps into the shop. He stood facing her, his face as plain as paper. All trace of his earlier distress had gone.

"Can I make you a cup of tea?" Fiona still felt guilty about ruining the lad's peace.

Stewart slowly shook his head and produced a paring knife from his pocket, gripping it tightly by his side. "You know, I really wish you hadn't said those things about my dad being innocent."

"What are you going to do with that?" Fiona took a step back, bumping into the table behind her, almost knocking the cake off. A deluge of dread descended over her along with a grim realisation. She was right about Oliver being innocent. But the killer wasn't Gail — it was Stewart.

He reached up and flipped off the lights. "We need it to be a bit darker for what's coming next."

He stepped further into the gloomy shop, shaking his head. "You've left me no choice now. You're going to take your theories to the grave. But first, more important things. Have you told anyone else, like Sue or Daisy?"

Fiona shook her head rapidly. Blood raced in her ears. "No, no one."

"I think you're telling me what I want to hear. How do I know you're not lying to protect your friends?"

"I swear, honestly. I swear. I haven't told a soul."

Stewart twiddled the knife in front of him. "You need to convince me. Otherwise, I'll have to kill them too."

Fiona wanted to be sick. This wasn't how she had imagined her life ending. She thought it would be in a nice retirement home, playing bridge, nipping sherry and looking forward to a gentle spot of afternoon jazzercize. Swallowing down her nausea, she tried to think. Convincing him of her friends' innocence could be a good thing. If she could string it out, keep him talking, she could buy herself some time until someone came in. However, the "Open" sign on the door was turned to "Closed", as it always was before opening hours. There was no way any passers-by would venture in. To Southbourne's polite residents, a "Closed" sign was as much of a deterrent as barbed wire and machine gun towers. Fiona was on her own. She looked across at Simon Le Bon for help. He just sat in his bed wagging his tail at Stewart, normally the bringer of cake. He would be no help either.

She needed a backup plan. Actually, she needed *any* plan. Preferably one that was foolproof, and she knew just where to get it. This had started with telephones, and she would end it with them.

She had briefly considered grabbing the cake off the table behind her and throwing it at him, slapstick style, but quickly dismissed this. She didn't have Partial Sue's wicked right arm and doubted her aim even at such close range. Knowing her luck, it would land on a heap on the floor and become fodder for Simon Le Bon's next gut complaint.

Instead, she casually slipped both hands in her pockets. With her right hand, she wrapped her fingers around her phone. She dearly wished she still had her GPS alarm, but she'd handed that back to DI Fincher weeks ago. However, she was still in possession of her phone. All she had to do was wait for the right moment.

"So, tell me the truth, how many people know about your little theory?" Stewart waved the knife at her, his eyes fixed on hers and, thankfully, not the whereabouts of her hands.

"I already told you, nobody knows. I've kept it to myself. I haven't told anyone."

"How do I know that?"

"Because it's extremely unpopular to unpick something that's already sewn up neatly. Police have got their man. Nobody likes to upset the apple cart." Fiona was back to mixing her metaphors again.

"And how were you planning to upset this particular apple cart?"

Fiona thought for a moment, her terrified brain attempting to think clearly. She needed to be convincing, otherwise she'd be putting Daisy's and Partial Sue's lives in danger. "It's too neat and tidy. Too planned. That photo of your dad appearing in the *Southbourne Monitor* a month after we discovered your technique for using the telephone cabinets to disconnect victims' landlines. You sent that picture in, I presume?"

Stewart bowed. "Guilty. And I just happened to drop his keys on the floor in front of you, hoping you'd spot his old telecoms tools."

"You set up your own father for all those murders. *Why?*"

"It's complicated. He was just a means to an end."

"What end?" Fiona had to keep him talking.

Stewart stepped forward, raising the knife. "Not important."

"Who's Fran?" Fiona asked, desperately hoping to stall him.

It worked. Stewart halted, an impish grin playing on his lips. With the knife still in his hands he performed a slow clap. "Well done, Fiona. You cracked the code. Well, it's only half the code. I never got to finish it, thanks to you. To be honest, I didn't think it was that difficult, using dominoes to send a simple Morse code message. Maybe I underestimated people."

"Who's Fran?" Fiona asked again.

"It's not a person. It's a statement."

"What statement?"

"Oh, just another bit of playful toying with the police. A vague clue to keep them occupied and distracted but not enough to make sense of. The phrase I was attempting to spell out was 'frankly unfayr' — unfair spelt with a 'y' and an 'r' — I was a bit restricted with what letters I could use. There are only a handful of dominoes that translate into Morse code."

"Frankly unfair? What was unfair?" Fiona asked.

"My circumstances, of course." A slight temper crept into Stewart's words, as if he were annoyed that she had to ask.

Trawling through her mind, Fiona's memory came up blank. He clocked her confusion and huffed out his answer. "I'm heading towards thirty and I live with my dad in a tiny box room. I should have my own place. I did mention it several times, but none of you were listening."

Then it clicked. He had told them. Every time he flashed a daft new app he'd created, he'd always boast about how he was going to make a fortune selling it and buy his own pad. "So you framed your own father for murder just so you could get his flat?"

"Well, like I said, he was a means to an end. I wanted my own place and I needed him out of the way to get it. But also, he was asking for it. I've had to put up with him and his stupid temper all my life. Do you know what it's like walking on eggshells every minute of the day and being criticised, wondering when he's going to kick off at something stupid and trivial? But now he's gone, life is sweet. I have my freedom. My rules. My way of doing things. Just got to tie up a loose end — that's you, by the way."

Fiona had to halt him fast. "Why not just kill your father to get him out of the way? Why go to such lengths to get him arrested?"

Stewart screwed his face up, unimpressed. "Oh, come on, Fiona. I wouldn't kill my own father. And if I had, the police would have looked straight at me as the main suspect. It had to be a lot more sophisticated than that. More convoluted to keep the attention off me. Put me above suspicion."

"Is that why you set up all those different people?"

"Of course."

"Why them in particular?" Fiona asked. "Why Malorie, Sophie and Saint June?"

"If you're going to all the hassle of committing murder, why not make a few others sweat, just for the hell of it? I made sure I chose awful people. Malorie is a browbeating cow, everyone knows that. When she found out we donated cakes to all the charity shops, she wanted — no, demanded — that we give free cakes to the community centre. She got shirty when we pointed out that she's not a charity and gets funding for things like that. Doesn't like being wrong, that one. So I swiped a couple of dominoes I needed from the community centre. Security's not exactly tight there. Then I found out that the numbers in Saint June's profile name matched the first two sets of dominoes I'd planned to use. That was pure coincidence, but too good an opportunity to pass up. I left the dominoes on the first two bodies, setting up two old birds with one stone, and starting my Morse code sequence, all at the same time — who says men can't multitask?" Stewart looked proud of himself.

"So you never intended that they would be found guilty?"

"Nah, like I said, sow a bit of confusion, make them sweat for a bit. Keep the police looking in the wrong direction."

"Why frame Saint June?"

"Because everyone thinks she's a saint, when she's really just a miserable old witch, a hypocrite. And then there's Sophie, who thinks she's Queen of Southbourne. She criticised my baking when we offered to donate cakes to her shop. I mean, talk about looking a gift horse in the mouth. With Sophie I thought I was doing the community a favour, taking her down a peg or two."

"Why not just kill Sophie, Malorie and June?"

"Same reason as I didn't want to kill my dad. There's a chance it would lead back to me."

"My name was on a domino. You wanted to kill me?"

Stewart smiled innocently, as if he'd just spilled his drink. "Don't take it personally. I just thought it might spice things up a bit, especially with you and Sophie being at each other's throats. Good opportunity to set her up some more." He gripped the knife by his side tighter, moved forward.

Fiona was backed up against the table with nowhere to go. She desperately needed more time, had to keep him talking.

"One thing I never got was the choice of people you murdered. What connected them, apart from them living on their own and being older? We couldn't figure out the pattern."

Stewart grinned. This was good. He wanted to gloat and show off. People were never in a hurry when they were gloating and showing off.

"Okay. I'll let you into a little secret. There was a connection, a big connection, but at the same time there was no connection."

Fiona's brain became befuddled. "What? I don't understand."

"I targeted them, but to a certain extent it was also random, to keep everyone guessing."

Fiona frowned. "I don't get it."

Stewart's eyes glittered. "Let's start at the beginning. I'll tell you where I got the idea first. Have you ever played the lottery?"

CHAPTER 64

Fiona shook her head. "I've never played the lottery in my life."

"I have. Got obsessed with it. Thought I could win it if I played the odds, you know, worked out the stats. Nothing worked, of course, or I wouldn't be here pointing this knife at you. But I did learn about human nature. Humans are incapable of true randomness. We can't help ourselves. We find patterns everywhere. It's the advantage of our species. However, try to choose six or seven random lottery numbers, and we end up unconsciously throwing in birthdays or a house number or grouping certain numbers together. Patterns. That's why the lottery introduced the Lucky Dip option. You need a computer to generate random numbers because humans can't do it. Our brains can't handle it. Now hold that thought. Think about what the police do when they're hunting a serial killer. What do they look for?"

"Well, it's actually all about locality—"

Stewart became irritable. "Yes, I know. Apart from that?"

"Patterns, they look for patterns and connections between the victims, motivation."

"Exactly. They're chomping at the bit to find them. Tripping over themselves to find hidden links between the victims. But they can't handle randomness. I've always thought it'd be so easy to misdirect the police, give them tons of patterns and themes for them to play with and get hung up on. Tie them up, looking at things that actually don't mean anything. Bit of chaos theory. Completely random . . . well, random-ish. That's the clever part. My technique was random with a pattern."

Fiona was none the wiser. The two ideas seemed to contradict each other. How could you have a pattern of murders that were also random?

"I still don't understand."

"What did you notice about the names?"

Fiona drew a blank. Then she thought back to Daisy's comment about how dull all the names were. Unmemorable, everyday names. No one called Jemima Glockenspiel, as she put it. "They're all quite normal."

"Exactly."

They should have listened to Daisy. Her leftfield thinking had hit the nail on the head, and they'd dismissed it as a bit of silliness.

Stewart continued. "Lots of people with those names. And that means lots of choice. It also means it's very hard for the police to throw a protective net over all of them. More opportunity to get away with murder. I'd just pick one at random initially, disconnect their landline, then throw on one of Dad's old hi-vis vests and call at their house, telling them that their line had a fault. They'd be pleading with me, almost dragging me inside to fix it. So easy."

"Then you picked Sarah Brown just because she had a common name?"

"Yeah, nothing more common than the name Sarah Brown. Best one to start with. However, I also knew she'd been none too happy about the minibus being scrapped. Good opportunity to set up Malorie. So I started with her. My guinea pig, as it were. Tried out my technique, did my thing. She opened the door, and the Domino Killer was born."

Bile burned its way up Fiona's throat. She swallowed it back down, wincing. Had to hold it together. Keep him talking. "So that time you targeted me, at Partial Sue's house, you got spooked by DI Fincher being there."

"That's right. So I just moved on to a different Fiona Sharp. Easy. That was the beauty of my plan. Randomness has the ultimate flexibility. If I had any doubts about my intended victim, if it felt too risky, or someone was hanging about, like DI Fincher or a witness, I'd just walk away, move on to someone else on the list a day or so later. Had loads of names to choose from. Sometimes I'd leave it a week or two. I could do what I wanted, strike whenever the time was right. I could slip out without Dad knowing."

"But suppose the detective hadn't been outside when you targeted Sue's house, and you'd have knocked on the door. Weren't you worried we'd have recognised you? You wouldn't be able to do your telecoms deception with us. Weren't you worried about that?"

"Wouldn't matter. I'd have sweet-talked my way in, then killed both you and Sue." The words of a cold-blooded killer.

Fiona shivered. She had to stay strong and continue. "So it was literally the luck of the draw which people were getting murdered. No motivation behind their deaths whatsoever, other than to frame your dad and shame a few others so you could get your own place?"

Stewart smiled playfully, then shook his head. "No. There was a big motivation behind each victim. A pattern. But it was camouflaged with my random-choice technique. To make it appear haphazard. Hiding my main reason for killing some people on the list while leaving others alone, but none of you spotted it."

"You went for older people."

"No, that was obvious for anyone to see. Again, it's this wood-for-the-trees business. My reasoning meant they were more likely to be older, that's all. You all missed what was staring you in the face, even the police."

Fiona had another stab at it. "They were retired. They didn't have to work anymore."

Stewart shook his head. "Last victim wasn't."

Fiona was clueless. The only link they'd identified with their limited information about the victims was that they were all older. "They lived alone."

"Getting warmer. I'll give you a clue. My motivation was jealousy. Why would I be jealous of them?"

Fiona rolled her eyes. It was obvious, of course it was. "They owned their own homes."

Stewart shook his head and growled, irritated that Fiona hadn't got it right. His temper rose. "All of them, including you, lived in great, big empty houses. Rattling around with all that space to yourself. What a waste. Shameful. Why should all of you get to have big houses while I have to live in a shoe box? It's not fair. I bet you all looked down on me. Thinking that you're all better than me."

Fiona didn't dare answer lest she provoked him any further. Clearly this was the source of his bitterness. The reason that had driven him to murder and set up his own father and the others. A simple but galling resentment that he'd never own his own house, especially not a big, comfy, spacious one he could call his forever home. There were plenty of those in Southbourne, avenues and avenues of them, which would have cranked up his bitterness every time he passed their mansion-like exteriors and huge leafy plots.

His chest rose and fell rapidly, expelling his fury. Gradually his breathing returned to normal. A calmer, more rational Stewart returned. "Still, like I said, it's far better now I've got the whole flat to myself, but that doesn't let the rest of you off the hook, having those empty rooms that you never use. And gardens. I'd kill to have a garden." His eyes lit up at that idea. "Maybe that could be my next venture."

The light in his eyes turned murderous. He squeezed the knife in his hand, ready to use it on her.

Fiona thought fast. "How did you get the idea for disconnecting the phone lines?"

323

"You know, Dad never stopped moaning. Complaining about how tough his last job was, working for the phone company. How they only gave him so much time to fix each fault. He'd bore me to death with his diagnostic procedures. I couldn't shut him up. Had no choice but to listen, but I learned. Found out how to disconnect a landline from a cabinet. That's where I got the idea from. So it was his own stupid fault. Anyway, back to business."

He closed the small gap between the two of them. She could smell his breath on her face. Prawn cocktail crisps. She hated prawn cocktail crisps.

Fiona had to delay the inevitable. She was running out of options fast. "How did you create your alibi? DI Fincher had proof you were at home in the evening playing games during some of the murders."

"I did a really good job with my clumsy computer-nerd routine, didn't I? 'Ah, bless him,' I bet you all thought. The harmless idiot with his useless apps. Thing is, I used those same skills to create a bespoke AI-mimicking program. I would just log into an online game using my computer at home, putting me in my room at the time so it had the right IP address. Then before I slipped out, I'd run my AI program in the background. It copies how I play, same keystrokes and everything. So it looks like I'm at home killing players online, while in reality, I'm out, killing people in the real world. Like I'm going to do right now."

He reached into his pocket and pulled out a domino. "I got you your own domino at last. We should move into the storeroom for this, close the door. Wouldn't want anyone to see me stabbing you. Come on. Chop, chop. It's time to die."

Fiona's head swam and her knees buckled beneath her.

CHAPTER 65

"Y-you're not going to kill me like that, are you?" Fiona held both her hands up.

"Oh, yes. Stab you in the back, then leave this domino in your hand. Got to be consistent. Now, come on, move."

"But you can't do that."

"Er, I think I can. Done it lots of times before, remember? Had lots of practice."

"No. Think it through. The Domino Killer has already been caught. Your dad's in custody. You kill me like that, it will give your dad the ultimate alibi. The police will know the real killer is still out there."

Stewart's mouth dropped open, eyes searching, cogs whirring until the penny dropped. He burst into manic giggles, repeatedly pounding his forehead with the domino in his fist. "Oh my God. You're right. How could I be so stupid? I can't kill you like that. You're a smart one, Fiona. But I have been a complete dumbass."

While he was distracted with berating himself, Fiona fumbled with the phone in her pocket, never taking her eyes off him. Making a call was out of the question. Far too tricky, but like a lot of smartphones, hers had an emergency feature for occasions such as this one, when you couldn't risk looking at the screen or didn't want anyone to know you were calling for help. Hold down the power button and the volume up button, and it automatically called 999. Or was it the volume down and the power button? Maybe it was the power button and the home button. She couldn't remember. Fumbling away, she tried all the combinations she could think of.

Stewart had ended his self-flagellation. He suddenly noticed the determination on her face as her hand struggled with her phone deep in her pocket.

"Hey, what are you doing? Take your hands out of your pockets."

She withdrew them, showing him empty palms.

With his free hand he delved into both pockets and retrieved her phone.

Disappointingly, the display showed the home screen, as it always looked — no signs of an emergency call in progress whatsoever. For all that effort, Fiona hadn't managed to get through to anyone.

"Were you trying to call someone?"

There was no point in lying. "Yes, I was. Can you blame me?"

"No, I suppose not." He tossed the phone on the table and forced Fiona to the back of the shop, the tip of his knife at her chin.

Desperately attempting to hinder him, Fiona said, "Wait, aren't you going to smash my phone or at least take out the SIM card, just in case I manage to overpower you and call for help?"

"Don't need to." Stewart reached around and unclipped something from the back of his belt. He held it up in front of Fiona's face. Similar to a large, old-school mobile phone, or perhaps a small walkie-talkie, it had four thick rubber antennae on the top. "Know what this is?"

Fiona's shoulders slumped. Unfortunately, she did. Partial Sue had described one of these when they were discussing theories. "It's a mobile phone jammer."

"You get top marks for that. I had this with me every time I did a murder. Victim had no landline and no mobile phone signal, GPS or Wi-Fi. No way of calling for help and neither do you. Clever, eh?"

Fiona didn't respond. All hope had gone. Her mobile phone had been her last line of defence. This was it, the last minute or two of her life before a demented baker with property envy cut it short.

Stewart reclipped the phone jammer to the back of his belt and slipped the domino and knife into his back pocket. He glanced around the shop at the displays nearby. In the dim light, he sifted through the jumble of items as if he were a customer. "So, I wonder if you could help me?" he asked. "I'm looking for a new murder weapon. Something effective but easily concealed. Do you have anything?"

Fiona shook her head.

"I'm going to need better customer service than that. What about this?" He held up a cheese grater then put it down again. "No, far too messy."

While Stewart was busy browsing for something to end Fiona's life, over the road she saw a fleeting sign of hope. The door to the Cats Alliance opened and Gail emerged from within. Fiona wanted to signal to her, but it was impossible with Stewart so close and Gail so far away. And if she could, would Gail even see her in the shadows at the rear of the shop? And what signal would she make? What was the international sign for "Help, I'm about to be murdered by a serial killer just as soon as he finds a suitable charity donation that also doubles as a murder weapon"? All she could do was stare wide-eyed out the window, hoping that Gail would somehow notice the strange goings-on in the darkened shop. Curiously, she spotted that Gail was holding a walking stick, of all things. Not for support, just clutching it by her side.

"Aha!" Stewart blurted out, making Fiona jump. He turned to face her once more. "I think we have a winner, but I'd like your opinion."

He held up a hefty, spherical glass paperweight with little dolphins inside.

"It's a bit tacky," Fiona remarked. Here she was on the point of her life ending and she couldn't help judging the tastefulness of the chosen weapon.

"I plan to bludgeon you to death with it, not put it on my mantelpiece." He made pretend actions of bashing it on her head.

Over his shoulder, Fiona watched Gail step into the empty road and start to cross. Fiona didn't dare hope, but it looked like the woman was heading this way. She desperately wanted to wave her hands or scream but Stewart was standing directly in front of her, holding a glass paperweight the size of a shotput.

She needed to keep him talking. There was still a chance that Gail would find out what was going on and call the police, as long as she was out of range of Stewart's phone jammer.

"Er, there's a problem with using glass as a murder weapon," Fiona said, trying to hold her nerve.

Stewart regarded her with genuine question in his eyes. "Go on."

"Well, it can get messy."

"Yes, murder usually is — for the victim."

Fiona stole another glance. Her heart thudded. Gail was on her way, she was sure of it. "Not for me. For you."

"How so?" Stewart narrowed his eyes.

"Well, you have to consider the nature of glass." Fiona was curtailing her replies on purpose, not giving him full answers to string things out. Gail was halfway across the road, still heading in their direction, walking stick in hand. Close enough for Fiona to see that it was a vintage wooden hiking cane, its sturdy shaft covered in little metal shields. Like Scout badges, people would collect them to show off the famous places they'd trekked. It was definitely a donation, and highly collectible, but had probably never seen the light of day thanks to Sophie's strict "edit". But what the hell was Gail planning to do with it?

"How so?" Stewart repeated. Fiona had become distracted. Gail had appeared outside the front door.

Fiona had to keep him talking. "Er, well, because glass smashes easily. You could end up cutting your hands to ribbons. Police will no doubt find traces of glass in my injuries. They'd put two and two together, seek out anyone who had corresponding injuries or bits of glass embedded in their hands."

"That's a good point. I need something less breakable."

Fiona's mind raced ahead. If she convinced him not to use the paperweight, he'd go looking for another weapon, at which point he'd see Gail at the door, and then it'd all be over, perhaps for both her and her would-be rescuer.

"But then again, it might be fine," Fiona said. "It's probably toughened glass. If you examine the base, there should be a symbol on it somewhere." Fiona had no idea if this was true or not. She had to keep him distracted, occupied.

Stewart held the paperweight up to his eyes, searching for markings of any kind, not helped by the lack of illumination. Over his shoulder, Fiona witnessed Gail gently nudging the door open with her right hand while holding the hiking cane in her left. It was at that point that Fiona spotted a problem. When Gail opened the door fully, the little bell above would ring, alerting Stewart to Gail's presence. Any second now, its joyful jingle would give the game away and it would be curtains for them both.

But it didn't happen, and Fiona found new respect for Gail's capacity for foresight. It quickly became clear what the hiking cane had been for. Holding the stick high above her, Gail jammed the rubber stopper on the end into the mouth of the bell, muffling it and preventing it from ringing. She quickly slipped inside.

Not bothering to close the door, she retracted the hiking cane and moved forward rapidly and stealthily through the shop, not making a sound.

Whether it was the draught from the open door, or the sudden increase in noise from outside, Stewart sensed something had changed. His eyes flicked from side to side. Something was different, something was wrong.

In the split second it took for his brain to analyse this new stimuli, Gail adjusted her grip on the hiking cane. She now held it like a baseball bat, cocked and ready.

Aware that someone was behind him, Stewart turned around and caught the brunt of the hefty hiking cane full in the face. For such a slight person, Gail had one hell of a swing on her. It only took one hit to render him unconscious, and he collapsed to the floor.

As he fell, Fiona caught the paperweight before it dropped and smashed. After all, why ruin a perfectly good piece of merchandise, albeit a tacky one, even if it had almost been used as a murder weapon? She could easily fetch a fiver for it.

CHAPTER 66

Fiona later discovered that two things had alerted Gail to her perilous predicament. Gail had been taking a breather from cleaning the floor of the Cats Alliance, which Sophie insisted should be clean enough to see her face in or there'd be trouble — a mystifying and impossible task when one considered that the floor was covered in carpet. But that was Sophie for you. She ran a tight, hygienic ship. As Gail had switched off the hoover, she'd happened to notice Stewart leaving the bakery and heading into Dogs Need Nice Homes. She hadn't seen the knife, but she had noticed him go in and abruptly turn off the lights. It had seemed a strange thing to do, unless he'd gone to show off the luminous dial on his watch like kids used to do at her school in the seventies. But she had doubted it was that.

So, flicking the lights off hadn't been enough to set alarm bells ringing, but as he'd entered the shop, Gail had got a clear view of his back and spotted what was clipped onto his belt. Being an electronics expert, she knew a mobile phone jammer when she saw one. To the untrained eye, it would have looked fairly innocent — just an odd, chunky thing that most people would have thought was a walkie-talkie. But Gail knew better. Anyone carrying a device for disrupting mobile phone signals into a darkened shop was definitely up to no good.

"I bet it felt good, cracking him round the head with that hiking cane," Partial Sue said.

Gail took a massive bite of chocolate cake. "'S'right."

They'd arranged a celebratory tea in Dogs Need Nice Homes in Gail's honour. If it wasn't for her, Fiona wouldn't be alive, and the real killer would have got away with it. Again. They'd pulled out all the stops, offering a vast selection of cakes from Waitrose (they'd had to resort to shopbought cakes, as no one had seen Oliver after he'd been released), and they'd even splashed out on a tablecloth, all to say thank you.

"I really owe my life to you, Gail," Fiona thanked her for the umpteenth time. "If there's anything I can do to repay you, anything you need . . ."

And for the umpteenth time, Gail refused. "'S'right."

Daisy raised her teacup. "How about a toast to Gail?"

"That's a great idea," Fiona agreed.

They raised their teacups and clinked them together. "To Gail!" they chorused heartily.

Gail flushed with embarrassment. Being the centre of attention was an alien concept to her. She clearly wasn't comfortable and didn't know where to look.

"Now, I have a question ask you, Gail," Fiona said gleefully, catching Partial Sue and Daisy's eyes. "How would you like to be part of our little investigative trio?"

"Make it a foursome," Partial Sue suggested.

Daisy screwed up her nose. "That sounds wrong. A quartet."

"Yes, quartet. How would you like to be the fourth wheel of our investigative quartet?"

Gail went quiet, not that she was ever loud or said anything consisting of more than one or two syllables.

"You're not sure," Fiona said. "I get that."

Gail nodded.

"You need some time to think about it," Partial Sue added.

"'S'right."

"Of course. Take all the time you need." But Fiona could tell that the answer would be no, regardless of how much time she took. Gail was a loner, and happy to be so. That was absolutely fine. Some people just preferred their own company. But despite this, she wanted Gail to know that she wasn't alone. She had friends, people she could turn to, even if she never socialised with them. Emergency friends, as it were.

"On another matter," Partial Sue said, "if you ever get fed up with Queen Sophie, you know you're always welcome to work here."

Gail smiled and blushed some more. All this attention and offers of jobs were overwhelming for someone who didn't get very much of either.

Speak of the devil. The bell above the door rang as Sophie flung it open, never one to shy away from making an entrance.

"Hello, ladies. What's all this in aid of?"

"None of your business," Fiona replied.

"Maybe, maybe not. But I'll tell you what is my business — Gail, you need to come back to work. You've had your fifteen-minute lunch break."

"I think she's allowed more than fifteen minutes," Partial Sue pointed out.

"Not on my watch. Come on, Gail. Off we go."

Gail took the hiking cane from her side and placed it deliberately and carefully on the table in front of her. After the incident with Stewart, she'd taken to carrying it every-where, and not to aid her walking. More as a talisman or a badge of honour and, in Sophie's case, a warning.

The manager of the Cats Alliance grimaced at the sight of the stick covered in little metal badges naming places such as the Brecon Beacons, the Lake District, the Yorkshire Dales and other famous UK walking spots. This was the cane that had knocked out a serial killer, wielded by someone who might be described by an American, as "a bit of a badass".

Sophie gulped hard. "But I'm sure a few more minutes wouldn't hurt."

"I think Gail can take all the time she wants," Fiona suggested. "Don't you agree, Gail?"

"'S'right."

"Fine." Sophie turned tail and exited the shop as fast as her expensive spiked heels would carry her.

All four ladies around the table burst into fits of laughter.

After Gail had left on her own terms, when she felt good and ready, Fiona, Partial Sue and Daisy cleared away the cups and plates and ensconced the leftover cake into Tupperware boxes. They'd made a good job of demolishing most of it.

Daisy was about to embark on the washing-up in the storeroom when the doorbell signalled a customer. Rather sheepishly, a middle-aged man stepped inside.

"Good afternoon," the ladies said in unison.

The man nervously glanced around.

"Are you looking for something in particular?" Fiona asked.

"I'm not sure," he replied. "To be honest, I'm not here to buy anything. Actually, I don't even know if I'm in the right place."

"What place were you hoping to be in?" Daisy asked.

"Well, I've heard there's a charity shop in Southbourne with three ladies who are very good detectives. That wouldn't happen to be you, would it?"

They all looked at one another, never ones to blow their own trumpet.

Fiona cleared her throat. No point in beating around the bush. "You're in the right place. This is the Charity Shop Detective Agency. How may we help you?"

THE END

ACKNOWLEDGEMENTS

I have a confession to make. When I wrote this book, I was on the brink of giving up. You see, my writing career hadn't exactly gone to plan. I didn't really have a career if I'm being brutally honest. After nearly fifteen books, trying my hand at all sorts of genres, from YA and sci-fi, to urban fiction and crime, the rejections had stacked up and up over the years, forming a teetering tower.

Undeterred, I'd dabbled in the indie route for a while with my John Savage action thriller series, and had some success, even getting longlisted for a CWA Dagger Award. Armed with that accolade and the fact I'd briefly hit the number-one spot on Amazon in Canada and Australia in that genre, I was convinced I'd get a publisher. Try as I might, the publishing world didn't seem to be interested in an ageing, balding, slightly overweight, tea-drinking Jack Reacher type with a sarcastic British sense of humour. So I tried writing something different and submitted a couple of high-concept fiction books. The result was the same. The teetering tower of rejections turned into a skyscraper.

"Why am I bothering?" was a question I was asking myself more and more. I made a decision. After getting a tip-off from Sam Missingham that cosies were about to be big

(big thanks to Sam — everyone should follow her), I'd have one last crack at it with *The Charity Shop Detective Agency* and if that didn't work then I'd call it a day, take up gardening or something. First set of rejections came in. *Here we go again*, I thought. But then an incredible thing happened. Steph Carey from Joffe Books read the whole manuscript. Then she asked if I could have a call with her and Jasper Joffe, the owner of Joffe Books. They offered me a deal there and then, and I've been pinching myself ever since. So my biggest and most heartfelt thanks must go to Steph Carey for believing in my books and pulling me back from the brink. I am in your debt and certainly would not be in this privileged position without you and Jasper Joffe. You don't know how much this means to me. Thank you, thank you, thank you. In fact, the whole team at Joffe Books have been brilliant from start to finish.

Writing crime can be a tricky business, even when it's cosy. Once you brush the cake crumbs away and wipe up the tea stains, there needs to be some solid police work beneath it all. For that I always turn to Sammy H.K. Smith. Not only is she a real-life kickass police detective, she's also one hell of a great writer and is published too. The perfect combination. She's always the first to receive my rough draft, and over the years I've not only come to rely on her technical expertise but also her suggestions regarding plot. Really I couldn't do this without her.

Getting a second opinion and a third and a fourth is vital in writing. Having honest and sharp-eyed beta readers is essential and I am lucky to have the best and most supportive you can imagine. They are Suze Clarke-Morris, Kath Middleton, who's also a great writer, and Terry Harden. I totally rely on them for every book I write.

Massive thanks must go to Cat Phipps, who has done a simply amazing job editing the whole manuscript and making it the best it can possibly be, and to Anna Harrison for her copyedit and Emma Jobling for her proofread.

And to Nick Castle, who has done an absolutely splendid job on the cover.

My wife has been the biggest supporter of my writing over the years, and I can honestly say I wouldn't be in this position without her. It helps that she's a writer too, a prolific and accomplished one, and knows exactly how challenging the whole process can be. She's also had to put up with me through all the disappointment when things didn't go my way, which was more often than not. Her positivity and belief got me through it. Thank you so much, Sha.

Keeping things in the family, I also have to thank Dan, my clever son (the Dan in the book is based on him). Maths isn't my strong point, but it's Dan's superpower. He helped me with all the numerical sequences, making some very complicated things easy to understand for someone who is totally maths illiterate. Thanks also to my daughter Billie, who is the one I always turn to when it comes to questions of style and taste, and testing out whether the jokes are funny or not.

Big thanks must also go to other people who have helped and encouraged me. They are David Gilchrist and Lucy Sampson from the UK Crime Book Club, Sarah Hardy, book blogger and book tour organiser, and Helen Boyce at The Book Club.

Thanks to everyone. Because of you, the Charity Shop Detective Agency will be open for business again very soon.

Thank you for reading this book.

If you enjoyed it please leave feedback on Amazon or Goodreads, and if there is anything we missed or you have a question about, then please get in touch. We appreciate you choosing our book.

Founded in 2014 in Shoreditch, London, we at Joffe Books pride ourselves on our history of innovative publishing. We were thrilled to be shortlisted for Independent Publisher of the Year at the British Book Awards.

www.joffebooks.com

We're very grateful to eagle-eyed readers who take the time to contact us. Please send any errors you find to corrections@joffebooks.com. We'll get them fixed ASAP.